Laura and Jimmy became mates while studying journalism at Sheffield University, so sitting in pubs talking about life and love is something they've been doing for the last ten years. Now they're writing books together they just take their laptops and write it all down, but little else has changed. Jimmy still tells Laura off for always being late, and Laura can still drink Jimmy under the table.

Their friendship survives because Laura makes tea exactly how Jimmy likes it (he once took a picture of his perfect brew on Laura's phone so she can colour match it for strength) and because Jimmy noted Laura's weakness for custard creams and stocks up accordingly.

Laura Tait is a writer for *Shortlist* and *Stylist* magazines and Jimmy Rice is a freelance journalist. Both live in London.

Follow them on Twitter at @LauraAndJimmy.

www.transworldbooks.co.uk

THE BEST THING THAT NEVER HAPPENED TO ME

LAURA TAIT & JIMMY RICE

CORGI BOOKS

TRANSWORLD PUBLISHERS
61–63 Uxbridge Road, London W5 5SA
A Random House Group Company
www.transworldbooks.co.uk

THE BEST THING THAT NEVER HAPPENED TO ME
A CORGI BOOK: 9780552170710

First published in Great Britain
in 2014 by Corgi Books
an imprint of Transworld Publishers

Addresses for Random House Group Ltd companies outside the UK
can be found at: www.randomhouse.co.uk
The Random House Group Ltd Reg. No. 954009

The Random House Group Limited supports the Forest Stewardship
Council® (FSC®), the leading international forest-certification
organisation. Our books carrying the FSC label are printed on
FSC®-certified paper. FSC is the only forest-certification scheme
supported by the leading environmental organisations, including
Greenpeace. Our paper procurement policy can be found
at www.randomhouse.co.uk/environment

Typeset in 10½/13½pt Meridien
by Kestrel Data, Exeter, Devon.
Printed and bound by
Clays Ltd, Bungay, Suffolk.

6 8 10 9 7 5

THE BEST THING THAT NEVER HAPPENED TO ME

Prologue

ALEX

May 2010

'They say you should never go back but everyone does. Everything comes back for a second go. Look at flares. And Wispa Gold. And Take bloody That.'

I lie flat, my back pressed against the grass, not caring if any midges bite me as the embers of the day's sun warm my face and arms. By my side is Holly, who is sitting cross-legged, sowing a daisy chain with her hands.

'What are you on about, Al?'

'Me and you. It's like we've come back for a second go. Reformed.'

Holly remains focused on her project, but I can see in my peripheral vision that she is suppressing a smile. 'Flares might have come back into fashion in Mothston, Alex, but nowhere else.'

'I'm being serious,' I persist. The origins of my theory are in the can of cider resting on the grass beside my right knee, but it still feels profound somehow.

'You're saying me and you are like Take That?'

'Yes, like Take That, but without all the money and screaming fans.'

Finally Holly looks at me, smiling. 'You'd be Gary Barlow. All straight-laced and sensible. And better looking with age.'

'You'd be Robbie.'

'The one that used to be fat?'

'No.' I laugh. 'The rebellious one that ran off the first time round.'

Holly resumes her chain, but with a more thoughtful expression than before, as though her heart isn't really in it any more.

'It's true, though,' I add. 'This is like our reunion tour.'

'Al?'

'Yep?'

'Pass me another cider, would you?'

I shake my head and reach into the plastic bag with the cider in it, throwing a can into her waiting hands. I smile to myself, happy to be here, Holly and Alex, and I try to ignore the fact that the sun is starting to disappear. I've waited for this moment so long, and I do not want today to end.

Chapter One

HOLLY

September 1999

When I wake up the next morning, I feel different.

Admittedly not the kind of different I was prepared for. Not the happy/spring-in-my-step/seeing-the-world-through-new-eyes type different.

But I know what I need to do.

Thinking about anything from last night makes the painful knot in my tummy tighten – even the earlier bits when I was having fun. Downing pints of Turbo Shandies (50 per cent lager, 50 per cent Smirnoff Ice, 100 per cent NEVER AGAIN) and grinding to DJ Luck & MC Neat around the garden with Ellie. It was pretty warm by September's standards – it was gone midnight by the time the party moved into her house.

My call to Alex came a good few hours after that. I can't believe I decided a drunken call in the middle of the night was the perfect time to tell him how I feel. That I want to be more than friends. That I've wanted it for ages. Thank God he never answered. Not because I've changed my mind about wanting him to know. I just

9

think it's sort of important that I'm not out of my tree when I say it.

I pull off my T-shirt and avoid looking in the mirror as I grab my bathrobe and sprint to the bathroom. I had a burning-hot shower when I got home last night and I have another now, enjoying the sting and the reddish tone my skin is turning, then force myself out, dressing in boot-cut jeans and a navy vest top – Alex always says navy is my colour – before bounding downstairs into the living room.

'Mum, can you give me a lift to Alex's?'

'Sure, Hols. *Diagnosis Murder* is nearly finished.' Her eyes flick from the telly to me and back again. 'I have a theory. You see that man? Everyone thinks he's killed his wife but I think she's faked her own—'

I can't take this right now. Whether a random fictional character killed his wife is the very least of my problems. Thank God she was in bed when I got home last night. I can pull it together today, but I'd have to be the best actress in the world to have pulled the wool over her eyes last night.

'It's all right – I'll walk.' Least it will give me a chance to work out what I'm going to say.

Shall I just come out with it? Or should I start with an explanation? Tell him about the worst night of my life – how even thinking about what happened makes my eyes screw up, my skin crawl and my brain hurt – and that the only person I wanted to see at the end of it was him. That he's my best friend and that while I've always known how much I cared about him, these past couple of years I've more than cared about him.

I've never admitted this to myself until now. I am

completely in love with Alex Tyler. LOVE. My best mate, who always puts everyone before himself – his dad, his mates, me – even though he's had a tougher time than anyone over the last couple of years. I love that I can talk to him about anything, and that he tells me what he really thinks instead of what he thinks I want to hear. I love that he still always offers to carry my bag, no matter how many times I tell him I'm perfectly capable of carrying it myself. I love that he wears woolly jumpers – and not even ironically. Could I grow to love his geeky hair? Sure. I can always send him to a proper hairdresser if not. I love how when I make us a sandwich he follows me around cleaning up the mess with a Dettol wipe. I love how he knows so much about stars and music and books – stuff that other boys don't put any thought into. I love how he alphabetizes his CDs. I love how he alphabetized *my* CDs – although I laughed at the time. Did I even say thank you? I'll mention it today after I've told him I literally love him to bits. (I even love that he tells me off for my misuse of the word 'literally'.)

What will he say when I tell him? Say it back? Knowing him, he'll want to talk about it first. Over-analyse it Alex-style to make sure it's definitely what I want.

Or maybe he'll look horrified, and awkwardly tell me that he could only ever see me as a mate – a sister, even – and that he's flattered, thanks, but NO, it's never gonna happen. I remember the first day of sixth form, not long after his mum had died. We were talking on the way to school and somehow got on to the subject of his mum and dad and, because he looked so sad, I went to hug him, but the look on his face . . . You'd think a rabid dog had leant in for a cuddle.

11

The memory still stings, but not enough to make me turn around, go back upstairs and climb into bed. I need to know either way, and it might be the last chance I get.

OK, the timing is not the best, with me about to start uni in London and him staying up in Yorkshire. Not that I'd have based my choice of uni around him – I'm not THAT girl. It is a bit frustrating to think we've been living a few streets away from one another for the past seven years. Why didn't I pluck up the courage to tell him? I should have listened to my mum all those times she joked about us getting married. Everyone else did too but I always told them to shut up – that we were just mates. I guess for ages it was because I thought that was true. And then later because I was terrified that if I didn't protest enough, everyone would know how I really feel, and make fun of me.

I don't care what anyone thinks now. And if Alex wants to, we can make the long-distance thing work. I'll be back in all the holidays, and we can chat on the phone – we chat for ages on the phone now anyway. And we can send loads of love letters – it'll be well romantic. And when I go off travelling Alex can come with me. I read something about Brits teaching English abroad – he wants to be a teacher anyway.

It's bloody freezing – I guess that's summer officially over, then – so I walk quickly and distract myself with daydreams of weekend reunions. I'm stepping off the train and running straight into his arms, and he lifts me up and I wrap my legs around his waist. And even though in my fantasy it's an old-fashioned steam train I'm getting off, it won't be any less romantic when I step off the Midland Mainline and drag my wheelie case towards him before the jumping-into-his-arms bit.

'Oh hello, Holly.' Alex's dad moves aside to let me in. 'No coat? It's getting chilly out there. Want a cuppa?'

Usually I'm all for a natter with Alex's dad – I think he's pretty lonely these days – but I tell him no and try not to notice his disappointment.

'Son! Holly's here,' he shouts up the stairs. 'Go on up, love.'

Alex clearly didn't hear – he's in the shower singing something about being a creep and a weirdo to a tune I vaguely recognize from his car, so I sit on his bed and wait.

Alex's room is as familiar as my own. The big Che Guevara poster over his bed. His college books in precise piles on his desk. Crease-free pyjamas where they always are – folded neatly on his pillow.

I can't believe there was a time I used to think it was stuffy. A bit boring, if I'm honest. But after his mum died, I used to come around and try to cheer him up and we'd talk late into the night, until I'd fall asleep, fully clothed on top of the covers, and I started to see his room differently. It's warm. And safe. A cocoon from the outside world. Like bad things can't get you in here.

'Uh, hi,' Alex says. He's at the door with a towel around his waist, and I feel myself blush. Droplets of water are glistening on his recently filled-out chest and dripping down to his slim waist, and when I try to say hello my throat is dry and my voice croaky. Get a grip, Holly. You've seen Alex without a top on before. With wet hair and eyelashes, and smelling all soapy.

I've never wanted to hug someone so much in my life.

'What can I do for you, babe?'

BABE?!

I ignore his random greeting and reach out to take his hand. 'There's something I need to tell you.'

'About last night, right? How was it?'

Is it my imagination or is there something a bit sarcastic to his tone? I try to catch his eye but he drops my hand and looks around his room like he's trying to find something, which is weird because his room is spotless and everything is always in its place. I shove my hands into the pockets of my jeans to cover up my embarrassment.

'Actually, that's what I want to talk to you about. I tried to call you last night. I—'

'Oh yeah – sorry, I didn't answer the phone.' He grins as he rolls deodorant under his arms. 'I had a date and let's just say I was otherwise engaged. If you know what I mean.'

In case there's any doubt about what he means, he gives me an elaborate wink.

What the hell is going on? This is totally un-Alex-like behaviour. The Alex I know is kind, thoughtful, sweet . . . and, more to the point, who the hell was he on a DATE with?

'Who were you on a date with?'

'No one you know. Her name's Jane. She's well fit. Big boobs. Good kisser.'

Right, something weird is going down. That's the kind of shit Kev comes out with. And when he does, Alex covers his face with his hands and shakes his head.

There have been loads of times I've tried to picture what it would be like telling Alex how I feel, but I never

14

pictured myself being this nervous. I can ask a guy out. I don't need to do that lame, pathetic, girly thing of waiting to be asked. And he can't have strong feelings for this Jane girl – they must have only just met. It can't be anything compared to what we've got. Can it?

'So, are you planning on seeing her again?' Say no, say no, say no.

'Yep, hoping to see her tonight, as it happens. Hence the shower.'

He winks again and my heart stops, through jealousy or embarrassment I don't know. Is this all a COLOSSAL error? All this time thinking that I love Alex when I'm actually in love with some fictitious version of Alex I keep in my head, and I don't actually know him at all? Like a few years ago when, after years of fancying Mr Abel, the French teacher, and an entire summer holiday daydreaming that I was a twenty-five-year-old meeting him in a coffee shop in Paris where we fall in love over a croissant, and kiss under the Eiffel Tower, I walked into his first lesson in September both excited and nervous to see him. As soon as he walked in, with his freshly grown moustache and his conjugating French verbs chat, I thought: Quelle the hell was I thinking?

Maybe this pain isn't my heart breaking. Maybe it's just painful disappointment that Alex is like other boys after all – acting as though they really like you just to get what they want, motivated by their willies.

But I wouldn't care this much if my feelings weren't real. And I can't have got him all wrong this entire time, surely? I attempt eye contact again.

'What are you staring at?' he says, laughing, and I feel my cheeks burn. I don't even have time to style it out

15

before he continues . . . 'What is it you were going to tell me, babe?'

OK, where did this 'babe' crap come from? I've never heard him call anyone babe in his life – he sounds weird saying it. Am I that generic?

It's me! Holly! I want to remind him. But I can't. I can't say any of the things I really want to say, because this isn't how this was supposed to go.

Instead, I swallow the lump in my throat and give him a resigned smile. 'I just came to say goodbye. I'll be tied up with packing over the next few days, and then Dad's going to drive me down to London. Then who knows when we'll see each other next?'

I study his face, waiting for a reaction, but it's expressionless. Still, when he opens his mouth to say something I allow myself a moment's hope that it's to ask me what I'm talking about – that of course he'll see me in the next couple of days, even if it means he has to come and help me pack. And obviously we'll visit each other loads. And then he'll pull me towards him for a hug and . . .

'Who knows?' He shrugs. 'Maybe Mothston Grammar will have a ten-year reunion. You'll be back from your travels by then, married to some Australian hunk and with a load of kids.'

'Yeah, maybe.' I laugh softly. 'Although you'll be headmaster someplace else and too busy with your own school to come back to ours.'

'Maybe.'

I take his hand in mine and we stare at each other for about seven seconds, before he pulls away and pushes his wet hair back off his face. Then he starts tugging at a stray thread on his towel, looking as awkward as I feel, so I mumble one last goodbye and leave, shutting the door behind me.

It's not until I'm walking down the stairs and out of the front door that the tears start falling. I don't know when or if I'll ever see Alex Tyler again, but one thing I do know is that I can't wait to get as far away from Mothston as possible.

Chapter Two

ALEX

January 2010

ONOMATOPOEIA.

I turn and ask my year sevens what the word on the board means. Eight hands shoot up. The usual suspects.

'Yes, Isabella?'

'Onomatopoeia is a word that sounds like the thing it describes,' she volunteers, as if reading from a textbook. 'Like bang or slap.'

'Good,' I say dutifully. 'Now, can anyone think of any other examples of onomatopoeic words?'

This time I avoid eager stares and instead seek eye contact with the less forthcoming kids.

'Jack?' I say hopefully.

Jack Couchman is the nearest we've got to a tearaway at Mothston Grammar, though refusing to tuck in his shirt and the odd bit of backchat is as bad as he gets. Over the last few years I've often found myself wishing the kids here had more zeal for rebellion. I long to catch one of my year nines smoking pot along the dead-end path behind the technology block, or to discover some minor vandalism in one of the IT suites. Not that I did any of those things when I was a pupil here, stationed at the desk now occupied by Isabella Smart.

'How about vulva, sir?' says Jack, see-sawing a Biro between two fingers. The minority who rarely put up their hands snort their approval, and I let Jack bask. He's no trouble if you cut him a bit of slack occasionally. Plus, my heart isn't really in rudimentary linguistics this afternoon. I'm nervous about tonight.

'Why are we doing this, sir?' queries Jack, when the snorting subsides. 'Like, why do we have to know about onomatowhateveritis?'

I peer out of the window for inspiration, but it's one of those days that even the weatherman would struggle to describe: neither wet nor sunny, cold nor particularly pleasant for the time of year. I've lost count of the times over the last six years I've been asked why we're doing something, and yet I still cannot summon a more satisfactory answer than 'To pass your exam'. Which, granted, is all most of the pupils at Mothston Grammar ever have to worry about, but still.

When I used to dream about being a teacher I'd picture myself as one of those inspirational types you get in movies – Coach Carter meets John Keating from *Dead Poets Society*. But somehow I can't imagine Samuel L. Jackson or Robin Williams getting embroiled in a discussion about onomatopoeia. Or vulvas, for that matter.

Five hours after the final bell of the week I amble into Mothston railway station, where the shutters are down at a greasy spoon once owned by my mum's friend, Sue. Sue had a nervous disposition, which made carrying a cup and saucer a noisy affair, and she eventually sold the cafe following a breakdown. She took up hairdressing, and Mum would invite her into our kitchen to practise on yours truly, as if I needed any assistance repelling women.

I pass the cafe, inspect the electronic screen to see when the next York train is due and settle by the ticket dispenser. That's where we arranged to meet. I catch myself nervously patting my hips with my fingers, and so I pocket my hands while I glance up at the glass ceiling and see that it's plastered with pigeon droppings. Constellations appear before my eyes, and I wonder how I've never noticed this faecal universe before. I'm just thinking that it's kind of like gazing at the stars when a shadow darkens my view.

It's her. Fiona. My first internet date. Dressed in tight jeans, a belted overcoat and a spirit-level fringe that makes her look like the kind of woman who has something interesting to say.

I know how it sounds: online dating. The only reason I signed up last month was because I began to wonder how I'd ever find a girlfriend in a town where every eligible woman knows my life story, including how as a teenager I once got an erection during RE. I didn't get an erection during RE – my new cords had scrunched up at the crotch. But as soon as Dean Jones shouted 'Alex Tyler's got a boner' I'd had it.

So here I am, holding the door for Fiona as we enter The White Horse.

'You look really nice,' I tell her, but she doesn't acknowledge the compliment.

I chose The White Horse because it's one of those

quaint little pubs with trinkets hanging from beams and, importantly, lots of quiet corners where you can get to know someone without being gawped at by the locals.

'Alex!' heckles a middle-aged voice when we approach the bar, a voice I immediately attribute to my dad's pal Rod. He places his tankard on the bar, examines Fiona, and offers me an approving wink that's about as subtle as David Bowie's trousers in *Labyrinth*.

Mortified, I pay for a bottle of red wine and apologize to Fiona as we settle at a table in the empty back room.

There are two types of town in this part of the north: towns that are famous for something (cakes, a TV show or a strong support for the BNP) and towns that aren't. Mothston is the latter, and the only reason people live here is because they've always lived here. Like me and Rod.

I wasn't one of those who couldn't wait to get away while growing up, but I never intended to stay so long either. Mum died just before sixth form and, when it came to choosing universities, I didn't feel I could abandon Dad.

'You'll be reading about me in here soon,' he told me when I mentioned I was considering Exeter. He was scouring the obituary section of the local paper at the time. When I queried whether you could get the *Herald* in Exeter he retired to his room with a bottle of Diazepam, and I ended up commuting to York instead.

Four years later I graduated and although Dad was off the pills, I knew he couldn't cope on his own. My dad who still refers to the internet as the Information Super Highway, my dad who adds an 's' to the end of the word 'cashback'. And so I applied for a job at Mothston Grammar.

I used to resent him, to blame him for the things I never did, but the older I got, the more I found myself able to imagine how it must have been for him, losing the person he loved most in the world. I'm not surprised he lost the plot.

I decide against sharing my life story with Fiona at this stage, and instead we sit and allow the first sips of wine to insulate our throats while four blokes wearing football jerseys jostle through the door. I recognize them as Leeds United colours; Dad used to own a season ticket.

'You're not into football, are you?' tuts Fiona, the word 'football' infused with contempt, as if she was talking about Hitler or paedophilia or Piers Morgan.

'Not really,' I answer with a placatory smile. My Saturday afternoons were spent on the sofa reading Penguin classics and drinking hot chocolate with Mum.

'Is it asking too much that you're not?'

'Nope.'

'Why are men so obsessed with it?'

'I'm not.'

'My ex never shut up about Arsenal this and Arsenal that. In the end I said to him, "It's me or bloody Arsene Wenger."'

'Which did he choose?'

'Arsene Wenger.'

Fiona sits back, rubbing the length of her arms as if she is cold and, before we know it, we're in the midst of our first awkward silence. It's like a black hole – the further we go into it, the harder it is to escape.

'So you enjoy teaching, do you?' she offers, and I take a sip of wine before answering.

Some teachers enter the classroom because they graduate and can't think of anything else to do. And that's fine. Some of the best teachers I know did that. But I'm one of the others, one of the naïve sods who believed he could make a difference.

Fiona directs two fingers towards her tonsils when I explain this, and I'm aware of how clichéd it sounds, but that's how you think at twenty-two.

'All right,' I say, to catapult us from another cosmological vacuum. 'You mention on your profile that you love reading. What book would you take to a desert island?'

'*How to Make Friends and Influence People*,' she blurts without pausing for thought, and I try not to appear taken aback.

'Why would you need that on a—'

'You should definitely read that if you want to make a difference at school.' Fiona swallows the remainder of her wine. 'Or do what I did: set up a printing business. A hundred and twenty grand – that was my turnover last year.'

I was hopeful about tonight. The website said we were compatible and our messages were frequent and long. But so far our date has felt like a nesting bird, desperately flapping its wings as it tries to take off for the first time.

Each of us dispatches a mute smile across the table and I suggest going for food, to help us relax. First she wants a cigarette, which she smokes as if recalling some hardship from her past: exhaling sideways through thin

23

lips, eyes defiant as they stare blankly through the windows of the vacant shop that used to be Woolworths. I fill the hush by asking if she has a 'type', and discover that her ideal man is six feet two (I'm six feet one), has short dark hair (dark but hanging over my ears), toned (nope), successful (still live with my dad) and gets on with her friends (not sure I'm ever going to meet them).

I listen patiently as she relays her list of boxes to be ticked. Personally I just want someone I find attractive, someone who wants to do something with her life, and someone who gets my sense of humour. Is that asking too much?

Fiona extinguishes her cigarette with a twist of her foot while the metallic sound of smashing glass signals trouble nearby.

'The working classes, eh?' I joke.

'I'm working class,' says Fiona, misinterpreting my tone completely and glugging any remaining hope I had that this could be the start of something.

I allow a mischievous notion to expand in my mind, a notion where I quicken my stride before accelerating into a sprint. I run without looking back, the cool air of late January countered by the warmth of the exhilaration I feel at having made my escape.

I've almost reached home when a waiter hands me a laminated menu. And that's when Fiona and I cross the event horizon of our final black hole – the point from which there is no return.

'When are you going to learn that no one goes on dates any more?' mocks Kev, as I approach the end of my story.

'There's more,' I say, with a jaded smile. I recall how,

24

once we arrived at the restaurant, Fiona declared that she was a vegetarian.

Kev places his pint on the tatty maple surface and coughs into the palm of his right hand. 'So?'

'So, when I ordered steak she told me I had to get something else.'

'Er, she *told* you?'

'Yep, and she suggested the spinach lasagne.'

'What did you do?'

'I changed my order.' I wait for his mouth to open in contempt. 'I got a mixed grill instead.'

I don't accept his high-five, and not because I object to high-fiving (though I swear he once punished me with a dead arm for attempting one at school). It's the germs he's just deposited into his palm. And the fact I don't much feel like celebrating.

'Who paid for the meal?' he asks.

'I did.'

'And that came to what? Fifty quid?'

'Just over.'

'That's you personified, that is. Always a mug where women are concerned.'

'How can a person be per . . .' I give up. An ex-girlfriend taught me that you need to be at least fifty to get away with correcting people's English outside of the classroom. It's almost enough to make me excited about middle age.

'Anyway, what do you mean people don't go on dates any more? How else do you find a girlfriend?'

'Er, you fuck, Alex. You fuck and then you fuck again. And if it's still fun after the fifth time, she's your girlfriend.'

25

'Sounds like a fuck buddy to me.'

'Have you ever had a fuck buddy, Alex?'

'Nope, and neither have—'

'Well then, shut the fuck up about fuck buddies.'

Why do I still humour Kev? Why do I still come to The Lion every Saturday afternoon? Probably because there's bugger all else to do in Mothston. There were three of us once, but Rothers entered social retirement when he got engaged.

The outlook was brighter for Kev a few years ago, when his skinhead was voluntary and his belly wasn't something you could rest a pint on. As for me? I still sleep in the same bedroom where I used to hang posters of the periodic table. I guess I've been waiting for someone to share a mortgage with, and now, in the dregs of my twenties, I'm stuck in a catch-22: no girlfriend, no chance of affording a house; no house, less chance of finding a girlfriend.

Kev clenches his empty glass and shakes it near my face, and when I return with drinks my dad has appeared from somewhere, positioned next to Kev, restlessness disturbing his posture. He asks how my date went, even though I never mentioned it to him. Kev shrugs as if to say, *Don't look at me*.

'What are you doing here?' I ask, but instead of answering he scratches his palm, eyes alternating between me and his hand. Eventually he takes a lungful of musty air, holds it for a second and in the act of exhalation announces that he is selling the house.

'What do you mean, you're selling the house?' I chortle.

'I've bought a boat.'

'You've bought a boat?' Now I'm laughing. This is

obviously some kind of ruse orchestrated by the two of them. I expect a TV crew will reveal themselves in a second.

'A canal boat.'

'I can't live on a canal boat.'

Kev reclines and crosses his arms, relishing the drama that's unfolding.

'It'll take me a few months to sell the house so it's not as if you're going to be on the streets.'

I stare at him, incredulous.

'What on earth are you talking about? Since when have you wanted to live on a canal boat?'

'Me and your mother used to talk about it a lot. I've been waiting for you to leave home but, well . . .'

'You've been waiting for *me* to leave home?'

Dad offers a smile that I interpret as forgiving, as if he holds no malice towards me for stalling his dream for all these years.

A thousand words of indignation bottleneck in my throat. Nobody says a word for a minute or two until Kev slaps both hands on the table.

'I've got it,' he says, turning to me excitedly. 'The answer to all our problems. You should move in to my place. It's not as if my parents are ever moving back from sunny Spain. We can split the rent, turn it into a proper bachelor pad. What do you say, cockermouth?'

Chapter Three

HOLLY

'Hello, you massive, sad, old cat lady.'

As far as 'Happy birthdays' go, it's not THE friendliest I've ever had. It's Jemma saying it, though, and if I took offence at every offensive thing she said I'd constantly look like the dude on the bridge in *The Scream* painting.

'Just one more year until the big three-o, eh? I'd hate to be you,' she continues in her broad Glaswegian tones, shrugging out of her denim jacket. 'What are you doing here anyway? We don't start work for another forty-five minutes.'

'I'm always here at this time. You're just never here to see it. More to the point, what are you doing here? As in, EARLY.'

'I came in to decorate your desk with balloons, and those little Happy Birthday things that you'll still be finding in every orifice for weeks to come.'

'Bless you,' I say, though I'm cringing on the inside.

'Don't bless me – I left the decorations on the tube by accident.'

'Never mind – it's the thought that counts.'

As much as I love her, thank God Jemma doesn't get here this time every day. I love the first hour before everyone else arrives – I can power through my work with no distractions. Melissa is usually here early too but she's not one for idle chit-chat.

'Can't believe my boss is in a breakfast meeting the one morning I'm in early.' Jemma pouts in the direction of Martin Cooper's door. 'I could have done with the Brownie points – I swear he thinks I'm a crap PA.'

She is a crap PA, but I let it slide.

'I'll just email him instead so he knows I was here.' She starts tapping at her keyboard. 'What about your guy – is he in yet?'

As if on cue, Richard Croft walks out of his office.

'Morning, ladies. You look nice, Jemma – have you done something different with your hair?'

'Actually, I'm trying a new shampoo and conditioner,' she gushes, whipping her highlighted locks over her shoulder. 'How lovely of you to notice.'

'No problem. Holly, do you want to come in for a catch-up?'

Richard is nearly back at his door when Jemma calls out: 'It's Holly's birthday, by the way. If you want to give her a wee birthday kiss or something.'

'Oh, yes. Er, happy birthday, Holly.' Richard pauses for a split second then strides back to my desk and gives me history's quickest peck on the cheek, before heading off again.

'Um, thanks,' I mumble to his disappearing back.

'Hols, you're blushing,' Jemma giggles, as soon as he's gone. 'Man, I'm so pretending it's my birthday tomorrow and getting a kiss from Richard Croft.'

'I hope you choke on your croissant,' I tell her fondly, and follow Richard in.

'Well, that was awkward,' he says as I shut the door.

'God, I know – I'm sorry about Jemma. Also, lamest birthday kiss ever. Can I have my real one now, please?'

Richard stands up, laughing as he grabs me by the waist with one hand, and places the other on the back of my head. He starts with small, soft grazes at the sides of my mouth. His lips get fuller and firmer when they reach mine, and that's pretty much the point of no return – we're shooting up the Richter scale of passionate abandon.

I suddenly realize the kiss is over but I'm still standing here with my eyes shut, not saying anything. I've come over all unnecessary. I'd better say something, lest he thinks I'm dead.

'Thanks again for my present – I love it,' I tell him, resting my palms on his firm chest. He took me out for dinner last night and gave me a soft-leather, black Mulberry tote bag. It's the most expensive bag I have ever owned. By a mile. Even if all my previous bags got together and ganged up on it, they still couldn't take it in a fight. Part of me thinks I should keep it in my wardrobe in the drawstring bag it came in so it never gets ruined, such is its beauty, but I don't want Richard to think I don't like it.

'You're welcome, sweetheart. Anyway, I'm going to a client pitch meeting with Martin this afternoon so I just wanted to say happy birthday while I had the chance.'

'Thanks. You should have woken me this morning, though – I would have come in with you.'

'But you looked so beautiful sleeping there – I didn't want to wake you.' He tucks my hair behind my ear and kisses me on the forehead. 'Besides, I checked with your boss and he agreed you deserved a lie-in on your birthday. You've been working so hard – we wouldn't have a hope in hell with this pitch if it wasn't for you. This place would fall apart without you, you know. I was telling Martin as much yesterday.'

I wave a dismissive hand and smile bashfully.

'I mean it,' he says. 'I want him to keep you on his radar. Don't let him pigeon-hole you as a PA.'

Straightening his blue silk Hugo Boss tie, he sits back down at his desk.

'You sure you can't make it tonight?' I ask casually, straightening my navy wrap dress.

'Babe, I really wish I could. But I couldn't say no yesterday when Martin asked me to work late with him – it's not like I can explain why. I'm so sorry.'

'It's fine,' I say quickly. 'It's only that Leah, Rob and Susie are dying to meet you – and Susie's bringing her new man to meet us too.' I don't add that I'm not looking forward to playing gooseberry on my own birthday.

'I know. I'm gutted I won't be there.'

'Really, it doesn't matter. There'll be other chances.'

Nine months into our relationship and he still hasn't met my two best friends. At least they know about us, though. No one else does. That's the problem with keeping our relationship on the down-low. Still, I suppose the down-low is better than telling everyone and becoming one big clichéd boss-shagging PA in their eyes.

It's not like that at all. It's not like he's married and

31

it's not AN AFFAIR – we were both single when we got together.

He's not OLD or LETCHY. He's thirty-five, in good shape and only touches me inappropriately when it's appropriate.

I am not trying to SLEEP MY WAY TO THE TOP. Even though Richard is always encouraging me to push myself within the company, I like being his PA – we're a good team. The only reason we agreed to keep it a secret when we got together was because we didn't want people misreading the situation in any way. And all the sneaking around has been kind of hot.

So, if you think about it, it actually doesn't have all the hallmarks of a big cliché at all. More all the hallmarks of a classic love story.

Boy meets girl. Girl falls for boy. Boy falls for girl even though he shouldn't, and together they overcome life's hurdles to be with one another against the odds.

Just see if we don't live happily ever after.

Everyone has made it to their desk now and I walk back in to a chorus of 'Happy birthday, Holly' and 'Happy birthday, Hols' and 'High-five, wrinkly!' (Danny) and 'Guys, quieten down' (Melissa). I grab my pad and start my To Do list.

I love a To Do list. Some people get their kicks from shoe shopping, or Krispy Kremes, or Facebook. I get mine from writing down the things I need to do, then crossing them out once they're done. It's been this way since university. Leah and Susie used to take the piss. They used to take it in turns to add things to my list when I wasn't looking, like 'Clean the toilet' and 'Make my flatmates' tea' and 'Get a life'.

I call the restaurant to change tonight's dinner reservation from six people to five, then satisfyingly run my pen through CALL RESTAURANT, just as Martin Cooper's six-feet-five frame casts a shadow over my and Jemma's desks.

'Ahoy, sailors,' he booms. 'Jemma, can I touch base with you in my office?'

He disappears behind his wooden, name-plaqued door while Jemma locates a notepad amongst her piles of rubbish.

'OK, I'm heading in,' she says. 'But if he even attempts to touch my base I'm calling HR.'

I've crossed another three things off my list by the time Jemma reappears and Danny rolls himself over on his swivel chair.

'Alwight, Essex?' mocks Jemma.

'Hello, Scotland,' he replies, badly attempting Jemma's accent. 'I have a question for you, ladies. Would you rather have a missing finger or an extra toe?'

'Too easy,' says Jemma. 'Extra toe. Your foot is hidden most of the time and your hands are on show almost always.'

'Plus, where are you going to find a four-fingered glove?' I add, not looking up from my computer. 'Socks, on the other hand, don't compartmentalize your toes so it makes no difference.'

Danny nods, satisfied. 'Fair enough. Good points, well made.'

We like Danny, despite the fact he finishes every third sentence with 'y'know what I mean?', even though nothing he says is remotely ambiguous.

'OK,' Jemma says. 'Would you rather never be able to

have an orgasm again or never give an orgasm again?'

'Have,' I say.

'Give,' says Danny at the same time.

'Selfish,' I say.

'Liar,' he says at the same time.

I'm not lying. Not that it's something I need to worry about with Richard. He'll keep trying until I get there, even if it takes all night. Sometimes it feels like it does. I used to be vocally averse to women who admit to faking orgasms but recently I've learnt that sometimes it's just plain necessary. The truth is, I don't always come. Doesn't mean I don't enjoy it. And Richard is the first bloke I've been with not to accept this, which is very sweet. Just a bit inconvenient at times.

Of course, to tell Danny all that would be spectacularly oversharing, and he's wheeling himself back to his desk anyway, upon the simultaneous opening of Martin and Richard's doors.

'Time to swallow the frog,' Martin explains, by way of a goodbye.

'Enjoy the rest of your birthday, Holly,' adds Richard, with a secret wink that gives me goose bumps. 'Get off a bit early if you like.'

'Thanks, Richard,' I reply in a tone that I hope is polite and friendly enough to display an appropriate amount of respect for my boss, but doesn't in any way imply that I've ever let him tie me to his bedpost with that blue Hugo Boss tie.

It's a fine line.

'Reason number ninety-four why your boss is better than mine,' Jemma moans as she watches them leave.

'Yeah – nice of him to let me go early.'

34

'Sure, that too. I was talking about his arse.'

I crack on with my list until about 4 p.m. when I see a few people gather around my desk with fake subtlety. They're clearly waiting for a cake to appear so they can sing 'Happy Birthday'. I hate this. It's so embarrassing. Do I acknowledge them, and look like I'm expecting a cake, or do I pretend I haven't noticed? Finally they burst into song, and I can blow out the candles.

'Sorry it's not up to our usual standard,' Jemma says as she slides a chocolate sponge next to my keyboard. 'But it would have felt wrong to ask you to bake your own so we had to settle for a Tesco Metro number.'

I usually bake the cakes for colleagues' birthdays. It was Danny's twenty-third birthday just after I started at Hexagon Marketing and I learnt about the ridiculous tradition where people bring in cakes on their OWN birthday, so I offered to make his. And so I inadvertently became cake lady. Now people actually email me requests about what kind they want, then still act surprised when Jemma presents it to them.

'Yum – that was a-mazing,' states Melissa, dropping her napkin into the bin and wiping crumbs from her desk, looking about as amazed as one might look upon hearing the weatherman announce it might rain this winter. Jemma winces. I never noticed until Jemma pointed it out that Melissa only expresses emotion vocally, without it ever actually registering on her face.

'More?' Jemma asks, once I've polished off my slice.

'No thanks, doll.'

She cuts herself a second fat chunk. 'Which is why you're a size ten and I'm not.'

That's not true. It's more to do with the thrice-weekly

gym workouts. I never really exercised until I started university and it can't be a coincidence that that's when everything shrunk. Even my bum – gone are the days you could host a tea party on it. Anyway, the way Jemma talks you'd think she was a size twenty-two rather than a fourteen. She told me over lunch on my first day working here that her diet started tomorrow, and it's been going to start tomorrow ever since.

'Might as well treat myself today,' she says, licking her fingers. 'Diet starts tomorrow.'

When the last of the cake-eating stragglers have dispersed, I get back to work and manage to finish everything that's urgent by 5 p.m. on the dot, at which point Jemma jumps up.

'Right. Get your coat – you've pulled. You havnae really. I could do better. But do get your coat – we're going to the pub.'

'I can't.'

'Course you can – your boss said so and mine never has to know.'

'I have to feed Harold.' Because Richard was meant to be coming, I didn't tell Jemma about my birthday dinner even though I'd have liked to. We've been good buddies ever since my second week here, when I gave her an emergency make-over for a last-minute date using the portable hair straighteners and make-up I keep in my drawer. That relationship didn't last the week but mine and hers was cemented, and these days she regularly helps herself to my beautification resources.

'You're running off home to feed your retarded cat?'

'Harold's partially blind, Jem, not retarded.'

'And depressed.'

'Yes. And I think possibly bulimic.'

'Then what's the point of feeding him?'

'HER.' When Harold first started turning up at my back door I thought she was a boy and the name I gave her stuck. 'Good point. But I still should – sorry, Jem.'

'Fine,' she mumbles, not unhuffily. Then she groans and I think she's dragging it out a bit, until I realize who's approaching my desk.

'You off, Holly?' Melissa says nicely. 'God, I envy you girls, being able to leave early. Not that I blame you. I wish I didn't have so many responsibilities and could escape at this time. Enjoy!'

Too dumbfounded to remind her I work late every single other night, I stare at her retreating back.

Jemma just makes V-signs at it.

I pop back and feed Harold – who is clearly pissed off that I'm going out again – before heading round the corner to meet my mates in Blackheath Village.

I spot them when cheers erupt as soon as I walk into the tiny Italian trattoria. There's a six-seater table in the corner – the girls on one side and the boys on the other. I drop my new handbag onto the seat opposite mine and kiss them all hello.

Chapter Four

ALEX

Mr Henderson reaches across his desk to receive the envelope from my hand. He tears the seal with his index finger and reads, his expression not changing. Once finished, he arches his weight back into his chair.

'London, eh?' he says blithely.

I remember my first morning as a Mothston Grammar teacher – a former pupil like Mr Henderson. 'Look how far you've come,' he pronounced without irony. Now I'm informing him I won't be returning after spring break, and he seems ambivalent. It's a pin to my ego.

Looking back now over the last few weeks and months, it wasn't Dad announcing he was selling the house that finally drove me to leave Mothston. It was my date with Fiona and her question: did I enjoy teaching? She inadvertently reminded me why I became a teacher in the first place and, over the next few days, it dawned on me that the nesting bird that couldn't take off wasn't just the story of our evening together – it was the story of my life. At school I was desperate for sixth form, but in sixth form it was all about university. Four years later I'd completed my teacher training and thought life would really begin. I'd meet the woman of my dreams and teach generations of kids to love Shakespeare. It was only during my cheerless date with Fiona that I realized I'd wasted years of my life waiting for something that I thought was just around the corner.

Suddenly I knew I had to leave Mothston, the incubator of my unfulfilled dreams. So I started applying for jobs in Oxford and Leeds and London.

'There was something about this other school,' I explain to Mr Henderson. 'It's in a deprived area and . . .'

'Your chance to change the world?' Mr Henderson removes his spectacles, cleaning them with the inside of his blazer before replacing them on his face. 'You remind me so much of your mother.'

Neither of us fills the silence that ensues, and it's as though someone has pressed pause on our conversation while we remember her; a quiet capable of condensing days or weeks or even years into a few seconds. Mum was Mr Henderson's deputy until she was offered her own headship at a special-needs school near York. He often recalls how she set up a campaign fund and rescued her new school from closure when everyone told her it was hopeless. As if I need reminding. I swear I've still got blisters on my hands from manufacturing placards on the kitchen lino.

I can't help wondering what Mum would make of all this. My first memory is of her explaining that whenever our burglar alarm sensor flashed in the living room, it was Father Christmas checking if I was being good. And so as a kid I always had a sensation of being watched over, and this continued long after I stopped believing in Santa Claus.

When Mum died she became the person watching over me, as silly as that sounds, and I know she'd urge me not to hesitate now, but I'd give anything to talk it all through with her. The thing that makes me most sad when I think of her is that I knew her only as a child knows his mum, and not as an adult; not how Mr Henderson knew her. What was she like as a colleague? What was she like after a couple of drinks? I'll never know.

'I'm chuffed for you,' says Mr Henderson. 'I often wish I'd moved on myself.'

I try to conceal my surprise. I suppose every generation presumes their elders never had real ambition, as if dreams were invented the day *they* were born.

Before I can ask Mr Henderson what kept him in Mothston, the school secretary knocks to report an incident in the school library.

'Take every chance you get in life,' concludes Mr Henderson, rising to his feet. 'Some things only happen once.'

It's not just Whitford High, my new school, I'm excited about. I'm excited about London itself: the Natural History Museum, Kew Gardens, the West End, Shakespeare at The Globe. I doubt I'll be doing much online dating.

Kev declared that I wouldn't last two minutes outside of Mothston. His way of saying he'd miss me, I expect. I'm still establishing whether the feeling is mutual. I reckon you have two types of friends in life: first, those you hang around with because you enjoy the same things and have a similar outlook. I'm hopeful of meeting people like this in London. Then there are those friendships where the foundation is in history and circumstance. Kev is the latter, and while I love him to bits, I'm not sure I like him very much.

Still, it was kind of him to help me find a house share, even if he soon became agitated as I vetoed people who'd posted online adverts for appearing too laddy, too messy or too bohemian.

'Er, you do realize that whoever you live with is going to find you too OCD, too geeky and too analytical, don't you?' he surmised, once we'd arranged a third and final appointment in Deptford, right by my new school.

And so here we are, boarding a tube at King's Cross having decided against driving through the capital.

'Oi,' he says, concern burdening his face. 'You're not going to start saying "Gorblimey" and "Al'white, guv", are you?'

I lift my eyebrows in his direction. 'Not unless you start saying "Eeeh by gum" and "Ay up, lad".'

I glance around at the other passengers: a huddle of Chinese tourists, a teenager dressed like a Topman mannequin and a skinhead with a ring through his septum. No one makes eye contact, and I absorb the anonymity with relish.

'Ay up, lad,' says Kev, prodding his brow towards the skinhead. 'That fella looks a bit like Bobby Shepherd.'

Bobby Shepherd was a prematurely bald headcase who took umbrage when I received a new bike with more gears than his for my fourteenth birthday. One afternoon he loitered outside the school gate with Dean Jones, and I was due to be pulped until Kev interjected, asking Bobby if the two of them could have a private chat. The sight of Bobby's throat jerking as he listened

41

to what Kev told him still sends a shudder of relief down my body, but to this day he won't reveal what passed between them.

'I promised Bobby I wouldn't spill,' he says when I probe him about it again now.

'That was fourteen years ago. He joined the army, he's fought in war zones. The Taliban are his enemy now, not me and you.'

Kev ponders.

'Consider it a leaving present,' I add, and his pupils expand.

'I wouldn't have to buy you anything?'

'Nope.'

Kev checks left and right, for some reason wary of eavesdroppers.

'Right, well, you know Bobby's dad was banged up?'

I nod. 'Yep, for armed robbery.'

'And how do we know that?'

'Because Bobby told everyone.'

'Exactly.' Kev waits for me to catch on, but I shrug, still not having a clue what he's on about. 'Come on, it was Bobby who told everyone his dad was some kind of armed bandit – but you would say that if he was actually inside for flashing at grannies, wouldn't you?'

I stare at him sceptically.

'It's true. My uncle Mick's a guard at Wakefield prison, isn't he? So when Bobby started on you, I threatened to write what I knew on every blackboard in school.'

My look of scepticism is replaced by one of admiration.

'No big deal,' concludes Kev. 'I mean, everyone's got a skeleton or two in the closet, haven't they?'

'Speak for yourself.'

42

Kev sticks his little finger in his ear, inspects the discharge and wipes it on his jeans. 'Sorry, I forgot about that time when my ma caught you playing with yourself in our downstairs toilet.'

Here we go.

'How many times do I have to tell you – I thought I had a lump.'

'Having a sly danger wank, more like.'

I shake my head. 'Kev?'

'Yes?'

'Let's have a bit of quiet time, yeah?'

The first place we're viewing is a second-floor apartment in the centre of Greenwich. I'd be sharing with a freelance illustrator named Carl, who owns a 52-inch plasma TV and looks like he plays bass in an indie band.

Kev raps his knuckles against the bedroom wall. 'Plastering's good.'

An unemployed builder is never off duty.

'Why would I care?' I say, making a show of rolling my eyes so that Carl knows not to judge me by anything Kev utters.

'In case you want to put a dart board up.'

'I don't play darts.'

'Er, I'm just saying that if you wanted to start, the plastering's good. You don't know anyone here – you'll need something to fill the time.'

This kind of nonsense is why I was reticent about bringing him. Although he does have a point – I am going to need things to do down here. I was thinking of starting a book club at my new school. And I'm definitely going to buy a bike.

'There's a few decent pubs around here,' interrupts Carl, flicking his long, diagonal fringe away from his eyes.

Kev slaps my back. 'There you go, you don't even need a dart board.'

Once the tour is complete, we say our goodbyes and begin the short walk to our next appointment.

'That's going to take some beating, ball-splash.'

'I can't live there.'

Kev stops dead. 'Why?'

'Didn't you see him when he sneezed?' I enquire, walking ahead.

'For fuck's sake.'

Kev catches up.

'I can't live with someone who doesn't cover their mouth. It's liquid bacteria whooshing out at a hundred miles an hour.'

Kev leers at me as if, rather than stating a perfectly valid point, I've just confessed that I've a penchant for wearing women's underwear.

Russell is our host at appointment number two. The first thing he does is point to the Pink Floyd T-shirt Kev is modelling.

'You a big fan?' he asks, and it's like a starter gun for the two of them.

Ten minutes later we're still in the hallway and they're still outdoing each other with boasts of their dedication to 'The Floyd'. Russell wins. His wife threatened to divorce him if he saw The Wall Tour on their first wedding anniversary. Hence he's looking for a new housemate.

44

It's only when I point out that we're running late for our next viewing that we're shown around.

'Not sure there's any point going to the next one, is there?' Kev concludes as we leave.

I wait for him to stop waving, and for Russell to shut the door. 'He had a life-sized poster of four men on his living-room wall, Kev.'

'They're not *just* four men, mate.'

That may be so, but it's irrelevant. If I'm honest, the real reason I couldn't live with Russell isn't his Pink Floyd obsession. It's the fear that I'd never see the last of Kev.

Our final appointment is in Deptford, where my potential housemate is an air-stewardess called Suzanne. Kev sweeps his tongue across his bottom lip when she answers the door, undeterred by the crusty make-up in the creases of her nose.

'Would you mind if Alex had a friend to stay once or twice a month?' he quizzes, and before I can protest, Suzanne frames her lips mischievously.

'You two aren't . . . ?' She hesitates. 'Are you a couple?'

Kev is agog at the suggestion he may be gay. Personally, I'm more affronted by the idea that I'd fancy him.

'Look, Susan—' interrupts Kev.

'Suzanne.'

'Sorry. Bet you get that all the time, eh?'

'Not really.'

'Well, anyway.' Kev leans towards her to confide something; Suzanne folds both arms tight against her chest, a tortoise retreating into its shell. 'Alex here likes a bit of the other.' I allow my head to crash into my hands.

45

'But hopefully me and you can get to know each other if he moves in?'

'Okaaaaay . . .' Suzanne ducks out of his way and leads us into the living room, with its shag-pile rug and modern chaise longue. Her place is homely and, based on our small talk while Kev relieves himself in the bathroom, she seems pleasant. I can picture us having dinner parties, with hors d'oeuvres and cinnamon-based desserts.

Once we're on the train home Kev uses the back of a receipt from two bottles of water to write a Pros and Cons list.

Pros of living with Suzanne (according to Kev)

1/ She looks dirty
2/ No problem with friends staying
3/ Nice house
4/ She'll probably have fit mates
5/ Five-minute walk to work
6/ She looks dirty

Cons of living with Suzanne (according to Kev)

1/ Potential girl talk
2/ Toilet seat isn't fitted properly – need to hold it up while having a wee
3/ You'll never get any sleep

'OK, a few questions,' I say, examining the list.

'Go on . . .'

'Firstly, shouldn't number two in the pros list actually be in the cons section?'

'Hilarious. Next . . .'

'What does "Potential girl talk" mean?'

'You know, when girls get home from work they tell you every detail of their day, like what they ate for lunch and how many times they went for a wee.'

'You mean conversation?'

'All right, Casanova. Any further questions?'

'Yep, just the one: why won't I get any sleep?'

'Er, because living with a girl that fit you'll be lying there with a raging boner every night.'

Of course, a raging boner – why didn't I think of that? Oh well, even without sleep the pros outweigh the cons, so I eagerly scroll down to Suzanne's number.

'Oh, hi.' She sounds surprised to hear from me.

'I've had a think and, if it's OK with you, I'd like to take the room.'

'Oh, right.'

'It's still available?'

'Yes, but—'

'But what?'

The line goes silent for a second and I'm wondering what the hell is going on.

'Don't get me wrong – you seem like a nice guy. It's your mate.'

Acrimony begins to consume me but I try to level my voice with calm. 'What about him?'

'He's a creep.'

'What's that got to do with anything?'

'I don't want to give you the room knowing he'd be staying once a month. Or staying at all, actually.'

47

I want to explain that it's fine, and that I wouldn't want Kev visiting either, but in all likelihood he wouldn't consult me before booking a train ticket.

I stare blankly through the window as we finish the call. I cannot believe he has found a way to spoil this for me.

'Well, come on,' he says. 'What did she say?'

I tighten my grip on my bottle of water, searching for the words.

'If you must know . . .' I sigh, still averting my eyes. But it's no use. I can't do it. He's no more ready to hear what the opposite sex really thinks of him than I am. And it's not as if I'll have to put up with him for much longer. 'Some bloke came around after us and he's having the room.'

'Oh. Sorry, man. I could easily have imagined myself shagging her on that funny little sofa thing as well. So what's it going to be: bacteria or Pink Floyd? You've left it a bit late to find anywhere else, haven't you?'

I'm still debating what to do the following day when I see Sally Barrowclough in the chippy. Sally and I sat next to one another in A-level English. She was one of those girls who had a boyfriend in his mid-thirties, which I thought was cool at the time. Then I got a bit older and realized it was about as cool as Gary Glitter.

I tell Sally about moving to London.

'You know Holly Gordon lives down there, don't you?' she interrupts. Her tone is suggestive, and I'm not sure what exactly she's insinuating, so I accept the information with a simple, noncommittal nod.

48

'Her mum comes into my salon. You and Holly used to go out, didn't you?'

The heat of the fryers starts to burn my face. 'Nope.'

'Are you sure?' asks Sally, handing over a ten-pound note to the girl behind the counter.

'I think I'd remember.'

Sally grins to herself as she collects her order, and grins some more as she says goodbye, and it all feels a bit juvenile.

Of course I knew Holly lived in London, but it's a big place. I'm hardly expecting to bump into her on the Underground. And even if I did, what exactly does Sally suppose will happen?

I think little more of our conversation until a couple of days later when the landline rings and Dad answers. He nods and looks faintly surprised and after a minute or so he mimes writing something on his hand to inform me that he requires a pen and a piece of paper.

'Who was that?' I ask once the receiver has been replaced.

'Joan Gordon.' There's something hidden in the smile that accompanies his answer, something I can't quite put my finger on.

'I didn't know you still spoke to her.'

'I don't, really. Christmas cards and what-have-you.'

I'm still confused.

'So what did she want?'

'She's heard you're moving to London.'

Finally I twig. Joan must have been due a haircut. Sally Barrowclough always was a blabbermouth. She used to tell everyone about the dirty things she let her older man do to her.

49

'She rang to pass on Holly's email thingy.'

I realize there is nothing mysterious hidden in Dad's smile at all – it's just a smirk. Like Sally in the chip shop. And I shouldn't have expected anything else. This is Mothston, after all. A place where no one has got anything better to do than interfere in other people's business.

I make a show of nonchalance as I accept the piece of paper with Holly's email address, but all the while a sequence of recurring questions come to mind. Why didn't she stay in touch? Why didn't she ever tell me when she was visiting?

I've searched for her on Facebook, trying to match one of the 263 Holly Gordons with the girl I remember. My eyes were always drawn to her lips, which were framed in a permanent smile, like she might burst into laughter at any point. The other girls at school applied make-up like they were taking part in an art project, or wasted away on The Cabbage Soup Diet (the common room was not a place you wanted to spend any time during those few months), but Holly was different, and yet she always looked incredible. If my eyes were drawn to her lips, then my mind, when I was alone, focused on her figure: curvy, a caricaturist's dream.

I feel a surge of regret as it occurs to me that maybe I can't find her on Facebook because she isn't Holly *Gordon* anymore. Maybe she married that Max fella I heard she was dating. I can't even remember who told me about him.

Over the next few days I draft and re-draft an email, trying to find the right tone. I know from bumping into Mrs Gordon the odd time – she was probably the one who told me about Max – that Holly lives in London and works in the City, but there are so many gaps. How long did she spend travelling? Did she ever open that cake shop in Paris? Or was it an English pub? It escapes me now. We didn't have a 'Girl most likely to . . .' at Mothston Grammar, but if we had, Holly would have been a unanimous choice.

Yes, I would've streaked through Mothston town centre to be with her back then, and I guess it couldn't have been more obvious. But Holly never saw us that way, so I did what you do, I tried to move on, and I've had plenty of broken hearts since, although it never hurt quite as much. They call it 'The one that got away', don't they – the person that never leaves your mind completely. And that's why I got flustered in the chippy with Sally. They're always there, like a time capsule you bury in your garden as a schoolboy. And now, all these years later, it feels like I'm about to dig mine up.

Chapter Five

HOLLY

'Who do you think Richard is fucking?' Jemma plonks a cup of tea on my desk.

Ohmygodohmygodohmygod. How does she know? Does everyone know? Did I leave my knickers in his in-tray? Knock his phone off the hook when we were doing it and speed dial Martin Cooper's voicemail by mistake?

'What makes you say that?' I mutter, eyes on screen, forehead screwed up, like I'm concentrating really hard on the email I'm reading.

'Look at him. Self-satisfied smile. That swagger. I walked into his office the other day and he was WHISTLING, Holly. As if he'd be that smug if he wasnae getting any.'

I breathe again, but my relief is half-hearted – there's a good chance the secret will be out soon anyway. In a spectacular fashion, as it goes.

I should be on day three of my period, yet for the third day running: nothing. Not even a little tell-tale cramp. The painters aren't in and haven't even called to say they're on their way.

Shameful confession: Richard and I haven't been

totally, 100 per cent careful during those office en-counters. Heck, on a couple of occasions we've been downright reckless.

So of course I'm entirely freaked out. Well, not entirely. Which is a bit weird. OK, if you look at it that I'm potentially knocked up by my boss after an illicit fumble on his desk it sounds BAD. On the other hand, I might be a twenty-nine-year-old woman pregnant by my thirty-five-year-old totally respectable boyfriend.

I had a scare two years in with my last boyfriend, Max, and I just couldn't picture the scene. Walking around with a bump, shopping for cots, changing nappies – any of it.

But when I make myself think about it now, the images come easily.

It's not like I settled just because I'm at that age everyone expects it from you, and Richard happened by chance. He was just back from holiday when I started temping here. I'd been an executive PA to the CEO at a bank when the recession hit and my boss – and, therefore, me – was made redundant. I should have seen it coming. I mean, considering the fact my boss was earning a small fortune to do sweet eff all. They say everything happens in threes, and not only was it the night after Max moved out, but that morning my hair straighteners broke mid-use and I had to go to work with half a head of frizzy hair.

I holed up in my flat for a week, moping. Not about the hair thing – although I still get upset thinking about it – but about suddenly having no direction. The only conversations I had were with Harold. It was a depression-off. I won. I got so bored I sat in tartan pyjamas reading my old teen diaries. The fourteen-, fifteen-, and sixteen-year-old me couldn't wait to get out of Mothston and see the world, apparently. And then it hit me. That was the only thing I'd never managed to cross off a To Do list. Why was I moping? I'd never given up on my dream to see the world and I'd just lost the two things stopping me.

So I drew up a list of destinations and took some soul-destroying temp jobs to boost my travel fund. The only thing keeping me going by the time I landed the three-week stint at Hexagon was the Lonely Planet books piled on my nightstand.

Then at 9 a.m. on Monday, there he was. I think I did an actual swoon.

'You must be my new PA,' Richard grinned, shaking my hand firmly.

'I love you,' I replied. But not out loud.

And that's how I met Richard a year ago. And he seemed like a pretty good reason to stick around.

'How long ago did he break up with Rachel?' Jemma continues. 'Must be a good six months, right?'

Bleeuuurrrrgggggghhhhhh. His ex.

'Nine months.' Those two words remind me of the box wrapped in a chemist's bag in my top drawer. With something halfway between fear and excitement I gulp down half my tea.

'Wow, you didnae even need to think about that,' Jemma smirks. 'Someone's monitoring the situation.'

'Not at all,' I protest. 'I only know because it was around the time of my three-month probation.' And a week before our first kiss.

I'd stayed late to help him on a presentation and

when we finally aced it at 9.15 p.m. he got over-excited, grabbed my face with both hands and kissed me on the lips. Then we had this weird movie moment where we looked at each other for what felt like ten minutes (in reality about four seconds) then slowly came together for a proper snog. Richard is what you would call An Excellent Kisser. I told him that once but there was no hint of surprise in the smile he responded with, so I assume it wasn't new information.

'You fancy him, though, right?' Jemma demands. 'You work hard because your boss is hot. That's the only way I can justify that I don't.'

'Not at all,' I lie defensively.

'So how come you're single? You're a fittie. We're the unluckiest people in love ever. If we're still single at forty let's become lezzers.'

'I thought you were seeing someone?' I deflect.

'I'm pretty sure that's over.'

'What makes you say that?'

'He texted me saying "It's over". I'm fine, though,' she adds, before I can administer sympathy. 'I got the phone number of a cyclist who nearly knocked me into the path of a moving bus this morning and I'm definitely gonnae marry him.'

'Really? That time we agreed that men on bikes were sexy, you pissed yourself laughing when you realized I was talking about bicycles and not motor bikes.'

'Yes, but his business card says he's an investment banker, so his other wheels are probably a BMW.'

'Why don't you stay single for a while?' I ask, not for the first time. 'Focus on yourself. Prove you don't need a man to be happy.'

'Oh, but I do,' she whines. 'Preferably a rich one so I can give up work and just have babies.'

'You go, sister!' I reach out for a sarcastic fist bump but Jemma whacks my hand with her ruler instead.

'You feminists do my head in. Don't get me started on those bra-burning sixties wifies – they thought they were doing us all a favour proving we're men's equals, but all they did was create a society where those of us who just WANT to raise a family and keep a perfect home aren't allowed to admit it.'

Before I have a chance to ask how she intends to keep a perfect home when there are still remnants of cake on her desk from my birthday, Melissa is at my desk.

'Holly, hi. I need a word with Richard – is he in his office?'

'Sure, go on . . .' She marches off without waiting for me to finish. '. . . in,' I mutter, rolling my eyes.

'There's someone who'd be pleased to know you're no' into Richard. Less competition.'

'Melissa?' I can't keep the surprise out of my voice. I'm far from the crazy jealous type, but the thought of Melissa flirting with Richard makes me feel a bit sick. She's one of those knows-what-she-wants-and-doesn't-stop-until-she-gets-it sorts.

'Oh aye, totally fancies him. Whenever she has a meeting with him she nips to the loo first and reapplies her make-up. Look, she's about to come back out. Watch her.'

'I'm *so* excited about this project,' she's saying, with a look conveying a level of excitement most people reserve for queuing for the ATM, while touching Richard's bicep.

Damning evidence.

Not that I'm threatened by Melissa. She's blonde and tanned (both from a bottle) and relatively pretty, I suppose. If you like that sort of thing. She's also as much fun as dental surgery. 'See?' Jemma lowers her voice. 'I'm telling you, if you threw her knickers against the wall they'd stick.'

'Right,' I laugh and swig the last of my tea. 'If you've finished speculating whether or not my boss has a girl-friend, I've got work to do.'

'Oh, I dinnae think he's got a girlfriend. I just think he's getting his end away.'

Two hours later I still don't need a pee. How is that even possible? I feel sick with anticipation. Or is it morning sickness? Can you get morning sickness in the after-noon?

'EARTH TO HOLLY.'

'Sorry, Jem, what?'

'Would you rather marry someone really clever but well ugly *or* gorgeous but thick as two short planks?'

I don't overthink these dilemmas ordinarily, but this feels pertinent. I glance at Richard, standing in Martin Cooper's doorway gesticulating animatedly with his hands. Looks are genetic. Is intelligence? I don't think it is, is it?

'Clever and ugly,' I say anyway, because it feels like the only acceptable response to that question.

'Oh, get your head out your arse. I'd go for the stupid fitty. I'm going to email Danny and see what he thinks.'

I'm about to get up and buy peanut M&Ms from the vending machine (effing hell – a craving!) when an email pops into my inbox.

From: <alexpatricktyler@hotmail.com>
To: <holly@hexagon.co.uk>
Subject: Hello

Hello Holly,

Remember me? Your mum passed on your email address. I'm a teacher now and just got a new job in London. I guess your mum thought it'd be good for us to meet up. Where exactly are you living? I'll be in Greenwich.

I can't believe it has been so long. We're nearly 30! I hope you're doing all the things you wanted to. It really would be nice to have a catch-up some time. Anyway, best crack on – loads to do with the move and everything. Hope to hear from you soon.

Alex x

Oh my God – Alex!

'Who?' Jemma looks around and I realize I said it out loud.

'A guy I went to school with in Yorkshire – he's just emailed to say he's moving to London.'

I read the email again, my heart pounding. He wants to meet up? I haven't heard from him in eleven years. It would be nice to see him. Or would it be weird? Why did he choose today of all days to get in touch – I can't think straight.

'You don't sound like you're from Yorkshire.'

'We moved up there when I was eleven, and I moved away again when I was eighteen so I never really—'

'That's nice. So, is he single?'

I shrug. We haven't spoken since I left Mothston. He

probably married that Jane girl he met just before I left. Right after they bought their house and just before she bore his first child. He was the sort to do things in the right order.

'Aren't you Facebook friends? Oh, I forgot. You're the only person on the planet not on Facebook.'

'Richard's not on Facebook.' What am I doing? Shut up, Holly. I carry on before Jemma asks how I know that. 'What's the point? It's just a way for people to stalk each other.'

'That *is* the point. Just think – without Facebook I would never have known that guy I met was a member of the group PEOPLE WHO LIGHT THEIR FARTS, and I probably would have gone out with him. It's also great for getting back in touch with people.'

'I'm in touch with everyone I want to be.'

'And you get to see which girls you went to school with got fat. Anyway, what's his surname?'

I tell her.

'There's shit loads of Alex Tylers,' she complains after she's typed it. 'What does he look like?'

'Um, skinny. Badly cut hair.'

'And you weren't interested? Shocking.'

I laugh. There was much more to Alex than that. He was a good mate, even though my other mates thought he was dull and studious, because he didn't bunk school, disrupt lessons or smoke behind the gym, as was the cool kids' way. He'd also analyse things to death, but he was a good listener. I could tell him anything. Until that time I really needed to tell him something, and he was a bit of a knob. So, I couldn't tell him everything it turns out.

59

'Can you search by location?' I venture. 'Maybe try Mothston.'

'Oh, you lost me at badly cut hair. I'm playing Online Scrabble now.'

Fair enough.

I tap out a quick reply to Alex's email, hastily changing my suggestion of a beer to a coffee when a tug at my bladder reminds me of my potential situation, then within a minute and a half I'm sitting on the loo.

With the lid down.

And my pants up.

I can't do it. Not the actual act of peeing – that would be easy. Too easy. I'm in danger of having an accident if I leave it much longer. But I can't have this moment here, like this.

If it's positive, I'll remember it for ever. Do I want to tell little Jeremy or Jemima (note to self: check if Richard was also a big *Chitty Chitty Bang Bang* fan growing up) that I was alone in a disabled toilet? Richard should be here. Is it irresponsible to tell him before I know for sure? We might not have talked about kids yet, but he must have thought about it. That's what you do when you get involved with someone – think about the future.

I can't stay here much longer thinking about it because if there's someone outside in a wheelchair I'll hate myself, so I pee without taking the test out of my bag and then head for his office.

Come Sunday, still no period and I still haven't told him. When I walked into his office he got in there first with some exciting work news: Hexagon are in talks with an

60

American marketing firm about a potential merger.

I'm playing fast and loose with the word 'exciting' there, but it excited the pants off Richard – it could mean a promotion, heading up a new department dealing with American clients.

Today's the first time since then that I'll be alone with him, and I'm stuffing a lemon into the backside of a chicken when the apple of my eye calls.

'Hiya, handsome!'

'Hey, gorgeous. I've good news and bad news.'

The good news being that the company we're potentially merging with want to fly him to their New York office tomorrow to meet him.

The bad news being that he needs to prepare, so won't be round for me or my roast chicken.

I tell him it's fine. It isn't, but he wasn't to know what I had planned for him: a romantic unveiling of a stick covered with my wee.

'Thanks, babe. I'll make it up to you. I'll . . . What is that racket? Are you in a church?'

'*Songs of Praise.* I was just flicking through the channels.'

I don't know why I said I was flicking – it's a lie. I like *Songs of Praise.* I like how the words are on the screen so you can sing along. It's like religious karaoke.

He laughs. 'I'd better go.'

I won't see him until Tuesday now. I can't wait that long to take the test – I'll go crazy.

'Looks like it's just me and you, Harold.'

Oh really? she asks, all beady eyed. *Am I supposed to be grateful? Just because you've got no one else here? Well, screw you,* she says, and storms off.

She'll be back once the chicken's done.

Sat on the loo with 'How Great Thou Art' blaring in the background, my mobile rings next to me, scaring the bejesus out of me.

Richard calling to tell me how he's going to make it up to me?

I check the screen.

'Hi, Mum. It's not a good time – can I call you—'

'Hey, honey. So, there was a woman on *Jeremy Kyle* who found out her daughter, who visits every weekend, not only steals money from her, but sleeps with her husband. And you know what I thought?'

'That you should get out more?'

'Very funny. No, I thought how lucky she is she sees her daughter every weekend.'

Most mothers would just ASK when you're coming to see them. Mine likes to dress it up and disguise it as a topic of conversation.

At least she got to it quickly this time. It's worse when we talk for ages first, and I don't know which subject will turn out to be a prelude to this. A bit like when someone is hiding and you know they're going to jump out on you any minute – it's the anticipation that gets you.

'I'll come up soon, Mum. I really have to go, though—'

'Anyway, the real reason I called,' she interrupts excitedly, 'is to tell you Alex Tyler has moved to London.'

It must be the talk of the town – nothing this big has happened in Mothston since the post office got a greetings card section. I got a phone call from Mum about that, too.

'I know, he emailed me about meeting up. Thanks for handing out my address willy-nilly, by the way.'

She ignores that last bit. 'So, have you met up?'

'Not yet.'

'Oh.' She sounds disappointed. 'I'd have thought you'd be dying to see him.'

'It's been eleven years,' I point out. *And I'm a little distracted by the potential imminent existence of your first grandchild*, I don't point out.

'Then you've a lot to catch up on. And he probably doesn't know anyone in London.'

I assure her I'll sort something and hang up.

Once the test is finally underway, I distract myself from clock-watching by singing 'Shine Jesus Shine'. I'm just getting to the bit where I'm telling him to flood the nations with grace and mercy when my phone goes again. Richard . . . ?

'Hello, Mum.' The only explanation I can think of as to why I bother answering is that there's a small part of me that doesn't want to be alone for this moment.

'It wasn't her dad, by the way.'

'Eh?'

'The girl sleeping with her mum's husband. Her parents are divorced and it was her mum's new husband. Just in case that wasn't clear. Though on that show you never know what to expect.'

I'm barely listening. I'm too busy staring at the little white stick.

Chapter Six

ALEX

'AHCHOOO!'

Carl rises from his armchair, eyes damp and swollen, while I scan the immediate area to establish which items have been contaminated. Most of the coffee table's a write-off: a charcoal pencil that rests on an A2 drawing pad, remote control, small rectangular tin that I suspect contains weed.

'Bloody hay fever.' He sighs, using his right foot to locate a pair of loafers beneath the sofa. 'I'm gonna pop out for some antihistamines. You want anything, buddy?'

Antibacterial wipes? A handkerchief? A shotgun?

'I'm good, ta.'

I finished unpacking an hour ago and already I'm unsure whether I'm cut out for flat sharing. I ended up tossing a coin between Carl (bacteria) and Russell (Pink Floyd), figuring I could always find somewhere more suitable once I'm settled. But then Carl requested an £800 deposit, non-refundable if I vacated within six months, so now I'm trapped in his viral pit, watching *Songs of Praise* on 52 inches of plasma because I'm worried what I'll contract if I try to flick channels.

I forget the TV and switch on my laptop. I haven't had a chance to check my emails all weekend, what with the move, and it takes me a few seconds to spot it among the teacher newsletters, Amazon receipts and messages from the Nigerian opposition leader asking for my assistance in the war against his oppressors. When I finally do, my chest constricts.

It's surreal reading her name in Courier New. No one in Mothston had heard of emails last time we saw each other. We still knocked on people's doors if we had something to tell them. I click on her message and am unexpectedly overcome by a familiar feeling. The same feeling I got whenever Mum or Dad would call up to my room informing me Holly was at the door. I'd tiptoe to the bathroom mirror, my heartbeat accelerating as I checked my breath against my palm. One final gulp of air at the top of the stairs and then . . .

From: <holly@hexagon.co.uk>
To: <alexpatricktyler@hotmail.com>
Subject: re: Hello

Hi Alex,

Hope all's well.

That's great that you're teaching now, just like you always wanted – good for you. I live in Blackheath, which is actually right next to Greenwich. I should be able to fit in a coffee in a couple of weeks – drop me a line when you're settled and I'll check my diary.

Good luck with the move,

H

I read her email again for clues, something to tell me whether she was pleased to hear from me. It all depends where you put the emphasis: the 'should' or the 'coffee'.

Maybe it's the coffee thing that has left me feeling deflated. Like she can only spare five minutes or whatever. I envisaged an evening reminiscing about old times over a few proper drinks, chatting until the early hours like we used to. I don't know – I was probably expecting too much. Some things never change.

After fifteen minutes I decide there's at least a slight chance I'm being an imbecile, so I make her 'coffee' jaunty and enthusiastic as I reply, asking when she's free and supplying my mobile number. Then I shut my laptop and fall back onto the sofa, allowing nerves and excitement to do their worst as I ponder what's ahead tomorrow.

A right turn from Deptford station sends me along a high street where a halal butcher's and an Afro-Caribbean food store are opening for trade. I smile at one of the shop owners; he doesn't appear to see me.

The spring air is still, the temperature hinting at summer. I remove my jacket and sling it over my shoulder as I follow the road until reaching a block of council flats where satellite dishes are suspended on different-coloured balconies. I begin to spy pupils: year sevens with untucked shirts and rucksacks hanging low; older girls wearing hooped earrings and stern expressions. There's far more bling than I'd imagined. During the last few weeks I've had visions of a Polish boy with holes in his shoes and no money for books. In the daydream I hand him my personal copy of *Michael Robartes and the Dancer* by W.B. Yeats and smile selflessly as he thanks me in broken English. The narrative then advances fifty years and the boy, now Poet Laureate, is guiding me around his personal library dressed in a burgundy smoking jacket. He places into my hands a book masked by thick wrapping paper, and later I realize it's the same Yeats collection I bequeathed to him all those years earlier.

I admit it's probably a tad romantic.

I complete one more left turn and there it is: my new school. I stand rooted, absorbing my surroundings. The principal building is a huge box with three layers of concrete and three layers of windows. Some of the kids gawp at me as they walk past, no doubt wondering who the fella with the massive grin is – but I can't help it.

A receptionist leads me to my head of department, Mr Cotton, who has arranged to spend the morning outlining protocols, pastoral care and other such matters.

Once all this is done he asks how I'm feeling about my first lesson this afternoon.

'Eager, keyed up, lots of other adjectives that don't quite suffice. I suppose a little bit scared as—'

'You've got your year nines first, I believe?'

I examine my timetable, even though I could recite it verbatim. 'Yep, I think so.'

'Well, don't let them see you're "a little bit scared" – they'll eat you alive.'

I laugh at his joke but Mr Cotton's face remains stony. His sallow complexion, comb-over and long, rigid nose make him look like a character from *Guess Who?*.

'I'm deadly serious,' he says as the bell tolls, standing and ushering me towards the door with an outstretched arm. 'That lot were one of the reasons your predecessor left.'

'Settle down please, settle down. My name's Mr Tyler and I've taken over from Miss Marsden.' Someone at the back of the room yawns. 'Now, I know it's difficult getting a new teacher at this stage of the school year but hopefully together we can make it work.'

A pale boy with a gravy stain down his shirt and a sovereign ring on the middle finger of his right hand draws an elastic band back from his Biro. He holds, aims and fires into the forehead of a classmate three seats across. I scan the electronic register. Gareth Stones.

'Come on now, Gar—' A latecomer breezes in. Even with an afro, the boy is a good few inches short of five feet. He limps past me in an oversized blazer that doesn't bear the school crest.

'Kenny's gonna get in one of the lockers at the back, sir,' warns a girl whose bleached hair hangs from jet-black roots. Juliette Jacobson, according to my screen.

Flustered, I shuffle from behind my desk and glance at the teaching assistant, Ms Pritchard, but she looks as bewildered as me.

'Can I ask what you are doing?' I enquire, but it's like he's in his own little world, a world where it's perfectly normal to manoeuvre yourself into a metal box. He fits with room to spare.

'Look, can you please come out of the locker?'

Still nothing. Gareth pings another elastic band, this

time into Juliette's cranium, while I walk tentatively over to the lockers.

'Come on,' I implore, pulling open the metal door that has swung shut. The boy recoils, banging his elbow on the back of the locker.

'You hurt me,' he bawls. 'I'm calling Injurylawyers4U.'

'Oi, Mr Tyler!' shouts Gareth in a voice somewhere between cockney gangster and camp TV entertainer. The rest of the class are distracted from their copies of *Hamlet*. 'I was just wondering where you is from? Harvey reckons Newcastle, Stacey reckons Uranus.'

Most of the kids laugh and I decide to use the same tactic that worked with Jack Couchman at Mothston Grammar: letting Gareth be the centre of attention for a moment rather than taking every opportunity to admonish him.

Gareth sinks further into his chair and cackles into his hand when I tell him where I'm from, a not un-common response. It's the way it sounds: *Moth*ston. I suspect the people of Grimsby and Bognor Regis get the same reaction.

'Where's that, then?'

'It's in Yorkshire.'

Gareth straightens himself once more and adopts a northern accent: 'It wa' either teaching kids in London or down t'pit.'

The class erupts, and Gareth celebrates by standing up and taking a bow.

'Very good, Gareth.' I smile. 'But down t'pit is where you might end up if we don't do some work.'

For some reason this causes another round of raucous laughter, and by the time they've all quietened down our hour is up.

Once my year nines have disappeared, I draw my phone from my pocket and am faced with one new message from a number I don't recognize.

Chapter Seven

HOLLY

A load of passengers pile into my carriage at Canary Wharf and I notice the woman who's just got on and started clutching my headrest is wearing a BABY ON BOARD sticker. Everyone else in seats pretends to be engrossed in their *Evening Standard* so I jump up.

'Here, sit down.' I shuffle into the aisle to let her in. She's at that stage where she could easily go either way in the Pregnant or Fat conundrum. I wouldn't have risked it if it wasn't for the sticker. She thanks me with a grateful smile and eases herself down with her hands on her belly, and I can't help but think she's milking it a bit.

Still, she's welcome to the seat. There's no baby on board THIS commuter.

If there was even a flicker of doubt about the accuracy of the rather blunt NOT PREGNANT result on my test, it was knocked on the head by the arrival of my special friend, strolling in two hours later like it was no big deal. *Only me – sorry I'm a bit late . . . What did I miss?*

I waited for relief to hit me, but nothing. Guess I'd got carried away with the idea. Just as well Richard wasn't there to share the moment after all – what if he'd been overjoyed at the prospect of being a daddy? I'd have felt terrible.

I don't know if it was my promise to my mum or my need of a distraction that made me get in touch with Alex, but if the latter, it has worked.

Looking forward to it. Holly x

That's how I signed off my last text to him. It's what you say to someone when you've just made arrangements to see them. It doesn't matter if it's been eleven years since you last saw them, or that you barely know a thing about what they've been up to since, or even that you parted on quite dodgy terms. It's just social etiquette, isn't it? And generally politer than the truth.

Not that I'm dreading it exactly. It's just that I don't know what to expect.

Alex is two different people in my head. There's the sweet, loyal, self-conscious, a bit OCD, clever, funny Alex who always had my back. Then there's the slightly odd, bit creepy Alex who went all laddish at the first hint of sexual attention from a girl.

There are far more memories of the first Alex.

But the second Alex was the one I saw just before I left Mothston, and has stayed with me since. And what if that was just the beginning of the change? What if he carried on in that direction for the next eleven years and he's just a big old slime-ball now?

Slightly daunted by it. Holly x

That's what I'd have said if I was being really honest.

Or: Hoping it's not awkward. Holly x

'It's quite straightforward,' Jemma insisted earlier. 'Why don't you just check him out from the other side of the road, and if he's a total minger then text him and tell him you're too ill to come, then just never arrange to meet him again?'

'Well, Jem,' I countered, 'my reasons are threefold. Firstly, we're meeting inside the pub, so I won't be able to see him from across the road. Secondly, I'm not a terrible person. And thirdly, you're totally missing the point. I don't care what he looks like. It's not a blind date – he's an old mate and I'm just scared we'll have nothing to talk about.'

'Oh, come off it. You're single and you're meeting up with a guy you haven't seen for years, who also might be single. I dinnae believe for a second you haven't wondered what he looks like.'

OK, she's right. Not about me being single, obviously, but I do wonder what he looks like. Eleven years is long enough to acquire a pot belly and a receding hairline. But what if he is still nice-looking? How will I feel when I see him? The sisterly way I did for the early years of our friendship, or the tingly way I used to feel standing close to him after I started teen-crushing on him? Not that it makes a difference either way – I'm all good on the man front. But it's hard not to wonder.

A few days after I last saw him, I spent the car ride from Mothston to London convincing myself I'd got my feelings for him wrong. Never has a journey felt so meaningful. I didn't just feel like I was leaving Mothston behind – I felt like I was leaving behind the girl I'd been there. It was a journey into adulthood. But being an adult wasn't as exciting as I always thought it would be – it had responsibilities and consequences. The carefree me dancing in Ellie's garden just a few days before was like a stranger to me, and I hadn't seen her since that night.

And what I'd felt for Alex wasn't real, grown-up love – it was that girl's young, naïve idealism of it. Probably.

I was telling Jemma the truth. My biggest worry really is that we'll have nothing to talk about, which is ironic because we never stopped talking back then – he loved to talk things through. It was his thing. But what if all we've got in common is our history? I don't want to spend the night talking about the good old Mothston days. I shut a door on that part of my life a long time ago, and it's not one I particularly want to open again.

I'd talked myself in and out of cancelling by the time I got on the DLR at Bank. The fact is, I do kind of want to see him. I'm curious as to how he turned out. Mum had mentioned he was a teacher but she didn't seem to know any details. Is it what he expected? Or is he one of those disillusioned teachers who secretly hates all the kids? I can't picture that, but I'm guessing I'm not how he pictures me either. He probably expects me to still have mental hair. Thank God GHDs were invented. And he has no idea I discovered the gym so he'll be expecting more junk in my trunk. It's going to be a bit like the big reveal on one of those extreme makeover shows.

I feel good until I catch two girls on the train squeal as they recognize each other and then meet in the aisle for a kiss, which gives me a whole new thing to panic about. How should I greet Alex? A hug? A handshake? We never really had a habitual greeting for each other back when we were mates.

It's not that we weren't tactile – we'd sometimes hug each other if one of us was upset, and give each other a kiss on the cheek on our birthdays. But we never really felt the need to have a thing. Not like Ellie – good old air-kissing Ellie. Every time we said hello and goodbye the air two inches either side of my face was treated to a red-lipped smacker from her, and an exaggerated vocal *mwah*. What was the point in that? A high-five would have been more intimate – at least it involved actual bodily contact.

What a weird week. Yesterday I was facing the possibility of jumping forward several stages in my life. Being a mother – that's proper adult stuff. And now, as the DLR hurtles into Cutty Sark station, I feel I'm on my way back into 1999, where I'm eighteen again.

I don't know which is scarier.

Chapter Eight

ALEX

Even as I amble into the pub at eleven minutes to seven, a portion of my mind is adamant that I've made some kind of error, that I've dreamt Holly's text message, and that in half an hour I'll be ambling out again, past the unsubtle sniggers of those who witnessed my folly.

I survey the room and am happy with my choice of venue. When Holly suggested Greenwich for a proper drink instead, this place sprang immediately to mind. The one time I've walked past it was full of girls wearing polka-dot dresses with Doc Martens, and boys cultivating various lengths of beard. I figured it was the kind of quirky place Holly would like.

I pay for a glass of red wine and sink into one of the not-as-comfy-as-they-look sofas. The clock hanging above the bar reads eight minutes to seven.

I decide to call someone, a diversion to anaesthetize my nerves. All I'd get from Kev is 'Make sure you give her one from me', so I continue to R in my contacts.

'Alex, mate,' says Rothers enthusiastically. 'It's been too long. How's London?'

When Holly emigrated from my life, I didn't have any-one to confide in. I remember my second year at York. Holly hadn't been in touch and I was finally ready to meet someone new. Along came Charlotte McCormack, with her vertiginous legs, ironic glasses (she would deny they were ironic) and biography of Chairman Mao on her bedside table. I thought we might get married one day, but a week after we donned our caps and gowns Charlotte announced that she needed to 'go find herself' in Thailand. Eighteen months later and where had her journey of self-discovery led to? A council house in Bradford where she resides to this day with her two little boys, but that's not the point. The point is that after she left I couldn't finish a meal for a month. Loneliness isn't something you can comprehend as a kid. You feel boredom and you feel longing, but you are never alone, not truly, and especially not in a town like Mothston. And if I did need a hug, Holly was around. But after Charlotte left I was alone. I'd always missed Holly but until then I hadn't understood how much I'd lost when she absconded. I'd call Rothers at his digs in Manchester but it wasn't the same.

'Yep, good – it was my first day tod—' I say.

'JACOB, PUT THAT VASE DOWN, WILL YOU? Sorry, Alex, Megs is away at a conference and Jacob has decided now is a good opportunity to turn into one of the Children of the Damned. What were you saying?'

'Nothing, just that it was my first day at school and then tonight I'm—'

'I WON'T TELL YOU AGAIN, JACOB.'

A group of eight or nine students skulks into the pub,

each of them hanging back from the bar so as to not get stuck buying a round. Eventually they break away in ones and twos to get their own.

'Look, shall I call you back another time, mate?'

'No don't be— RIGHT, IT'S THE NAUGHTY STEP FOR YOU, YOUNG MAN. THIS SECOND, PLEASE. Sorry, Alex – it might be best if you call back. Sorry.'

Rothers is the only person I know whose life has gone precisely to plan, and so whenever I dial his number I always feel a little bit like a pest. I can't remember the last time we spoke for more than a few minutes now he's back near Mothston with a wife and kids and a partnership at a legal firm in York.

I dispatch the phone into my pocket and, without any distractions, my body becomes overwhelmed with angst, as though I'm about to sit an exam. I inspect myself. What a stupid idea to leave my work suit on. I had plenty of time back at the flat to get changed but reasoned that I look better in a suit than in any of my casual clothes. Now I feel hopelessly overdressed.

Two minutes to seven.

A reunion with my childhood sweetheart – or the girl I wish had been my childhood sweetheart. Instead, I had to make do with being best friends, but over the years I've wondered if perhaps I got that wrong too. Did I exaggerate the frequency of those nights we spent chatting until the early hours? And why did she never call if we were as close as I thought?

I look again at her final text message from this afternoon, reassuring myself that this really is happening. At least she seems excited now, and I feel excited too. I feel curious, about the past and the present. I feel nervous about what could happen in the future.

My phone seems to vibrate but when I look, no one is calling and no one has messaged.

Eleven minutes, eleven years; they don't seem so different right now. Sometimes, when we were teenagers, it felt like I'd spend my whole life waiting for Holly Gordon.

I take a large gulp of wine to settle myself, place the phone back in my pocket and, as the clock above the bar strikes seven, set my eyes anxiously on the door.

Chapter Nine

ALEX

September 1997

I loiter outside Mr Sawyer's store, waiting until I see Holly turn the corner of her road so that I can time my walk to coincide with hers, and so that our paths will cross at the start of Brickfield Road and we can walk to school together.

I feel like an idiot standing here like this, but I haven't seen Holly for two weeks, and I haven't spoken to her because it was late when she got back last night, and I couldn't wait until lunchtime or tonight to see her.

When she eventually turns the corner, running late as usual, dressed in our brand-new sixth-form uniform, adrenalin floods through my body. I set off, quickening my pace after a few seconds and getting to the corner of Brickfield just in time for it to look like pure coincidence.

'Hey. How was Turkey?' I open casually, not quite sure how to greet her after so long. 'Thanks for the postcard.'

'It was fun,' Holly says. 'I just wish my dad didn't insist on going all-inclusive. You travel all that way and end up seeing nothing but the hotel.'

She looks at me properly for the first time. 'Anyway,' she says, smiling. The holiday sun has brought out a cute little cluster of freckles around her nose. 'It's good to see you, Al. How's your dad bearing up?'

My mum and my dad. No one else mentions Mum dying, or asks how Dad is coping. I think they're worried I'll start to weep on their shoulder. Holly is the only one who doesn't seem worried.

She's always been there, an only child like me, someone to sneak off with at family parties. That's how we met: Holly's family had just moved to Mothston and Mum decided to throw a party so Mr and Mrs Gordon could make some friends.

Holly was like no one I'd ever met. When I was little, Mum would complain that I'd take too long to eat my tea. I'd spend ages deciding which item on the plate I liked the most so I could save it until last. Holly was more of a scoffer. I don't mean in an Augustus Gloop kind of way, she just didn't think about things. She got on with it and, even then, even though she was only eleven, she seemed to have her entire life planned out. I've been trying to make myself a part of her plan ever since.

And now, after Mum got cancer, after the worst thing I could ever imagine happening happened, the one good thing to come out of it is that Holly and I have become closer.

'He's . . .' My sentence falters before it gets going, and from nowhere tears start to form an unorderly queue at the top of my cheeks. Holly stops walking and I stop too, and she is staring at me intently. She begins to offer me a hug but, even though I can't think of a single thing in the world that I want more than a hug from Holly right now, I pretend not to notice her gesture and start walking again. It's the only way I can stop the tears coming.

Rothers traces my gaze to the door of the school canteen. 'Who you waiting for?' he asks.

Kev replies on my behalf. 'The girl of his wet dreams.'

His answer isn't strictly accurate. I've never actually had a wet dream. Whenever they're mentioned my face goes red and I have to pretend I know what people are on about.

'I should've guessed,' says Rothers, and I roll my eyes as though they're *way* off the mark.

Truth is, I am waiting for Holly. I want to see her to make sure we're OK after things got a bit weird this morning.

'What you've got to realize is that Holly isn't going to shag a lad who wears cords,' jibes Kev, and I pat my fingers over a pretend yawn.

'You haven't seen us when it's just me and her.'

'Obviously.'

I tut. 'We chat about everything, Kev.'

'Do you tell each other about your periods?'

He bursts into a chorus of 'Ooooooh Bodyform, Body-form for yooooouuuuuu', swinging his arms as if he was rollerblading. I tell him it was the Tampax advert where the woman wore rollerblades, not Bodyform.

Kev spits on his right hand. 'Two squid says I'm right.'

I wince. 'We don't need to shake on it.'

'Actually,' says Rothers nonchalantly, 'I believe both adverts had rollerbladers in.'

I steal a look at the door again, but am distracted by the sight of Dean Jones locked in an arm wrestle with

Shaun Harmston. As an illustration of his confidence, Dean pours ketchup on his chips with his spare hand.

'I've got to admit,' says Kev, stabbing his fork into a whole sausage and craning it towards his gob, 'she's got a cracking pair of mammaries.'

'Shut the fuck up, will you?' I snap.

Rothers freezes mid-chew.

'Bloody hell,' says Kev. 'Who's pissed on your chips?'

An uneasy silence settles among the three of us and I realize it's my fault. I overreacted when, actually, all this is a relief. The 'nice' Kev who revealed himself after Mum died last term – the one who didn't make up nicknames for me containing references to genitals, the one who didn't make a ritual of laughing at my cords – was disconcerting. I'm just irritated by his refusal to believe anything could happen between me and Holly.

'Have either of you ever had a girl try to stick a finger up your arse?' says Kev.

Neither I nor Rothers answer him.

'It's happened to me a couple of times now. I've had to cut things short and say, "Sorry, I'm not into that."'

He looks at us for a reaction but doesn't get one. We know Kev is a virgin, but ever since Megan Robinson let Rothers go to final base two weeks ago, Kev has been boasting about his own non-existent conquests.

'I reckon one of those women's magazines must have written that we like it, or something. A whole generation of female minds corrupted in one fell swoop.'

I zone out, thinking about the postcard Holly sent me last week: *Wish you were here xx*. I injected her 'Wish' with a dose of longing, and every time I've closed my eyes since then she's been there, stamped on my eyelids, lying stomach down on a sunlounger, using a hardback book for support as she penned my postcard with sorrow in her eyes.

I might not have had a wet dream, but that doesn't mean I don't lose whole weekends daydreaming about Holly lying naked in my bed, her wild hair strewn across my pillow; whole weekends scripting the conversation where I tell her. And it's not the fear of rejection that stops me, that means I'm suddenly jaw-locked. It's knowing that if I am wrong and Kev is right then things would never be the same again.

'Oi, oi,' says Kev, eyeing the door where Holly is standing with Ellie and some other girls I recognize from a collage of photos on her bedroom wall.

Without being instructed to do so, my left arm springs into a wave, and in my peripheral vision I can see Kev is shaking his head pitifully. Thankfully Holly comes over.

I stare at her in wonderment. Despite being best friends, we've never really hung out much in school, and the pressure of having an audience tightens my throat. Kev offers me a glare and I realize I need to say something but, before I do, Holly points towards the kit bag on the floor by Rothers.

'You going to football training after school?' she asks him, and when he nods, Holly says she is too.

'But you hate football!' I intervene.

'I do, but the posters says it's boys only.'

'So what? You're going to prove a point?'

Holly nods and Rothers laughs a little too hard for my liking. He's been so cocky these past few weeks. I have to suppress an intense urge to shove him over as he rocks back on two legs of his chair.

84

'Did you get a key-ring?' I ask. My way of telling the others that Holly is my friend and that I know loads about her that they don't. Like how she has a massive collection of key-rings – one for every holiday she's ever been on, including the week our families spent together in Camber Sands when we were twelve.

She shows us her steel pendant of Turkey and I ask if she's joining us, sliding my tray towards Kev to create space to my right.

Holly flashes her eyes towards her mates, who've congregated near Dean Jones and his gang.

'I'm going to sit with Ellie,' she says, biting her bottom lip apologetically. 'We've got a party to plan. Start of sixth form and all that. But hey, why don't you guys come over?'

Sit with Dean Jones? Us? I think not. Bobby Shepherd might have left to apply for the army but that lot still treat us like gypsies who've set up home in their garden.

A minute or two later I glance at where Holly and her friends have coalesced. She's in hysterics – hands on belly, mouth ajar – at something Dean Jones has said, and in that moment, for the second time today, something approaching a sob rises through me. I have to stop myself looking at Kev, because one sight of a knowing smile that I'm almost certain will be on his face might be enough to make me punch him in the nose.

Chapter Ten

HOLLY

April 2010

Wow – it's like my favourite scene from *Pretty Woman*. The one where Edward walks into the hotel bar to meet Vivian, and as he scans the room looking for her his eyes skip back to the beautiful girl with perfectly styled hair and an elegant cocktail dress sitting on a barstool. Then he tries to hide his surprise when she turns around and – OMG! – it's Vivian.

Except Alex's cords and woolly jumper have been replaced by a slim-fitting dark blue suit, rather than his miniskirt and thigh-high boots being replaced by a lacy black dress. And he no longer looks like a self-conscious teenager. As opposed to no longer looking like a self-conscious hooker.

But apart from all that it's EXACTLY the same.

'Holly!' He jumps up from the sofa and holds out his arms, evaporating my greeting anxiety. I fall gratefully into his hug, breathing in aftershave tinged with red wine – scents I've never associated with my old school friend – as his unfamiliar stubble grazes my cheek.

'Look at you!' He doesn't elaborate. Look at you – you look well? Look at you – what the hell happened?

I look at me. I'm in a white fitted Reiss shirt tucked into charcoal-grey high-waisted trousers. Hair is straight, make-up reapplied on the DLR, two dress sizes smaller than when he last saw me – heck, let's assume it was a compliment.

'And you,' I reply, shrugging off my coat. 'You look great. Totally working a suit.'

I've only ever seen Alex in a suit once, at his mum's funeral, but – and I say this fondly – at the time he looked like a refugee who'd been to a car boot sale. This jacket doesn't hang off him, but fits snugly to his slim frame.

'Why thanks.' He tugs on his lapels. 'It's one of Topman's most exclusive numbers. Let me get you a drink.'

'Lovely.' I nod towards his wineglass, suddenly excited about this. 'Same please.'

I've never been here before and it's clear why. It's a student pub. Its faux-traditional interior is full of modern replicas of traditional beer signs, and instead of a friendly landlord behind the bar who knows everybody's name, there's a bored-looking twenty-something who looks like he'd struggle to remember his own. Why did Alex pick here? We both look out of place in our smart attire compared to the eclectically dressed casual crowd, ordering their individual drinks despite being in groups.

While Alex waits patiently to be served I lower myself onto the leather sofa he'd been sitting on and immediately slide back into it. I'm still trying to sit up when Alex gets back from the bar – bottle of wine in one hand and two glasses in the other.

The fact I'm about to drink wine with Alex is surreal –

it feels too sophisticated, like we're kids playing at being grown-ups.

'Cheers.' We clink glasses, like we'd done with tons of alcopops in the past, while Alex attempts to position himself at the front of the sofa in the same way I did a moment ago.

'Good first day?' There are a thousand questions I'm far more curious to know the answer to, but none of them feels like an appropriate way to kick off a conversation with someone I haven't seen in ages.

'Yep, so far so good,' he enthuses. 'It's everything Mothston Grammar wasn't, which is perfect.'

I have to stop myself going in for an exploding fist bump like we used to do when I aced an essay or he accessorized well, even though I'd forgotten until this moment that we used to do that. It's a shame his mum isn't here to see how he's followed in her footsteps – she'd be well proud.

If it felt weird when my mum told me he was a teacher, it feels even weirder hearing him talk about it. I keep picturing our teachers. They were PROPER adults. If I saw any of them now, I'd still feel like I had to do what I was told. Not that I ever did as I was told at school. Unless it was Mr Abel, the French teacher, but that was only because I fancied him. All the girls did at some point. We used to roll our skirts from the waist to make them an inch or two shorter before his lessons.

I wonder how many teenage girls roll up their skirts before Alex's lessons. He laughs when I ask him if I have to call him Mr Tyler, revealing straight, white teeth. No surprise there – he's the only person I've ever known to floss every day. To everyone else it's a universal lie we tell our dentists. But Alex's OCDness has definitely paid off.

'I'd prefer "sir", actually.' His smile – wide and genuine, deepening the little creases beside his eyes – lights up his face. Not literally, like a glow worm. Just one of those smiles that means he always looked good in photographs.

'What about you?' he asks. 'Your mum said you work in the City but she didn't say what . . .'

'I'm a PA.' I shrug dismissively. Why did I do that? I love my job – I've never dreaded going in. My colleagues are a laugh, it's a good company to work for – I've got BUPA and a decent pension. But when I see a flash of surprise cross Alex's face, which he tries to take back by scratching his head above his raised eyebrows, I realize that's what I was trying to avoid. Him being disappointed for me.

I can't blame him. He was the one I told every time I changed my mind about what I wanted to do when I grew up. There was the English pub I was going to run in New York, with a big office out the back to do paperwork, although sometimes I'd serve behind the bar, where regulars would tell me their problems while I topped up their whisky. Or the cake shop in Paris, where I'd do all the baking, and serve bottomless cups of tea and leave the daily papers on all the tables. Or the bra shop for women with big boobs, where you could get pretty underwear even if you were above a C cup, rather than those ugly beige contraptions I had to make do with when I was sixteen.

But fickle as I was, none of my career plans ever involved opening someone else's post.

'I never saw that coming either,' I insist, gazing at my

fingers as I twirl strands of hair around them. 'It was never really a decision I made – I just fell into it while I was waiting to wake up one day and suddenly know what I wanted to do.'

I drop my hair and divert my eyes to Alex. He's listening intently, one elbow resting on the back of the sofa, one side of his head resting in his palm. The space between his eyebrows is furrowed slightly and I wonder what he's thinking.

I've never said all this out loud before. Not sure why I am now. I used to do this with Alex when we were younger – volunteer more information than I did with anyone else. He wasn't like my other friends, butting in after every sentence with their opinion. He listened without judging and made me see myself more clearly. Like I was seeing me through his eyes or something.

'And then it just worked out,' I clarify, breaking eye contact and sipping my wine. 'I'm happy at Hexagon. And me and Richard – my boss – we make a great team.'

I want to tell him we're a great team in the non-professional sense too but Richard is a bit funny about people knowing. Which is understandable – it wouldn't reflect well on either of us.

'So what's he like? Your boss, I mean?'

'Oh, he's great.' I sip my wine again to disguise the way the corners of my mouth are twitching involuntarily. 'We're actually kind of together.'

Well, what was I supposed to do? He practically dragged it out of me.

'Oh, wow.' Alex leans back and folds his arms, and I can't quite read his expression. I tell him more, before he jumps to any wrong conclusions. I tell him everything actually, aside from the teeny tiny detail about it being a secret. Because while I totally get why we don't tell anyone, I'm not sure if I can summarize it eloquently enough to make him get it.

'That's great, Hols.' Alex smiles warmly when I'm done. 'I knew you'd be settled down.'

It feels like an odd thing to say, but before I can dwell on it, he asks what it is Hexagon does.

'It's a marketing agency. Richard thinks that blah blah blah blah, blah blah-blah blah blah blah-blah . . .'

I don't say blah – I use actual words – but this is potentially what Alex is hearing. Why are we back on Richard? Have I become one of those smug, annoying girls who turn everything around to be about their boyfriend?

Anyone: 'Can you pass me a napkin, please?'

Me: 'Richard uses napkins, you know.'

Pause.

Anyone: 'Er, OK.'

'What about you?' My eyes flick to his left hand. It's ringless. 'Is there a future Mrs Tyler on the scene?'

'Nope,' he says matter-of-factly. 'Looks like I'll be turning thirty single, but I'm not fussed.'

It's evident he's cool with his relationship status from the way he meets my eye. I still can't get over his newly found self-confidence, which he manages to pull off without being remotely cocky.

Alex is definitely boyfriend material. Not for me, obviously, but maybe I should try to set him up with Jemma. On second thoughts, I'm not sure he'd be able to cope with her potty mouth – he's still so polite.

Who'd have thought I'd be sitting here trying to think

91

of potential girlfriends for Alex. It makes me want to ask about something I've been wondering for the past eleven years. I hadn't planned to bring it up tonight if he didn't mention it, but then I didn't plan to tell him about Richard either, so what the hell – in for a penny . . .

'So how come it never worked out with Jane?' I take a drink as I say it because somehow that makes it seem a bit more of a casual enquiry. The few seconds it takes him to answer seem to stretch on for ever, and my tenterhooks are such that the sound of crashing coins as the bloke on the fruit machine next to us wins the jackpot sounds earth-shatteringly loud.

'Jane?' Alex screws up his forehead in confusion.

'That girl you starting dating at the end of sixth form,' I remind him. 'Well fit. Big boobs. Good kisser.' I do that last bit in his thick Yorkshire accent.

'Oh her.' He sounds surprised. 'Wow, Jane – I'd forgotten about her. I think we only went out once or twice. How did you . . . ?'

But he doesn't finish his sentence.

He barely remembers her. All these years I've considered Jane to have contributed to the way my life panned out. She's gone through several incarnations in my head – from pretty, bookish brunette to sexy, blonde sporty-type to a stylish, raven-haired fashionista. And Alex barely remembers her. Would it have made a difference if I'd known the Jane thing would go nowhere? Maybe I'd have told him what I went round to tell him. Still, if anything had changed the course of my life I might not have ended up where I am today with Richard, so I guess everything happens for a reason. I decide to let it go.

I ask Alex how he's finding London, and his face brightens in the same way it did when he was talking about school. He gushes about the museums and theatres with the optimism of someone who's just moved here. I won't kill his buzz, but I'll remind him of this conversation in three months' time when he's complaining about it taking an hour and a half to visit a friend in the same city and fighting an urge to tut loudly at tourists who stand on the left side on escalators.

By the second bottle of wine we've both given up trying to sit upright, leaning back instead with one elbow each on the back of the sofa, facing each other, while he fills me in on who still lives in Mothston, who's left and who's dead. I've been waiting for a lull in the conversation so I can nip to the loo, but there hasn't been one.

'What about Mr Sawyer – the dwarf that ran the paper shop. Is he still . . .'

I pause and wait for Alex to correct me.

'What?' he asks, confused about why I've stopped.

'Aren't you going to remind me Sawyer is a midget – not a dwarf?'

'Nah.' He shrugs, drinking his wine.

'Wow, you've changed,' I tease. 'That would have annoyed the hell out of you eleven years ago. That's why I said it.'

He smiles. 'Yep, he's still there. Do you remember when I asked for a quarter of cola cubes off the top row, then after he'd spent half an hour going up his ladder to get them then down again, you—'

'Asked if I could have a quarter too? Yes! He thought I did it on purpose – he wasn't happy.'

'Nope, he wasn't. He was Grumpy.'

I get his joke just as I'm swallowing wine, and my unexpected laughter makes me spit it everywhere.

And then I blink and by the time my eyes are open again Alex has been to the bar and asked for a towel. My cheeks flush a little and I hope he doesn't notice. I don't know why I'm embarrassed – this is the guy who once held my hair back while I sicked into a wheelie bin.

'Actually,' I say, grabbing the towel and whipping him with it, before wiping the table, 'Grumpy and Happy were dwarfs and Sawyer was a midget.'

'Right, sorry.'

I'd forgotten how funny Alex was. He was never one of those people who always tried to be the clown, all gag, gag, gag. He doesn't even laugh at his own jokes. You'll miss them if you're not listening carefully enough.

He tells me about his housemate sneezing with genuine horror, like he's revealing he's found dead babies in his basement or something, and I realize that I've gone from noticing how much Alex has changed to thinking how he hasn't changed at all.

His eyes are as wide and white as I remember, but the lines around them when he smiles are new. His hair hasn't actually changed since school but he's grown into it. While most lads at school had French crops, crew cuts or curtains, he wore his long and shaggy, hanging over his ears. A bit teacherish. But teacherish suits him now he's a teacher.

'Did your old key-ring get too heavy to lug around?'

'Sorry?' I follow the direction of Alex's eyes to the table, where my silver heart-shaped key-ring with my door keys attached is spilling from my bag.

'You used to keep your keys on that holiday key-ring collection.'

'Ah, I stopped using that at uni. I still have it, but to be honest it isn't much bigger than the last time you saw it.'

I fill Alex in on my holidays since school. There was Magaluf with Leah, Susie and a couple of other uni mates. Then there was Crete with Max, Leah and Rob. Then Max and I went to Barcelona on our three-year anniversary.

That's it.

'You're kidding!' exclaims Alex in genuine surprise. 'How come?'

Because you can't have everything. I explain how I met Max at uni and we couldn't afford to travel. That never changed for him when he became a sporadically working music journalist. And then along came Richard.

'I'll see the world one day, though,' I insist, if only to get rid of that slight look of pity on Alex's face, which I can't bear.

'With Richard?'

An image pops into my head of Richard wearing a backpack and sandals, checking into a hostel. I almost laugh out loud. I guess I'm a bit old to do the backpacking thing anyway, but we'll take loads of holidays, I'm sure.

'Maybe.' I squirm in my seat, then stop myself before Alex reads anything into it. 'I don't know. Things are easier when you're younger, aren't they? Even if you aren't doing anything exciting, you can at least look forward to doing it. When you're approaching thirty you have to accept you might never do it.'

We both sip our drinks, experiencing something resembling an awkward silence for the first time. I try to

95

shake off my defensiveness and think of something to say, but Alex beats me to it.

'How come you're never back in Mothston?'

'Did my mum tell you to ask that?' I narrow my eyes at him. He laughs and shakes his head but it wouldn't surprise me. They used to gang up on me all the time.

Mum: You're not SERIOUSLY going out in that belt, are you?

Me: Yes, and it's not a belt – it's a skirt.

Alex: It is a bit short, Hols . . .

Mum: Have you started that history essay yet, Holly?

Me: Nah, I've got loads of time.

Alex: Um, it's due tomorrow, Hols . . .

To be fair, there were photos of my bum cheeks from that party, and my late coursework brought my history GCSE down a grade.

'I just need to get round to it,' I tell him, putting my hand on his knee to lever myself up. 'I'm just nipping to the loo.'

When I get back Alex is pulling pound coins out of his wallet.

'Fancy it?' He nods at the quiz machine.

'Sure.' I pick up my glass and unsteadily follow him over, watching him attempt to balance his glass on the tilted top of the machine a couple of times before settling for the windowsill behind it. Thank God I'm not the only tipsy one.

Alex feeds in the coins and I poise myself for button pushing.

'Stop choosing Entertainment, you,' he complains after the third question he doesn't know the answer to.

He gently shoves me away, buying himself long enough

to select Art & Literature, hitting the screen before I have time to finish reading the question. Then he picks Art & Literature again.

In which Shakespeare play was Don John the sinister half-brother of Don Pedro?

'*MUCH ADO ABOUT NOTHING*!' My finger is on the button before Alex gets a chance.

'Why are you shouting?'

'I DON'T KNOW.'

'Well done on that answer, though.'

'It was easy.' He does not need to know I only remember that because Keanu Reeves played him in the film.

'So, do you know any Shakespeare characters that weren't brought to life by Keanu Reeves?' He gives me a sidelong smile, which I use as an opportunity to hit Entertainment again.

'NOOOOO, you div!' I slap his arm when he picks Will Young as an *X-Factor* winner. 'He was *Pop Idol*. Well done – game over.'

'Wow, it's been years since anyone called me a div.'

'Yeah, to your face maybe. Ooh, you should come to the pub quiz opposite my work one Wednesday – we suck at the Art and Literature questions.'

And the History ones.

And Sport.

And Politics.

'Aw thanks, I'd love to. Let's play again. I'll get us another drink and we can use the change from that. Same again?'

I'm about to say yes but then see that the clock above the bar says 10.30 p.m. – I didn't realize it was that late. It's going to take fifteen minutes to walk over the heath.

If I go now I can be in bed by 11 p.m. I feel surprisingly reluctant to leave and consider relenting to just one more, but if Richard calls when his flight lands I don't want to have to take the call here.

'I should go. Let's do this again soon, though – it's been fun.'

'Definitely,' he says, a little taken aback.

'It really was fun,' I say again, squeezing his arm. I mean it – it was the most fun I've had in ages. Nothing about the last time we saw each other in Mothston came up – thank God – so it was just like the times we hung out before that. I forgot how effortless I found his company. But work will be busy with Richard being back in the office, and I could do with an early start.

'It's fine. A hangover on my second day wouldn't go down well anyway.'

I don't think I've seen Alex with a hangover. He was a rare sort of teenager who knew when to stop. That was on the few occasions he even started.

'You sure you don't want to jump in a taxi?' Alex asks me for the third time as he hugs me outside the pub. I assure him I'll be fine, and he makes me promise I'll text him when I get home.

My feet start to hurt after five minutes, so as soon as I get onto the grassy heath, I take off my shoes and carry them. The stiletto heal will also double up as an excellent weapon should an attacker strike. Bonus.

I recall Alex telling me off when I took off my shoes to walk home barefoot after a night out in Mothston. He said I might stand on a broken bottle and cut my foot and when I wasn't worried he said I might stand on a junkie's dirty needle and get AIDS, and I pretended not

98

to be worried so he took his socks off and made me put them on.

I'm still smiling at the memory when I stumble through my front door and trip over Harold, who has clearly been clock-watching. When I climb into bed I turn up the volume on my phone in case Richard calls but it's not long before I'm in a deep, uninterrupted sleep.

Chapter Eleven

ALEX

The streets of Greenwich are the colour of Halloween pumpkins as I walk home. Beyond the glow of lamp-posts is a cloudless night sky, and I recall someone once telling me that most of the stars visible to the human eye don't exist any more; they've burnt out, but because of the time light takes to travel, you can still see them. So really, you never know if you're witnessing the real thing or not.

I enter the flat, finding it unlit and silent, but as I hop, skip and jump around piles of books to undress, the sound of a key turning in the lock is accompanied by a female voice. Giggling and clumsy footsteps are interrupted by a sneeze. And another and another. Poor woman. Moments later Carl's bedroom door creeks shut and that's the last I hear of them.

I settle into bed myself but feel restless. It's not even 11 p.m. when Holly texts to say she is home safe. Still, it was nice seeing her again. It wasn't awkward and my jaw didn't lock once. I discovered what she's been doing since leaving Mothston and heard all about her boyfriend, who wasn't Max, and who she spoke about with such ardour that I got the impression she was warning me. *I knew about your pitiful crush back then, Al; please don't get any ideas this time.* But you know what? That's all right. It's different now. She's different.

When she walked into the pub my arms opened involuntarily. Blimey, I thought. All this time I've carried a Polaroid in my head, a photograph of Holly in her combats and navy-blue vest top. But here she was in ten megapixels: office clothes Photoshopped onto her slimline body, hair digitally enhanced to remove any trace of a curl, freckles vanquished by time or make-up. I instantly wished I'd chosen a smarter pub.

Don't get me wrong: she looked great. Just not like the girl in the Polaroid. Isn't it weird how things turn out? If you'd asked me before tonight what I thought Holly would be doing for a living, PA wouldn't have been top of the list. It wouldn't have even been on the list. It would have been on the definitely-not-on-the-list list alongside roofer, M16 spy and Bosnian folk singer. But then my career hardly warrants an episode of *This Is Your Life*. I was more shocked that she didn't have any stories of swimming on Bondi Beach or camping on a mountain in Peru. It's like when you grow up and then one day you visit your primary school, and it seems tiny compared with how you perceived it as a kid. Maybe Holly wasn't the person I perceived her to be. Maybe she was never the free spirit I thought. The free spirit I loved.

She is happy, though. Back in the day it was seeing the world and parties that caused her pupils to dilate – these days it's Richard and work. And I enjoyed hearing about it; enjoyed being with her again; enjoyed looking at her without feeling the swell of any feelings in my stomach. It was quite liberating. And if right now I feel a bit flat, it is only because I allowed my imagination to run away with me a little.

I've got a friend down here. I should be delighted. Now I just need to find some single friends; friends who are around on Saturday nights and other occasions reserved for couples, when having a blank diary feels like watching a play in which everyone else has got a part. Bank Holidays alone are probably my least favourite thing about being single, closely followed by the obligatory conversation with my Auntie Pauline every Christmas:

AP: Have you met a nice girl yet, Alex?

Me: Nope, not yet, Auntie Pauline.

AP: Oh well, you're no age.

Dad: He's almost thirty, Pauline.

AP: What happened to that girl you were seeing? The tall one?

Dad: She left him.

AP: I liked her.

Dad: We all liked her.

Me: Me and Charlotte split up almost seven years ago, Auntie Pauline.

AP: And you haven't had a girlfriend since then?

Me: There was Debbie. You met her. She came for Christmas dinner one year, remember?

AP: What happened to her?

Dad: She left him.

Me: She didn't leave me.

I feel tired but I cannot seem to drift off. I flip my pillow so it's cool against my cheek but it doesn't help. I've got too many thoughts going around in my head.

I pass her on my way to the kitchen. A brunette straight from the pages of a fashion magazine. She's heading out of the flat and offers a casual, polite smile with glossy lips.

'That your other half?' I say to Carl, who is leaning against the kitchen sideboard, a plate in one hand and a slice of toast in the other.

'Sophie? God, no.' He looks genuinely horrified at the thought. 'We just have an arrangement.'

Unsure what to say, I nod interestedly.

'I'm not ready for anything heavy,' he elaborates in between bites of toast. 'Soph's the same. It suits us both.'

Now neither of us can think of anything else to say. Carl stands there munching his breakfast while I construct my packed lunch.

'You get up to much last night, then?'

I tell him about Holly and deflect his predictable question about whether there is anything between the two of us. I can sense he is sceptical. What is it with people?

'You're probably right not to commit yourself,' he says, placing his empty plate on top of a stack of *his* dirty pots in the sink. 'I reckon women are a bit like bacteria: once you've got one on the go, they start to multiply.'

I smile and Carl starts to laugh. I think he thinks I'm smiling in admiration for his theory, but it's not that. I'm just relieved that he knows what bacteria is.

*

I once asked Mr Scrafton, chemistry teacher at Mothston Grammar, what caused hangovers, and he explained about chemicals formed during alcohol processing called congeners. It's these little buggers that make your belly cower, your throat wither and your head gyrate. Dark drinks like brandy, red wine and whisky contain loads of congeners, whereas clear spirits like white rum, vodka and gin don't, and so cause hangovers less frequently. Mr Scrafton and I concurred that chemistry lessons would be far more useful if information like this was on the syllabus.

My problem is that I started drinking red wine in my early twenties in the hope that Charlotte McCormack would think I was sophisticated, and I got a taste for it. Hence bringing my year nines to order this morning is even harder than it was yesterday. I struggle to make myself heard over Stacey Bamber, who is telling Bhumi Khan about visiting her cousins in Peckham, where it's all 'pow pow' (she makes a gun with her fingers) apparently.

'Can we settle down, please?' I say, circulating sheets for a *Hamlet*-themed spelling test.

As I navigate the room Gareth Stones draws his iPhone from his trouser pocket and uses its reflection to review a face that's long and thin and colourless. His deep-sunken eyes are a little too close together, making him resemble a cartoon ghost.

'Oi, Hairy Muff,' he squalls at Mary Hough. 'How's my hair?'

'I swear to God, I'm gonna fuck you up in a second,' she answers.

I warn Mary about her language and ask Gareth to

put his phone somewhere I can't see it, then glance hopefully at Ms Pritchard, the teaching assistant, as the test begins. Most of the kids work quietly, though Stacey uses the time to sketch a penis in red ink. The detail is quite impressive, but her scale is way off. At least, I hope it is.

'Laertes sounds like something I'd catch off you, Hairy,' shouts Gareth, and the silence is broken by a chorus of 'Ooooh!'.

Mary gawps at me. 'How can I not cuss when he's such a tosser all the time, Mr Tyler?'

It takes me a few minutes to settle the class but the pattern repeats itself: I'm just getting into something when either Gareth or Stacey misbehaves and I have to start over. It's like navigating one of those electric buzzer games, and today, because of the congeners, I just can't keep a steady hand.

'OK, what do we think prompts Hamlet's outburst at Ophelia's graveside?' I venture.

Silence. Torpid silence.

'How about you, Kenny?'

Kenny hangs his head low throughout class, and when he does look up his eyes are glassy with disinterest.

'Come on, remember we talked this through yesterday?'

Gareth commences a low chant of Kenny's name. Paul Keogh joins in. I shush them.

'Want me to buy you some earplugs?' says Gareth, but I manage to zone out the laughter that ensues and focus on Kenny.

I give him one more chance to answer amid the din.

'Look, I don't fucking know, all right?'

He shoves his desk forwards with force, instantly hushing the room. He stands and slides a hand down his trouser front menacingly, and I feel panic consume me. I take a tentative step towards him. He eyeballs me. For the first time in six years I feel totally out of my depth in a classroom. Holly wouldn't be so proud of my teaching career if she was witness to this. Kenny's arm slowly withdraws up past his belt. Teaching deprived kids to love English – who was I kidding? I'm going to have to restrain him.

Then he whips it out.

An afro comb.

He stabs the implement sideways into his hair and sulks out of the room with a limp.

Flustered, I follow him, asking Ms Prichard to cover while I shadow Kenny through the door. I'm soon accelerating into a jog, striding past the toilets before going back on myself to inspect the cubicles. No sign. I shuffle outside onto the concrete yard where the pupils spend break and lunch, and that's where I spot him, in the far corner, crawling underneath a wire fence that has come loose at the roots. He's walking towards four or five older boys. They're wearing baggy jeans and most of them have at least one hand tucked into their pants, and they greet him with a mixture of elaborate handshakes and simple nods. I watch them slope off away from the school grounds, and in that moment resolve to make Kenny Sonola my first pet project at Whitford High.

When the last of my year nines has disappeared I fall into my chair with a tired breath. If I'd been teaching years seven or eight, the room would smell of sweat; a lot of eleven- and twelve-year-olds haven't been introduced to Lynx yet. But once they get to thirteen and fourteen they leave behind a whiffy amalgam of celebrity perfumes, marker pens, fake tan and lethargy.

'I can't stop thinking about what happened with Kenny before,' I tell Ms Pritchard.

'It was hardly your fault,' she consoles in a melodic Irish accent that makes everything she says sound like she's tucking you into bed. 'That boy's got issues.'

It turns out that at the age of fourteen Kenny already has as many letters after his name as I do. Kenny Sonola SEBD SAP, to give him his full title. Which means he has Social Emotional Behavioural Difficulties and is on the School Action Plus programme. Ms Pritchard doesn't know much about his home life, other than his mum died when he was young and he's spent some time in care.

'You know what I thought when he put his hands down his trousers?' I say. 'I thought he was going to pull out a knife.'

'So did I – that's what anyone would have thought.'

I was too caught up with everything to notice yesterday, but her wavy auburn hair, pale skin and constant smile give her a beauty that's enhanced by the fact she seems oblivious to it.

'Yep, and that's my point. He's black and he's not engaging in class so he must be a wrong 'un. I saw him outside with some other black boys and instantly I thought, *He's in a gang.* I can't believe I've fallen into that way of thinking.'

'You're being too hard on yourself.'

Ms Pritchard places a comforting hand on my forearm

107

and I thank her with a dejected smile. She crouches for her handbag and in doing so a scarlet thong inches ever so slightly over the back of her trousers. It's hard not to stare. She doesn't seem like the type who'd dispatch such an overt sexual gesture, but then if my boxer shorts were on view above low-riding trousers, I'd know about it, wouldn't I?

'I guess I'll see you later then,' she says, grinning as I hold the door open.

Then I'm on my own, and suddenly I don't feel so tired or weary or hungover.

The DLR to Greenwich is sliding into the station and I'm sidestepping towards where I think the doors are going to stop when I'm distracted by a female voice.

I swivel round and . . .

'Ms Pritchard – I didn't know you got the—'

We step onto the train together.

'Please, call me Cassie. Short for Cassandra but I only get that when I've been bad. I guess you're Alexander when you've done something wrong, right?'

She chuckles to herself while I try to recall the last time anyone called me Alexander. Several years at least.

For a moment I imagine her hair strewn across my chest: we're in bed together, her head is resting on my shoulder and it's the morning after the night before, a night in which she called me Alexander numerous times.

'Alex!' she calls, waving her hand in front of my face as we pull into Cutty Sark. 'I'm getting off here.'

The train is just gathering speed again when a hooded boy who got on with us at Deptford Bridge turns around.

'All right, *Alex*.'

Gareth Stones allows a piece of chewing gum to hang from his lips.

'You shagging Ms Pritchard, are you?'

Chapter Twelve

HOLLY

'So have you and Richard had The Talk yet?'

I peer around the office to make sure no one is listening in to my conversation.

'Shit off with your TALK nonsense, Susie,' I whisper forcefully into the phone.

'But when is—'

'Why don't you ask him yourself at Chloe's wedding?' That shuts her up for a second and a half.

'He's coming?'

'Course.'

'As in coming coming, or as in your-birthday-meal coming.'

'Coming coming. Now I have to go – I can't talk about this here. Love you, bye!'

She returns the sentiment and I hang up.

So, Richard and I have never had The Talk. The talk most of my mates think is necessary to promote their bloke from This Guy I'm Seeing to My Boyfriend.

They obsess about it for ages, meticulously plan the time and the place they're going to have it, practise the conversation in their head thirty-two times then breezily ask . . .

'So, where do you see this going?'

Then hold their breath while waiting for confirmation that this *is* a relationship, *or* a stammering no-eye-contact assertion that This Guy They're Seeing isn't really looking for anything serious with *anyone* right now.

Or that he thinks she's awesome but he's just found out that his company is about to move him to its Dubai office for two years and he leaves next Tuesday. Jemma doesn't know I saw the guy who told her that buying wine in Waitrose a month later.

Anyway, I've never bought into The Talk. I've never got to a stage when I've felt like I needed it, which is lucky because it sounds as much fun as poking my own eye with a rusty compass.

At school it was easy – you were the rightful owner of a boyfriend after the conversation:

'Will you go out with me?'

'Yes.'

Then Max saved me from any fleeting worries that we might need The Talk. Three weeks after we met, I over-heard him on the phone telling his mate he was out with his girlfriend. I panicked for a second, looking around to see where this girlfriend he spoke of was, before I realized it was me.

But how can Richard refer to me as his girlfriend when the whole idea is that no one knows? Still, I've never felt the need to resort to 'So, where is this going?'. But ever since my birthday dinner, Susie has taken to calling me daily to convince me otherwise.

Leah inadvertently started it after her husband Rob let slip that Max had a new girlfriend, Felicity, so she elbowed him to shut him up.

Rob and Max are best friends. Leah and I met them in the student union and, six years later, while Leah and Rob were getting married, Max and I were breaking up. Literally at the wedding. We looked at Leah and Rob, looked at each other and realized that there would never be a time when we could stand there and promise to be together for ever. It was pretty amicable. We don't stay in touch but I let him share custody of Leah and Rob without him having to dress as Spiderman and scale a tall building.

'Oh, sorry.' Rob looked embarrassed.

'Don't be silly – why would I care if he has a girl-friend?' I meant this. 'The break-up was mutual.'

'Yeah, but no one likes to lose the race,' Susie joined in, as she beckoned the waiter over. 'I'll have another vodka, soda water and lime, please. Fresh lime – not cordial. Thanks.'

'Um, lose the WHAT now, Susie?' I asked once the waiter had disappeared again.

'You know – after a break-up. Everyone wants to be first to get with someone else.'

'Firstly, that's crap, Suze – there's no race. And apart from anything else, I've been with Richard for nine months.'

I won the race by a mile. I could have stopped and danced the Macarena at the halfway point and still Max wouldn't have caught up with me.

'Yeah, Susie.' Leah smiled encouragingly at me. 'She has her thing with Richard.'

'Um, can we really class her and Richard as an actual thing, though? No one apart from us even knows they're together.'

'How come?' asked Jamie, Susie's new man. He's her usual type – sweet, amiable, easily walked over.

So far, we like him. By we, I mean me, Leah and Rob. And Susie tolerates him, so that's promising. It was touch and go when he offered her half his butter-laden garlic bread. Seriously, dude? Tempting her with an amalgamation of carbs AND fat? The rest of us stopped breathing for about a minute while she glared at him. But we got past it, and I feel like we're all closer for it.

'So let me get this straight,' said Jamie, once I'd filled him in. 'He's never met your mates, you've never been on holiday together – in fact, you rarely go out together – and the first three months of your, um, relationship, you only ever slept together at work.'

'Yep. What's your point?'

'It just seems—'

'And don't forget that Suze and I still have the "Sooooo, what do you think of Jamie?" conversation to come later.'

'No point. Just making sure I'm following.'

'Have you had The Talk?' asked Susie, before I had a chance to change the subject.

'What talk?'

'The one in which you establish you're boyfriend and girlfriend.'

'Well, no – we were going to, but then we remembered we're not fourteen.'

'Yeah, and why would he be sleeping with her if he wasn't serious about her?' added Leah.

113

'Sure,' said Rob drily, while Jamie nearly choked on his garlic bread. 'I can't think of any other reason.' He grinned in my direction but something in my face made him change it to an apologetic smile.

'So have you told your mum yet?' Susie asked, knowing I haven't.

'No. Now can we quit the Spanish effing Inquisition and you all give me presents please?'

'Hols, come watch this video of cats being dicks on You-Tube,' Jemma is saying, as Danny walks away, wiping a tear from his eye.

'I'm busy,' I call, turning back to the work on my screen.

I mean, it's not like I don't understand why my friends don't get it. I can see how it looks from the outside. But they don't see us when it's just the two of us.

I'd never tell anyone this, but whenever I'm in a relationship I make a little montage in my head and put a song to it. Like in a film. In the early years with Max, the song was Savage Garden's 'Truly Madly Deeply'. The scenes playing in my mind were things like us lying together in my single bed in halls of residence, facing each other, propped up on our elbows as we talked late into the night. Or snogging in the sea on holiday in Crete, while Leah and Rob played with a ball a few metres away shouting, 'Get a room!' Or in the kitchen at a house party; me sitting on the worktop and leaning on his shoulders while he stood between my legs, facing outwards as we laughed with friends.

Then in the last couple of years with Max, after

we moved in together, the song changed to 'End of a Century' by Blur. Us sitting at separate ends of the sofa watching *EastEnders*.

We would LITERALLY kiss with dry lips and then say goodnight.

Every boyfriend – right from my first in sixth form – has had a soundtrack montage.

Anyway, after the first night I kissed Richard, and in the following few weeks, my mind mingled scenes of us making meaningful eye contact in the office with him grabbing me passionately and throwing me down on his desk – all to the tune of Etta James's 'I Just Wanna Make Love to You'.

But it's different now.

The song is 'Better Together'. The scenes are me with my legs over his lap, talking about our day. And us dancing to the radio around his big kitchen while we cook dinner – him chopping veg and me scraping it off the chopping board into the wok, then clinking our big wineglasses together. High-fiving after finally completing a project following a late night at the office. Him grabbing me passionately and throwing me down on his desk.

Because, in the words of Jack Johnson, we really are so much better when we're together.

Feel free to vomit.

The point is: it's real.

He wouldn't be coming to Chloe's wedding otherwise.

Admittedly, Susie's cynicism has got to me – I'd even started worrying she was right and that I've blown the relationship out of proportion in my head. But then I told

Richard I was thinking of taking Alex as my plus one, and he was quite taken aback that I hadn't thought to invite him. I realized it was silly assuming he wouldn't want to come. Chloe's an old mate from university so there won't be anyone who knows him, and that's the only issue.

'Can I ask your advice or are you still too busy?' Jemma pouts at me.

'Go for it.' I smile. I can multitask.

It turns out Jemma has invited Jonny, that banker who nearly ran her over on his bike – who she's now had three dates with – to the quiz tomorrow. Which isn't a problem in itself, except that after an initial hot date she's feeling a familiar lack of enthusiasm from him the last couple of times, and is relying on tomorrow to bring it back from the brink.

'I need your help, Holly,' she whines. 'I'm so *bored* of being single. How long have you been single?'

My eyes flicker to my boyfriend's office door as I answer . . .

'About a year.'

'Have you been on any dates?'

'No.'

'Wow – have you even had sex in that time?'

'Um. No?'

I've never had so much sex. Richard is one of those people who is ALWAYS in the mood.

Way to congratulate him after he nets a big account? Sex.

Way to cheer him up when client negotiations fall through? Touch his willy.

Way to alleviate his boredom? Take your clothes off.

116

Way to help him relax after a stressful day? Cook him dinner and serve it with Scotch and a shoulder rub.

He's not a piece of meat, after all.

'Wow, a year. That's depressing,' Jemma says.

Actually, the most depressing my sex life has ever been was Max's final year. It wasn't like we never did it – we were doing it about once a week towards the end, but it was more out of maintenance than passion. Like bleeding the radiators or cleaning the oven.

'What's my sex life got to do with it? I thought you were asking me for advice.'

'Oh, yeah. Well, it sounds like it'll be the blind leading the blind, but you've at least *had* a long-term relationship so you must have had it in you at some point.'

I find it hard to advise Jem as I truly have no idea where she goes wrong.

'Did you kiss him?'

'Course.' Then she slaps her forehead dramatically. 'Is that where I'm going wrong? Do I need to stop acting like a big whore?'

'Nah, it's important to be yourself.'

'Oh HA HA HA.'

'Maybe that's it.' I clutch at straws. 'Guys love a challenge. Try it – no kissing on the first date.'

'Great – thanks for the advice.' She picks up her phone receiver. 'Hi, is that Doctor Who? Hi, Doctor, I was just wondering if I could borrow your Tardis so I can go back two weeks and four days so I can *not* snog the face off Jonny on our first date.'

'Well, obviously it's too late for that,' I laugh as she slams down the phone. 'But maybe just hold out for a while before you sleep with him.'

She picks up her phone again. 'Hi, Doctor, I was just wondering if I could borrow your Tardis so I can go back two weeks and three days . . .'

Then she notices Danny has got up to go to the loo, so she sneaks over to tip the contents of his hole punch onto his keyboard.

'Can I get some relationship advice?' Danny stops at my desk on his way back from the loo and perches himself on the edge.

'Why not? I'm putting out fires all over the place to-day. What's up?'

Danny comes across as a bit of a lad with his tales of debauchery in Romford nightclubs, and waking the next morning in some unknown girl's bed – but he's a softie when he falls for someone. Which he does approximately four times a day. He's currently hung up on Carla – the twenty-one-year-old temp who covered for Jemma when she was on holiday. They've been joined at the hip for the three months since, but on Saturday she leaves for a year in Australia.

'So I want to ask her to stay but I keep bottling it because I'm scared she'll say no and I'll look like a twat, y'know what I mean? Now I'm scared it's too late. Should I turn up at the airport by surprise and beg her to stay? Girls love that shit, right?'

He needs to stop reading so much into his dates' reactions to chick flicks. I tell him so.

'We love it in films but in real life, Danny, we'd think it was kind of awkward and a bit stalkerish. Let her go. A year will fly by and if it's real, you'll pick up where you left off when she's back. If you don't, it was never going to work anyway. That's better than her staying, then ending up resenting you for the fact she never travelled.'

'Yeah. You're right.' He looks pained for a moment then forces a smile and ruffles my hair. 'Cheers, Holly. You're like the big sister I never had.'

'Aw, and you're like the little brother I never wanted.' I comb my hair with my fingers, trying to rectify the damage.

The clock strikes 5.30 p.m. and we're surrounded by a chorus of the DA DA DA DUM of Windows shutting down, so Danny leaves to turn his own computer off.

'See you tomorrow, ladies,' he says a minute later, stopping next to Jemma to empty her box of paperclips all over her desk. 'Are we still quizzing tomorrow night?'

'Wouldn't miss it for the world.' Jemma slips on her denim jacket without acknowledging the paperclip situation. It has made no difference to the state of her desk, so the joke's on him really. 'Oh, and I'm bringing a friend. A boyfriend, actually. So if you could act like I'm God's gift to men for the evening I'd really appreciate it.'

'Sure – I did GCSE drama so I'm a good actor. Holly, you in?'

'Yeah – I'll probably have my friend Alex with me too.' As I say it I mentally slap my forehead. Alex doesn't know Richard is a secret. I should have told him, I know, but it seemed easier not to have to explain.

'But he's not her boyfriend,' Jemma clarifies. 'Just a *boy* friend. So there's no need to be nice to her too.'

'What about you, Mel?' Danny asks Melissa, who has just strolled out of the meeting room.

I shoot him a look but compose my face quickly, while

119

Jemma continues to glare at him like he stabbed her granny.

'I can't tomorrow night – I've got yoga,' Melissa replies, a hint of surprise in her voice. 'But I can pop in for one drink before I go.'

'Excellent,' smiles Danny.

'Excellent?' Jemma and I say in unison once Melissa's gone.

'What? I couldn't not ask her when we were all talking about it. Besides – she's all right. I don't know what you lot have against her.'

'I don't know what you've got *for* her,' Jemma is saying as they traipse out of the office.

I'm getting ready to leave myself when my phone rings.

'Hexagon Marketing? Oh hi, Mum.'

'You need to come home soon,' she's saying. Uncharacteristically direct. I'm impressed.

'Yeah, I will. The next few weeks are a bit busy, but after—'

'No, I mean you have to come within the next three weeks. I have some news, you see. Your dad and I have bought a house in York! We're moving next month.'

WHAT?

Apparently now that my dad's retiring from the police, they fancy a change. I don't know why I'm surprised. My mum's like me – she'd take a city over a small town any day. I'm sure she'd still be in London if she hadn't married my city-phobic dad, but she must have put his happiness first.

'But I don't want you to move!'

'Why not?'

Well, for a start, she clearly wants me to go up and clear out my old room but I roll with one of my less selfish reasons . . .

'Because it won't be the same. I love that house. All my childhood memories are there.'

'Whatever, dear.' My mum sighs. 'You just can't be bothered to come and clear your old bedroom out.'

'Why would you even think that?'

I'm obviously more attached to my old home than I realized. As Mum reminds me every opportunity she can, I rarely go to that house, but I like knowing it's there. Maybe I'm just feeling nostalgic after my catch-up with Alex but it feels like the end of an era. Even though the era ended eleven years ago.

'There's a spare bedroom at our new place, so you'll always have somewhere to stay when you visit. *If* you visit, I should say. It's a smaller room, though, so you're going to have to go through your stuff and decide what to throw away.'

'OK, OK,' I concede. 'It's Chloe's wedding this weekend but maybe the weekend after.' I flick through my Filofax. 'Yep, that's fine.'

'Great. I'll cook your favourite. Let me know what your favourite is – it's been that long since I've cooked you anything other than Christmas dinner. I bet Terry Tyler didn't have to work this hard to convince his only child to help him clear out his house when he moved. How is Alex, by the way?'

'He's fine.' I twist the telephone cord around one finger as I try to think of a summary. 'Exactly the same as he used to be. But totally different to how he was. If you know what I mean?'

'No, no idea. But I'm glad he's fine. Lovely boy, just like his mum. She'd do anything for anyone, and never complain.'

I felt sorry for my mum when Julie Tyler died – she was her best friend. My mum was miserable when we first moved to Mothston. It was my summer holiday between primary school and secondary, deemed the least disruptive time to move me. Dad had wanted to move back to his hometown for years, and Mum has since admitted that she thought it would be like living in *Emmerdale*, but it didn't take long after she got there to realize that, minus the affairs and murders and plane crashes and stuff, *Emmerdale* would be rather dull. But then Julie took her under her wing, helping her settle with coffee mornings and dinner parties. She's been a bit lost there since losing her friend.

I feel bad for pissing on her bonfire, especially as she was obviously hoping for a big chat about the move, so I ask her some questions about the new house.

'It sounds lovely, Mum,' I say with deliberate warmth.

'It is. Anyway, you are the Weakest Link . . . goodbye!'

And she's gone. OK, then.

I sigh, and add to my To Do list: *Book train ticket to Mothston.*

Text from Holly to Alex

fyi no one at work knows about me and R so don't bring it up x

Chapter Thirteen

ALEX

Mr Cotton is watering a cactus on his window sill when I arrive for a review of my first two weeks at Whitford High. He doesn't avert his attention from the plant, so I remain standing.

'Low maintenance,' he finally says, inviting me with a sweep of his hand to sit. 'You can leave them for months and they'd still be going strong.'

I can't think of anything to say, so I keep it zipped. Eventually Mr Cotton sits, shuffles some papers and goes: 'Mr Tyler.'

'Hello.'

'Mr Alex Tyler.'

I adopt a silly voice to joke: 'That's my name, don't wear it out.'

'Pardon?'

'Sorry, just something we used to say as kids.'

Mr Cotton's computer emits an email notification. He leans right into his monitor to inspect the correspondence for almost a minute before returning to his previous posture.

'We're not here to reminisce about your childhood,

Mr Tyler; we're here to talk about your present. How are you settling in?'

'Fairly well, I'd say. I—'

'Problems with any classes?'

'I was going to say, my year nines are quite boisterous. I think it's just a case of making a connection with the few who are stopping everyone el—'

'Bottom set, no?'

'Yep, but—'

'Give them easier work. They'll feel in control and give you less bother. Then everyone else can get on with achieving the grades we need.'

I gawp at Mr Cotton with as much incredulity as I think I can get away with. 'But if it's easy they won't learn anything?'

'Yes, but if giving them difficult assignments means they get restless, Mr Tyler, what's the solution?'

'I'm sorry but I—' Mr Cotton picks up a ruler from his desk and bends it with his hands, causing my throat to clench. 'All I mean is, surely you can't give up on the kids because they're hard work? Like Kenny Sonola – he was off today and when I spoke to Ms Pritchard she said he's always off on non-uniform day.'

'His attendance is above ninety per cent – there's no cause for concern. Mr Tyler, some of our pupils are spiky creatures – like my cactus here.' His ruler becomes a pointing stick. 'Over-water them and they'll die; get too close and they'll prick you.'

I stay quiet, even though there's a small part of me that feels like sticking Mr Cotton's measuring device – and cactus – somewhere the flickering light bulb above our heads doesn't shine.

124

'Anyhow,' he continues, shuffling the same papers he shuffled when I came in, despite the fact he hasn't touched them in the interim, 'I didn't call you in for this. I notice you haven't sent me any incident reports. Remember: anything extraordinary occurs, you email a report sheet. If it isn't in my inbox, it didn't happen. Clear?'

If that were true, then these three events would never have occurred:

1/ My admission of ignorance, while watching a Channel 4 documentary on teenage pregnancy with Charlotte McCormack, about women having a separate hole for weeing;
2/ My phase at university of calling people 'love';
3/ My decision sixteen years ago to chance a quick you-know-what in Kev's downstairs toilet while he went to purchase some Pot Noodles. His mum was meant to be doing a big shop.

My phone grunts angrily in my pocket as I'm walking home. It's Kev. I tell him about Kenny Sonola.

'Out of your depth. I warned you.'

'They're not bad kids – just high-spirited. I'm properly enjoying it.'

'You remind me of my grandma. She's always telling me she loved the war because Granddad was away for five years and he drove her crackers. But I'm like, "Granny, it was a war."'

'I've got no idea what you're talking about.'

'You wouldn't,' he huffs. 'Anyhow, you haven't been replying to my texts so I thought I'd ring to find out whether you've seen Holly Gordon starkers yet?'

I roll my eyes and explain that Holly is in a relationship – and that she's different now anyway. He doesn't respond.

'We're mates. I'm off to a pub quiz with the people she works with tomorrow.'

'Mates?' he spews. 'Yeah, I believe that's all you want.'

I groan. Does he seriously think I'm clinging to some desperate crush? I'd never give him the satisfaction of divulging this but, yes, there was a millisecond when I met Holly in the pub that I wondered. Back in school the first thing I'd check out was a girl's chest; these days it's her wedding finger. And I admit it: at the start of the night when I glimpsed Holly's left hand and saw the bare finger, there was a pang. But as the night evolved I realized it was just nostalgia. She's not the same Holly. And you know what? I'm not the same Alex.

To shut Kev up I tell him about the thong incident. He wants to know if Cassie has given me any other signals.

'I've noticed she touches my arm a lot,' I say.

'Ah, pre-sexual contact,' he says, and sensing my puzzlement adds: 'It's what two people who are gonna have sex do before they get to the stage of ripping each other's clothes off. Touching your arm is akin to a hand job.'

'Where do you get this shit from?'

'It's called the University of Life, my friend, and I graduated with an A star.'

I don't know why I'm still indulging Kev with this nonsense. He's right – I have been ignoring his texts. I guess part of me didn't see our friendship lasting once I moved to London, that we'd just drift apart the way we would have if we hadn't been stuck together in a town like Mothston. But he seems intent on making long-distance work.

'You sure she's single?' he enquires, and then sucks air through his teeth when I tell him that I've seen her several times chatting to Ted Rodgers, one of the PE teachers.

'What?' I ask, and he sighs.

'Let's be realistic,' he says. 'If it's a choice between some buff PE teacher and you . . . All I'm saying is, don't get your hopes up.'

Good job I didn't join one of those dating websites where a friend writes your blurb – I dread to think what Kev would have come up with.

'Women look for more than just thick arms, you know.'

'You've read too many books, Al.'

'You say that like it's an insult. And what about the arm-touching? You said that meant we were going to have sex?'

'Maybe she's just touching you the way a kindly care worker touches an elderly patient.' Once he's finished laughing to himself he adds: 'Regardless, it doesn't really matter whether this Cassie girl likes you, because you like Holly.'

I thank Kev for his advice and try again to change the subject by telling him about Carl's theory.

'He thinks women are like bacteria?' balks Kev. 'Sounds like a right sexist twat.'

I have to make an effort not to choke on my own saliva. 'Yes, Kev – awful, isn't it?'

He doesn't respond to my sarcasm.

127

'Having said that, he does seem to fare better than either of us.'

Kev releases a phlegmy, dismissive snort. 'Er, actually, I was getting the eye from some bird on the train back from the Job Centre earlier. Through the reflection in the window, like.'

This is typical Kev. A girl so much as glances in his direction and he infers that she wants to procreate.

'Good, well keep me informed of that one, won't you?'

'Will do.'

Neither of us has anything left to say, and the silence stretches for a little more than is comfortable.

'All right, I guess I'll speak to you soon, then,' I say.

'In a bit, mate. Oh and—' I hear Kev go to say something else but it's been a long day and my thumb is already hovering over 'End call'.

When I arrive for the quiz Holly smiles and holds out her arms as if she's about to take possession of a large box, and a couple of seconds later I'm being introduced to her workmates. I meet Jemma (a wave hello), Danny (sideways handshake) and Melissa (double kiss on the cheeks).

Holly insists on going to the bar, leaving me to nod and laugh at the appropriate moments while they mock someone called Martin. Melissa – the only one who isn't amused by whatever Martin did this afternoon – lends me an empathetic smile. She has one of those faces that holiday reps have – happy to help. Further up, her immaculate blonde hair sways as one entity whenever she turns her head. As for her clothes – they're like Holly's but with more revs: puff-sleeved jacket and short skirt, shirt ironed rigid, patent heels that must have taken practice to walk in.

She asks what I do for a living and when I tell her I'm an English teacher she lays a hand on the chest above her heart. 'That's amazing,' she gushes, lolling her head wistfully. 'I used to love learning Shakespeare.'

I'm about to ask which plays she studied when Holly reappears with our drinks.

'Here you go, Mr Tyler,' she interrupts, and Melissa excuses herself. She returns a minute or two later hooking her arms into a beige mac.

'Hope to see you again,' she tells me, executing another set of kisses. This time her hands cup my elbows.

Once she has clip-clopped out of the door I realize the others are eyeballing me.

'Were you just flirting with Melissa, Alex?' asks Holly teasingly.

The attention makes me blush, even though they're way off. Melissa is pretty, but I've never gone for the archetypal blonde.

'I wasn't flirting,' I tell them. 'Not intentionally anyway. But she does seem very . . .'

'Fit?' offers Danny decisively.

'I was going to say "nice", but yep, you can't deny she's attractive.'

Holly's head retracts. 'Yeah, in a conventional kind of way,' she says, and Jemma supports this notion with a nod.

'You're right,' say Danny, also nodding. 'Conventional attractiveness – that's the worst kind.'

A few minutes later Holly spots a table that's about to be vacated, and we stand over the departing group as if their seats were in the front row of the Royal Albert Hall rather than next to a table full of empty bottles, torn crisp packets and little lakes of spilt cider. I'm pleased when Holly ushers me to sit next to her with her eyes, while opposite us Jemma saves a place for a bloke she's dating. He's late, and she spends the first few rounds stalking her phone, while Danny's sole contribution to the quiz is bawling incorrect answers to throw rival teams off the scent. It's Holly and I who come up with most of the answers.

'What was the full name of Kylie Minogue's character in the Australian soap opera *Neighbours* before she got married to Scott?'

'Charlene something or other,' offers Jemma.

'It was Mangel,' says Danny. 'Or was it Robinson?'

I've never sat through an entire episode of *Neighbours* in my life but I know the answer. Holly used to love Kylie, despite my attempts to introduce her to Radiohead.

'It's Mitchell,' I tell them. 'Charlene Mitchell.'

Danny and Jemma look sceptical.

'Are you sure?' they say together, but Holly alleviates any doubt by scribbling my answer.

'He's right,' she confirms with a smirk.

Jemma tells me I can come again, a declaration that elicits a proud nudge into my ribs from Holly. The wine must be going to my head because for a second it's like we're teenagers again and I'm pleased at winning her approval.

'Right, that's it.' Jemma chucks her phone into her handbag and grabs Danny by the arm. 'I've obviously been stood up. No reason not to get ratted now.'

They head to the bar, and once they're out of earshot

my mind turns to Holly's text. I guess I was flattered when I read it. Holly always used to confide in me about various boys, unaware of how it would make me ache.

'I got your message,' I say, anticipating a revelation. Richard has a wife and children. It's an affair but he is going to leave them soon. He got married too young.

It has to be something big, or else why wouldn't she have mentioned it in the pub a couple of weeks ago?

'We both just want to keep things low key, with it being work. It's for the best.'

She keeps an eye on Jemma and Danny at the bar. Beside them, a man in a pinstriped suit whose slackened tie hints at drunkenness is letching onto a reluctant woman. I watch Holly watching the sleaze as he drops to one knee for a mock proposal. The woman's previously contemptuous facade softens.

'It's complicated, but it won't be a secret for much longer.'

As the man gets back to his feet he stumbles into Jemma, who dispatches him with an elbow to the spine.

'We've been waiting for the right time to do the whole friends and family thing—'

'I meant your message with directions to this place,' I interrupt, grinning.

She looks at me for the first time since Jemma and Danny went to the bar and smiles. 'Sorry, I'm just aware that some people would see the whole thing as a massive sleeping-with-the-secretary cliché.'

Had that thought occurred to me? Yep, but whose business is it but Holly's? And from listening to her now, it's clear that what she and Richard have is the real thing. She's happy.

'Did you see that arsehole at the bar?' says Jemma, releasing a packet of Scampi Fries from her teeth. 'The poor cow should run a mile.'

A few minutes later the results are revealed and we narrowly miss out on the prizes, finishing a respectable tenth out of eleven. Jemma turns my way and cups her mouth at one side so Holly can't hear or see what she's about to whisper.

'I bet you any money she checks her watch within the next minute,' she says. 'Always does after the results.'

Jemma and I exchange mischievous glances for about thirty seconds until Holly kinks her left wrist, winning a roar of laughter from Jemma.

'Oh, shut your face,' says Holly. 'I was just seeing what time we're at. And for your information I was just about to go to the bar.'

Jemma snorts doubtfully but Holly is true to her word, scooping her handbag so that it hangs from her shoulder and striding to the bar.

'Actually,' confides Jemma as Holly flashes four fingers to the barman with one hand and points to a bottle of Sambucca with the other, 'I've never seen her drink so much on a work night. She's like a different person with you around.'

I take an extended sip of wine to hide a round of blushes.

'And I meant what I said earlier,' she continues. 'You should come again.'

Chapter Fourteen

HOLLY

It's the first time I've seen Max since he moved his stuff out almost a year ago.

Richard has his arm wrapped around me outside the church after Chloe's wedding. He's all smiley – probably because we've been chatting about what our wedding day would be like. We're looking loved-up and sickeningly happy when . . .

'Holly!'

'Max!' I notice him walking towards us, trailed by his reasonably-pretty-if-a-little-unglamorous girlfriend. His hug lasts longer than necessary, until he remembers Felicity and Richard are there too.

'You look great,' he tells me, checking me out after everyone's been introduced. It's true – I do. I swear yesterday's spray tan makes my legs look longer and my arms thinner.

'So do you,' I reply charitably, even though his once ruggedly sexy stubble is now slightly too long, and his blond hair could do with a chop. It's almost like he's not quite as concerned about his appearance these days.

'So, I guess we'll see you at the reception?' I say

warmly. Max meets my eye and smiles but I wouldn't say it was a happy smile. More – and obviously I'm guessing here – a smile of wry reflection. *Ah, Holly Gordon. The one that got away.*

So anyway, that's how it goes down in my head.

The reality is a bit different.

Richard not being here is a setback of colossal proportions. It means I'm standing outside the church with Susie and Jamie, trying hard not to listen to their argument (Jamie forgot to remind Susie to charge her camera) but to appear to everyone else like I'm involved in the conversation so I don't look like a loner, when . . .

'Holly!'

'Max!' He's strolling over, his arm draped around the toned shoulders of a girl who looks like she should be on a mountainside, dressed in Lycra, advertising muesli.

'This is Flick,' he announces. 'Flick, this is Holly, Susie and . . .'

He's holding his hand out to Jamie and while Susie's introducing them I see Flick eyeing me up.

Does she know who I am?

I don't want to come across like a hostile ex-girlfriend. Need to say something nice.

'I love your dress,' I gush. 'Where's it from?'

I wish I could say I'm just being polite. Unfortunately, I genuinely do love her layered, coral-pink fringe dress and matching fascinator. The colour complements her tan.

I had to cancel last night's spray tan appointment because I was preoccupied booking train tickets as Richard would no longer be driving, the unreliable git.

134

Flick is telling me the name of some exclusive boutique in Chelsea where she buys, like, ALL her clothes but I'm finding it hard to concentrate on what she's saying because whilst the breeze is blowing her blonde hair away from her face like a wind machine in a modelling shoot, it's blowing mine onto my face from behind, making it stick to my lip-gloss.

'Where are the others?' Max looks around.

I'm not sure whether he's just referring to Leah and Rob, or if it's my plus one he's asking after.

'Getting the car,' says Susie. 'Rob drove so he's giving us a lift to the hotel.'

'Richard couldn't make it,' I add. 'Big work thing. Couldn't be helped.'

Max looks like he's about to say something (ask who Richard is and why I'm telling him the whereabouts of this random person?) but Flick pipes up.

'Darling, shall we . . . ?'

She doesn't finish her question but Max seems to comprehend because he tells us he'll see us there, smiles, and leaves.

A happy smile, if I'm not mistaken.

'Well, that wasn't at all awkward,' I say to break the silence that descends as soon as we pile into Rob's Corsa. I'm joking but it prompts attempts of subtle glances between the other four. Are they kidding me? I'm wedged in the back between Susie and Jamie, and sitting forward almost level with Leah and Rob's seats. They literally have to LEAN AROUND ME to subtly glance at each other.

I chuckle in case there's any doubt I meant it light-heartedly.

I can see how they'd be confused. I am a bit sulky. It's nothing to do with Max, though. It's Richard.

My stomach lurched as soon as I saw his name appear on my BlackBerry screen last night. He was supposed to be three hours into a Gatwick-bound flight – how could he be calling?

Had he got an earlier flight from NYC so he could get an early night to be all rested and sparky for my friend's wedding?

Like hell he had.

I tried to be understanding as he apologized his head off, explaining there were still people he had to meet. And I know this promotion is important, but eff it – I'm so gutted he's not here. I've played out today in my head so many times.

Holding hands in public.

Dancing to romantic songs.

Introducing him to my friends.

Just the little things that couples do.

'They're your friends,' he said. 'You don't need me there.'

'I do need you there!' I screamed. In my head. But of course I couldn't say that out loud because it would sound NEEDY and PATHETIC, and I'm pretty sure they're not on Richard's list of top qualities for a girlfriend.

And the Max thing? I just wanted him to know I'd moved on. Not because I still have feelings for him. I've not a speck of regret about our break-up. I want him to be happy.

It's just, well – and I would never say this out loud – it just feels pretty crappy seeing him happier than he was with me.

That's not something I could tell Richard. Nor could I tell him I've made a massive deal about him coming to my friends.

'I've never understood why people called Felicity shorten their names to Flick,' Susie says eventually, staring out her window. I love her for it.

I'm over my bad mood by the time we get to the hotel. It'd be selfish to walk around with a face like Posh Spice when it's Chloe's wedding day.

Best day of her life, and all that – I'd hate to spoil it. Besides, the awkward bit is over and it's not like it can get any worse.

But then it goes and gets worse.

On our table is me, Susie, Jamie, Leah, Rob. And Max. And Flick. And an empty seat for that inconsiderate bastard, Richard.

'I hope this is one of those one-in-three marriages that ends in divorce,' I say calmly to Leah, who's just appeared at my shoulder as I ponder the seating plan chart at the entrance to the function room.

I know Chloe wouldn't have known I'd be solo, but to stick me on the same table as my ex? Seriously?

I'm going to have to suck it up. It'll be fine – I'll just be friendly, and non-moody, and charming, and very, very drunk.

I lift two glasses of champagne off the tray of a passing waitress and hold one out to Leah.

'No thanks, I'm not drinking.'

'What do you mean you're not drinking?'

We've never had this conversation this way round before.

'I said I'd drive so Rob can drink. Come on, let's sit

down – and don't worry, it'll be fine. Just have fun.'

I neck the first champagne and follow her to our table clutching the second.

Just have fun.

I try. I really, really do.

I laugh along with everyone else when Max reaches the finale of yet another story about his nights out with bands I've never heard of . . .

'So then I woke up in this random stranger's house at six in the morning . . .'

Why didn't I just bring someone else?

'. . . and the place looked like it had been burgled . . .'

Jemma would have been a laugh but I already told her I never got a plus one.

'. . . empty bottles everywhere, wonky pictures on the wall . . .'

Or Alex? I'd considered inviting him in the first place until Richard volunteered himself, and he still doesn't know many people in London so it's not unfeasible he'd have been free at the last minute. And he scrubs up well, so he would have been a match for Flick in the plus-one stakes.

'Then I found the bass player at the sink washing dishes . . .'

Or Harold? Ha ha.

'. . . stark naked . . .'

I hope I left Harold enough food.

'. . . with a tea cosy on his head!'

Max always was the life and soul of a party. It was one of the things I loved about him. Most of the time. Sometimes dinner parties started turning into *An Audi-*

ence With Max Brown, and I'd know it was time to tell him we were out of beers.

But at least he was there when I needed him, which is more than can be said for Richard, undependable fiend that he is. I really thought he might be looking forward to today. Could he really not have got back on time, if he genuinely wanted to? My throat constricts as if I'm going to cry so I take a swig of water and push my relationship doubts out of my head, channelling back in to the conversation at the table.

Max works in music PR now – apparently Flick knew someone who knew someone.

'I told him it's about time he got a regular job with a regular salary.' She rests a hand on the back of Max's neck and smiles proudly, like a mum who's just weaned her child off his dummy.

I top up my wine.

'I like Flick,' I tell Leah and Susie's reflection in the loos later, sucking in my cheeks to apply my blusher. 'She's a bit controlling, though, isn't she?'

Leah's mascara wand and Susie's lipstick freeze in unison.

'She just seems to do everything for him. It's like she's his mother.'

'Oh, that reminds me, I have a message for you,' Susie says, her eyes meeting mine in the mirror. 'It's from the kettle. Stop calling it black.'

'What do you mean?'

'You totally did the same.'

'I did not!'

'You did too, Hols,' says Leah. 'It's not a criticism –

I mean, this is Max we're talking about. I love him to bits but he couldn't organize his way out of a paper bag. Remember that one time at uni when we made him take a turn at organizing the film night?'

We'd ended up watching the *Eurovision Song Contest* because Max had forgotten to get any films. I was still trying to impress him at that point so I didn't let on I was secretly thrilled about this development.

'That's why you two worked,' Leah continues. 'You love organizing and he needed to be organized.'

I'm about to argue but stop myself. Is she right? Did I do that?

Maybe I did.

That was then, though. Thank God I'm in an adult relationship now. And to be fair to Richard – although I don't know why I should be, the selfish moron – at least he's independent and doesn't need looking after.

'I really am OK with Max being with someone else, you know,' I tell them, scooping everything back into my make-up bag.

'Yeah, we know you are,' says Leah, just a split second too late for me to believe her. I want to argue but what's the point? She's right. None of this feels OK.

'I just wish Richard was here,' I admit unhappily. 'You don't think Max is sitting there feeling sorry for me because he thinks I've been stood up, do you?'

'Nah.' Susie shrugs. 'He probably thinks you made Richard up.'

'Oh God, I didn't even think of that!' I gasp. 'Like in *Romy and Michele's High School Reunion*? You know – that film with Phoebe from *Friends*, where she and her mate pretended they invented the Post-it note so their

140

old classmates wouldn't realize how lame their lives got? No? It's funny – you should watch it. But seriously, what if everyone thinks I made up a boyfriend so they wouldn't think I've turned into a loser?'

'I was kidding, hun. No one would think that. And no one is feeling sorry for you. If anyone's the loser it's Richard.' Susie tries to take the sting out her words by pressing her freshly painted lips against my forehead to leave a bright red kiss mark, then breezes out of the loo, just as Chloe bursts in.

'I'm going to throw the bouquet – come on!'

'I'm already married,' Leah reminds her.

'I'm . . .' The ten gallons of champagne I've drunk mean I can't think of a valid excuse to get out of it so I wipe the lipstick off my head and reluctantly follow her to the dance floor, where she thrusts me between a teenage cousin who's already sporting a big diamond on her engagement finger and a girl about my age, whose boyfriend is hovering with a face like a defendant on a murder charge waiting for the verdict.

Chloe turns her back on us, lowers the bundle of cream-coloured roses, and then flings them high into the air.

I catch them. Of course I do. God clearly HATES me because I actually see the bouquet CHANGE DIREC-TION to find me.

If I'd have had time to think about it I would have batted it away like a volley ball, but it happens so fast that suddenly it's in my hand, and I'm forcing a smile until I get face ache, before pushing my way through the small gathering.

'Why did *she* go for it?' one resentful-looking girl asks

141

another with her eyes. 'She doesn't even have a man.'

'Oh *apparently* she does,' the other girl's eyes respond bitterly. 'Not that anyone's ever actually seen him.'

Then I'm back at my table just in time for yet another coupled-up dance-athon.

As much as we were all 'why the rush?' about friends who got married in their early twenties, their weddings were undeniably more fun. Once the first dance was over, it wasn't dissimilar to a Saturday night at a cheesy club. But in posh frocks. All dancing in big circles, and flinging each other around the floor.

Tonight it's all dancing in couples. Even the singles have paired off, aside from a handful of girls tapping their feet to the music like those dateless extras sitting at the back of the hall at the prom in *Grease*, waiting to be invited to dance.

Rob and Jamie are taking turns to drag me up, which is sweet of them but I have to put a stop to it because it's all getting a bit humiliating.

'I'm fine here . . . No, honestly, I'm fine . . . I am having fun . . . My feet just hurt a bit that's all . . . You go dance . . . Yep, I'm sure.'

They stop asking after approximately the thirty-ninth time, which is lucky because I'm one 'I'm fine' speech away from beating myself to death with my new bouquet.

It's not just today I'm feeling humiliated about. The more I think about it, the more I think I must have this Richard thing all wrong – Susie was right. This isn't a serious relationship to him, or he'd be here. Or he'd at least bloody understand why it's wrong that he's not.

God, tonight is going slowly. I honestly don't know how much longer I can pretend to enjoy myself. When

142

my phone rings I almost hope it's a neighbour calling to say my flat is on fire so I've a valid reason to leave, but it's Richard.

He's landed then, the self-centred fool. I should ignore it.

'Hello?'

'Hi, baby. Are you having fun?'

'Yeah it's fine. I just—'

'Hang on, I can't hear you . . . What?'

'Yeah, it's fine. I—'

'Hang on, what?'

'NO, I'M NOT ACTUALLY – I—'

'Then we better do something about that.'

I'm confused. That didn't come from the phone, it came from behind me. I spin around.

And there he is.

RICHARD.

Suited up and beaming and handsome and HERE.

I jump up and throw my arms around his neck. A combination of shock and way too much champagne makes tears spring to my eyes.

'I can't believe you're here,' I whisper as we hug.

'I caught an earlier flight so I could make it,' he says, pulling away and looking me up and down. 'You look stunning, by the way.'

'You scrub up pretty well yourself. Now come and meet the others.'

Richard is charm personified with my friends. Leah gives him a warm welcome, and even Susie defrosts after the first couple of minutes. Max is a tad uncomfortable-looking during my boyfriend's enthusiastic handshake, and I wonder whether that's about me or about the fact that Flick got all pouty-mouthed and fluttery-eyed when she met him.

I can't believe I almost wrote us off. It's this whole secrecy thing messing with my head. And as Richard spins me on the dance floor I'm totally convinced of one thing: it's time we went public.

I don't want to get out of bed when I wake up at 7 a.m. However, it's clear I'm going to die of dehydration if I don't. And with a boyfriend having an important promotion to prepare for and a cat with trust issues, dying isn't convenient right now, so I drag myself to the kitchen.

'Morning, Harold,' I say, when I've downed a pint of orange squash.

Really? is her riposte. *That's all I'm getting? All day by myself yesterday, shut out of your room all night because that friend of yours is over, and the best you can do is a 'Morning, Harold'?*

I assume what happens next is that I curl up next to her on the couch, because before I know it it's 10 a.m. and Richard is shaking me awake, bearing tea and toast.

God love him.

Harold meows angrily and runs away as Richard squeezes next to me and puts his arm around me.

I snuggle into his bare chest, and attempt to approach the subject of us coming out of our non-gay closet.

'Thanks again for coming yesterday,' I murmur.

'That's OK, babe.' He kisses my forehead. 'I know it was important to you. Besides, I'm back out to New York next weekend, so I'll get everything else done then.'

The tiny little drummers going at it nineteen to the

144

dozen inside my skull mean it takes me a moment to work out what's wrong with this sentence.

When I do, I try to sit up but the drummers get angry so I rest my head back on his chest to ask . . .

'Next weekend? But what about Harold?'

'What about him?'

'Her, not him – and you're meant to be feeding her next weekend.'

His face is blank.

'While I'm at my parents, remember?'

'Oh shit, sorry, Holly.' One hand flies to his forehead. 'I totally forgot.'

OK, be reasonable. I can't expect him to ruin his chances of promotion to feed my cat.

It's just, well – would it hurt him to have at least remembered?

'I really am sorry. I should have put it in my diary.'

'I did put it in your diary,' I tell him weakly, no longer in the mood for a relationship chat. 'But it's fine. I'll sort it.'

I'll have to ask Jemma. Although if there's one thing she dislikes more than coming south of the river, it's cats.

I could always ask Alex, I guess. Or is that a bit cheeky?

Maybe there's some sort of school fête I could make cakes for in return. I mull it over while I nibble my toast.

Chapter Fifteen

HOLLY

November 1998

I could always ask Alex, I guess. Or is that a bit cheeky?

He did say as soon as he passed his test that if ever I wanted a lift then just ask him. *Any time, any place* were his exact words. Though I'm not sure a random house party a few miles out of Mothston, at – I shut one eye and squint at my watch – 2.23 a.m. is exactly what he had in mind.

Sitting on the hallway stairs, I try to check my reflection in the full-length mirror opposite but I'm struggling to focus. I sit up and tuck in the curls that are falling out of my bun. Damn it – I spent forty minutes earlier trying to make my hair look like I'd pinned it up haphazardly in seconds.

I could get a taxi home, I suppose, but Mum would FREAK if she knew I'd lied about being out with Alex tonight. It was the only way I could get away with staying out this late – and if (when) she looks out of the window when she hears a car pull up it'll look well suss if it's not Alex's rusty Ford Fiesta.

'There you go, Hols-Bols.' Ellie thrusts a watermelon Bacardi Breezer into my hand and sits on the stair in front of me, clutching a Moscow Mule bottle.

There's no room for her to sit next to me, skinny as she is, because there is a line of girls pinned up against the wall with boys attached to their faces.

Her glittery dress is both low-cut and short, even though I keep reminding her that the rule is boobs OR legs. I may have to keep checking my nipples aren't trying to escape my boob tube but I'm wearing it with baggy hipster jeans.

I take a glug of my drink, even though the room is already a bit spinny, and wonder if anyone will notice if I take off Ministry of Sound's *House Anthems* and put *Now 40* back on. I want to dance again. Then I remember I want to go home.

'Whose house is this again, Ells-Bells? I need to ask to borrow their phone.'

'Fuck knows – just use it.' She reaches out to grab the cordless phone from the hallway table but falls onto her hands and pushes it off the table with her head. We laugh until our tummy muscles ache – her still lying on the floor where she fell. We've just calmed down when she looks up at me.

'I've got Moscow Mule coming out of my nose.' And we crack up again.

'So . . .' She clutches the table to pull herself to her feet, smearing her mascara as she wipes the tears away, and sits on the stair again. 'I think I'm going to get off with Dean Jones tonight.'

My mouth opens a little bit in shock, but she can't see because her back is to me. She's licking her finger

147

and wiping a smudge off her high silver sandals, which she refuses to take off, even though the pointy heels are leaving dents in the carpet of whoever's house this is. I can't tell if she's waiting to see if I react or if she genuinely doesn't think there's anything wrong with the fact she's after Dean.

Even though she knows I already got off with him.

Even though I told her that he'd been talking to me a lot at school recently, and that I'm wondering if he's going to ask me out, and I asked her what she thought of him, and she shrugged and said: 'He's all right.'

Even though last week, after me and Dean were lab partners in science, I joked that we had chemistry.

We've been silent for a good minute and a half now so she says, 'I saw that guy in the red polo shirt you were chatting to for ages – he's *cute*.' She pronounces it ker-ute. 'You should so get off with him.'

He's not cute. Ellie doesn't think he's cute either – he's about three foot eight with acne the colour of his polo shirt – and Ellie knows full well that I was talking to him because I'm polite, because unlike her I don't only talk to boys I think are fit.

Maybe I should remind her about me and Dean? Maybe she's forgotten.

'I didn't fancy that guy,' I say, playing with her straight blonde hair. I love her hair. I asked her if I could have it once and she said she'd swap it for my boobs.

'Actually, I've been thinking I might say yes to Dean. You know, about going on a date with him. But it's not like he's my boyfriend or anything and it was just one kiss so it's not like I can stop you doing—'

'Oh, I know – it's not like you've actually been on a

148

date with him. Obviously, I'd never steal him off you if you guys were a thing. That would be well out of order – you're my best mate.' She stands up and kisses me on the cheek, then struts into the living room. I get up to pick the phone off the floor where Ellie left it, and as I do I glance through the living-room doorway just in time to see her squeeze her tiny bum onto the sofa next to Dean.

I wonder if he fancies her. She's skinny and blonde – what's not to fancy? I thought I'd seen him checking me out when I was bumping and grinding to R. Kelly's 'Bump n' Grind' earlier, but he could have easily been watching her dancing next to me. And if he was, fine! I'm not going to fight a mate for a man. As if!

I dial Alex's number, grateful that he has a phone next to his bed and his dad doesn't.

'Two seven zero seven?' he says after two rings.

'Hello, two seven zero seven.' It sounds like he's yawning. 'Sorry, did I wake you?'

'Yes! I mean no. I mean, yep, you did but I wasn't properly asleep or anything. You all right?'

'Actually, I was wondering if you'd do me a MASSIVE favour.' I manage to turn the five-word asking of the favour into a five-minute monologue. I'm not so drunk I don't realize I'm over-enunciating the way drunk people do when they're talking to sober people, but I'm too drunk to stop.

'Holly!' Alex interrupts – actually, I think it might be for the third time. 'The address?'

I have to run outside to check both the house number and the street name, and although he doesn't know exactly where it is he says he'll look it up in the *A-Z* in his glove box and be with me as soon as he can.

Once I've hung up and replaced whoever's phone I've just used I do a little equation to work out how long that's likely to be. Maths was my one A* at GCSE so this shit is easy. It took about twenty minutes to get here in a taxi but when you take into account that Alex has to get dressed and look up the address (add ten minutes) and the fact that it's Alex who's driving (reduce average speed by one third) I decide I definitely have time for another drink.

There are no more Bacardi Breezers so I settle for a Diamond White. Bobby Shepherd, who's sitting on the worktop next to the fridge, grabs it and uses his teeth to pull the top off, before proudly handing it back to me.

'Good skills.' I smile. 'No wonder you've been accepted into the army.'

He doesn't pick up on the sarcasm and now he's asking me if I've ever got high by pouring vodka into my eyeballs. I give him an honest 'no', and he asks if I want to try it and I give him an equally honest 'no', and when he goes to show me how it's done I'm wishing someone would come and pull me away. And then as if by magic Dean appears at the doorway.

'Um, Holly?' He looks at me apologetically. 'Ellie's asking for you – she's not well.'

When Dean leads me through to the living room, where Ellie is sitting with her head in her hands and lumpy orange-coloured puke on her sandals, I'm wishing I was back in the kitchen with Bobby-vodka-in-his-eyeballs. The two girls stroking Ellie's back run away gratefully as soon as they see me and as I get closer, the smell of ginger beer and sick hits me in the face.

'Ells,' I say gently, crouching next to her and putting my arms around her.

'Hols,' she sobs into my shoulder. 'I think I'm dying.'

'You're fine,' I tell her. 'Alex is on his way – he'll drop you home. You can sleep in the back all the way there.'

'I ruv roooo, Hols.'

'I love you too, Ellie.'

As I stand up, Ellie flops across the couch. I get our coats from the upstairs bedroom and drape one around her shoulders and the other over her legs, before going to get a cloth to clean the carpet where she was sick. Worried I'll throw up soon myself, I wash my hands, then head out the front to wait for Alex.

'That can't have been a fun job.' Dean has followed me out, and drops down next to me on the porch step.

'Can't have been much fun for you either.' I grin. 'Hope she realized she was going to be sick in time to get her tongue out of your mouth.'

'What? We didn't do anything,' Dean says quickly, putting his beer can down and gently laying his hand on my knee. 'Um, actually, I was in the middle of asking her whether she thought I was in with a chance with you.'

Wow, no wonder she threw up.

Is the hottest guy in sixth form really sitting here asking me to be his girlfriend? I don't know where to look. I'd have been fine half an hour ago when I was really pissed, but nothing sobers you up like cleaning up someone else's puke.

'Holly?' he says, using his hand to turn my face towards him. 'Can I ask you something?'

'Yeah, course,' I say lightly, even though I think I

know what he's going to ask and I still haven't decided my answer.

'Will you go out with me?'

I smile and look away shyly. What girl in my school wouldn't want to be me right now? I might not have that feeling I have when I sit this closely to Alex, all tingly and desperate to close the gap between us. But I don't know him as well as I know Alex, so maybe we could get there. He's so good-looking – everyone thinks so. Ellie included, it turns out. And I can't sit around my whole life waiting for Alex if he doesn't want to close the gap.

In the end Dean saves me from having to answer by pulling my face towards his so that our lips mash together. He tastes of beer and fags and is kind of a good kisser. I wonder what he's thinking. Am I a good kisser? I wish I'd known this was going to happen – I've got Polos in my handbag. My neck is starting to hurt a little bit now because of the angle my head is turned at but I don't dare stop. Then a car horn blares.

'Is that a yes?' Dean asks.

'Yes,' I laugh, rubbing my neck. 'Call me tomorrow, OK?'

'Wicked. Is that your taxi?'

'No, it's Alex Tyler – he's giving me a lift.'

'Ha, you're kidding. Isn't it past his bedtime?'

'Shut it, Jones.' I slap him gently on the arm, hoping he'll take the hint and actually shut it.

'You know he's trying to have it off with you, right?'

'He is not!' Is he? No, of course not. Is he? 'He's a mate.'

'He's a bloke. He might be a bit of a girly bloke but he's still a bloke, and that means the only reason he'd drive

152

out to pick up a girl in the middle of the night is if he thinks he'll eventually get into her knickers.'

'You're wrong. Seriously, Dean – lay off him, OK? And help me get Ellie.'

'Fine, but he better keep his hands to himself.'

Alex's hands are the least of my problems. I'm more worried about his reaction when I tell him he needs to let a sick-covered Ellie into the back of his car.

'I really am sorry, Alex,' I say again.

He agreed without hesitating to give Ellie a lift – even getting a blanket out of the boot to cover her with, which I'm 99 per cent sure he'll just bin when he gets home. But he's been really quiet the entire journey so I think it's safe to say he's a bit pissed off.

'It's fine,' he says again, then starts singing along to Stereophonics's 'More Life in a Tramp's Vest', as if to prove he is indeed fine.

I stare out of the window, trying to think of something to talk about to ease the tension, and notice a twenty-something couple staggering along arm and arm – him carrying her high heels and her carrying a handful of those red roses that sellers carry around restaurants, guilt-tripping blokes into buying for their dates.

'Yuk,' I laugh.

'What?' Alex's eyes flick to me.

'Red roses. The world's biggest cliché. I'd dump a bloke who was that unoriginal. Sunflowers maybe. Or Roses chocolates. But not red bloody roses.'

'I wouldn't worry,' he says after a minute or two. 'I don't think Dean Jones is a red roses kind of guy.'

'You saw that?'

153

'Yeah, I saw.' He pauses. 'So was it just because you're drunk?'

I glance at the back seat to check Ellie is still sleeping. She's drooling all over the seat.

'Actually,' I watch his face closely as I turn back to him, 'he asked me out.'

I notice Alex's jaw clench a little.

'He's bad news, Holly. Him and his mates – they're always smoking weed and bunking off school and stuff.'

'Look at you getting all big-brotherly on me.' I force a smile and pat his leg affectionately, then lean my head back and close my eyes.

'I just think you're too good for him, that's all.'

My heart speeds up a little. Is Alex trying to tell me something? I look his way and wait for his eyes to meet mine, but they stay on the road while he starts singing along to 'Local Boy in the Photograph', and I realize he's not trying to tell me anything at all.

Chapter Sixteen

ALEX

May 2010

The tinny fallout of iPods spills from the corridor as someone enters the staffroom. I tap a Biro between my teeth, keeping my eyes on my crossword.

Nonsense; an expression of disagreement. Seven letters, sixth letter E.

Someone stands in front of me and blocks my light. I wait for them to move. They don't. Impatient, I look up, and my face instantly softens. Cassie is smiling down at me, waiting to be acknowledged. She smoothes the back of her flowery, knee-length skirt as she falls onto the ripped leather seat beside me.

'Thank God it's Friday, eh?' she says, and I place the newspaper and pen on my lap. 'Got any plans for the weekend?'

'Feeding a mate's cat,' I reply. 'I'm so rock 'n' roll.'

Cassie nods in sarcastic agreement.

'How about you?' I say.

She shakes her head. 'Nothing in the diary. Expect I'll

just curl up on the sofa with a book. Unless I get a better offer.'

Cassie glances my way, and the glance lasts a second or two longer than I expect.

'Four down,' I say, because it seems easier than asking what she's staring at. *'Nonsense; an expression of disagreement.* Seven letters, sixth letter E.'

Cassie finally stops looking at me and thinks for a second. 'I'm rubbish at crosswords.'

'And you work in the English department?' I grin, and she punches my arm teasingly so that I stop thinking about the crossword and try to establish whether we've just engaged in pre-sexual contact, or whether Cassie is a kindly care worker and I'm an elderly patient. And then I realize. The funny way she looked at me. It was me. It was me who was supposed to give her a better offer.

'Afternoon, Japseye,' says Kev when I answer the phone.

Working day complete, I'm on my way to feed Harold. The bus is packed, and squeezed in next to me is an old lady with one hand resting on a tartan trolley that's obstructing the aisle.

'Just thought you should know, I had sex last night.'

Baloney. That's what it was. Four down. *Seven letters, sixth letter E.* Why did I leave my newspaper in the staff-room?

'Pull the other one, Kev.'

'Seriously, remember the girl I told you about who was giving me the eye on the train?'

'Whatever you say.'

'I swear. We fucked like rabbits. Twice.'

'How on earth did that happen?'

'Well, Alex, I took my trousers off, gave it a bit of a slap and stuck it in.'

'That's a lovely image, Kev – but what I meant was, how did you get to a situation where she . . .' I lower my voice to a whisper. 'Where she let you stick it in?'

'Saw her again on the train back from the Job Centre, didn't I? Except this time she didn't just perve at me. She came and sat with me. And you know me, Alex – women love my banter, don't they? So we ended up going for a drink and then—'

He finishes his sentence with a whistle.

This all sounds like bullshit to me, especially as he claims he won't be seeing her again. I ask him why, trying to prise open the cracks in his story.

'Because when I woke up this morning, guess what I saw in her bathroom?'

I really can't be bothered with this. I've still got a headache from an hour with my year nines and I just want to get to Holly's.

'I've absolutely no idea.'

'Just guess.'

'Fungal cream?'

'Worse.'

'I really don't care, Kev.'

'Come on, think – what's the most horrifying thing you could find in your lover's bathroom?'

Without warning a cyclist swerves in front of the bus, then flicks his middle finger when the driver honks his horn.

'Tena Lady?' I say, prompting the old lady to glance at me sourly, stand up and move to another seat that has

157

just been vacated. I try to appease her with an apologetic smile.

'Worse,' says Kev.

'I give up, mate – I can't be—'

'Snow globes.'

'Snow globes?'

'About a hundred and fifty of them. From Canada and Lapland and one from Skegness. Weird or what?'

I was wrong. He is telling the truth. Not even Kev could fabricate this.

'A bit, I suppose.'

'Alex, it's scoop-de-loop. Bunny-boiler shit. Fucking psycho.'

The old lady is now glaring at me as if I represent *everything* that's wrong with society today. 'So to conclude, you're not seeing her again because she collects snow globes.'

'Correct.'

'Good. I'm glad you've got all this off your chest, but I'm going to hang up now. I'm getting funny looks from someone's grandma.'

'Well, if she comes and sits next to you, ask her if she collects anything weird before going home with her.'

I must have wandered into the wrong flat.

This is the girl whose bedroom was a notorious pigsty, her floor quadrupling as a clotheshorse, a desk and a CD rack. She would tell me that life was too short to waste time cleaning your bedroom. Hence my shock at seeing four corduroy cushions balanced symmetrically across the sofa in her open-plan living room and kitchen. A set of matching enamel mugs that look like they were bought

158

at a flea market hang from a rack above a barren work surface. Her DVDs are divided into sections: musicals, black-and-white movies, concerts by bands like Erasure and Take That. The contents of each section are sorted alphabetically (my books and CDs are currently ordered by year of release), and she's included all shows or films that start with 'The' under T. I contemplate correcting her mistake, but she'd probably call me a freak.

The sole deviation from neatness is in the corner of the kitchen belonging Harold. There, soggy bits of cat food mingle with stray pebbles of litter. I open the cupboard under the sink in search of a dustpan and brush when the culprit herself limps towards me and tilts her chin in lieu of a scratch. I stretch my hand to oblige but she snubs it and trots towards the refrigerator, where a note marked 'Alex Patrick Tyler' is being restrained by a cat-shaped fridge magnet. I'd forgotten how using my middle name amused her.

I free the note from its feline captor:

Help yourself to tea/coffee. And don't even THINK about cleaning the mess Harold has inevitably left in protest at my absence. You were going to, weren't you? Ha, I knew it! See you soon – and thanks again, you STAR.
   Holly x

I carefully fold the note in half and place it in the inside pocket of my coat before scooping Harold into my arms and offering her a neck scratch. Within a few seconds she's purring with a stoned glint in her eyes.

It's while cradling Harold around the flat that I notice a photo of Holly with a man. It must be Richard. The

159

frame looks expensive and modern, in contrast to her other belongings, which generally have a vintage feel to them. The photo was taken by Holly with an outstretched arm in what appears to be a trendy bar with barely any customers. She is laughing; Richard has his arm crested around her shoulders and is peering into the lens with a pouty smile. A good match for the Holly I've come to know over the past couple of weeks, I conclude: professional, handsome and immaculate, and I can see from the bicep resting on her shoulder that he too spends a lot of time in the gym.

I should have guessed I'd encounter something like this and braced myself for the melancholy it would induce, but the jolt doesn't last for more than a minute or two. Harold and I exchange a smile, though her expression turns a little sorrowful as she realizes I'm saying goodbye. I decide to stay with her for another five minutes.

I glance over the room again, Holly's world, and shake my head at how neat it is. And meanwhile I'm living with Carl who, I've realized, is OCD about not cleaning pots. This morning I couldn't find a spoon for my cereal because they were all submerged in scummy water, shipwrecked beneath pots and pans and a cheese grater. I can understand leaving dishes – though isn't it better to do them as you go along? – but why abandon them in dirty water? You're as good as saying, 'Hey, bacteria, there's a party over at my place tonight, tell all your friends on Twitter.' I know I sound like a killjoy; I know there are more important things going on in the world. But it's every single day.

As if that wasn't bad enough, I almost broke my leg

getting dressed this morning when I tripped on a stack of books. I still haven't decided who is liable: Carl for not having any shelves in his entire flat or J.G. Ballard, J.R.R. Tolkien and other authors who released books in 1984 for being in my way. I settled on the first and resolved to look for somewhere else to live. Balls to my deposit.

Chapter Seventeen

HOLLY

Most of my train journey to Mothston is spent mentally kicking myself for my lost opportunity to talk to Richard. I was so close. I'd got as far as standing up and tossing down the pen I'd been tap-tap-tapping on my To Do list for twenty minutes. Grow some balls, Holly, I told myself. Just march on in. Ask him if he has five minutes. Say you need to talk to him. It's not hard.

'Does Richard have five minutes? I need to talk to him.'

'Um, yeah, he's—' I stammered at Melissa, who was suddenly in front of me.

'Great.' She marched in. By the time she was out I barely had time to say goodbye to Richard.

As the train pulls away from my penultimate station, I try to shake off my feeling of foreboding by gathering my bags and waiting by the door. It doesn't stop long at Mothston. It's like they don't really believe anyone would want to get off there. As ever, I'm tempted not to. But after practically throwing myself off the moving carriage onto the platform, I wheel my case to the front of the station.

Dad's there already, sitting in his car, reading the

paper. He'll have been there at least half an hour. Early to a fault. I used to share my mum's over-optimistic approach to time management, but at some point my dad's influence must have rubbed off because you can set your clock by me these days.

'So are you excited about the move?' I ask as we pull out of the car park, partly to break the silence – he's not a man of many words, my dad – and partly because I genuinely have no idea how he feels. He'd never been as happy in London as he was in Mothston. He got a job with the Met Police to be near my mum – she was doing a design course down there, but it wasn't a patch on his hometown in his eyes. Maybe he just hated London. York's not nearly as intense.

'It'll be something new, I suppose,' he says, taking his eyes off the road for a moment to give me a tight smile.

Ecstatic, clearly.

Mum is already at the door in her flour-covered apron when we pull up at my folks' semi.

'There she is.' She holds her arms out for me, kissing the top of my head as we hug. 'Come in, come in – make yourself at home. But not too much at home – it's not our home any more, ha ha ha. Now run up and get out of your work clothes while I put the kettle on. We had no biscuits in so I'm just baking some.'

Upstairs, I open my bedroom door and step into the 1990s. Red and yellow striped wallpaper on the bottom meets plain yellow on top, split midway by a red floral border. Bang on trend when I helped my dad decorate it. I'd just wanted a red colour scheme but the addition of yellow was the compromise to make it, in Mum's words, 'less brothelly'.

163

There's never been much point in updating it – I rarely spend time in it. I've only ever been back at Christmases – and that's just the years Max and I didn't spend it in London by ourselves. Even then it was just somewhere to sleep when I arrived late on Christmas Eve until my dad drove me into York on Boxing Day to get the train back, because the Mothston train doesn't run on Boxing Day. At least the move will save him a journey.

I look around, and even though the only change is the pile of empty boxes stacked in the corner, a roll of bin bags propped up against them, it feels like the first time in years I've noticed its contents. Like it's all so familiar I stopped seeing it.

My pin-board is covered in photos, curled at the corners with age, and a small but comically chunky television sits on a stand in the corner on top of a VCR player, with videos in a messy pile next to it. The empty case of *Friends* Series Two, episode 7–9 sits on top of the pile, with *Take That and Party* visible underneath it. A huge map of the world dominates the wall above my bed, red pins marking the countries I've been to and a load more gathered in the bottom left corner, waiting to be placed.

Deciding not to think about packing until morning, I sit late into the evening at the kitchen table catching up with Mum.

'So she knows about the affair but she's scared that if she confronts him he'll leave her,' she's saying. 'You know, in spite of everything, she still loves him.'

'I see.' I nod, reaching over to the biscuit tin for my hundredth cookie and dipping it in my tea. I should have brought my trainers to go for a jog in the morning. 'And does he love her?'

'Who knows?' Mum shakes her head sadly, nibbling a biscuit. 'I think so, but he's probably never going to be able to keep his ding-a-ling in his trousers.'

'So what's she gonna do?'

'I don't know. That's where it ended. It's on again at nine this Wednesday, so I'll keep you posted. I've made far too many of these, by the way.' She holds up her cookie. 'You better take some home or your dad's teeth will fall out.'

'Thanks, I'll take some for Alex.' She nods and gives me a smile that I'm not sure how to take, so I clarify. 'To say thanks for feeding Harold.'

Mentioning Alex was an error because now he's all my mum wants to talk about. If I'm seeing him soon. If we're going to see much of each other. If he's single. It's actually great having him around – life is a bit more colourful with him in London – but I dread to think what Mum would read into this if I told her.

Just then my BlackBerry beeps and, before I have the chance to grab it, my mum notices the name on the screen.

'Richard? Your boss? Bloody cheek texting at this time. You're allowed a life outside the office, you know, Holly – you shouldn't be at his beck and call night and day.'

I quickly scan Richard's message.

Just about to board my flight gorgeous, miss you already xxx

'It's fine, Mum,' I reassure her, smiling involuntarily. 'He's just telling me something I need to do on Monday as he's on his way to New York.'

'Oh, I loved New York.' She brings her hand to her chest. 'Remember when we were there?'

Vaguely. I was nine when my mum and I went for a long weekend just before Christmas, while Dad was working.

'All I remember is shopping, and seeing *Beauty and the Beast* on Broadway.'

'That's all we did, love. No wonder your father didn't fancy it.' Her smile fades slightly. 'Anyway, I hope your boss enjoys it while you're here doing his dirty work.'

I momentarily contemplate telling her the truth. By the time she meets him, it won't be a secret any more anyway, and she can stop worrying I'll grow old alone with my cat, and lose any crazy notions that Alex and I might start something up now we're back in touch.

But knowing my luck she'll call me at work and it'll be the one time in his life that Richard answers his own phone. And Christ knows what she'll say.

So I just tell her not to worry then kiss her goodnight, before she has a chance to imply that the reason I don't have a boyfriend is because my boss is a slave driver.

Chapter Eighteen

ALEX

Carl is spreadeagled on the sofa when I return from feeding Harold, his dirty dishes still garnishing the sink. I planned to bring it up as soon as I saw him, but in this moment I cannot think of any words that wouldn't resonate with anal retention. Which is bizarre, because it's not anal at all. The two of us are bound to catch typhoid or something.

Instead of coming straight out with it, I nurture a hostile expression and restrict conversation to a simple 'hello', hoping he'll sense my annoyance, realize what it's about and wash up without me having to say anything. But he doesn't. He makes small talk about a fake blonde he's hoping to charm into nudity tonight.

'Sorry to be anal, mate . . .' I interrupt.

What's with the anal? This is not anal.

'. . . but I was going to rustle up some tea in a bit . . .'

'Rustle'? Who have I become?

'. . . and was wondering if you wouldn't mind clearing the sink so I can . . .'

I begin to wonder if I'm doing the right thing. I'd underestimated how awkward this conversation would become.

'I'm doing a pasta bake. You can have some, if you like?'

This last bit is to show that I'm a cool flatmate really, but it's superfluous, because after initially appearing startled, Carl says, 'Yeah, course, I'd forgotten about them', and trots over to the sink.

I feel proud for asserting my authority. Who knows how long it'll take me to find somewhere new, but at least I've made Carl consider what it means to cohabit. He may never be considerate, but if he's going to make more of an effort from here on in then I'll meet him halfway.

I buzz across the flat, resisting the temptation to break into a whistle, but as I enter my room, something is amiss. For the second time today it's like I've sauntered into the wrong place. I gawp at the large object that has been left in the middle of the carpet.

A set of dark wood bookshelves that I have never seen before in my life.

'Listen, mate, I'm really sorry about the thing with the pots before. I guess I'm still getting used to this flat-sharing thing. I'll chill out a bit.'

Carl sips his pint before releasing a smile that implies the episode barely even registered.

'And thanks again for the bookshelves – really thoughtful of you.'

Carl invited me for a night out with his mates in Islington shortly after explaining how he'd noticed the books on my floor and bought the shelves from a junk shop in Lewisham. Several hours later we're standing in a wine bar with jazz music and low-hanging lampshades the shape of Chinese hats. Not the kind of place you'd find in Mothston – and for that reason I like it. Hopefully Cassie will too. Egged on by Carl and his bacteria theory, I texted her, and it turns out I was right: she obviously had been waiting for me to ask her out in the staffroom.

She arrives just after half-nine looking effortlessly pretty in tight jeans and an open-neck top that makes her breasts resemble something from a period drama starring Kate Winslet – ample yet suppressed, aching to be liberated. I focus on not staring at them as she kisses me hello, and then the two of us head to the bar, Cassie clinging to my elbow as we side-step through the din. When I twist my neck to present a warm smile, the gesture is returned in kind, and it feels like we're saying something without words, though I can't quite establish what.

We commandeer a sofa and spend the next couple of hours drinking red wine and talking about how annoying it is when people compare James Joyce's *Ulysses* to Jack Bauer's *24*, and how Mr Cotton forced IT to remove the dot from his email address after one of the kids saw it and started calling him Dot Cotton.

When finally there's a break in conversation I head to the toilet, hypnotized by how well things have gone for me over the last couple of months. I take my place at the urinal and direct my flow at a discarded piece of Hubba Bubba. It's stubborn, but the little bugger does not bank on me having four glasses of wine in my system, and eventually it succumbs, sliding along the stainless-steel bed before disappearing into the drainage system. Alex Tyler one, Universe nil.

When I return Cassie is staring at her phone, and my

buzz is killed by a ludicrous, paranoid thought: she is messaging Ted Rodgers, the PE teacher I've seen her with in the canteen.

Spotting me, she locks the device and slips it back into her handbag.

'What are you just standing there for?'

She pats the seat next to her, and any paranoia is expunged when she tucks herself into me on the sofa. She turns to face me and somehow we both know that it's time. My face begins to fall in slow motion towards Cassie's, and she doesn't retreat or do anything to defend herself.

I try to calm myself, focusing all my attention on Cassie's lips, which feel cold and sticky, and I submit as she takes a drunken lead, cushioning her mouth with mine, accepting a clumsy stab of her tongue.

For the last few hours I've had a nagging feeling that she might be too good to be true, but I was being an idiot. Soon we're seated in the back of a black cab on the way to her house, and my thoughts turn to all the things that could go wrong. What if she notices my nipples are disproportionately small and laughs in my face? What if I accidentally tell her I love her during orgasm?

I was nineteen when I discovered that Mr Gaffney's diagram of the female perineum was as helpful as Google to a Chinese dissident searching for the truth, because the things I learnt during sex education bore no resemblance to what I was presented with in bed with Sarah Cross. I managed to get through it without feeling too humiliated – but I never got undressed with my back to her again, because she never returned my call.

I've slept with seven women since Sarah but, if I'm

170

totally honest, I've never got to a point where it hasn't felt like I'm blagging it – and I'm worried that one of these days I'm going to get found out. What if it's tonight?

I fix my eyes on the red neon lights of the meter, trying to relax and ordering myself to stop being a prat. This is good. This is what I wanted. And Cassie obviously feels the same. By £7.60 she is nibbling my ear; at £21.00 the button to my jeans has been undone. Before I know it I'm telling the driver to keep the change from £30 and I'm considering it money well spent.

Chapter Nineteen

HOLLY

The house is quiet when I wake up so I get myself a coffee and make a start on my room. After twenty minutes of emptying cupboards, pulling stuff out from under my bed and turning drawers upside down I realize something.

I was a HOARDER. Seriously. Did I not throw anything out AT ALL in the first eighteen years of my life? There's so much crap. One cupboard alone produces a belted snakeskin-patterned coat I'd never be seen dead in again even if it wasn't too big for me; too-small ice skates that can't have fitted me for the past twenty years; CDs from boy bands that, quite rightfully, disappeared into oblivion; eight ugly troll dolls with varying hair colours and outfits; cinema tickets; a bottle of Lou Lou Blue perfume that I might even have saved deliberately when it was discontinued but now smells rancid; and a cork. Why did I keep a cork? What kind of useful or sentimental reason made me think that one day I'd reminisce over a cork?

I hate clutter these days – I toss everything I no longer have a use for. But for some reason I have to force myself to be ruthless here. Filling more bin bags than boxes, I work my way through it until 10 a.m., when Mum pops her head in to offer me a fry-up.

'Just a little bacon sandwich then?' she offers when I say I'm not hungry.

Eventually I concede to toast, which she brings on a tray with a cup of tea, a glass of orange juice, a slab of butter, a small jar of jam and a jar of Marmite.

I try to turn on my old FM radio but after a frustrating five minutes twiddling the dial, I can't find a clear station so I pick up a CD from the top of the pile. Bad Boys Inc. I can't for the life of me remember what they sang, but I recall fancying all of them so let's roll with it.

I'm rediscovering Ace of Base by the time I pull down my pin board and sit cross-legged on the floor, unpinning the photographs and dropping them into one of the boxes to store at Mum and Dad's new place. There's a strip of passport photos of me and Alex that makes me laugh, so I tuck it into my handbag to take home.

The final tattered picture is of me and Ellie, dancing at a house party. Ellie is looking at the camera, one hand on her hip and the other pointing at the photographer, with me just behind her, arms in the air, hair whipping, eyes closed and clearly unaware I was having my picture taken. I don't recognize the house but that's not unusual – familiarity with the host was never necessary. As long as the parents were away, it was fair game. I remember the night, though. It was the first time I snogged Dean Jones. Nausea grips the pit of my stomach and I tear the photo in two before tossing it in one of the black bags, before getting up to shake the pins and needles out of my legs.

All that's left on the walls now is the world map. The

memory of Mum presenting me with it in my newly decorated bedroom with a dramatic 'Ta-dah!' makes me smile. I was preparing myself to politely thank her for hideous frilly cushions, so when this turned out to be her 'surprise' I was ecstatic. We stood and marked everywhere I'd been on holiday. A cluster of pins mark Turkey, Mallorca and the Canary Islands – Dad vetoed anywhere unlikely to have a British or Irish bar – with the furthest flung pin in New York. I update it with the places I've visited since I left Mothston, which takes all of five seconds, my smile fading as I run my hand over the pin-free expanse of Australia, Asia, Africa, South America – all the places I was itching to cover in pins at the time. My eyes well up unexpectedly. What happened to my dream of travelling the world?

Oh grow up, Holly – you're not married to Mark Owen, either. No one does all the things they dreamt about when they were young.

I pull out all the pins, take the map off the wall, roll it up and, after a few moments' deliberation, chuck it in the bin.

A few sweaty, dusty hours and crap CDs later I look around at my room, neatly boxed up – no clothes slung across the mirror or bottles scattered across the dressing table – and feel a pang of sadness. All that's left is a BHS carrier bag that had been tucked under my bed. As soon as I empty its contents on the carpet, I remember what it is. Alex left it in my porch the morning after that final visit to see him, full of stuff I'd left at his. I'd barely looked at it before shoving it somewhere out of sight, still stinging from the hurt and humiliation of his rejection and having resolved that after everything that'd happened in those few days, I needed to close a door on Alex and Mothston and that part of my life.

Hair clips, a bracelet that was once silver but is now a greenish colour, Frizz-ease hair serum and a clip frame containing a picture of the two of us. The picture was actually his mum's, but he clearly had no use for it once his mum was no longer around – and he was always a bit embarrassed about it. It was taken at my fancy-dress twelfth birthday party. I'd made Alex be the Jason Donovan to my Kylie Minogue and the pair of us are sporting stonewash jeans – his teamed with a white T-shirt and black leather jacket and mine with a little black suit jacket, my hair blow dried curly and held in a side ponytail with a scrunchie. If that wasn't quite humiliating enough for him, I then talked him into singing a duet with me, making him copy down the words to 'Especially For You' from the back of my old Jason Donovan LP and learn them off by heart, and in this picture we're looking at each other, singing into our microphones.

I grin and am about to add the photo to one of the boxes when I notice there's something stuck to the back of it. It's an A4 sheet of lined paper folded four ways and it comes away easily from the dry, yellowing Sellotape attaching it to the frame. I unfold it, and as I read the words my heart catches in my throat. Written in faded blue Biro in Alex's unmistakable teenage scrawl are the lyrics from 'Especially For You', with an additional scribble written sideways in the margin.

Sorry I was a moron yesterday, Hols. You were trying to tell me something and I wasn't listening. What was it? I know you're leaving today but I just went and bought a mobile so that if you want to talk – any time, any place – then you have my number: 07588876098. Yours always, Alex xxxxx

Chapter Twenty

ALEX

Cassie is lying with her back to me, duvet tucked into her neck, knees craned towards her belly. I decide not to spoon her. Let her sleep.

To think I was worried about Ted Rodgers. What kind of name is that anyway? Ted Rodgers wouldn't be able to identify the print on her bedroom wall as *The Lady of Shalott*. Nor would he be aware of the poem of the same name by Tennyson. How could he? He's a PE teacher.

Ted Rodgers. Pah!

Here I am in Cassie's immaculate bedroom, where the pastels of cushions and rugs and sheets are still suffocated by the cinders of night. The sun will rise soon, and maybe then I'll ask Cassie if she fancies doing something together. A day out in London. The British Museum, perhaps. A first proper date.

I lie there for several hours, content, listening as she breathes slowly against her pillow until finally, just before 10 a.m., she yawns herself awake.

'Morning, sleepy,' I say, placing a hand gently onto her elbow.

She twists her body around, eliminating any contact

between us, and uses both hands to rub the sleep from her face. Her eyes remain closed.

'Did you sleep OK?' I ask, but a reply isn't forthcoming.

Minutes go by without either of us uttering a word. The wail of a baby can be heard from another house down the street. It is Cassie who speaks next.

'I was so drunk last night.'

Unsure where she is heading, I follow her lead.

'Yep, me too.'

Cassie groans and sinks back into the duvet, once again tucking it into her neck. The silence becomes unbearable but I cannot think of anything appropriate to say. I find myself pianoing my fingers against the bedframe to punctuate the quiet.

For fifteen minutes we remain dormant, and then Cassie announces that she's getting in the shower, and when she returns she asks me to look away while she gets dressed. Me who saw every inch of her pale body just a few hours ago, albeit under the shadows of her duvet. Me who stroked the thighs I'm now banned from seeing and who caressed the breasts that are now covered by a defensive right arm.

Crestfallen, I convince myself that she's just embarrassed about the whole situation: sleeping with a colleague, a proper teacher, someone she sees every day and who could influence her career. I should have guessed she'd feel a little uncomfortable afterwards. We were bound to end up sleeping together eventually, but Cassie isn't this kind of girl any more than I'm that kind of guy. Obviously we got carried away with the occasion.

I decide the best course of action is to give her some

space. Then we can resume whatever this is next week.

Cassie smiles gratefully when I tell her I need to leave. She trails me out of her room and down the stairs, accepting a kiss on the cheek and a hug goodbye, while simultaneously reaching for the door latch.

I sense her eyes tracking me as I pass through her iron gate until, a little sooner than expected, her door slams shut.

'I feel like I've been used,' I say wryly, taking a chip between my finger and thumb and examining it.

'She's probably just embarrassed about sleeping with you on a first date. And the fact she'll now be working with someone who has seen her vagina.'

The barmaid asks if everything is OK with our food. Holly is treating me to a pub lunch to say thanks for feeding Harold, even though she already brought me round some of Mrs Gordon's famous biscuits last week.

'You weren't in our English class last Monday. She didn't say a word to me for the whole hour. I don't understand how a woman can go from inviting me into her bed to treating me like I'm on the Sex Offenders' Register.'

'This is just like old times – me listening to you over-analysing everything.'

'What do you mean, over-analysing everything?'

Holly laughs tenderly. 'Look, did you try to speak to her?'

Fair enough. I didn't speak to Cassie either, but I did attempt eye contact several times, and of the two smiles I executed, one elicited a contemptuous swerve of the head and the other was ignored completely. To compound my embarrassment, the latter was witnessed by Gareth Stones, who, having spied us together on the train that time, took it as a cue to pelvic thrust into his desk.

'He sounds funny.'

Holly rests her chin in both hands. It's the first time since I moved to London that I've seen her without make-up. I want to tell her that she looks better for it but, worried she'll take it the wrong way, I refrain.

'Funniest of all was last week when he handed in his assignment on *Hamlet*, and all he'd written was "SMD".'

'SMD?'

'I had to look it up on youthslang.com. It stands for "Suck my . . ."'

Holly bites her lip to suppress a laugh.

'I suppose it is quite funny, but I'm worried that I'm totally out of my depth down here. My big idea was to implement a seating plan, except then it became a choice of Gareth and his mates sitting next to each other and talking or Gareth and his mates shouting across the room to one another.'

Holly listens intently, nodding when nodding is appropriate and offering advice here and there.

'It's as if most of the boys have already decided they've failed: they've given up. Like Kenny. His mum died when he was little and he's got so much aggression in him, but you can't do anything. It's not like *Waterloo Road* where you can go around and talk to their parents. I'd get fired. Everything has to go through the pastoral team and ours is diabolical. What an idiot, thinking I could have an impact in a school like this.'

Holly takes her opportunity to interject. 'You should

sit him down. Kenny. After one of your lessons. Tell him you're on his side. Shit, you of all people should be able to connect with a kid like that.'

I look at her doubtfully. Sure, my mum died when I was young but that's about the only thing I've got in common with Kenny. It's hardly going to be credible if I try the old 'I know what you're going through' routine.

'What have you got to lose?'

'I don't know,' I say weakly. 'I guess it's not just school. It's not even Cassie. She's hardly up there with some of the heartbreaks I've had.' As soon as the words leave my mouth I realize it's too close to home, but, mercifully, Holly doesn't respond. 'I can't believe I'm saying this, but for the first time this week I actually missed Mothston. Everything's weird down here. I haven't met one Londoner who knows anything about the geography of the rest of Britain. Pubs think they can get away with serving you four chips by describing them as chunky and triple cooked.' I pick up my last remaining chip, which has somehow become a symbol of my discontent. 'And no one queues at bus stops, which along with wanting to avoid Gareth Stones on the train, is another reason I've bought a bike.'

Holly steals the chip from my fingers and pops it into her mouth, whole.

'So you're still loving London then, yeah?' she says, and her smile proves contagious. We both shake our heads at my ridiculousness and Holly reaches over and places a hand on mine. It's just for a second or two before she retreats and signals for the bill, but in that moment, moving to London doesn't feel like such a dumb move after all.

I gaze outside, where the sunset has turned the sky the colour of Fruit Salad sweets. It is Spring Bank Holiday – summer is not far away now. I watch Holly wrap her navy blue cardigan around the back of her chair, exposing bare arms that are thin and goose-pimply.

'What are you staring at?' says Holly, checking her forearms.

I snap myself out of it. 'Nothing. I was just thinking that navy always was your colour.'

Holly reviews me with intrigue but I pacify her with a blank expression until she gives up and changes the subject.

'Another thing you'll find with London. People who visit are either afraid of everything here – the tube and the roads and the people – or else they dismiss everything by saying, "That may be the way things are done in London . . ."'

'Your dad?'

Holly nods, but I can tell she wouldn't have it any other way.

'How's yours?'

'Loving life on water. Except for his barny with the Mothston Barge Association. They won't accept his membership until he changes the name of his boat. They're supposed to be called things like *Lady Rosebery* or *Haste Away* or *The Duchess of York*.'

'And what's his called?'

'*Terry's Barge.*'

Holly claps her hands together in delight.

'And you say Kev's met a girl too?'

'Well, he had sex.'

'So maybe it was *you* holding *them* back?'

Holly greets me with two mischievous eyes as she downs the rest of her drink.

'Come on, let's go find an old man's pub. Somewhere the regulars will stare at us when we walk in. It'll be like you're back in Mothston.'

'Aren't you in work tomorrow?'

Holly ignores me and leads us on to the street.

'Talking of work,' I say, reminded of the friend request I received a while back. 'Your workmate added me on Facebook.'

I'd anticipated a reaction – it was clear at the quiz that Holly isn't Melissa's biggest fan – but she accepts the information with little more than a nod. She's busy eye-balling a STOP sign ahead of us, mirth hatching from the corners of her mouth.

'What?' I say.

'Don't tell me you've forgotten?'

Holly regards me expectantly until at last the memory surfaces. We must have been thirteen or fourteen. Holly had persuaded me to share a plastic bottle of White Lightning under a three-quarter moon in Weelsby Park – Holly matching each sip of mine with a gulp of her own – and we were on our way home when Holly produced a black permanent marker from the pencil case in her school bag.

'Give us a leg-up,' she said, surveying the STOP sign in front of us.

'What are you doing?' I whined.

'You like school work, don't you, Al? Let's call this an art project.'

She removed the lid from the marker, rebellion drawn across her face.

'Someone'll see,' I protested while simultaneously locking my fingers to create a step. It was Holly, after all, and to this day I remember how, as I was straining to hold her in the air, I found myself getting an erection, and I couldn't make it go away no matter how much I thought of Grandma, but I think I got away with it, because by the time she disembarked we were both too absorbed in her handiwork.

STOP, HAMMER TIME

'Your turn now,' she said, thrusting the marker pen into my belly. 'What's it going to be?'

We traipsed around for half an hour before another sign caught my attention. I'd never done anything that could have got me into serious trouble before but I didn't want to disappoint Holly, so, with her as a lookout, I approached McDonald's and commenced work on their Drivethru banner, meticulously adding a roof to the 'u' so it became an 'o'. Then, one by one, I scribed the 'ugh' so the sign was now dictionary perfect: 'Welcome to McDonald's Drivethrough'.

Panic set in as soon as I'd finished – what if someone had seen? – but Holly was so impressed that I didn't really care if I got caught. A few days later my artistry featured in the *Mothston Herald*, appearing on the letters page with praise for our enterprise from a pensioner named George Riley.

'I found a copy when I went home,' says Holly. 'I should have brought it with me.'

As we keep walking a wistful look comes over her. I follow her gaze but it leads to nowhere in particular in the distance.

'What are you thinking about?'

184

At first I wonder if she has heard me because it takes her about thirty seconds to reply.

'Do you believe in fate, Al? That some things are meant to be and others aren't?'

It seems like a strange thing to ask. I glance at her again but her focus remains off in the horizon.

'I believe that everyone is meant do a certain thing, to follow a certain path. Whether that's fate or not, I don't know. I think it's just a concept people use to give things meaning.'

Holly doesn't say anything.

'What about you?' I ask.

She thinks for a moment. 'There was probably a time when I did.'

'And now?'

'I think life's just a million different coincidences and accidents that lead you to where you are. Not very romantic; but true, I think.'

Holly brings us to a halt outside a pub called The Woodman. She peers through a dirty window but a shake of the head tells me she doesn't fancy going inside.

'Fuck it,' she says, finally coming back into the moment. 'We should get a six-pack and go to the park instead.'

'A park?'

'You know, trees and grass. Sometimes they have swings, too.'

I examine her face, trying to establish the source of her newfound abandon, but I never could work her out.

For the first time since we saw the STOP sign Holly turns my way. 'Why are you looking at me like that?' she says. 'Let's get drunk. What are Bank Holidays for?' She invites me to link arms. 'It's not as if I have to get home to Richard. He said he was too tired to come around after helping his mum decorate her new extension. Bless his cotton socks.'

'Fair enough.' I hook my arm into Holly's with a contented grin. 'Let's do it.'

'All dry,' I say, inspecting the ground near an ancient oak tree with the flat of my hand, and for the next hour or two we sit cross-legged in Greenwich Park drinking cans of cider and talking about the old days like we're drawing our pensions already. The sky shifts through the spectrum of purple and blue but the air remains still as we remember familiar names and the week our families spent together in Camber Sands. Holly tells me that it was there she kissed a boy for the first time, and I wonder how it can be that a revelation like this still provokes jealousy in me all these years later. I've no idea, but it does.

We reminisce about the time Kev fell into a lake while trying to disprove the theory that geese can break your arm. Right now, here in the park, it feels just like it used to. I feel just like I used to.

I disregard the thought; erase it from my mind. I'm drunk on cider and nostalgia and the smell of car fumes mixed with freshly mowed grass. Holly and I are friends and that is all we will ever be.

'There's something I've been meaning to ask you,' says Holly, in a tone that prompts my chest to squeeze in on itself.

She draws out the moment so that I'm wondering what on earth it is she wants to know. Finally she places her hand on top of mine and says with amusement in her eyes: 'Do you still carry wet wipes to clean toilet seats?'

'That's it? You want to know if I still carry wet wipes?'

She replies with laughter.

'If you must know then, no, I don't. Charlotte McCormack forbade me.'

'Charlotte who?'

'One of my exes. She's also the reason I stopped correcting people's grammar. She said it made me a tosser.'

Holly smiles. 'You should have hung onto her, Alex.'

I explain how I didn't have a lot of choice, and then I explain about Debbie and how that ended, and then it's Holly's turn to provide the relationship history. She talks me through all her exes with the exception of Dean. I guess I know all there is to know about him.

'And now it's Richard,' she concludes, fingering the catch on her third can of cider.

When we eventually stand up and brush the grass from our legs, my head feels dizzy, and an ominous tightness begins to rise through my throat.

'I think I'm going to be sick.'

'You've hardly drunk anything!'

'Three cans of cider and the best part of a bottle of wine.'

'You never could hold your—'

I scurry to the oak tree, pressing my hands against its tired bark while my head hangs like a bell from my neck. Soon a fierce contraction zips through my body. And then again.

I'm sick three times before I look up to witness Holly standing two or three feet away, hands cupped over her

187

mouth, eyes wide with sympathy. Once she's sure that I'm done, she steps closer and places a hand lightly on my shoulder.

'Do you need some TLC?' she asks softly.

Unable to speak, I look at her, smile gratefully, and sink my head back in my hands.

And then Holly starts to sing a song. A song I recognize from sixth form about a woman who doesn't want a scrub. The lyrics confused me at the time and they are confusing me now. There isn't anyone else around, but her singing is loud enough for me to feel self-conscious.

'What are you doing?' I croak.

'Singing. I asked if you wanted some TLC. That's one of their biggest hits, Alex. "No Scrubs".'

Holly bites her lip to stop herself laughing.

'That is among the worst jokes I have ever heard,' I tell her, turning my back to her and stepping away. She begins to sing again, even louder than before.

'You're about as funny as Gareth Stones,' I yell back, but despite myself I can't stop the laughter seeping through my lips.

And once it starts, I find it almost impossible to stop.

Chapter Twenty-one

HOLLY

I saw this documentary once about a woman who loved the Eiffel Tower.

Not loved it in a nostalgic sort of way – she was actually in love with it. She married it. True story. It's called objectum sexualism, or something.

I remember watching it and thinking she was a bit of a mentalist, but I've just decided I love my bed. LOVE it. I would definitely marry it if that meant I got to stay here for ever.

My reverie is shattered by Lady Gaga.

'Oh, eff off,' I groan out loud, slamming the snooze button on my radio alarm.

Incidentally, there was also a woman on the programme who claimed to be making love to her stereo, but that's just ten thousand degrees of wrong.

Urgh – this is no normal hangover – I'm actually dying. I didn't think I was as hammered as Alex in the park, but I seem to remember defacing a To Let sign on my way home by putting an 'i' between the two words with eye liner and sending a photo of it to him on his mobile.

It's only now I notice he's replied with a picture of

Queens Road, but with an apostrophe before the 's'. Ha ha! It's getting more and more like old times. That's why I decided against telling him about the note I found. I don't want things to get weird and awkward, like they did that last time I saw him in Mothston.

Not that it's easy, saying nothing. What did he mean? He knew I liked him and was sorry he didn't feel the same? Were the Jason and Kylie lyrics his way of letting me down gently, of trying to cheer me up? Or was there a message in the lyrics? Was he trying to tell me he feels the same way? What would have happened if I'd found the note at the time? I don't suppose I'll ever know now – Alex probably doesn't even remember it. But I just wish I knew what—

OH, HOLY MOTHER OF CRAP. I wish I hadn't looked in the mirror. I lean closer to check for leaves, given that I was clearly dragged backwards through a hedge in my sleep.

Scraping my hair into a messy ponytail, I practise the *Britain's Got Talent*-worthy ability I recently discovered I possess to get dressed, apply mascara and brush my teeth all at the same time.

'Meow.'

'Morning, Harold. I'm LATE. Do I look remotely presentable?'

Whatever, she says. *Just feed me.*

The dried cat food comes out of its box too quickly and spills over the side of Harold's bowl, but I'm out of the door by the time it hits the floor so I'll have to clean it up later.

*

'You look proper shite.' Jemma sounds impressed.

'Thanks.' I sink into my chair and peer around the office. It's like the *Mary Celeste*. All the computers are on. Half-drunk coffees and open newspapers lie next to keyboards. But other than Jemma, there's not a soul to be seen.

'Where is everyone?'

'Martin Cooper was late for his breakfast meeting because I forgot to book his car. Again. Richard Croft is in his office, probably simultaneously typing up his own letters, answering his own phone and craving a coffee, given that his PA has only just seen fit to drag herself in. And the team are in the conference room. Melissa gathered them there half an hour ago going: "Guys, guys, can we have a quick pow-wow in the den – we need to get our ducks in a row."' She swaps her Glasgow accent for an exaggerated posh London one to impersonate Melissa. 'Anyway, why were you late? Out with Alex?' Said suggestively, complete with predictable wink.

Jemma doesn't believe that my relationship with Alex is purely platonic. But then why would she? As far as she's concerned we're both single. Out of everyone, it's hardest keeping Richard a secret from her. It's not that I don't trust her. She'd never intentionally spill the beans. She's just one of those people whose face gives everything away. If someone suspected something and asked her, her voice would say no – but her face would say, *Aye, they're totally at it – and look! They did it right there on that desk!*

'Yeah, I was, and I hear you added him on Facebook. Hope you're not going to start stalking—'

'Jemma,' Melissa is out from her meeting and suddenly by our desks, 'I want to start having weekly catch-ups

191

with the team re our strategy staircase. Can you put something in the diary, please?'

'You're such a wanker, Melissa.' That's what Jemma's face says.

Out loud it's: 'Sure thing, Melissa.'

'Great, thanks. We need to get everyone into the habit of pre-preparing and forward planning.'

'As opposed to other forms of preparing and planning,' Jemma mutters.

'What?' Melissa snaps.

'What?' Jemma says innocently.

'Er, nothing.' Melissa turns to me and smiles. 'Afternoon, Holly!'

'Sorry, slept in,' I mumble. No idea why I'm even apologizing. It's only a quarter to effing ten, and I stay late often enough. And apart from anything else, SHE'S NOT MY BOSS.

'Oh, I'm only kidding. Do me a favour and ask Richard to ping me an email rearranging lunch, would you?' She waves one hand dismissively. 'He'll know what it means.'

'Well, thank fuck Richard will know what it means,' Jemma says, once Melissa's out of earshot. 'Don't know about you but I was really struggling to decode that message.'

I laugh, but these little lunches and meetings Melissa keeps commandeering Richard for are doing my head in. It's happening a lot lately. I'm not insinuating they're DOING IT or anything – I know what they're talking about. I asked Richard about it the week I got back from Mothston.

We'd been lying between his king-sized charcoal-grey Egyptian cotton sheets in woozy post-coital bliss. His bed is like everything else in his Docklands apartment – expensive, luxurious and unnecessarily large considering he lives alone. His television screen could give the local Odeon an inferiority complex; you need a degree in physics to work out how to play a CD on the stereo system that takes up half a living-room wall; a dining table that could comfortably seat a family of twelve stands next to a wine rack containing enough bottles of high-end plonk to keep the lot of them drunk for a fortnight.

I had been lying there wondering whether I'd end up moving into his or whether we'd get a place of our own. I mean, it's nice enough and everything – the complex had just been built when Richard moved in three years ago, and it has its own bar and gym. But there's just something so characterless about it. It's a fine bachelor pad, but I picture us in a house with a garden. Especially when we have kids.

I'm not sure how I went from thinking all this to blurting out my question about Melissa. The word 'characterless', I expect.

'Well – and this is strictly between me and you, mind – she got wind of the merger.' Richard folded both hands beneath his head. 'She's keen on being part of my new team.'

Huh! I bet she is, the manipulative cow.

'Huh! I bet she is, the manipulative cow.'

I honestly hadn't meant to say that out loud, but I was riled. Not only because she's blatantly trying to get her claws into my boyfriend, but also in a professional sense. I'm his PA. And until I'm not, if she wants to speak to Richard about work matters, she should arrange it through me.

Though it's more the trying-to-get-her-claws-into-my-boyfriend thing.

'What's your problem?' Richard laughed. 'Oh wait, sorry – I forgot.'

'Forgot what?'

'About you irrationally disliking Melissa.'

'I do not!'

'You do – you can't stand her.'

'No, I mean it's not irrational. No one likes her.'

'I like her.'

'OK, none of the girls like her. Every bloke in the office is completely oblivious to how annoying she is, though – what's WITH that?'

'She's a nice girl. Did you know she wants to get into golf? She asked if I could teach her the basics.'

'That's crap!' I protested, remembering how Melissa had rolled her eyes a few days earlier when Jemma said Richard was in Martin's office talking about golf. 'Boring,' she'd said. It was the only time I'd ever known her words to match her tone of voice and facial expression.

'Aw.' Richard draped an arm around my shoulders and pulled me into his chest. 'Are you jealous of Melissa?'

Jealous of Melissa? JEALOUS of Melissa? Jealous of MELISSA?

'What would I have to be jealous about?'

Does he think she's better than me? Prettier? Cleverer?

'That she might be working with me after the merger but you won't?'

With his genitals in such easy reach, he's lucky that was his answer.

194

'Oh that. Not at all. I'll be far too busy personally assisting your replacement to think about you.'

I changed my tone of voice to make the words 'personally' and 'assisting' sound as dirty as possible, then waited for him to get affronted so I could tell him I'm joking, then prove it by kissing him.

'That's all right,' he half smiled/half yawned. 'I'll have some hot new secretary tending to my needs anyway.'

I'd asked for that, I suppose.

Maybe it's Melissa and her little lunches, or maybe it's being too hungover to have the energy to fob off Jemma about why I'm not interested in Alex, but a niggling insecurity I sometimes feel with Richard comes bubbling to the surface. Why *doesn't* he want anyone to know? If I was on the outside looking in, I'd feel sorry for me. A woman approaching thirty trying to force commitment from a man who's clearly not that into her. Who won't hold her hand in the street or take her to meet his mum. That's the reason I've stopped talking to Susie and Leah about it – Susie makes no secret of the fact she's not convinced, and Leah does the same with her silence. When the eternal relationship optimist can find no words of encouragement you know what she's thinking. The only person I can talk to is Alex – he just listens, and doesn't judge. No one else sees what Richard is like when it's just the two of us there, and he *is* that into me. He couldn't be more affectionate.

But it's like that tree in the woods debate – is a relationship real if there's no one there to see it?

I've never really given it another shot since my failed attempt at The Talk the Friday I left for Mothston.

Richard's even busier than usual with work, and I've been seeing more of Alex, which has kept my mind occupied.

But it's getting beyond a joke. I stand and . . . woah. I sit back down again.

'Head rush,' I respond to Jemma's inquisitive look, before I attempt it again, but in slow-mo.

'Baby?' I close Richard's door and sit opposite him at his desk, clutching the notebook I grabbed from my desk to maintain the facade. I need to think of a topic that will lead seamlessly into the conversation. Can't just blurt it out and put him on the spot.

'Let's tell everyone. About us, I mean.'

Oops.

I try to look casual and breezy, like I have only a slight passing interest in what he's going to say, while all his possible responses run through my head.

'*Fan*tastic Jazz !' he booms.

OK, not ALL possible responses had run through my head.

'Are you a *fan* of Jazz? JazzEast . . . are you a *fan*?'

'What are you on about, Richard?'

He explains. One of our clients is JazzEast – an annual open-air Beer and Jazz festival in Shoreditch – and Richard is proposing to promote this year's event by giving out paper fans to sweaty commuters with the email address on. He's trying to come up with a slogan to get printed on them.

My eyes scan his office for inspiration, skipping over the copies of *Men's Health* and *GQ* littering his otherwise tidy desk, and falling on a motivational poster behind his chair, in which four men are lined up in a rowing boat holding oars.

TEAMWORK. Together we achieve more.

Exactly. That's why I spend so much time trying to come up with crap puns. Words have never been my forte but two heads are better than one, and all that. I look at the poster next to it.

ACHIEVEMENT. It is hard to fail, but it's worse never to have tried to succeed.

This picture shows a lone smiling man on top of a snowy mountain with his hands in the air. Doesn't that totally contradict the teamwork one?

'JazzEast: this summer's COOLEST festival?' I offer.

'That,' Richard says, giving me an energetic arm-stretched finger snap and point, 'is why I love you.'

My heart stops beating. He's never told me he loves me before. This is momentous. I'm about to reciprocate with the obvious response when I realize he's distractedly jotting in his notepad. He's not waiting for a response. He didn't mean it like that.

'I think it's about time we tell people about us.'

'Why?' he asks, still scribbling away in his notepad. 'Pass me that document off the printer would you, babe?'

'*Why?*'

'Because I need it to send the—'

'Not that.' I grab the paper off the printer and pass it across the desk. 'What do you mean "why"?'

He leans back in his chair with his hands behind his head. 'In a couple of weeks I'll be moving upstairs and you won't be my PA any more. Why would we stir things up at the last minute?'

I breathe a sigh of relief. The reason it's not been getting

197

to him is because he can see the end is in sight. There's no reason to keep it a secret once he changes roles. He's right. We've done nine months of secrecy so another few weeks won't make much difference.

'So, you're feeling pretty confident about this job then, eh?'

He flashes me a grin that implies it's so much in the bag my question isn't even worth answering and so I match his grin, and we both sit there grinning until the door flies open and Martin Cooper flashes us a grin of his own.

'I'll leave you two to it.' I jump up and wave my notebook. 'We've finished here.'

I try to get away at 5.30 p.m. because I've invited Alex over for comfort carbs – he's suffering too.

'Holly, can I see you in my office before you head off, please?' Richard pokes his head out his office. 'I need you to take down some dictation.'

Dictation/pants, tomato/tomayto.

As soon as his door is closed he's kissing me.

'Martin cancelled tonight's conference call,' he murmurs, nuzzling my neck. 'So I'm all yours tonight.'

'Nice as that sounds,' I murmur back, 'I have plans. Alex is coming for dinner.'

'Oh?' Richard pulls away, knitting his eyebrows slightly. 'Can't you cancel? You saw him last night, didn't you?'

'No, I can't cancel – it wouldn't be fair on him.' Plus, I don't want to cancel. I like hanging out with Alex. 'I thought you were busy. It's no big deal; he's just coming for dinner. I'm making lasagne and I always make way too much.' I don't know why I'm justifying it. 'You should join us.'

I wait for him to decline.

'All right then,' he nods.

'Great,' I say, hiding my surprise.

I head home to cook while Richard finishes at work. I couldn't say no to him after the amount I've gone on about wanting him to get to know my mates. And why would I want him to say no? Them meeting is a good thing. Burying my inexplicable uneasiness, I'm about to call Alex to give him a heads-up when the doorbell goes, and in comes Richard brandishing a bunch of red roses.

'For the host,' he says, handing them over with a kiss before he goes into my room for a coat hanger for his suit jacket.

'Aw, bless you,' I call, chuffed (he's never bought me flowers before), and put them in a vase. He fills me in on the latest on the merger while I prepare the lasagne (leaving out my usual layer of sliced mushrooms, because Richard doesn't think they belong there) and I've just stuck it in the oven when the door goes again.

If Alex is still suffering, you wouldn't know from looking at him, all fresh and bright eyed having cycled over from Greenwich.

'Guess who's here?' I whisper.

'The police?' he whispers back, peering around me. 'They've finally tracked down the phantom graffitist? If so, I'm off – you're not taking me down with you.'

'No.' I giggle, pulling him in and closing the door. 'It's—'

'You must be Alex?' Richard appears at the living-room door, extending his hand. 'So nice to meet you finally – I've heard so much about you.'

That's not quite true – he never asks anything about Alex.

'Alex, this is Richard,' I offer, in case it's not obvious.

'Of course. Richard, hi.' Alex quickly casts off his slight look of surprise and shakes Richard's hand.

I usher them both into the living room nervously – why am I nervous? – and ask who wants what to drink with a single clap of my hands – why am I clapping?

'I brought this.' Alex holds out a bottle of red wine.

'Here, let me.' Richard takes it off him, and picks up the bottle opener from the table.

'Good choice.' He nods approvingly, reading the label.

'Right,' I tell them, shuffling towards the kitchen. 'I need to grate the cheese for the top of the lasagne, so you boys just hang out and, um, talk boy stuff.'

Back in the kitchen I add the cheese then start the salad. I feel flustered for some reason. The murmur of Alex and Richard's voices drifts through to the steamy kitchen, and I can hear Richard talking about a recent marketing conference he was on, and I surprise myself by silently willing him to shut up. That stuff isn't interesting to anyone who doesn't work in marketing. Christ, interesting is pushing it even if you do. It's always nerve-racking when you introduce two people who are important to you for the first time – especially when they have little in common – but I hear Alex's polite murmurs and follow-up questions, and feel myself relax a bit.

Thankfully, dinner goes well. It's weird witnessing Richard channel Mr Schmooze in such a small social situation. I kind of presumed it was a technique reserved for work purposes. Still, by the time we're mopping up the last of the tomato sauce on our plates with garlic bread, Alex is making us laugh with anecdotes about kids in his class, and we're all reminiscing about our own school days.

'I had no idea you were such a rebel,' Richard laughs, after Alex tells him about the time I skipped school to go to HMV in London with Ellie because Take That were there signing CDs.

'Only compared to you pair of kiss-arses.'

They both chuckle, then none of us says anything for a few moments too long before Richard leans forward and sits his elbows on the table, resting his chin in one hand and using the other hand to swirl his red wine around by the stem of his glass.

'So,' he begins. Thank Christ for that – I was worried it was turning into an awkward silence.

'Given that you guys go way back, have you ever . . . you know . . . got it on?'

Whoa, where did that come from? The grin on Richard's face and the twinkle in his eye indicate it's a playful rather than a confrontational enquiry, but he must clock my look of horror because he quickly adds, 'Back in the day, I mean. I wasn't suggesting now. I just wondered if ever you—'

'No.' Alex smiles gently, meeting Richard's eyes. 'Holly and I have never got it on.'

'No?' Richard laughs. 'That's impressive. Not even a cheeky snog?'

'No.' Alex shakes his head, while I will this discussion to end. 'Not even that.'

'Not even an almost moment?' Seriously, why are we still on this?

How I miss that sweet, sweet silence.

I'm conscious I still haven't spoken and I'm probably blushing. I need to do something that suggests this is as comfortable a conversation for me as it is for both of them, so that I don't give away what did happen back in the day. Or what never did happen, to be more precise. So I laugh. Slightly harder than I mean to, which sends me into a fit of hysterical giggles. They both look at me oddly.

'Me and Alex,' I sigh, wiping a tear away then holding out the lasagne dish. 'Anyone want any more?'

They both shake their heads and tap their tummies to signal they're stuffed, then throw compliments at me about how good it was. Richard picks up my hand to kiss it before standing up to get another bottle of wine from the kitchen. I allow myself a glance at Alex, who looks thoughtful, until he notices me watching him and smiles. I smile back, then Richard returns.

'You guys get a comfy seat while I clear the table,' I mumble.

'Let me help,' says Alex, starting to pile the plates.

'No, no,' Richard insists, taking the pile from him, gloriously oblivious to my discomfort. 'You're our guest.'

'Both of you leave them.' I continue the game of Pass-The-Plates by relieving Richard of them. 'I'll just get this cleared away and I'll be right with you.'

'Well, that's us told.' Richard raises his hands, laughing. They sit at separate ends of the sofa, and Harold crawls up onto Richard's lap.

'Hello you,' he coos, rubbing her under the chin and winking my way. I throw him a smile and disappear into the kitchen.

Chapter Twenty-two

ALEX

Richard shoos Harold from his lap and retrieves his glass of wine from the coaster beside his feet. He goes to take a sip but hesitates at the last second.

'Chianti is actually the classic accompaniment for lasagne,' he says, glass still hovering near his mouth. 'That's what they'd give you in Italy. You need a rich red with beef, and the pasta provides a superb canvas for the wine to strut its stuff. Then the tomato sauce and herbs are the ideal partner for the acidity and smokiness of the Chianti.' He finally takes his sip. 'You chose well!'

Holly's in the kitchen finishing the dishes, oblivious to our wine chat.

'All I know is that it was Hannibal Lecter's favourite. I figured it'd go with red meat.'

Richard laughs heartily and I spot Holly glance over to where we are sitting, just for a second, before returning her focus to the dishcloth and plate in her hands.

This has been the routine all night, each of us playing a role: me the submissive guest, Holly the housewife and Richard the veteran host with his shirtsleeves rolled up and two buttons loose down his chest. It takes an air of

Latin confidence, two buttons. I've never been able to pull off anything other than one. You have fewer options as a pallid northerner, though on occasion I've stood before a mirror, shirt fastened to the collar like a mod. I always bottle it before leaving the house.

When Richard came to the door and offered me a robust handshake, when I realized he would be joining us, I worried that it all might be a bit weird. Dinner with the girl I used to love and her secret boyfriend. But he put me at ease. He gave me compliments. And there hadn't been a single awkward moment until he asked if anything had ever happened between me and Holly. Did he know something? Was his jokey exterior a mask for trying to warn me off? I did my best to not appear defensive while Holly just laughed it off. Why did she have to laugh quite so hard? I understand she never felt the same as I did, but I didn't know she found the idea *that* ridiculous.

'I was reading an article the other day,' Richard says, as Holly wipes down the placemats and Harold, who has taken refuge under the dining table, licks her hind legs with long, thorough tongue strokes. 'And from what I can gather, the problem with kids at the moment is they all know their human rights. This article, I can't remember where I saw it now, but . . .'

A headache that afflicted me all morning and afternoon bubbles to the surface as Richard talks. My hangover is making it difficult to concentrate for any length of time. My eyes flick to a vase of roses on the windowsill behind Richard and, for a second or two, I lose myself in a distant memory.

'. . . if anything, I think you teachers deserve more holidays.'

204

I find myself relieved as the extractor fan that chugged throughout dinner is finally silenced, acting as a full stop on our conversation. We watch Harold tiptoe from under the dining table.

'So, how are you finding the girls down in London, then?' Richard wraps his arm around Holly's shoulders as she slips onto the sofa between us.

It feels like an odd question, especially after his earlier round of questioning about me and Holly, and I'm not sure how to answer, so I release a 'Ha!' in the hope that it will be enough, but the cramped hush that follows tells me it's not. Holly eventually intervenes.

'I should set you up with one of my friends!' she blurts, holding out her arm in invitation to Harold, who trots over for a neck scratch.

'Actually,' I tell them, stung by the idea that I'm a charity case, 'I was thinking about asking someone you know out.'

Holly looks up from the cat and glances at Richard as if I might have already confided in him while she was in the kitchen. He shakes his head. How could he know what on earth I'm on about when I'm not entirely sure myself?

'Who's that, then?' says Holly.

Still unsure where I'm going with all this, I direct a bashful smile at Holly, then Richard, then back at Holly. 'Melissa.'

Holly seems confused. 'Melissa who?'

Richard furrows his brow knowingly but it takes Holly a few more seconds to twig.

'We met at the pub quiz that time, remember? I told you she added me on Facebook.'

Holly lifts her body ever so slightly to adjust the waist of her pencil skirt, and then settles back again, arms folded.

'Oh.'

The three of us bathe in silence once again and it dawns on me why they're both concerned.

'Don't worry,' I assure them. 'Your secret's safe with me.'

As I turn and see two incredulous faces, I suddenly feel like a complete prat. I haven't exactly thought this through. I was as surprised as anyone when Melissa sent me a friend request, and again when she started 'Liking' all my statuses. Kev says she's marking her territory, like a cat spraying its house, but until now I hadn't seriously considered that there might be anything in it.

I guess Holly's offer to set me up confirmed something that has been nagging at me all evening. Seeing her and Richard together for the first time: it's made lots of things real in my mind. When I moved to London and we met up, I couldn't believe how much Holly had changed, but lately . . . I don't know. There have been moments over the last month or two where it's started to feel like it used to – or at least I have. But tonight has made it clear: it's not going to happen. This is Holly's life now and she's happy.

An awkwardness has settled between us, and it's this that seems to prompt Holly to reach into her bag.

'I haven't shown you yet, have I?' She produces a digital camera and shuffles closer to me, at which point Richard excuses himself to go to the bathroom and Harold jumps onto my thighs, eager to get a peep at the snaps herself. 'I took some photos of our old house with

206

everything boxed up. I never thought I'd be bothered but . . .'

I scroll through the photos, lingering on the ones of her bedroom for as long as I can without coming across as a weirdo. This place is to my teenage fantasies what Graceland is to Elvis, and although I barely even recognize it without all the junk on the floor, the sight of it still makes me syrupy inside.

After shots of the house come photos from a party.

'Ooh, these are from the wedding I went to a few weeks ago,' says Holly, and I feel obliged to continue.

I don't know anyone in the first twenty pictures or so until finally Holly appears with a bouquet in one hand and Richard in the other. She looks overjoyed at having caught the flowers, while Richard, his chin at a right angle to the lens, is sporting something of a pout. The pose is familiar from the framed photograph on the windowsill that I first saw while feeding Harold a few weeks ago.

'So I guess this means you and Richard are next then?' I venture, and Harold takes this as her cue to leap back onto the carpet, leaving a wig of cat hair on my trousers.

'Sorry about her,' says Holly, ignoring my question and taking it upon herself to brush the fur from my legs. Despite myself I start to blush and avert my eyes, because Holly Gordon's hands are sweeping across my thighs, and because I'm fairly sure this could constitute pre-sexual contact under Kev's definition.

I order myself to stop being absurd. Holly would brush cat hair from the trousers of any of her close friends, obviously.

'All done,' she says.

The bathroom door opens on the other side of the flat. Holly collects the camera from my palm and that would have been that.

Would have been that, but for the faintest, tiniest, most minuscule flicker of totally innocent eye contact that means when Richard walks back into the room, clasping his hands together for no apparent reason, I feel like a naughty schoolboy, as if I – we – have done something wrong.

A plastic bag wrestles with the bough of a tree to my left as I cycle around the heath and back to Greenwich. It's losing and I know how it feels. An evening of lasagne and wine and weird moments has left me with indigestion, and the previous night's frolics with Holly are refusing to be ignored. That's why I decided to call it a night.

I'm almost home when my phone vibrates and I have to stop pedalling and disembark so I can answer. It's Kev.

Steering my bike with one hand and holding my phone to my ear with the other, I tell him I've just met Richard and then listen as he reveals he went on a date last night. With Diane, the girl he met on the train. I crack up and he tells me to 'fuck off'. And then he tells me to 'fuck off' again.

I mean, it's good that for once in his life he isn't being shallow, but he was the one who thought the snow globes thing was psycho, and what happened to 'No one goes on dates any more'?

'She practically begged me, Alex. And anyway, I've been in a rare barren patch. I found myself looking up the skirt of a mannequin on the escalators at Marks and Spencer the other day.'

He recalls the date and how he avoided awkward silences by saving a list of things to talk about on his phone, revising whenever she went to the loo.

And they say romance is dead.

Of course there's a 'but'. There's always a 'but' where Kev's concerned, and here it's that when he tried to snog her at the end of the night, Diane exhibited her cheek. She's gone from sleeping with him to not wanting a proper kiss.

'Do you think she's using you for your conversation?' I say, but he doesn't bite. Which makes me think he might actually like her.

I hope he does. I hope he gets a steady girlfriend. I hope she makes him grow up a bit.

'So anyway, cocksplash, spit it out – what's Richard like?'

Kev pronounces Richard's name in the kind of dismissive tone that's usually accompanied by air quotes.

'He's . . .' I try to summon a definitive opinion. 'He's all right. I guess he's the kind of guy most girls go for. Prince Charming. Ticks the boxes.'

'What's that supposed to mean?'

'I don't know. Nothing. He was nice. Full of compliments.'

'Sounds like a tosser.'

We don't have a lot in common, but he's not a tosser. Despite the photo pose and the marketing chat, he's not. I think again about the way Holly laughed when Richard asked if anything had ever happened between us, and then I remember the vase on her windowsill and wonder if she ever really wanted all the things she talked about. Maybe that was my problem: I always listened to what she said, and presumed that was what she wanted, when from what I've seen tonight, it quite clearly wasn't.

'Can you stay behind for a quick word please, Kenny?'

The rest of the kids file out. Stacey Bamber tells Kenny to plead the fifth as she passes.

I perch against the desk next to Kenny's.

'I won't keep you long,' I begin. 'I just wanted to say that if you ever need anyone to talk to – anyone for advice or just to sound off to – then I'm here.'

Kenny grunts, then without looking at me says, 'If I wanted to talk, why the fuck would I talk to you?'

'Watch your language,' I tell him. He tuts and rolls his eyes. 'Look, I'm not pretending I know anything about you or how hard your life has been because I don't. But I do know how it feels to lose a mum.'

This is the first time I've ever told a pupil about Mum and it feels like I've got a marble stuck in my throat.

'Mine died when I was fifteen. It's not something you can ever get over, is it? There's always that hole.'

Kenny takes his hands from his pockets and folds his arms across his chest, and I begin to wonder if I was right to take Holly's advice.

'Like I say, I'm not trying to pretend I know what your life has been like.'

'Can I go now?' Kenny says abruptly, reaching down for his bag but waiting for a reply before picking it up.

'OK,' I tell him, trying to shield the deflation in my voice. 'I'll see you next time.'

As it turned out, I didn't have to ask Melissa for a date. She did the asking, a few days after my evening with

210

Richard and Holly. Did I want to go for a coffee near where she lives in Chiswick? She doesn't mess around.

Planned engineering works on the District Line mean I'm walking apace, hot and rushed and late, the midday sun making a midget of my shadow against the pavement.

She's waiting for me outside the coffee shop just down from Chiswick Park tube station. I spot her first, a dark brown dress wrapped around her figure like gravy on mashed potato. I check myself and realize I'm underdressed in jeans and loafers.

And yet I feel at ease. I know from our messages that we're going to get on. She likes Radiohead. And yes, she uses too many exclamation marks, but it shows she's a passionate woman. It shows she's interested in what I'm saying.

I know what Kev would say if he met her. He'd decree that she was out of my league. According to his football analogy, I'm Huddersfield Town, which I'm presuming isn't a compliment. Whereas he'd probably put Melissa in the Premier League. But as Kev says (and this is the most profound thing that's ever left his mouth), everyone is Manchester United to someone.

Melissa playfully checks an imaginary watch when she spots me, then takes charge of the greeting: a double kiss like the one when she left the pub quiz, but this time her hands linger on my elbows for a few seconds before she withdraws.

'Shall we get this started, then?' she says, placing her hand back on my elbow to weightlessly usher me into the coffee shop.

Chapter Twenty-three

HOLLY

'I'm so, *so* sorry, babe,' Richard repeats. 'No one's as gutted about this as me.'

'Oh, I can imagine,' I sigh into the phone, falling backwards onto my bed to stop my heart getting blood on my new shoes when it plummets to the floor. 'Watching Kasabian from the luxury of a box at the O2 while being plied with free champagne and posh canapés. Sucks to be you.'

'Don't be like that, Hols,' he chuckles. 'You know I'd rather take you out for dinner. The big boss didn't leave me much choice. When a client with a marketing budget that big invites you out to play at the last minute, you drop everything.'

It makes sense that Martin would rope Richard in. Let's face it, Hexagon is winning no business off the back of his own charm, so step in Mr Schmooze from Schmoozeville. It's not Richard's fault he's better at that stuff, endearing bastard that he is.

'I know,' I whine. 'But if you could just make a little effort not to be so bloody charming, he'll stop asking you.'

'I'll try,' he says with mock sincerity, 'I promise. And I promise to make it up to you.'

HOW? I want to ask, when he doesn't expand, but instead I tell him to enjoy it and hang up the phone, then take off my dress and hang it up in the wardrobe, gently kicking off the blue stilettos I'd bought especially for tonight, so rare it is I get to go on an actual date with my boyfriend.

Now what?

My first instinct is to call Alex and see if he fancies a bite to eat, but then I remember he has a second date with Melissa. Christ, she ruins my life on so many levels.

I'm about to get into my pyjamas when I catch sight of myself in my underwear in the mirror. Without having to weigh myself, I know I'm nine stone. I've been somewhere between eight stone ten and nine stone for the last ten years, and can tell just from looking that I'm at the latter end right now. It's unsurprising – I've been drinking a little more since Alex moved to London. I don't want to cross the nine-stone threshold, so I switch my PJs for my running gear, grab my iPod and head out into the night, happy to have a purpose.

I'd never run until I moved to London to go to university. Unless you count PE at school – and I always dreaded the athletics classes because sprinting made my boobs hurt. But after I moved out of Mothston I started monitoring my weight more. Not because I thought I was fat, but because I like the feeling of control that being able to maintain my chosen weight gives me.

My running playlist consists entirely of songs sung by the female leads in musicals. I keep myself entertained during this otherwise spectacularly boring pastime by picturing myself in the musical, playing the lead.

As I run across Blackheath I'm Eva Perón telling Argentina not to cry for me, then by the time I'm passing through the gates to Greenwich Park I'm Fantine from *Les Mis* dreaming a dream in time gone by, and while I'm running past the Royal Observatory and down the hill I'm assuring Joseph that he's doing fine, and him and his dreamcoat are ahead of his time.

It's an emotional roller-coaster, but the time flies by.

It's getting dark by the time I reach the park gates at the other side so I exit the park into Greenwich town centre. The street route from Greenwich to Blackheath takes me past Alex's flat. I drop my pace slightly as I pass and glance up at his bedroom window. The light is out. Is he still out with Melissa? Or much, much worse . . . are they both back and in his room, and THAT'S why his light's out? I hope not.

It's hard to tell someone they can do better without insulting both their taste and their pulling abilities. But Alex could definitely do better. That's my less selfish justification for secretly hoping that this thing between them doesn't work out.

The other is that Alex is MY friend and I don't want her to take him away.

I've run through the side roads and am nearly at Black-heath Road when I trip over one of my laces, which has come undone, so I stop, pause my music so that I don't waste the crescendo of 'Gravity' from *Wicked*, and crouch down to tie it.

What was that noise?

I pull one earphone out and listen. There it is again – a

low, crackling sound, like careful footsteps on gravel. I spin around.

'Hello,' I call. The noise stops. 'Is anybody there?'

Must have been a fox. Pull yourself together, lady. I stand up and am about to press 'play' again when a figure appears from behind a bush a few houses down and starts walking towards me. All I register is a man's frame in dark clothes, with a hood pulled up. Why didn't he answer me? I turn and start to jog gently away.

His footsteps quicken so I run faster. So does he.

I run across to the other side of the street, like we were always told to do in Stranger Danger talks in primary school if we suspected we were being followed.

The stranger crosses too. Oh my God – I'm in danger. My heart pounds and despite all my energy being spent already, I break into a sprint. I want to turn round and see how close he is but I don't want to give him a chance to close the gap, so I resist. My chest hurts and my breathing is all over the place but I make myself keep up the pace. What is he going to do to me if he catches up with me? Better not to speculate. I empty my head of all thoughts and focus on the rhythm of my feet, until I reach the corner of the heath. I can either cut diagonally across it – the much shorter, but more isolated route back to my house – or keep to the road surrounding it, which will take longer but at least there are street lights and passing cars and houses and a much better chance of someone hearing me scream.

I can hear his footsteps getting closer so I choose the roads.

I've made it all the way around before I have to stop and catch my breath, lest I drop dead, and look over my shoulder. Oh, thank God – I've lost him. He must have—

ARGHHHH. He springs from the darkness of the heath, making me scream . . . and runs right on past me.

In profile, a wire reaching out the top of his jogging suit up into his hood is visible. Headphones. No wonder he couldn't hear me. He's just out for a run. That must have been his own driveway he appeared from.

I'm an actual idiot. I don't know if I want to laugh or cry, but I do know that I need to hear a familiar voice before I get back to my front door.

Chapter Twenty-four

ALEX

'What do you mean you're being followed?'

Holly is out of breath, and panting, and generally not making any sense.

'I thought I was . . .' She pauses to take a lungful of air. I sit up on the sofa and mute the TV, rubbing the tiredness from my eyes with my free hand. I'd been about to go to bed when my phone started to ring. 'I'm OK now.'

'Where are you? Do you need me to come and fetch you?'

I stand and peer onto the road. It's well past rush hour but people and cars still clutter the street. London is relentless like that, and it sweeps you along, not giving you time to stop and think.

'I'm nearly home now. I'm all right. I thought I was being followed and it shook me up a bit.'

'Where have you been?'

'For a run.' Holly takes a couple of deep, composing breaths. 'I heard a noise and then saw a man appear from a driveway and start chasing me. Then I looked around again and a man was running behind me, so I sped up even more and then—'

'Tell me where you are and I'll come and get you.'

'I'm OK, really.' A street light opposite the flat is flickering on and off, adding to the sense of busyness outside. 'I'm on the heath now. There's no one around.'

I relax and retake my seat. 'You shouldn't go running on your own when it's dark.'

Holly doesn't say anything for a few seconds and I wonder if we've been disconnected, but then she goes: 'You're very sweet, you know that, Al?'

'I'm sure Richard would say the same – London's a dangerous city.'

There's another pause in the conversation, and I ask Holly if my reception is OK, but she doesn't answer.

'I like running on my own,' she says instead.

'Don't you find it a bit boring?'

'Nah,' she laughs, her breathing finally back to normal. 'I do this thing where I listen to musicals while I run and pretend I'm in them.'

I picture Holly skipping over Blackheath Hill singing 'Doe, a deer' and burst out laughing.

'I don't know why I told you that. I've just realized I've never told anyone that before.'

'Maybe try to keep it like that in future, yep?'

Holly tuts, pretending to be bruised, and I want to ask her why she's ringing me and not Richard. Did she try him first? Was he engaged, or did he just not pick up? Or didn't it even occur to her to ring Richard? Was I the first person she thought of? Not that I mind if I was, obviously, but what does that say about the man she is so clearly besotted with?

Jesus, Holly's right – I do over-analyse everything.

'Are you still there, Al?'

'Yep, sorry, I . . .' I stand by the window once more and watch a couple leave the pub across the road. The woman is wearing a tight, white dress with purple high heels, and her partner is having to hold her arm so she doesn't fall over. 'Where's Richard tonight?'

'He's at a work thing.'

'This late? Poor Richard.'

'Yeah, he's quite the martyr.'

I can't tell if she's being sarcastic or not, so I wait for her to continue, but she doesn't and I don't feel comfortable pressing further where Richard is concerned. We often talk for hours about every other part of our lives – and it's not as if she ever used to hold back when telling me about boys. I'm not sure what's different now, why it sometimes feels as though she becomes guarded where Richard is concerned.

'Anyway,' says Holly, banishing the silence before it becomes awkward, 'how did tonight go?'

It takes me a second to realize that she means my second date with Melissa. I guess this is another thing that I haven't had time to think about. Or maybe I just haven't had to. Melissa introduced me to cinnamon cappuccino on our coffee date and, after an hour or two, asked if I would like to have dinner sometime. Tonight was arranged, there and then. None of the head-scratching about how long I should leave it before I called; none of the anxiety waiting for the other person to text.

'We both had steak. Melissa wanted hers just short of raw.'

'Who would have thought?' Holly snorts to herself, and I can't tell what she means. 'So are you going to see her again?'

219

Tomorrow night. Melissa's got complimentary tickets for the new Leonardo DiCaprio film.

'I think so.'

Suddenly it's me being guarded, and I'm not exactly sure why. Holly knowing Melissa has made all this feel a bit like a love triangle, even though I don't love Holly and Holly definitely doesn't love Melissa, or me, and even though Holly is going out with Richard, so technically it would be a love square if it was a love anything, which it isn't. It just feels that way.

'So it's going well, then?'

I suppose it is. It's early days, but I like Melissa. She's independent and knows what she wants from life. And, as someone said at the pub quiz, she's conventionally very attractive.

'Really well.'

'Good,' says Holly, and I know she's being genuine, despite her feelings about Melissa, and despite her worries that I might let slip about . . .

'I'd never say anything, you know.'

'I know,' she says. 'You deserve to be happy, Al.'

Holly's words linger for a few seconds until I spot something in the sky.

'Are you still outside?'

'Yes, why?'

'Can you see that shooting star?'

The line goes quiet. 'I can't see it – where is it?'

I look for a signpost in the sky. The moon is behind a sheet of cloud and it's too early in the year to see Orion.

'Remember in Camber Sands I showed you how to find the North Star?'

220

Holly sounds unsure, and I recall what she told me in the park the other week, about her first kiss. How much of the time we used to spend together was like this: me banging on about stars and music and books while she was thinking about something else. How much of our friendship has been spent on crossed wires?

'I can't see it, Al. But if you can then make a wish.'

Prompted by Holly, I think about the thing I want more than anything else in the world. Radiohead to record a new album? Kenny Sonola to declare his Mr Tyler-inspired love for The Bard?

'Have you made one yet?'

'Yep.'

'Well, don't tell anyone – ever. Otherwise it won't come true.'

I promise Holly that I'll keep my wish a secret for eternity.

'Hang on a second,' she says. 'Is the North Star the bright one near the moon?'

'So you do remember?'

'That's a plane, Al.'

I inspect the sky. Sure enough, there's a plane right where I was looking. Gatwick, Heathrow, Luton – I do live under several flight paths. But I'm certain that what I saw was a star.

'No, I'm positive,' I tell her, pretending to be certain. 'It was definitely a star.'

I have to suppress a yawn as my year nines troop in. Holly and I were on the phone until Richard arrived at her flat. It was past midnight.

'Could you put your mobile away please, Gareth?'

Gareth Stones has wrapped his school tie around his head like a sweatband.

'One sec,' he tells me. 'Just sending a text.'

My mind wanders back to when we were teenagers, when phones had leads and there was the excitement at not knowing who would be on the other end of the line when you picked up. There was no such thing as free minutes, and if you were on the phone longer than ten you could expect your mum or dad to start shouting at you. If it was Holly on the phone I wouldn't care.

'Do you think it's fair that the rest of the class has to wait for you to send a text?'

Gareth doesn't flicker. He sits there, legs stretched out in front of him, composing his message. Once he's finished he slips his iPhone into his pocket and says, 'Next time, don't feel you have to wait on my account.'

I tell him that it's all very well acting like this now, but that one day in the not too distant future he's going to get a job and he won't be able to doss around on his phone and turn up whenever he likes.

'Yeah, but I'll be getting paid then, won't I? So I won't mind, will I?'

There was a time when an exchange like this would play on my mind, but I'm really positive about school right now. Things are turning around with my year nines – and I owe Holly a thank-you for some of that. It was her who emailed me a new version of *Hamlet*, one that tells the story in a series of Facebook statuses.

Horatio thinks he saw a ghost; Hamlet thinks it's annoying when your uncle marries your mother right after your dad dies;

222

*the king thinks Hamlet's annoying; Laertes thinks Ophelia can
do better; Hamlet's father is now a zombie.*

The kids were suddenly enthusiastic about the play.
Stacey Bamber no longer spends lessons drawing a
hangman with my head in the rope and even Kenny
Sonola is engaging in class discussions since our talk a
few weeks ago. He hasn't taken me up on the offer of
chatting, but he's at least doing the work now. I could
have hugged him when his latest assignment warranted
a D, but I didn't want him to threaten to 'fuck me up'
again so I settled on a simple 'well done'. It might not
sound like much, but I know for a fact it's better than his
grades in every other subject. I checked.

This is why I came to London, and I don't want the
term to end now, although I'm looking forward to
getting Kenny and the rest of them started on their
GCSEs in September. I know he's got a C in him – I'm
certain of it.

'OK, any questions?' I ask, at the end of another pro-
ductive lesson.

No one puts a hand up but a familiar voice makes itself
heard.

'Who let the dogs out?' gobs Gareth.

This is his new favourite hobby. At this point last week
he asked me how old a man had to be to stop finding
women his own age attractive. The lesson before that
he enquired whether I would lend him a tenner. The
one thing I've noticed is that each time, the laughter
his quips elicit has been more meagre, so that this time
there is barely a snigger in his direction.

'Thanks for that, Gareth,' I say. 'The rest of you, great

work today. Just a few more lessons before the summer holidays. I'll see you next time.'

Text from Holly to Alex

It was definitely a plane xx

Chapter Twenty-five

HOLLY

September. How'd that happen? Summer went down like the scene in a film when they're trying to illustrate how much time has passed, so they speed it up and you can see the season change before your eyes. The snow clears or leaves appear on the ground, and the characters start the scene in shorts and end it in woolly jumpers, and shit loads has happened since a minute and a half ago.

My mum and dad have moved to York. Hexagon Marketing has gone global. Alex and Melissa are in what can only be described as a serious relationship.

Not everything's changed, of course. Jemma's diet starts tomorrow and no one knows about me and Richard.

I thought the merger would kick-start the process that concludes in us telling everyone. Alas, no. Apparently I was being optimistic that Richard's promotion would happen that easily. He is still my boss. I am still his PA. And today he mainly needs some new pens and half a dozen foolscap folders.

'You finished with the stationery brochure yet, Jem?'

'Hang on – I'm concentrating.'

Christ, even she's changed. It's like we've had a role

reversal – she's got a hard-on for stationery and I'm starting to, well, NOT CARE. I don't know why. I used to love work but my enthusiasm must have been dwindling because today I realized it's pretty much non-existent. Maybe it's hanging around with Alex and hearing about him doing things at school that actually matter. How much of a difference do I make? The amount of times I've come into work drugged up to the eyeballs on Lemsip because I'd feel too bad calling in sick, but I've been flattering myself about how much anyone would care if I did. Richard would have to answer his own phone and everyone else would have to arrange their own meetings directly with each other. Whoop-de-do.

Leah calls me at lunchtime, which cheers me up for all of thirty seconds. Then she asks when I'm free to meet up because she's got 'news'.

'Ha – you're not pregnant, are you?'

Silence. Dear God, no . . .

'Leah?'

I wait for her to laugh but all I hear is the tapping of keyboards around me.

'Oh my God, I was joking, but you are! You're pregnant!'

'I wanted to tell you in person . . . but yeah, totally up the duff. Mental, eh?'

Mental is an understatement. How did our lives become so polar opposite? We were on the same page for years. Now she's about to have an actual family. And me? A depressed cat and a secret romance do not a family make. Why is everyone's life moving forward except mine? I should have worked it out when she didn't drink at Chloe's wedding.

'Hols?' Leah laughs nervously. 'You all right? You haven't said anything for like, a minute and a half.'

'Yeah, sorry – I'm just stunned.' Have a word with yourself, Holly, this is great news. 'Congratulations! I'm SO happy for you.'

I AM so happy for her. So utterly, completely, wholly, one hund . . . OK, 99 per cent ecstatic for her.

It's the other 1 per cent that makes me a terrible person. When I hang up I touch my desk with my forehead until a pair of black pointy stilettos alert me to the arrival of someone at my side. I recognize those shoes. Balls.

'You all right, Holly?'

'Yeah, just a bit of a headache, ta, Melissa.' I sit up again and start typing, hoping she'll take the hint. She doesn't.

'Oh, you poor thing. I hope you'll feel up to coming out with us tonight.'

Um, strictly speaking SHE'S coming out with US – Kev's down to see Alex so we're all having a catch-up – but whatever.

'Yeah, I'll be fine.'

'Brilliant. Let's get the tube together, yeah?'

'Good idea,' I lie. I don't know why Alex had to invite her – I haven't seen Kev for years, so we'll probably spend the night talking about school days and she'll just feel left out. And it's not like she and Alex don't spend enough time together.

He and I hang out a lot less since they got together. We still make plans for regular catch-ups but gone are the spontaneous lunches in local pubs and DVD nights at mine when Carl has a girl over and Alex wants to get out.

I don't know why I was surprised – it's not like it's the first time this has happened. He's been such a good mate since moving to London that I started to think it was my fault we'd lost touch before, what with that note I found under my bed in Mothston. That maybe I'd exaggerated his weirdness that day I saw him for the last time, and should have let him know when I was coming back to visit Mum and Dad, or invited him to stay with me at uni. Have I lain in bed at night wondering whether my life would be different right now if I HAD found the note at the time? Yeah, sure. More than once. But the truth is it probably wouldn't be any different, because this is what Alex does: prioritizes mates when he's single but re-strategizes when a girl he likes comes on the scene. I don't blame him, really. Blokes do that. I just miss him.

'Danny, get over here.' Jemma beckons, putting down the stationery brochure at last. 'Right, you two, would you rather . . . be fisted by Edward Scissorhands *or* have a man with a stapler for a mouth go down on you?'

'Scissorhands,' says Kev, after deliberating for five minutes. 'Actually, no – stapler. Argh, I don't know . . . I don't care if it's against the rules – I'm saying neither. They're both men.'

'They're both men? That's your issue?' Alex smirks as he sips his wine.

'Well, it's not yours, obviously, gaylord. Christ, Holly, this Jemma sounds like a right sicko.'

'She is. You two should really meet.'

Kev hasn't changed a bit. I wasn't sure what seeing him would be like. We were never friends in the way Alex and I were friends. Apart from just one time –

which I'd rather not think about – we never had any deep or meaningful conversations, and we never hung out together when Alex wasn't there. But we had a good laugh whenever we were all around. He would deliberately antagonize me with sexist comments, and then tell me to stop being a hairy lesbian when I got on my feminist high horse about it. Likewise, I would casually drop something into the conversation about how I was Alex's best friend, which would wind him up something chronic. Then we'd have a back-and-forth about why we each qualified as Alex's best friend, which would inevitably end with Kev whining 'Alex, *tell* her' like a five-year-old. I'm tempted to do it tonight for old time's sake but he's got eleven years on me now, and I'm not sure I can argue with that. Besides, an unspoken truce was formed between Kev and me during the last conversation we ever had in Mothston. It's almost a shame Alex can never know about it.

'What would be the point in us meeting? I've got a girlfriend now. That's my cooking, cleaning and shagging taken care of. Besides, she'd just get upset that I won't put out.'

'You won't?' I gasp. 'Gee, Kev, way to break it to a girl – I wish I'd known that before I bothered coming tonight.'

'So tell me all about this girlfriend of yours,' Melissa butts in, leaning across the booth to pat Kev's hand, and cutting off whatever retort he was about to give me. 'Alex tells me nothing and I want to hear all about her.'

So Kev tells us all about Diane, and Melissa keeps clutching her empty chest in the place where other people's hearts are located and telling him 'That's *so* sweet' whenever he says anything gushy.

Alex listens with the quiet, polite boredom of someone who's heard it all before. I listen with the quiet, polite boredom of someone who doesn't need to hear ALL ABOUT someone I don't know.

'Well, she sounds just adorable,' concludes Melissa, when Kev is done.

'Wait, that's it?' I interject. 'But there's still so much we don't know. Like, I dunno . . .' I pause to sip my wine. 'Does she collect anything special?'

When Alex cracks up, Kev coughs on his own hand and waves it near Alex's face, which has the desired effect of wiping the smile off it.

'You told her about the snow globes, didn't you? You bastard.'

'Snow globes?' Melissa's eyes narrow slightly as they dart from Alex to me and back to Alex, so Alex explains, laughing again, while Kev pouts huffily. I'm in hysterics until Melissa shoots me a small, patronizing oh-leave-him-alone smile and head-shake. She's kidding me, right? She's not actually trying to dictate how I act with someone I've known for eighteen years? Someone who knows me well enough to know it's harmless teasing, and who I know well enough to know he can take a ribbing?

'Yeah, come on, Holly.' Alex pulls himself together and forces a frown. 'It's snow joke.'

'That was terrible,' I say at the same time as Melissa goes: 'You're hilarious,' with an expression that looks sarcastic but, because it's Melissa, isn't.

We're in a back-street boozer and it's a Thursday so the atmosphere is low-key, but Kev's I'm-on-holiday mode is infectious and Alex isn't back at school until next week, so we drink steadily.

'My round,' says Melissa, pulling a long, cream-coloured wallet from her bag and departing the table with an unnecessary caress of Alex's bicep.

Alex smiles at her as she walks away, then turns his gaze back to the table, catching me watching him. Our eyes lock and hold. Suddenly my lips are dry but when I lick them I feel a rush of self-consciousness about the action, and I'm almost relieved when Melissa calls over: 'Give me a hand would you, darling?'

Alex blinks and scoots off to the bar, and Kev puts his feet up on the chair he's just vacated, leaning back in his own seat.

'So I'm going to this Elvis tribute act next week,' he says.

The barman is waiting to take Melissa's order but she hasn't even noticed his approach – she's too busy sucking Alex's face. I can't get over how rude she is sometimes – like the poor guy hasn't got other people waiting to be served.

'When I phoned up for tickets I had to press one for the money or two for the show.'

'Did you?' Why did she need a hand anyway? How hard is it to carry four drinks? Apart from anything else, there is a pile of trays RIGHT THERE.

'Er, no, it was a joke, Holly. Elvis – one for the—'

'Melissa!' I call. She separates herself from Alex and turns round. I nod towards the barman.

'Oh, God, I'm so sorry – I didn't see you there,' I hear her say.

'So as I said,' Kev is still talking, 'if you could keep that strictly between me and you about me being a secret caped crusader I'd appreciate it.'

'Yeah, course, I . . . Hang on, what did you just—'

'You haven't been listening to a word I've been saying, have you?'

I turn my attention back to Kev a second too late, because he's diverted his eyes to where mine have just been.

'Ah.' He chuckles, then leans his head towards mine and eyeballs me accusingly. 'You know, Holly, Alex is the happiest I've seen him in ages.'

'He is?' Get a grip, Holly. 'I mean yeah, he is. I know. Great, isn't it?'

'Is it?' Kev's face contorts, like he's trying to raise one eyebrow but can't quite pull it off. 'Because I'm not being funny, but could you look any more jealous?'

'Jealous? *Me?*'

'Oh, come on, it's been obvious all night. Luckily Alex isn't the sharpest pencil, so you're getting away with it, but you can't get past me.'

'Is it really that obvious? Shit, look they're coming back. Don't say anything to Alex, OK?'

'Course,' he says, looking pleased with himself.

Christ, I am jealous. How did that happen? What's not helping is the fact that Melissa has made more progress in her relationship in a few months than I have in a year – and she's done it by taking Alex. Before he came back into my life, it didn't bother me that I had no one to wander around Borough Market with on a Saturday morning, or to drag to the cinema on Orange Wednesdays to see some inevitably crap film, before taking the piss out of it over a pizza. But then he did come along, and we did all these things together, and now that we don't, it is bothering me that I can't with Richard.

'I got us a bottle as we're both on the white wine,' says Melissa. 'Sauvignon Blanc – that's what you were drinking, right?'

I'm tempted to pretend it was Chardonnay, even though she's right. But what would be the point in being vindictive?

'Thanks – here, let me give you some cash.' I reach for my bag but she shakes her head.

'Oh, don't be silly – I definitely owe you a glass of wine for keeping everything in the office ticking over in such ship-shape condition. Seriously, boys, I don't know what we'd do without her.'

I take it from the warm smile Alex gives her that the fact his girlfriend is a patronizing cow is lost on him.

Despite Melissa's presence, the rest of the night is a laugh and we even get to giggle over a few happy Mothston memories before Melissa finds a way of changing the subject to something she can include herself in.

Just like the first time Alex and I went out when he moved to London, chatting with Kev reminds me of how many good times we had. I wonder whether I would have had less of a downer on Mothston for the last eleven years if I'd stayed in touch with anyone after school and reminisced like this. As it was, whenever I thought about the place I always thought of how my time there ended and I've never really spoken about my school days much with anyone. Even Max, Leah and Susie – who know most things about me – would probably summarize my adolescence as growing up in a dull little town that I couldn't wait to escape. I'm starting to feel disloyal to the teenage me for giving such a negative impression of what life was like back then.

'Where next?' asks Kev.

'Home for me,' I hiccup. 'Some of us have got work tomorrow.'

'You've changed, Holly Gordon.'

Alex shoots Kev a look I can't quite read as Kev continues: 'The Holly I knew would be up at that bar demanding a lock-in.'

'We're in a pub opposite a police station – the landlord isn't stupid.'

'Well then, the Holly I knew would be listing our options for what clubs to go to.'

'It's a Thursday night. In Greenwich. Our options are nowhere, nowhere or nowhere.'

'Then the Holly I knew would be working out whose house we're going back to for a nightcap. You live alone, right?'

'Oh, but you have a cat, don't you?' Melissa intervenes. 'I have a horrible allergy to animal hair and I haven't taken any antihistamine – sorry, Holly.'

'Guess it's all back to Alex's then.' Kev stands up and drains his pint messily. 'Come on, team.'

I'm about to argue some more but suddenly I realize I'm doing it out of force of habit rather that genuine conscientiousness, and that I'm not actually particularly worried about the consequences of a hangover in the morning.

'All right then.' I salute Kev. 'I'm in.'

Chapter Twenty-six

ALEX

'Will I get to meet this sexist twat housemate of yours?' growls Kev, swaggering out of the pub with his hands in his pockets, an island of spilt lager soaked into his top.

'He'll probably have an orgy on the go,' I bait.

Kev sniffs and flicks his shoulders. He goes to make a joke – most probably about how any girls engaged in an orgy would take one look at him and threaten to quit unless he partook – but something causes him to hold back. Maybe having a girlfriend is having an effect. I'm pretty certain three months is a personal best for him. By about two months.

'Actually, he's in Barcelona with one of his girlfriends,' I say, but only Kev hears me. Melissa waited for Holly as she searched for something in her handbag, and we're walking slightly ahead now.

'You know what?' The last pint seems to have finished Kev off, because he is starting to slur his words. 'Maybe he was on to something.' He turns to look at the girls for a second. 'Maybe women *are* like bacteria.'

He looks at me and I humour him with a nod, and for

a moment it's like we're back in Mothston – me listening to his gibberish as we stumble home from a night at The Lion. How can it be that so much has changed, and yet here we are, and everything feels just like it always has done?

'I still find it weird socializing with Holly outside of work.' Melissa strips to her expensive lace underwear. 'I think she could of made a bit more of an effort with me tonight.' *Could have*, I think but don't say. 'She was just a bit . . . off.'

Holly has just left. Kev is out for the count, spread-eagled on the sofa. It's almost 2 a.m.

'I always get the feeling in work that she doesn't like me.'

'Nonsense,' I lie. 'Holly thinks a lot of you. I know she does.'

This seems to pacify Melissa, who slips into bed beside me, places a cold hand on my belly and nestles her cheek into my shoulder.

I'm fully aware of what Holly thinks of Melissa. She thinks she's false and patronizing, but maybe Holly feeling patronized has more to do with how *she* feels about being a PA. And maybe if she'd had a bit of Melissa's drive she wouldn't even be a PA; she'd have done some of the things she always talked about.

'It's like she sees me as a rival.' Melissa's words are marinated in too much alcohol. 'But it's not my fault I'm great at my job, is it?'

And anyway, Holly should be thankful. This thing with Melissa has been good for my friendship with her. I was becoming a burden, calling and texting her all the time when she's got her own life down here, with Richard and Harold. I came along expecting things to be exactly how they used to be and I ended up getting confused about what could happen. I needed to lay off a bit, to put just a little bit of distance between us, so that's what I've done. It's easier for everyone.

'Richard says the place would fall apart if it wasn't for me. You know he's been bigging me up to all the senior management?'

Finally I give Melissa my full attention. 'Say that again?'

'He's been bigging me up – says the place would fall apart if I wasn't there.'

I knew her words sounded familiar, and now I remember why: Holly mentioned how Richard said almost exactly the same thing to her. Is he spouting the same lines to every girl in the frigging office?

'Don't worry,' says Melissa, misinterpreting my look of disbelief. 'There's nothing between me and Richard.'

She's staring right into my eyes but, frustrated that I can't share my thoughts with my own girlfriend, I focus on the small crack of moonlight between the curtains. I've found it quite easy these past few months keeping what I know about Holly and Richard from Melissa – but right now I feel like blurting it out.

'I know there's nothing between you and Richard,' I say, biting my tongue. 'That's the last thing I'm worried about.'

Melissa detaches herself from me, insulted. 'I could have had him if I wanted him,' she says matter-of-factly.

'What's that supposed to mean?'

'It's not supposed to mean anything. I just didn't like

237

the way you said what you just said, as if Richard could never be interested in me.'

'That's not what I meant.'

'We kissed, as it happens. A couple of times, just over a year ago.'

I glare at her, unable to dispatch any words.

'Once when he had a girlfriend and then once two days after they'd split up. The next day he acted as if nothing had happened so I confronted him and he said he wasn't looking for anything heavy. Fine by me, I thought. I wasn't going to wait around for him.'

I do the maths. Holly told me she and Richard got together a week after his break-up. Which means there wasn't any crossover, but still, I can imagine her reaction to this.

'Sorry,' says Melissa. 'You're mad with me, aren't you?'

I need to think for a minute, but Melissa isn't having it. Her now warm hand is back on my belly – but this time it doesn't lie dormant.

I collapse onto Melissa, our clammy chests gluing together, all the words that could have marred the night now lost in elation.

Everything seems to have fallen into place since that day in The Lion when Dad announced he was buying a boat. School, my friendship with Holly, Melissa. It was after our third date that she came back to the flat. We fucked and we fucked again and somewhere along the line she appropriated her own drawer in my bedroom. I guess Kev was right after all.

Melissa sees what she wants and she gets it. A five-year plan to take her from an apartment in Chiswick to a townhouse in Kensington. And it's one of the traits I like most about her. It's refreshing.

I shift my position so that we're both lying on our backs.

'Are you happy, Alex?'

I swivel my head to look at her. She does the same. Our eyes now accustomed to the dark, she sees my smile and reflects it. 'What kind of question is that?'

'It's a question I want to know the answer to.'

She let me take her to the British Museum on our fourth date and was interested in the same exhibits as me, though she did attempt to ambush me for a piggyback as we passed a tomb from Lycian Xanthos.

'Do you know what the time is, Mel? You've got to be up for work in the morning.'

'I know I've got to be up for work in the morning but before that I want you to answer the question: are you happy?'

'Yep, of course I am.'

It's funny how things turn out. If you'd asked me when I was fifteen to imagine my thirtieth birthday, I'd have envisaged coming home from work to an unlit house in Derbyshire, somewhere off Snake Pass. When I walked through the door, my wife and friends and family would leap out from behind the sofa and shout 'SURPRISE!' And if I'm being totally frank, in this vision, Holly would more than likely have been my wife. I catch myself smiling at the thought.

'How happy?' resumes Melissa.

'Really happy,' I say, shrugging off the things I'd been imagining.

I look down the bed at our four feet standing to attention underneath the duvet. I shut my eyes and start to drift towards sleep. But Melissa hasn't finished yet.

'Alex?' she says, in a new, more serious tone. A sober tone.

In a couple of hours the sun will rise but for now we're stuck in the purgatory between night and morning.

'What is it?' I murmur sleepily.

Melissa turns her head and from her expression I sense what is coming a few seconds before it actually arrives.

Chapter Twenty-seven

HOLLY

By Monday I'm starting to feel human again. Friday was a wash-out. I fell asleep on the sofa when I got back from Alex's and woke up at half five, peeled my tongue off the roof of my mouth and got into bed, only to sleep through my alarm. I momentarily contemplated calling in sick, but then remembered I'd been out with Melissa the night before. She'd definitely know it was a hangover.

To make things a million times worse, when I rocked up half an hour late looking and feeling like death, the first person I saw was an immaculately turned-out and perfectly functioning Melissa. How can we have had the same amount to drink?

'Nice of you to join us, Holly,' she drawled sarcastically without meeting my eye, before marching into the meeting room by herself and letting the door slam shut behind her.

Not entirely unaffected by a late night, then.

'So sorry I'm late.' I took sanctuary in Richard's office. 'Last night turned into a bit of a late one.'

'Bit of a habit these days, isn't it?' Richard mumbled, without lifting his head from the report he was reading.

Not as habitual as my early starts and unpaid over-time, but I hadn't the energy to debate it so I settled on an eye-roll and let it go.

And that day went from bad to worse. Richard's attempts to steer Martin towards confirming his promotion failed so he spent the whole day being impatient, tetchy and, if I'm not mistaken, a bit pissed off at me. He made a couple of passing comments about me drinking until all hours while he was working on a presentation. I didn't know whether the digs were coming from my boyfriend or my boss.

Still, it's a brand-new week now and I'm channelling my energy – restored from an uneventful weekend – to make it a good one.

'Anything interesting to report?' I ask Jemma, as she strolls out of a mid-morning one-on-one with Martin.

'Work-wise or in real life?'

'Both.'

'Well, work-wise, Martin is gathering everyone after lunch for an announcement re the new Director of International Ventures.'

HALLE-BLOODY-LUJAH. Richard's promotion. I knew today was going to be a good day.

'"Re" is Martin's abbreviation, by the way – not mine. He's way too busy and important to say all three syllables of re-gard-ing. And how wanky is that job title?'

This is it. This is where the ball starts rolling. This is where Richard and I start moving forward. I can actually feel a metaphorical cloud lifting and all the negative 'where-is-my-life-going?' thoughts I had on Thursday suddenly seem distant and overdramatic.

'He called this morning to accept the offer,' Jemma

242

continues. 'Alas, he's not that handsome, unfortunately – I collected him at reception and directed him to the boardroom for his interview.'

Hang on . . . Who?

'I wouldn't sleep with him, and, as you know, I'm not that fussy. Poor Richard, though, eh? I think he thought he was well in there. Martin's taking him out for lunch today to break it to him. So, anyway, that's it on the work front. In other news, I don't think Robbie wants to see me again. I've texted him twice and he hasn't replied.'

As the implications of her words sink in I go cold. Richard didn't get the job. I didn't even realize that was a possibility. I don't think Richard did either. He'll be gutted.

'Oh my God, I can't believe this – it's awful.' I bury my face in my hands.

'I know, right? I thought it was just me being melo-dramatic but you're thinking the same. There definitely must be something wrong with me. Maybe I should see a therapist?'

'No, I mean about Richard not getting the job. I better go and see him.'

'Oh.' Jemma pulls a wounded face but then something else occurs to her and her expression becomes horror-stricken. 'You can't say anything. It's strictly confidential info until Martin announces it this afternoon.'

'But I have to prepare him,' I think out loud. 'He'll be humiliated if he waits to hear it from Martin.'

'No, seriously, Hols. Martin would fire me. He stressed that I wasn't allowed to tell anyone. His last words before I left his office were "I'm trusting you not to walk back to your desk and blab to Holly."'

'Well, I can't just do nothing!'

'Why can't you?'

But, of course, I can't tell her why. And, of course, I can't tell Richard. She's right, I get the impression from Richard that she's on thin ice with Martin anyway, and leaking confidential information might give him grounds to get rid of her. I wish I could believe that if I explained this to Richard, he would go through the motions at lunch and pretend to know nothing when Martin broke the news but, the truth is, I think he'd be straight into his office to have it out with him.

I have to do something, though. Perhaps stop him getting his hopes up, without letting on that I know anything.

After Jemma makes me swear on Harold's life that I won't tell him, I go into Richard's office and close the door, at which point he practically rugby tackles me (in a sexy way) onto his desk for a passionate snog.

For a moment I let myself forget that I'm here on a damage-control mission and get lost in his kiss, lapping up the intimacy. It's been ages since we've done this. There was a time when I'd always get a steamy welcome from him but they've been dwindling of late, replaced by merger chats and coffee requests.

'Wow, what was that for?' I ask, trying to get my breath back as we half sit/half lean on the edge of the desk.

'To say sorry for being such a dick recently. I didn't mean to be grumpy with you, I've just been working such long hours and not sleeping well, and missing you.' He kisses me on the cheek when he says that bit. 'But I shouldn't have taken it out on you. Sorry, babe.'

I study his eyes, screwed up slightly with sincerity, and his lips, which have formed into a small, guilty pout.

'That's OK.' I mean it – and somehow I know everything WILL be OK. I've been starting to worry that getting this new job is the be all and end all in his life, but clearly I'm important to him too. So, he didn't get it. Big deal. We'll have to suck up the fact that people might have opinions about us. I'm pretty sure shagging your boss isn't actually illegal. It's just a bit frowned upon. That will pass when everyone realizes we're serious about each other.

'And anyway, all that's about to change,' Richard continues. 'Martin's taking me for lunch today for a chat. He's going to confirm my promotion, I'm sure of it.'

Arghhhh.

'Well, whatever happens,' I say, taking his hand, 'good news or bad news, you've always got me.'

'Thank you, babe, though I can't see there being any bad news. It might mean me shooting across to the States once a month, but I'm cool with that. Maybe you could come and join me in New York for a weekend? Plus I'll have a bigger office here – they're dedicating the entire third floor to the new international department.'

'There's nothing wrong with this office, though. I mean, if you do have to stay here it's not the end of the world. And I like having you a mere twelve seconds from my desk.'

He responds to the kiss I lean in for then tells me jovially to stop being so bloody pessimistic and get him a coffee.

Well. That went well.

*

245

Jemma's booked them a table at some trendy new celebrity-owned steak house in the West End. Martin seems to think the disappointment will sting less if Richard is tucking into a perfectly prepared slab of expensive beef when he hears it, but the choice of venue just confirmed to Richard what he thinks he already knows: they've got something to celebrate.

It seems like they're gone for ever. I spend my lunch hour traipsing round the shops. The office doesn't seem to hold any distraction from this feeling of impending doom. Five minutes before I'm due back I realize I've bought nothing so I buy a pair of black, leather, knee-length boots just for the hell of it and head back to the office.

'These are gorgeous,' gushes Jemma, stroking the leather like it's a naked man's torso.

'A-mazing boots,' Melissa drones as she passes my desk. 'I've got a pair that are practically identical – they go with everything.'

Jemma waits for Melissa to be out of earshot. 'You kept the receipt, right?' she says, dropping them back into their box.

'Yup.'

'Good-o.'

It's at this point that both of our bosses walk solemnly back in, wordlessly making their way towards their respective offices and shutting their doors behind them.

Richard is sitting in his chair, elbows on desk and head in hands. The ticking from the clock behind his desk seems unnaturally slow and ridiculously loud.

'How'd it go?' I ask softly, to maintain the pretence

246

that I don't already know that it went very, very badly.

'They're bringing in someone new,' he says, his eyes staying fixed on the coffee mug on his desk. 'Someone with more experience in international marketing or some bullshit. Zero experience in Hexagon, of course, so he won't know his arse from his bloody elbow when he joins, but hey ho.'

'I'm sorry.'

He shrugs and screws up the top page of his note-pad – notes he'd been here late last night making – and hurls the paper ball across the office, missing his bin by a mile.

'There will be other opportunities, Rich.'

'Oh, there will, will there?' His voice drips with sarcasm. 'Then do tell me about them, because this is the first shot at promotion I've had since I joined here four years ago, and they're not creating any other new departments as far as I'm aware. And Martin doesn't look set to throw in the towel any time soon. More's the pity. But do enlighten me about these other opportunities.'

I try not to take offence at his tone – it's not me he's angry with. It's normal to take things out on the person closest to you when you're upset.

'Well, if not here then how about somewhere else? You should have no trouble getting something with your experience, and you'd interview really well.'

'There's not a lot of jobs out there, funnily enough. In case the news has escaped you, the economy is a bit shit at the moment. That's why it was so important we pulled this merger off – a company this size might not have survived on its own. That's the reason this new guy got in touch with Martin – he comes from a competitor on the verge of culling half their staff. I'd been front-runner up until that point but apparently this maverick is just too good not to snap up.'

He practically spits out those last words, and I cross the room to his side of the desk and put my arms around him.

'So what are we going to do about us?' I enquire softly after a minute or two.

'What about us, Holly?' He spins around aggressively on his swivel chair. 'Please don't tell me you're actually going to make this about you?'

'Not me Richard, us.' I take a step back. 'This affects us both. This was meant to be the turning point for us, so we could actually be a proper couple at last.'

'Says who?'

'Well, why wouldn't we? We can't let anyone know about us because they might think it's inappropriate because you're my boss – that's what you're always telling me. If you weren't my boss any more then what would be stopping us doing all the normal stuff couples do? You know – like going out for dinner, and going on holiday. Or moving in together.'

'Christ, Holly – just plan out our entire future, why don't you? I don't remember promising any of that.'

I feel like I've just been slapped around the face. And even if I had been, I don't think it would sting as much as Richard's words.

'Well then, what are we doing, Richard? What have we been doing for the past year? What's the point in any of this if it's not leading to anything?'

'To tell you the truth, sweetheart, that's the least of my concerns right now.'

I walk out without saying anything further and find Melissa hovering at my desk.

'Holly, hun, there's no paper in the printer.'

'It's in a box, next to the printer,' I mumble.

'Great. I need to print a report by close of play today, so as long as it's refilled by then—'

'Oh, just put the bloody paper in the printer yourself, Melissa – it's not rocket science.' I don't wait for her reaction before I storm off to the loo.

'You all right, Holly?' asks Jemma. 'I don't mean you going postal at Melissa – that was brilliant – but your face is all puffy and your eyes are red. I really hope you've been crying, because otherwise you just look like shite.'

'I'm fine,' I tell Jemma, attempting a smile.

'Really? You look even worse than you did on Friday on a hangover. And you looked terrible then.'

I've been silently bawling my eyes out in a locked toilet. Silently bawling your eyes out sounds like it would be quite difficult, but it's surprisingly easy. If someone had been listening outside the door they would have thought I was just a bit of a heavy breather. I'd just calmed myself down when I remembered it was the same toilet I nearly took a pregnancy test in a few months ago. And to think I thought that Richard might have been happy about it. What was I thinking?

I wish I could call Alex, but he's on a training day. I'll feel better after talking to him. He'll help me put things in perspective, and work out how to deal with all this. What would I do without Alex? It pains me to think that if this had happened a few months ago I wouldn't have had him to lean on. I wonder if he even realizes how much of a difference he makes to my life.

I try to think how Richard must be feeling. Between the job and our argument it's fair to say he's had better days, and I'm half expecting him to hide in his office when Martin gathers everyone together at 3 p.m. for the big announcement. But he strides out and stands next to his boss, smiling pleasantly at the news that a Shawn Walker will be joining the team as our new Director of International Ventures, and that other staffing shuffles will be announced in due course. Pretty much everyone glances his way to check his reaction to the news – it's no secret that he was the obvious candidate for the role – but his face remains impassive. It must look like he's taken the news on the chin, but I can tell it's killing him. For a moment all I want to do is hug him, but the memory of our argument keeps me at a distance.

When it's over everyone shuffles back to their desks, murmuring speculation about who on our floor might be working on the new team – and whether they'll get to go to New York if they do, and whether iPods are that much cheaper there, or if you're better off buying them on Amazon.

Melissa pats Richard's arm on her way back to her desk in a gesture of commiseration, and Richard replies with a silent little nod of gratitude. Oh, so she can comfort him without getting beaten around the head with the sarcastic stick, can she? A fresh bout of tears stings the back of my eyes but I fight them back.

He catches my eye on the way past. 'Can I see you in my office please, Holly?'

'Sure.' My voice is shaking. This is it. He's going to

finish with me. He's come to the conclusion that whatever this is, it's not worth it. Maybe he blames me. Maybe he thinks if I had just spent one or two more nights helping him with his work stuff rather than hanging out with Alex, he might not have been pipped to the post by Shawn Walker.

'I'm leaving at five thirty on the dot tonight, baby.' He rests the back of his head on the door he's just shut behind him. He looks knackered. 'I can't wait to get out of here. Will you stay at mine tonight?'

He sees my confusion and adds: 'I could really do with a hug.'

'But earlier—'

'I was upset earlier. It was the shock – I was so sure Martin was taking me out to tell me the job was mine. Sorry if I upset you.'

I fall into his open arms and let the relief wash over me, breathing in his familiar scent of Jean Paul Gaultier aftershave and waiting for it to intoxicate me like it usually does, making me forget everything. But it doesn't work. I can't forget everything that was said between us earlier. Even though I really, really want to.

Chapter Twenty-eight

ALEX

'Just one more item to deal with,' says the new acting headteacher of Whitford High, scanning his audience to ensure everyone is paying attention.

The official line is that Mr Stretford, the permanent head, suffered a cardiac arrest while changing the oil filter on his family saloon early in the summer holidays, but a counter rumour originating right here in the staffroom is that he was kidnapped by Mr Cotton, who buried him alive on the penalty spot of the school playing field before assuming control himself. Mr Cotton escaped justice because no email was sent about the incident. Therefore, it never actually happened.

'I know you're all desperate to go and put your feet up before the new term officially starts tomorrow, so I'll keep this brief.'

It's Monday afternoon and the staff of Whitford High are enjoying a training day that has consisted of updating wall displays, catching up on gossip and listening to senior staff 'remind' us of things they never told us in the first place in case Ofsted drops by.

'Some of you will already be aware of this . . .'

I drift off, back to last Thursday night, in bed with Melissa.

'I love you, Alex Tyler.' Her words floated in the air like Pac-Dots, waiting to be devoured. I stalled for time but the 'Game Over' sign appeared – the window I had to return her three words was closed.

Melissa woke the next morning and acted as if nothing had happened. She kissed me on the cheek and departed for work, and whenever I've broached the subject since she's talked over me about something insignificant like what she had for lunch or what I want for my birthday.

I'm sure I could fall in love with Melissa, but it's only been nine weeks. It's like listening to a great album – no one thinks it's great the first time they put it on. You need to absorb it, listen to it over and over, and only then does its genius become clear. Patience is required.

I just wasn't expecting it. I had other things on my plate: my first full year at Whitford High; lesson plans, strategies to build on the foundations laid with my year nines as they start their GCSEs.

'. . . but Kenny Sonola won't be returning for the forseeable future.'

I lift my eyes from the floor, redirecting them to Mr Cotton, his expression a recipe of smugness and indifference, as if he predicted whatever has happened all along.

'It's unclear at this stage what part Kenny played in the stabbing but his case will be going to court and, in the meantime, he's taken residence in local authority secure accommodation.'

*

253

'He was involved in a stabbing,' I report, still trying to process everything.

'Whoa!' Melissa's voice resonates as if she is speaking through a megaphone.

I shift my mobile to my other ear. 'The other boy is in intensive care. I don't think it was Kenny who had the knife, but he was at the scene.'

I hear cupboards being opened and closed on the other end of the line. 'Kenny is in intensive care?'

'No, the boy who was stabbed is. Kenny is in custody. Are you even listening to me?'

Kenny was making real progress before the summer but now . . . I trace back through the hours I've spent with him, trying to bring to mind anything I might have overlooked. I should have been more concerned that he was in with the wrong crowd when I saw him with those older lads after he stormed out of class. I should have counselled him again, tried to alter the course he was taking. I should have predicted this. But I didn't, and so all this – Kenny incarcerated and another boy critically ill – feels partly my fault.

The line clicks and becomes clearer. 'Sorry, you're off speaker now. I'm making spag bol.'

'I just feel like I've failed him, you know?'

'Aw, honey.'

'I really thought he'd turned a corner.'

'There's only so much a teacher can do. When I think back to my old English teachers – I used to give them hell. I hated English.'

My mind rewinds to the night I met Melissa at the pub quiz. 'I thought you said you loved Shakespeare at school?'

254

'Argh!' Melissa disappears behind the sound of clattering pans. 'The spaghetti is boiling over, I better go.'

'Were you lying about liking Radiohead too?'

'What? Look, Alex, I need to get off the phone. Try not to be sad. I'll cheer you up tomorrow night.'

'Tomorrow night?'

'My friend Rhian's birthday, remember? We're all going for a meal.'

Damn.

'I'd forgotten,' I say, to myself more than Melissa. 'I've just agreed to meet Holly. She's coming to mine.'

'Don't talk to me about Holly Gordon. She was so rude to me today. I felt like saying, "Drop the attitude, love – you're only a PA". But she's your mate, so I didn't.' I fail to conceal a sigh, but it doesn't register. 'Anyway, you'll have to rearrange.'

The line stutters. I think I've been put on speaker again.

'Look, my cooker top is starting to resemble the Serpentine. I'll see you tomorrow night, OK?'

I go to answer but by the time the words have formed in my mouth, Melissa is gone.

Holly rings the bell to the flat just before 8 p.m. I lead her into the living room, where she takes a seat on the sofa. Carl is doing caricatures at a party in Chelsea so it is just the two of us.

I start to pour the wine. 'So everything good with you then, Hols?'

One of the reasons I didn't want to cancel tonight was the tone of her texts yesterday afternoon. It was like she had something on her mind, but now she ignores my question. 'Has anyone ever told you you've got really spindly fingers?'

I examine my hand and allow my bottom lip to quiver in false desolation. Holly responds by offering one of her own tiny hands to compare.

'Come on,' she coaxes, and as our skin collides I try not to let it become any kind of moment in my head, but still I find myself avoiding eye contact.

'Anyone's fingers would appear long against yours,' I protest, once her point has been proven. She half-moons her eyes dismissively, then removes her shoes and leans into the opposite corner of the sofa from me with her knees lifted to her chest.

'What's new with you, Alex Patrick Tyler?'

My shoes already off, I emulate her posture and answer the question, filling her in on Kenny.

'I feel like Kenny was my first real test as a teacher and I've failed,' I say, trying not to notice Holly's foot starting to slip across the sofa. 'And if I fail when it really matters, maybe I'm just not cut out for it?'

'How many pupils pass through any given teacher's career?' She doesn't wait for my answer. 'Thousands. You can't get to all of them, Alex. You'd be a fool to set yourself that mission. You gave Kenny your time. Like you said, you were making progress. But he came to you when he was what, thirteen or fourteen? Most kids are in school, say, six hours a day for how many days a year?'

'One hundred and ninety-five.'

She regards my overly precise answer mockingly. 'So, six hours a day, one hundred and ninety-five days a year. The point is, they're not in school all that much when you think about it.'

Finally her foot touches mine but instantly she snatches it away.

'It doesn't help when half of them sit there bored all lesson.'

Holly refills our glasses without asking. 'You're concentrating on the wrong half. You can't solve all of the world's problems. I know what you're going to say – you're going to say that you came to London to make a difference, but if you ask me, if you just catch a few, if you just set a few on a better track, then that is making a difference. Not many people come close to that with their careers.'

She pauses, puts down her wine and then leans across, putting a hand on my shoulder and fixing her eyes onto mine. 'And anyway, you do make a difference. And not just at school. Just having you in London . . .' She hesitates. My eyes flick to her lips for a split second and I imagine myself kissing them. 'What I mean is, you've helped me remember who I used to be before . . .'

Her sentence trails off, and I'm left wondering what she means by 'before'. She is still gazing at me and her gaze is like a puzzle, but before I can solve it, and before I can ask when she forgot who she was and why, it is as though she remembers who she is, who I am, and takes her hand off my shoulder.

'You know what I did today?' she says, recoiling completely and talking breezily as if nothing had just occurred. 'I typed up a health and safety report for someone who shut their thumb in their drawer. Under the heading "Nature of the injury" I had to write "No injury".'

A sea of guilt washes over me for moaning about the job I always wanted. OK, Holly has never told me she is unhappy, but she didn't grow up wanting to be a PA, did she?

'I'm fed up of talking about me,' I say. 'What's going on with you? How's Richard?'

She sets her focus on the plasma screen. The TV isn't on, so all there is to see is a silhouette of the two of us positioned on the sofa. The distant way she's staring, it's like she's in another dimension.

'Has something happened?' I ask, and she shuttles back into orbit.

She bunches her hair into a ponytail with her hand before letting go. 'No, no. I just feel . . .'

I hold my tongue and wait for her to continue.

'I was on the bus the other day and I overheard this girl talking to her boyfriend and she was having a go at him. He'd put his PlayStation first again like he always does. I could tell it was a row they'd had loads of times and yet I was jealous. I was jealous because at least their relationship is real; at least their arguments are proper arguments.'

Holly sets about another refill but there's not enough left in the bottle for us both so she goes to the kitchen to fetch another. It's a school night and I'm just a few sips from insobriety, but I've spent half my life dreaming about nights on the sofa with Holly, so I hold out my glass and thank her with a grin.

'At first it was exciting, sneaking around,' she says, returning to her previous position. 'But that's gone now. I want a normal relationship. Everyone else seems to be moving on with their lives but me.' She inspects a lock of her hair for split ends. 'Is it slugs that can sleep for three years, or is that snails?'

I laugh. 'I'm really not sure.'

'That's what I'm starting to feel like: a slug, or a snail. I feel selfish and when I'm talking to him I can see in his face that he thinks I'm nagging, but am I really being that unreasonable?'

Holly's feet are inching towards me again.

'You're not being unreasonable at all. He's clearly a . . .'

Our eyes fuse fleetingly. I suppress the word 'creep' because that road is bound to lead me to Richard and Melissa. *Yep, your boyfriend's a creep and he's not looking for anything heavy right now. Ask Melissa.*

I decide to keep my counsel. This is the first time Holly has expressed real doubts to me about Richard, and I know it's probably just frustration. If I speak my mind now she'll never open up to me again.

'He's just a bloke, Hols.'

Holly takes another decisive glug of her drink, her blushed cheeks revealing that she too is tipsy. Her feet are touching mine now and this time she doesn't retract. Feeling a twitch from within my boxers, I shift my sitting position slightly to disguise any visible signs, all the while careful not to disturb our feet.

'I was supposed to be seeing Melissa tonight.'

Holly silently regards me. After all the fidgeting she's been doing, her hair looks like it used to: wild. Not for the first time since we met up again in spring, I have an intense urge to hug her, to hold my best friend in my arms, to press her chest against mine and to feel her breath warm the nape of my neck.

'Things have been going well between her and me,' I say.

Holly hints at a smile but doesn't put it into effect.

259

'She keeps going on about wanting to meet my dad. You know her own dad left when she was tiny?'

'Explains a lot,' Holly says into her glass.

I stare at our silhouettes once more. 'I just don't know if she and I want the same things. I thought we did, but lately . . .'

I stop myself. I don't want to talk about Melissa, not until I've figured out what I need to do. Our eyes meet again but now neither of us is willing to submit. I stare into Holly's brown eyes and I'm reminded – how did I forget? – of the peculiar ring of hazel that separates her pupil from her iris. I've never seen it on anyone else.

I want to ask her why she didn't respond to the note I wrote before she left Mothston, why she didn't get in touch at all for so long, and I want to tell her what I wished for that night I saw the shooting star/Boeing 737, but if I do it might not come true.

'I don't understand why anyone would want to keep you a secret,' I say, and I become aware that the atmosphere has changed, has become charged. 'Most men would shout it from the rooftops if they got to come home to you at night.'

Holly says nothing. She is still holding my gaze, her glass tilted against her chin, but I cannot read her expression. Then the facade breaks. A tear emerges from the corner of one eye and begins a solemn journey down her cheek. I move to hug her, to comfort her and ask what's wrong, but at the last moment her head turns so that her glass of wine, still propped against her chin, is all that separates our lips.

And then it is happening, and I'm holding her face in my hands, holding her face like it's the most precious

260

thing in the world. Still clutching her wine, she fumbles blindly for the coffee table, her lips not leaving mine, even as the glass shatters to the floor.

We inhale one another, our hands now exploring, and I think about how no one has ever been able to compare to Holly, not in eleven years. I think about all the times I've dreamt of *this*, and about the day all those years ago when I tried to make it – us – happen.

The day that could have changed everything.

Chapter Twenty-nine

ALEX

March 1999

I ring the bell and take a step back from the doorstep, not wanting to startle whoever opens the door. I put my hands in my pockets but immediately pull them out again, folding my arms before settling on putting them by my side.

A cramp starts to swell in my stomach as I wonder why no one is answering the door when the TV is on and they're clearly in.

I fold my arms again and realize that I have no idea what I'm going to say if it is not Mr or Mrs Gordon who answers the door but Holly.

Do I just come out with it? Or does there need to be a prologue, a few chapters, a slow build-up before the narrative accelerates and I tell her what I've been waiting to tell her from the very start.

After what seems like several minutes, and with my arms back by my sides, it is Mr Gordon who finally answers my knocks.

'Oh, hello, Alexander. Long time, no see. I thought you'd be Dean.'

Five months is all it's taken Dean Jones to usurp me in the Gordon family consciousness. 'What about Camber Sands?' I feel like saying, but Holly and Dean have just split up, so what does it matter?

'Well, you're always welcome here, no matter who Holly is courting.'

I know he means well, but he's clearly way behind the latest news, and I'm grateful when Mr Gordon sweeps his hand towards the stairs to indicate that I can go ahead. Now I'm here, I just want to get on with it.

Holly is sitting upright on her bed reading a magazine. She's dressed in combats and a white tank top, left hand pocketed in a packet of salt and vinegar Discos. Wavy tendrils of hair are escaping from the messy bun on top of her head, falling softly onto her neck and shoulders. She looks amazing.

'Hey, Al,' she says, holding out the crisps.

I shake my head. I'm not sure my stomach could take anything right now.

'So you said you wanted to talk to me about you and Dean?' I say, tiptoeing over the carnage of her floor to sit cross-legged on the end of her bed, already knowing what she's about to say.

I breathe in the scents of her room – hairspray, perfume, fresh sheets – and think about tomorrow. How I'm going to feel when I wake up in the morning. How different my life is going to be. Before Holly. After Holly. I realize that I won't need to say anything at all. I am on her bed, she is just there, close enough to take in my arms and kiss, under the light of a lava lamp. Some people actually believe it is real lava inside, when in fact it's a mix of wax and carbon tetrachloride in liquid.

'Well . . .' She pauses while she gets off the bed to shut her bedroom door. I'm almost certain that Holly can see my heart beating through this T-shirt. I focus on her lips, not really listening to her words now but preparing for what I'm about to do.

'I've been thinking of, you know . . .' She nods at her bed sheets, and though I see her gesture clearly, I don't immediately grasp what it means. I examine the two bodies of wax and carbon tetrachloride in Holly's lamp dancing around one another, both of them shaped like a number 8. At times they resemble two human beings poised for a hug, but the hug never happens. The laws of heat and density won't allow it.

'I just feel like the time's right for us to make the next step. It feels right, you know?'

I'm still not certain what Holly is talking about, but then I notice that her cheeks have become blushed, and that now she has turned away, slightly embarrassed, and in that moment my stomach collapses.

I realize what I'm hearing, realize that she's telling me she's going to sleep with Dean Jones, realize that *I'm* a blob of fake lava. Every time I get close to telling Holly how I feel, it's as though something stops me.

It is all I can do to concentrate on not swallowing, because if I swallow, my Adam's apple will confess everything. Why I came here, the lot. I keep my gaze fixed on the lamp, and the one thing I'm grateful for is that I didn't blurt it out or go to kiss her.

'Are you OK, Alex?'

Part of me wants to get out of here, away from the words I've just heard, but if I leave now things might become awkward between us. And she can't sleep with Dean Jones while I'm here.

I speak without thinking. 'But Kev said that you and Dean had a bit of a . . .'

'One of his mates, in front of everyone, started going on about the size of my tits. So you'd think Dean would tell him to shut it and tell everyone else to stop laughing and that they shouldn't objectify women like that. Especially not his girlfriend. But he doesn't do that. He laughs too. I felt like a right . . .'

I zone out, my own stupidity having dawned on me. 'He came after me and apologized. He's a big softie, really. I think he just . . .'

I distract myself by standing up from the bed and inspecting the map on her wall, pins dotted around the world.

'I can't imagine Dean getting his backpack on and doing the Inca Trail,' I interrupt, trying not to let my voice betray how I'm really feeling. I don't think I do a very good job.

When I turn back to the bed, Holly draws her knees to her chest and hugs them.

'What?' I say, noticing that Holly is giving me a look, a weird kind of look that I haven't seen before, as if I wasn't a person but a static object, a picture on a wall. She goes to say something but holds back.

Then eventually: 'I guess I don't know if me and Dean are going to be together forever. I'm not going to miss out on uni life by pining over a bloke for three years.' Her eyes flick to mine for a second, searching for support for

265

her principle. I offer it with a half-smile. 'I've just been thinking that I want my first time to be with someone special and . . . Oh, I don't know.'

I'm grateful when Holly stands up and suggests going for a walk, grabbing her keys and coat and then padding downstairs in front of me. I have no idea where we're walking to and I don't intend to ask. If I ask she'll plan a route, and routes always have an end. Whereas this way we might end up losing track of time and spending the whole night together.

The wind picks up as we pass a row of ivy-clad terraces, sending strands of her hair into flight. She zips up her jacket and giggles to herself.

'What?' I say, still feeling sorry for myself.

'You know whose house that is, don't you?'

Holly is jabbing her forehead in the direction of a detached cottage across the road. It's the biggest house on the street but, unlike the other houses, it doesn't have a front garden. It belongs to our headteacher, Mr Henderson.

'So what?'

'Remember when we used to knock and run?'

Holly is already crossing the road.

'It's still light – someone'll see.'

'Alex, we're not going to be able to mess around in Mothston for much longer, so let's make the most of it, yeah?'

It feels like a weird thing to say, but there's no time to ponder because Holly is less than three feet from the door now. She stops and inspects me for a second.

I step towards Holly, expecting her to wait for me to join her, but her fist begins to pound against the glossy black paint and before I can respond she is fleeing, trailed by an outstretched arm as if someone was about to hand her the baton in a relay. I don't have a baton, so the only explanation is that she's inviting me to hold her hand as we run away together, away from Dean Jones and all the words that have been spoken during the last hour. I start running, chasing Holly's long shadow and clasping her soft hand in mine. I keep one pace behind her so she won't let go until finally, at the gates of Weelsby Park, she slows, retracts her palm and falls onto the clammy grass, where she's overcome by breathless laughter. When she finally composes herself my stare is there to meet hers, and it's at least three or four seconds before this thing is broken and Holly begins walking again, trusting that I'll follow without instruction.

'I thought you'd said they'd had a blazing row?'

Kev is peering out of my window, facing away from where I'm stationed on my bed. 'You're paraphrasing a tad.'

'Everyone saw it, you said.' I lower my voice as Dad makes his way past my bedroom door to the bathroom. 'A massive scene, you said.'

'OK, so I exaggerated – sue me. What's it matter?'

'It matters because . . .'

But of course I don't want to tell him that it matters because I almost made a complete fool of myself.

'Something's gone on,' he says, turning to me and stroking his chin like Sherlock Holmes. 'You weren't in classes today and—'

'Who are you? My dad?'

'And you're acting strange. Stranger than usual. And it's clearly something to do with Holly.'

I take a gulp of air and exhale loudly. I don't know what to say to him. It's not his fault, really. I know that 90 per cent of what he says is bullshit. It's just that when Holly asked me around to her house to talk about Dean, I put two and two together and . . .

'Your mistake with Holly is that you made it impossible for her to fancy you. You're like a lap dog, always at her side, always ready to please, always obedient. I'm going to give you two pieces of advice, young Tyler.'

I want to tell him to shut up. I do. But where have all these years of doing it my way got me?

'Firstly, quit with all this "Hols" crap. Try "babe" or "darlin'".'

Kev grins gormlessly, waiting for me to acknowledge his genius.

I look at him wearily. 'You said you had two pieces of advice?'

'Er, what's with the 'tude? I'm trying to help you here.'

'Just get on with it, will you?'

'All right, keep your Y-fronts on.' He offers me a piece of chewing gum. I shake my head. 'My second piece of advice is that you need to move on, find someone new. Absence makes the heart grow fonder, right? So get absent.'

I stare at him blankly.

He resumes: 'Here's an idea – why don't you take Jane Ferrington out? You know she likes you – and it might make Holly stop and think.'

Jane Ferrington lives next door to Kev and is in the year below us at Mothston Grammar.

'I don't *know* she likes me,' I laugh dismissively.

'Alex, every time you're at mine she pretends to be washing-up so she can perve at you from her kitchen window.'

'She might just use a lot of crockery.'

'Just do it, Alex. Then next time Holly phones you at two in the morning, don't answer. And when she asks why, tell her you were manoeuvring your love prod into Jane Ferrington's murky cave of lust. That should make her see the error of her ways.'

'Murky cave of lust? This is the most ludicrous plan I have ever heard.'

'Fine, have it your way. Sit at home with a sock over your cock – but don't ever say I haven't tried to help you.'

With that Kev stands and coughs up some phlegm, which he swallows immediately.

'And one last thing, yeah? Stop dressing like Noel Edmonds.'

'Pardon?'

'Cords, Alex. I haven't seen a pair of cords since Noel Edmonds was on telly with Mr Blobby. That was yonks ago.'

Kev starts to walk away, but he turns and walks backwards for a few steps to finish sharing his thoughts.

'And the fact he wore cords is probably the reason why he'll never be on telly again.'

Chapter Thirty

HOLLY

September 2010

Alex slides his hand down my back, making me shiver. We're both lying stretched out on the sofa: our private island in a sea of discarded clothes, broken glass and red wine.

He gently sweeps my hair away over my shoulder to nuzzle my neck and I groan as he—

'Oi, slag bag. Are you listening to me?' Jemma snaps me out of my daydream.

WHAT AM I DOING? Every time I think about what happened in Alex's flat the other night, it goes a little bit further. I actually forced myself to break away about six and a half seconds into the embrace, mumbled an apology and ran away. But my mind has somehow turned it from the type of snog you get between love-struck teenagers on *Home and Away* to the dirty bits in *Sex and the City*. If I'm not careful we'll soon be re-enacting a scene from *Basic Instinct* in my head, and that'll just be awkward for everyone.

'Sorry, Jem, what did you say?'

'Do you reckon if two people who have only ever been friends get drunk and kiss it means they secretly fancy each other?'

WHAT?

'Why do you ask?' I gasp. She must know something. But how could she? Only Alex and I know, and it's not like he's going to call her up for a natter. But why would she ask that?

'Christ, chill out, doll – I'm only making conversation.'

Stop being paranoid, Holly. Jemma loves a hypothetical question, it's a coincidence. Albeit, a totally weird one.

She goes back to whatever she's looking at on her screen – Twitter, the last time I checked – and I resolve to think about this Alex thing logically.

Maybe my head is turning it into something it wasn't. I mean, it must be easy to romanticize it and confuse my desire for Alex as something more, but if I step outside the situation and look at the facts then there is probably an explanation. Richard and I are having a few problems. Between him working so hard and his disappointment over the promotion, he is feeling stressed and I am feeling neglected.

Because all this also means it's been a while since Richard and I had sex. We used to do it all the time. It's no biggie – every relationship has a dry patch – but if we're not doing it, and we're not going out, what are we doing, exactly?

That's why I got all confused. That's why I need to talk to Richard and make him realize that this has gone too far. It's time we acted like a proper couple, because then we can deal with our issues like a . . . well, a proper couple.

Apart from anything else, Melissa is still on the scene, so even if I did want to dump Richard and jump straight into Alex's arms – which I DON'T – then it's not an option anyway.

It would be easier on my conscience if I could blame Alex. I lay in bed the night it happened trying to feel angry at him. I'd been drinking! He knows I've got a boyfriend! He kissed me anyway! But then I remembered he'd drunk the same amount, I know he has a girlfriend and I kissed him too. Then my mind started wandering, and it was hard to feel angry at the things he was doing after he unfastened my imaginary bra. His long fingers caressing my skin as he moves the straps down my arms, and . . . RICHARD. I need to talk to Richard.

His door is ajar and he's reading something on his screen. I stand in the doorway and take a moment to study him – Christ, he's handsome – before knocking, making him look up and flash me a brief smile.

'Hey you,' he says. He looks tired.

'Hey yourself.' I shut the door behind me and sit opposite him at his desk.

'So, I've been thinking . . .' And I tell him what I've been thinking. Not EVERYTHING I've been thinking, obviously – only the bits about us. How I want to hold his hand in public, and have dinner in a restaurant with him without worrying that someone we know will walk in the door, and refer to him as my boyfriend. His face remains impassive, so I talk and talk until eventually he nods slowly.

'OK.' He shrugs.

'OK?' I breathe incredulously. He's agreeing?

'I want all that too.' He grins.

272

OMG, this is epic – he's actually saying we should tell people.

'I'm not saying we should tell people.' Oh . . . 'But maybe we can go away together.' Eh? 'I think we could both do with a holiday. Forget about this place for a couple of weeks.'

I allow the disappointment to wash over me before I really think about what he's saying. We can go away together. Not exactly what I was after, but an excellent start. We'll get used to holding hands and kissing in public, and once we get used to it, having that sort of relationship back home will be the natural step. And I've not been on holiday in ages . . . this will be ACTUALLY AWESOME.

'Let's do it,' I laugh, drumming my hands on the edge of his desk in excitement. 'Where shall we go? How about South America? I reckon we can fit in three countries in two weeks – we don't want to be rushing around too much. Brazil, Argentina and Peru could be a nice itinerary?'

He makes a face and cocks his head in a look I interpret as 'nah'.

'How about India, then? We should probably pick north or south as trying to cover both in that time will be tricky.'

He still looks underwhelmed.

'Thailand?' I venture. Come on, Richard, throw me a bone here.

'That's a good shout.' He nods enthusiastically.

'Yeah? Brilliant! We can travel around – there's a train that goes between Bangkok and Chang Mai but we're probably better off catching internal flights so we don't waste a day, and we should do a couple of the islands, too. Ooh – we can split the second week between Vietnam and Cambodia, and maybe even Laos if we—'

'Can't we stay in one place? I'm beat, babe. I just want to spend a couple of weeks lounging by a pool and not having to think about anything. Let's book a hotel for two weeks.'

'Oh, right.' Two weeks lying by a pool? When there's so much to get out and see? That sounds dull.

'We'll stay somewhere nice, though,' he says, like that's what I'm worried about. 'Five star. You choose it and I'll pay.'

I try to shake off the negative vibes taking hold and resolve to stop being an ungrateful cow. I have a handsome man instructing me to find the best five-star hotel in Thailand and he'll pay, and I'm sitting here pouting because it looks like I won't get to eat street food with the locals.

'Right,' I exclaim with forced cheer, heading for the door. 'I'll start looking.'

'Holly?' he calls after me.

'Uh-huh?' I smile back at him, though he's leafing through a magazine now and no longer looking at me.

'Find somewhere all-inclusive, yeah? That way we don't even have to leave the hotel.'

''Sup, buddy?' I subtly minimize sixthsensesresort.com/ phuket and maximize invoices.exe/september as I clock Danny hovering at my shoulder.

'Not much.' He sighs, perching himself on the edge of my desk.

274

He starts flicking through my stationery catalogue in what's clearly a show of acting casual.

'Dude,' I say, grabbing the book out of his hand, startling him. 'You're obviously after lady advice. Out with it.'

'I'm not,' he laughs. 'Well, not really. It's not advice I need, more of an opinion. Not for me, for a friend!'

'O-K,' I say slowly, watching him take a deep breath like he's trying to gather the courage to say what he wants to say.

'Do you think office relationships are a good idea or do you reckon they're doomed to failure?'

Oh, holy crap!

'What are you getting at, Danny?' I ask, more harshly than I intend to.

'Nothing. Don't worry.' He shrugs sulkily, practically running back to his desk with his head bowed, as Jemma gets back with our teas.

Why is everyone asking me weird questions today? And then it hits me . . .

'Oh my God, something's happened between you and Danny!' I cry, almost making Jem spill my tea over my desk.

'Shhh,' she hisses. 'Christ, Holly – I don't think Helen from accounts on the fifth floor heard you there.'

'That's all right, I'll bring her up to speed later in an all-staff email. Now tell me what happened.'

Jemma is uncharacteristically coy as she explains how she and Danny were the last two left after the quiz on Wednesday and, after several ciders, ended up having a hot and heavy snog in a doorway by Bank station.

'Aw, you guys are in love.' I smile, clutching at my heart.

'We're so not – urgh, as if.'

'OK.' I shrug, turning back to my screen.

'I mean, loads of colleagues get it on when they're drunk – doesn't mean they're gonnae get married.'

'True,' I mumble, not looking at her.

'And it's only because I was there – I could have been anyone.'

'Right, I hear you.'

'Why are we still on this? What's your obsession with my love life, anyway? Sounds like you need to get laid.'

Ain't that the truth . . .

'Let's never mention it again, all right?'

'Sure,' I say nonchalantly, sipping my tea and watching her out of the corner of my eye.

It's the first time I've ever seen Jemma blushing.

I carry on with my Thailand research, trying not to laugh every time I see Jemma or Danny surreptitiously glance at the other one, then revert their eyes to their own screens quickly when they get caught. After emailing Richard a few links to hotels, I research things to do in Thailand. I take it if Richard doesn't want to leave the hotel then he's not going to be up for an elephant trek. Shame. Could I do it alone? He might be a bit pissed off if I leave him lounging by the pool by himself. Plus, it kind of defeats the purpose of us going on holiday so that we can act like a couple.

My phone rings.

'Richard Croft's office?' I answer distractedly.

'Ten thousand pounds.'

'Sorry? Mum, is that you?'

'No, it's the banker.'

'Eh?'

'*Deal or No Deal*. You're Noel Edmonds.'

'No idea what you're talking about, Mum. I don't watch much telly.'

'No, me neither.'

'Ha, sure.'

'I hardly watch it at all these days, thank you, lady. I've got too much going on, which you'd know all about if you came to see us in York.'

Oh, here we go.

'I will, Mum,' I promise. 'I'm actually in the middle of booking a holiday with, um, a friend from work, and once I have the dates sorted I'll pick a weekend to come and see you.'

'You should do – York's a lovely place. We've been to some lovely restaurants we'll take you to when you visit, and we've joined a bowling team. I'm rubbish but your dad's pretty good. Ooh, when you come we can go for afternoon tea at Betty's Tearooms, just the two of us. It'll be fun. I don't blame you for never coming to Mothston, really. What a boring old dump that place was. But you'll like it here.'

'Mum!' I laugh in shock.

'Well, it was. I don't know why we stayed so long. Well, other than the fact your dad loves it.'

'Relationships are about compromising, I guess,' I sigh, my eyes flicking to my screen, where 'Things to do in Thailand' still fills the Google box.

'That they are. But you know what, Holly?' Her voice has gone uncharacteristically quiet and serious. 'Compromising works two ways. I should have put my foot down sooner about moving out of Mothston.'

277

'You've been happy though, right?'

She pauses a little too long for my liking.

'Mum?'

'Yes, of course I've been happy being with your dad. I wouldn't have wanted to be anywhere without him. But I can't pretend I don't resent the number of years I've wasted being stuck somewhere that never felt like home to me. Especially after Julie died. He's a stubborn man, your father. Never one to put others before himself.' Her light-hearted tone has returned, but I get the feeling she's not joking when she adds: 'I had to practically threaten to go by myself to get him to agree to move to York.'

We're both silent for a moment. I don't really know what to say.

'Afternoon tea sounds lovely, Mum,' I say eventually, a lump forming inexplicably in my throat.

'Great. Anyway I'd better be off – I have a Women's Institute meeting tonight.'

'You've joined the Women's Institute? Bloody hell, Mum. You're not going to turn up in one of those naked calendars, are you?'

'Fat chance,' she tuts. 'No one wants to look at this with no clothes on. Except your dad maybe.'

'Right, thanks, Mum – I have to go and throw up into my bin now.'

'OK, dear. See you soon.'

I hang up slowly, with a feeling of impending doom about the realizations going on in my head right now. Mum's right – Dad does tend to put himself first. Why have I never noticed that before? But that's not the worst thing. Richard is like that, ten times over.

He's never once put me first. It's all about HIS career, HIS holiday, HIS need for us to have a secret relationship. He's never once done something he hasn't wanted to do. Apart from turning up to Chloe's wedding two hours before it ended – whoop-de-fucking-do. If it was his mate's wedding I'd have been there for the duration. Why have I been kidding myself that was such a remarkable gesture?

That's why I love Alex – he's the only one who has ever put me first.

Oh my God, I love Alex. Without even realizing it, I've actually gone and fallen in love with him again.

He'll plan his weekend around feeding Harold, he'll change his radio station from 6 Music to Absolute Eighties whenever I'm over, he'll DRESS UP AS JASON BLOODY DONOVAN AND SING IN FRONT OF HIS CLASSMATES, for crying out loud. No man has ever put me first the way he has. Not Richard, not Max, certainly not Dean – not even my dad.

If Alex was in Richard's situation he'd have told everyone as soon as he knew it was important to me. And if people had thought badly of him? He'd suck it up.

Will Richard EVER do the same?

I don't hover at his door this time, I simply walk in and sit down.

'Are we ever going to tell people about us?' I demand.

'Sure,' Richard peers over the magazine he's still reading, blinking in surprise.

'When?'

'When the time is right.'

'When's that?'

'I don't know, Holly.' He sighs, tossing the magazine

gently onto his desk. He sounds exasperated now. I don't care.

'So, never then?'

He leans back in his chair, running a hand through his hair.

'Babe, it'd cause too many problems if people found out what's going on while I'm your boss. It wouldn't be worth it.'

Ouch!

'Quit then.'

'I can't quit,' he laughs, his eyes softening. 'You could, though? You're only a secretary – it can't be that hard for you to find another job, and I can easily get another PA.'

His words stun me for a few seconds. That's how he sees me. Not as his right-hand woman or the wind beneath his wings or any of the other crap clichés I've been fooling myself apply to us, but merely a robotic purveyor of random admin.

'Fine, I quit,' I whisper after a few moments.

'You don't have to do it right now.' Richard rolls his eyes and smiles wearily.

'Yeah, I do. I quit,' I say again, louder this time. 'All of it.'

'What do mean?' He looks genuinely confused, following me all the way as I jump out of my seat and storm out of his office.

'I no longer want to work for you,' I explain matter-of-factly, reaching my own desk and swinging my Mulberry bag over my shoulder. 'Or under you . . .' I don't know where that came from. 'OR over you . . .' What does that even mean?

It obviously made more sense than I thought because the last thing I hear as the heavy oak door slams shut behind me is Danny exclaiming, 'Have Holly and Richard been doing it?' and Melissa deadpanning, 'Oh. My. God.'

Right. What the fuck am I going to do now?

Chapter Thirty-one

ALEX

'Did you know?'

Not for the first time, Melissa jolts me with three little words.

'Did I know what?'

'Holly and Richard.'

How does she know? My mind assumes the role of quizmaster – Jeremy Paxman on *University Challenge*. Has Richard finally agreed to go public? Did Holly confess? Did she use our kiss to nudge him into submission? I'm going to have to press you.

I fill my lungs with a long, deep breath, sling my work bag onto the sofa and grip the phone between my shoulder and ear while guiding one arm from my jacket sleeve. I then swap ears until the other arm is free.

'She's my best friend. I promised her.'

'Yes, Alex, and I'm your girlfriend. We're supposed to share everything.'

I toss the remote control across the sofa and place myself in the spot where Holly and I kissed for the first time.

'How did you find out?'

'I felt like such an idiot. I had to act like I wasn't

shocked, that of course I knew Holly and Richard had a thing, that of course my boyfriend had confided in me.'

'What on earth are you talking about? What's happened?'

'Oh, you didn't know?' Melissa pauses, allowing her affected surprise to fossilize. 'I thought she was your best friend?'

I try to disguise the impatience in my sigh. 'Will you just tell me what has happened?'

'Holly blew her top at Richard in the office, just now, screaming at him that it was over. In front of everyone.'

Melissa details the scene, her voice an orchestra of different emotions. On strings we have shock. On percussion there's glee. Wind comes courtesy of disappointment. And let's not forget our conductor: indignation.

I zone out, filling in the gaps myself.

It's me. She has dumped Richard to be with me. She finally sees that we are meant for one another. The touch of her hand against mine, the night in the park, the kiss: preludes to this. Inside I feel like a can of lemonade that's accidentally dropped from the fridge, ready to burst.

'How could you lie to me all this time?'

'I didn't lie, I just—'

'Didn't tell me the truth. It's the same thing, Alex. Your loyalty should lie with me, not her. If I hadn't just found out about her and Richard, I'd have half a mind to think that something was going on between you and her.'

I scoff, for my own benefit as much as Melissa's. 'Don't be ridiculous.'

'It would be ridiculous. She's really let herself go lately.'

I remove the phone from my ear, pressing it against my

thigh and closing my eyes. After a few seconds I return it to my ear. Melissa is still talking.

'. . . times I think that your friendship with her means more to you, is more important to you, than what we have, and I shouldn't feel like that, Alex – no girl should.'

'I'm sorry,' I protest weakly. 'I'm sorry you feel like that.'

'Just tell me I'm wrong – tell me that I mean more to you than Holly.'

Now Melissa is Paxman, and I feel like a dumbstruck student from an old polytechnic that is up against Oxford Balliol. I should have seen the question coming but instead we're consumed by a level of silence that until now I didn't think was possible in the city of London.

'Anyone would think you were in love with her or something.'

I cannot think of the right thing to say, and the line goes quiet for a few seconds.

'Can you just be fucking honest with me, Alex? I want to know whether the man I'm supposed to be starting a life with has a thing for some slag from my office. So if you don't mind, I'd like you to tell me: is whatever is going on with you and Holly more important to you than what we have?'

I feel like I'm standing on the edge of a steep cliff, deciding whether to jump or to turn back. In the end I do neither. I stand still, submitting my back to the gusts, and fall without jumping.

'You're a fucking coward, Alex. A fucking coward. I'm not playing second fiddle to anyone, especially not some whore secretary who tries to screw her way to promotion.'

284

The line dies. I stand up from the sofa, dropping my phone into the indentation that I've just left in the cushion, and the guilt I feel at having hurt Melissa is matched only by the relief that has come with knowing our relationship is over.

Chapter Thirty-two

HOLLY

I could travel the world. I toy with the idea as I pull on my cardigan, realizing as I do that my shoulders are slightly burnt. It's sunny but breezy on Blackheath Common, and the kite flyers are out in their dozens around me. It makes me think of the end of *Mary Poppins* when Mr Banks quits his job and goes to spend time with his family, singing 'Let's Go Fly a Kite'. The symmetry makes me laugh out loud until I remember that I don't have anyone to fly kites with, and that I might have been a tad hasty in quitting my own job. And then I realize I have tears streaming down my face even though I'm still laughing, and I'm glad there's no one near enough to see me because they'd be scared for their life.

So if there's nothing here for me, travelling really does make sense. I have enough money. A decent enough salary coupled with an unadventurous relationship with a flashy boyfriend was at least good for my savings account. It was kind of earmarked for my and Richard's dream home, but I'll think of a plan B while I'm trekking through the Australian outback, finding myself. An old university mate, Jess, left recently to do just that. By the sound of her emails she's finding herself in a lot of Aussie men's beds. I could maybe catch up with her somewhere.

There's just one teeny-tiny thing complicating matters.

I don't want to leave Alex.

But just because I love Alex, doesn't mean I can have him. He's got a girlfriend, and I can't hang around playing third wheel to him and Melissa. But if he's serious about Melissa, why would he kiss me?

For a moment, I'm lost in the memory of the touch of his lips on mine, but then I force myself back to the present and jump up, brushing the grass off my dress. I have a plan. First I need to go home and feed Harold and rub cocoa butter into my burnt shoulders, but then I'm going to find out where I stand with Alex.

'Travelling?' he says, looking up quickly. His expression is unreadable. We're sitting at opposite ends of his sofa, drinking tea. He's said nothing while I've relayed my story about Richard and work, but his understanding nods and the occasional widening of his eyes have indicated that he's listening to every word.

And then I put the travelling idea out there.

'Yeah.' I shrug, my eyes not leaving his. 'I mean, there's nothing much here for me . . . is there?'

Say it, Alex. Tell me that there is something for me to stay for.

Silence.

I wasn't prepared for this. The whole way here I allowed myself to fantasize about the best-case scenario, in which he tells me there's no way I can leave, and then scoops me up in his arms, my legs around his waist, and

287

takes me to his bed to make mad, passionate love to me. Then tomorrow I get up and make tea wearing nothing but his pyjama top, and while I'm doing it he comes up behind me wearing nothing but the matching pyjama bottoms and wraps his arms around me. I turn around to kiss him and soon we're having sex on his kitchen worktop, and Alex doesn't give a crap how unhygienic it is because he wants me that badly.

That's pretty much where I was at when I rang his doorbell, my heart pounding with anticipation as I heard his slippered footsteps pad towards the door, thinking about what I would say when he mentioned what happened between us. He would ask what it meant, surely? How would I answer? Confess I wished I'd never run away? Or just show him by picking up the kiss where we left off?

'Travelling,' he says again, but this time it's not a question.

I'm not sure how long we stare at each other for but it's Alex who breaks our gaze.

'Excellent idea,' he says, necking the last of his tea and standing up.

'You think I should go?' I ask, stung. He's taken his mug straight to the sink and is washing it up with his back to me so I can't see his expression.

'God, yeah,' he says quickly. 'Are you sure you just want to go for six months, though? Why not a year?'

Bloody hell, he can't wait to get rid of me.

'Are you finished with that?'

'What?' I realize he's pointing at my mug. 'Oh, yeah, sorry.'

I hand it over with a shaky hand, watching his back while he picks up the dishcloth.

'What about you?' I ask casually, pretending he hasn't just thrown my heart against the wall and missed it ricocheting into his recycling bin. 'Did you sort everything with Melissa?'

As much as I don't really want to know, I have to. I have to know if the other night meant something. Because if it didn't, and it's Melissa he wants to be with, then I have to get away and pretend that these feelings I have for Alex don't exist. I've done it before, I can do it again. Distance did the trick the last time, and you literally can't put much more distance between us than London to Australia.

He turns around, leaning against the sink and crossing his arms. The distance between us is palpable and it's almost impossible to believe that just a few days ago, on this very sofa, there was no gap between our bodies at all. He hasn't even mentioned the kiss.

'Yep,' he chirps, his voice two octaves higher than normal. 'We're good.'

'Great.' That's not great at all. This isn't how this was supposed to go.

'Yeah.'

'So . . .'

'So.'

And that's that. It's not me he wants, it's Melissa. All this time – every heart-clutching look, every skin-tingling touch, every time he confided in me, or laughed at my jokes – it was just as mates. Don't cry, Holly. At least not yet.

'Well, I'd better go sort my life out.' I grin, wondering if Alex realizes how forced it is, and walk towards the door. 'I have so much to organize, plus I'll need to work out what to do about my flat.'

I stop at the door and turn back towards him, holding my arms open. 'See ya, then.'

'Yeah, see ya,' he whispers into my hair as he hugs me. I tighten the grip of my arms around his waist and feel him tighten his back, and I'm torn between wanting to get out before the tears escape, and never wanting to leave his embrace, ever.

I give him one final squeeze, then break away.

And for the second time in my life, I feel a sad sense of finality as I close the door on Alex Tyler.

Chapter Thirty-three

ALEX

The doorbell rang just shy of 9 p.m. Holly hadn't texted or called since Melissa's phone call but I knew that it was her. I pressed the buzzer to release the door two storeys below, all the while imagining our cottage in the Peak District. I was driving up our gravel driveway in second gear, pulling in next to the vintage campervan in duck-egg blue that we'd bought for weekend breaks to Totnes and Edinburgh. I surveyed the Derbyshire stone, the glossy black of the front door. The nights had drawn in for winter and the curtains were closed. It was my birthday. I turned my key, opened the front door and *surprise*!

'I'm thinking of going travelling.'

A sob rose through me as a new reality sank in. It was the first time I'd seen her since our kiss, which I'd decided not to mention. It would only make things awkward, and she'd think I was over-analysing. And anyway, we had enough to talk about. What I hadn't expected was *this*. But I should have, because I'd lived it before. Holly hadn't come to broadcast her love; she'd come to tell me that she was leaving, walking out of my life again, promising that she'd stay in touch, just like she did eleven years ago.

How could I have allowed myself to become so deluded again? At school Holly could explain what every button on a scientific calculator meant: nCr, ALGB, tan. Teachers said she was a natural when it came to maths, and more than once she commented that her love of maths and my love of English typified the difference between us. She liked hard facts, I liked to search for different interpretations. She could stare at a piece of art and enjoy it for what it was, I was always straining to find out what it meant. She lived life while I mulled it over.

You'd have thought I would have learnt my lesson first time around. Holly puts three kisses at the end of a text message, Alex has visions of gripping her hand in a maternity ward; Holly's foot slips across the sofa, Alex debates the practicalities of opening a joint account; Holly offers a drunken kiss, Alex imagines he is Menelaus reclaiming Helen of Troy from Paris. Holly breaks up with Richard . . .

I needed to start dealing in facts, not fiction. And one fact was clear: Holly was not in love with me. If she was, she wouldn't keep absconding.

I took her in, sitting on the opposite end of the sofa from me, just like she had been a few nights before, except this time she was upright, her feet coy, facing in on themselves. Her hair was restrained in a ponytail and there was a strand of grass on her skirt. Where had that come from? She stared at the floor for a moment and then at me, cheeks blushed, eyes expectant, as if she was waiting for me to respond, to tell her it was OK, that she should follow her dream.

The one thing I was thankful for was that I hadn't spewed out my emotions and that Holly would never know what I was imagining as I let her into the flat.

I listened to her footsteps as she descended the uncarpeted stairs towards the door that leads onto the high street. I tried to judge her emotional state from the rhythm of her steps but it disclosed nothing; her steps could have been anyone's. She stopped momentarily. A change of heart? Seconds passed, I could hear my own heartbeat. But her descent resumed, as unrevealing as before, until the front door slammed with a cartoon clunk, causing my insides to rattle. I glanced at the window but stopped myself from walking over and looking down onto the street, knowing that it would be all too much to watch her trail from my life again.

I wake to the sound of the dodgy plumbing downstairs – growling like Chewbacca – after someone flushes the loo. The moon is peeking out from behind a chimney on the other side of the high street, a paracetamol in the sky spilling a dose of light into the front room. I check my phone. It's 2.17 a.m.

My neck feels stiff from sleeping on the sofa and I'm uncomfortable. The heat of the day has left the flat stuffy. So much so that Holly's scent has lingered. Sun, chocolate, outdoors. Holiday smells. I remember her hair against my cheek, the faintest trace of damp, as if she'd spent the morning in the sea.

I hold my phone above my face while I navigate to my messages, reviewing our correspondence from the past months, scrolling backwards with my thumb.

Load earlier messages.

293

Meeting Kev in the pub. Our night in the park. Graffiti.

Load earlier messages.

Feeding Harold. The pub quiz. Don't say anything about Richard.

Tears start to roll down my cheeks, but I cannot stop. Soon there are no earlier messages to load, and I realize that these past months were just an interlude. Holly and I, our story ended eleven years ago, and all this has just been a bad remake of an old film that should have been left well alone.

It's approaching 8.30 a.m. when my feet hit the pavement at Deptford station and my phone begins to splutter inside my pocket. My mind allows itself to be fooled by hope, but the feeling is fleeting.

'Hello, Dad,' I answer, struggling to shield the disappointment from my tone.

'Expecting someone else, were you?'

I rub my stiff neck, wincing, and contemplate telling him that it is not a good time, but for some reason I feel a warmth towards Dad this morning that I haven't felt for a long time. It is as though last night made me realize who I can really depend on. Then again, maybe it's his fault I'm in this mess. Him and Mum, for lending me fanciful expectations of love. Terry and Julie, like the couple in The Kinks song; married at nineteen, expecting within a year. Everything in the right order. Till death do us part.

'It's a bit early for you, isn't it?'

'I've got bingo at 10.30 a.m.'

The halal butcher is erecting his awnings. I do not

acknowledge him as I pass. I gave up smiling at the shopkeepers on my third day.

'Bingo?'

'Don't mock it until you've tried it, son. I can't think of anywhere in the world with a more favourable female-to-male ratio.'

'You're playing bingo to pull?'

'You'd love it,' he says. 'The men's toilets are pristine. No one ever uses them.'

I smile to myself, at Dad and his bingo, at being cheered up when I didn't think it was possible.

'Anyway, I rang to tell you that Kev's better half is organizing a surprise party for his thirtieth. A week on Friday. I thought I might get to meet this Melissa girl of yours?'

Melissa – I'd almost forgotten about her over the last twelve hours.

'I'm not sure that's going to happen.'

'Don't tell me you've split up?'

The Afro-Caribbean food store is already doing a brisk trade. I went in there during my second week. The banana I bought for breakfast turned out to be a plantain.

'Not exactly but—'

'Can't say I'm surprised.'

'What's that supposed to mean?'

'Do you realize you've never actually told me about your girlfriend, Alex? Not mentioned her once in however many months it's been. The only reason I know is because Kev tells me when he and Diane pop around.'

'It hasn't come up.'

I can see pupils now. Familiar faces, mainly. These are

the people I convinced myself I was moving to London for, but there are schools like Whitford High all over the country. The reason I chose London was . . .

'Holly Gordon, on the other hand, you never shut up about. Holly this, Holly that. When are you going to sort yourselves out?'

Something invisible grips my abdomen, rendering me speechless. My eyes begin to well again.

'Look, I've got to go. I love you, Dad.'

There is a pause, the meaning of which my mind is too blurred to fathom.

Then he says: 'You too, son. I'll see you next weekend.'

Chapter Thirty-four

HOLLY

This is the most epic To Do list I have EVER written.

There are so many layers, subcategories and side lists to it. Firstly, it's all the destinations I want to cross off on my travels. I want to get around as many as possible, but I don't want to spend the next couple of months on planes and trains.

Then there's the To Dos for each destination. I decided on six months for my adventure, so I need to make sure I allocate the right amount of time to each place so that I don't miss any of the best stuff, without staying anywhere too long.

Then there's all the things I need to do to make it all happen. Buying, packing, booking, checking.

It's an A3 work of art – that's what it is.

I'm sitting with it spread out in front of me on the floor, and I've just run my pen through the two jabs and bikini wax I achieved this morning when Harold strolls onto the page and settles herself down on it, eyeing me with barely concealed resentment.

She knows something is going on. Her rebellion over the last week has included climbing into every container

I'm attempting to pack my house contents into, sleeping on the clean, freshly ironed clothes I've laid out ready to pack and peeing into my brand-new rucksack.

'Get lost, cat,' I groan, gently pushing her off my travel plan.

You'd love that, wouldn't you? she says, with narrowed eyes. *It would lessen your guilt about being the second owner to abandon me.*

I give in, tossing down my pen and rubbing behind her ears with both hands.

'Mum and Dad are taking you to York to live with them while I'm away, so don't give me all that.' Tears spring to my eyes, and I wipe them away with one hand while scratching her under the chin with the other. She'll be fine. She'll love it at my parents' – I went to see their new pad the other day, and it's much bigger than my place, and has a garden and there's already a cat flap from the previous owners so she can come and go as she pleases. Harold will be happy there.

I went so that I could tell my folks in person about going away.

Dad was a bit confused. He's a creature of routine, so the appeal of spending six months on several unfamiliar territories is lost on him. But he told me to enjoy myself and stay safe, before turning back to his newspaper. Mum was surprisingly supportive. Asked a lot of questions about where I was heading and what I was going to do there, oohing and aahing at my responses. She agreed to take Harold on the condition that I promised never to hitchhike, and that I would update her on what's happening in *Neighbours* when I get to Australia.

All my furniture is in storage so all that's left are boxes

of stuff for them to take to theirs when they pick up Harold. My flat looks bigger and cheerless without my belongings. This must be how it looked when Max and I first moved in, but I can't remember – it seems so long ago. So much has happened since then, despite how little I have to show for it.

A knock on the door interrupts that depressing thought, and I rush to answer it.

'Jem!' I cry, surprised but overwhelmingly happy to see her. 'Come in.'

'No, that's OK,' she insists. 'I just came to give you this. It's from everyone at Hexagon.'

She rummages in her bag for about three minutes, before producing a creased envelope with 'Holly' scrawled across it.

'If that's even your real name,' she says, folding her arms as I pull out a card.

'If you weren't planning on coming in you should have just posted it to me,' I point out, trying not to laugh.

'I wanted to double-check you do actually live here. I wasn't sure exactly how far your double life went. Besides, I left it too late for it to reach you before you leave.'

'I'm sorry, Jem,' I say, putting my hand on her arm. 'Like I said in my email, I did really, really want to tell you. But Richard didn't want me to and he kept making me think that it was only for a little while longer.'

'But I tell you everything!' she whines, pushing past me into the flat. 'I don't know how you could just let me sit there and babble pointless shit about my calamity of a love life and not mention the fact you're shagging your boss.'

After closing the door, I sit cross-legged on the floor,

299

leaning on the wall where my sofa once sat, and pat the space next to me.

'I'm all right standing, thanks,' she says, flipping her head to the side pointedly.

'Please, Jem – I hated keeping it from you,' I tell her. 'But I was in a bad place. I can't believe I let him convince me it was better kept a secret for so long. I feel so stupid now. And I've lost you and I've lost Alex and none of you can hate me more than I hate myself.'

Then I burst into tears.

'Oh, shush,' Jem says, the prickliness dissolving from her expression. She sits down next to me, putting an arm around my shoulders as my tears turn into full, convulsing sobs.

'Please stop crying,' she begs, after a little while.

'I'm so sorry,' I tell her again. 'I really did want to tell you.'

'Yeah, yeah, whatever – it's fine. But you need to stop crying. Seriously, Hols, you are one ugly crier. I don't think I've ever actually seen you cry before. Like, don't get me wrong – you're a gorgeous girl and everything, but right now your face is all swollen and blotchy, and you've got a big drip of snot.'

She hands me a tissue from her bag and I'm about to blow my nose with it when I notice that there are blue ink stains as well as some unidentified yellow splotches all over it, so I dab my nose lightly with it before discreetly dropping it on the floor by my leg.

'Now, what's all this about Alex?' she asks.

'Well, I went to see him after—'

'Sorry,' she interrupts, swivelling on her bum on the wooden floor. 'I hope you don't mind but I'm going to turn round this way while you tell me so I don't have to look at your face.'

'Hey.' I slap her arm, though I'm secretly glad she's facing the other way as it will make this easier to say.

'So, I realized I'm in love with Alex and—'

'*I knew it!*' She spins back round to face me. 'It was so obvious. That's why this Richard revelation totally threw me because I knew you and Alex are totally in love.'

'That's just it, though, Jem. He's not. I thought for a moment he might feel the same way so I went to see him the day I left Richard, but I was wrong. He wants to be with Melissa, and he didn't really give a shit when I told him I was leaving and I haven't even heard from him since.'

Fresh tears come. Jemma pulls a face.

'I don't believe it.' She sighs, sounding genuinely disappointed. 'I was sure he was into you. You should see the way he looks at you when you're not looking. And I don't know what he sees in Melissa – that bitch has got even worse recently. She screamed at me in front of everyone for forgetting to book the meeting room for her yesterday. I hope her next shite's a hedgehog. But you know what, Holly? Screw Alex! And screw Richard, too. As in to hell with them – not as in bone them both. Your trip sounds amazing and you're going to be off tangoing with handsome South American men and flirting outrageously with hot Australian surfers and you'll forget all about the pair of them.'

'I'm not going away to find a man.' I wipe the tears from my cheek with the back of my hand. 'I'm going to—'

'Holly, if you're about to tell me you're going to *find*

yourself I'll punch you in the face and then be sick on you.'

'I wasn't going to say that,' I laugh. 'But I kinda am. I just want to get excited about stuff again, and have new experiences, and do things for me and not for anyone else.'

'You're bound to get laid, though.' She grins. 'Long as you don't cry in front of them.'

'I honestly haven't thought about it.'

We sit in comfortable silence for a moment or two, then I glance sideways at her. 'I'm glad we're OK, Jem. When you didn't reply to my email I was scared you would never talk to me again.'

'Well, considering I've been here for forty-five minutes and you havenae made me tea yet, it's still a distinct possibility.'

I get up and make us some weak tea – I've only one teabag left and just a splash of milk – and return to the living room, where Jemma sits looking thoughtful.

'I need to do it too really,' she says distractedly.

'What?'

'Something. Anything. Just not resign myself to spending every day doing stuff for Martin Cooper.'

'Is that what you do?' I smirk. 'Really?'

'All right, smart-arse. Fine – I don't want to resign myself to spending every day realizing I've forgotten to do stuff for Martin Cooper.'

'You should come with me!'

'Nah, I can't be seen in a bikini until I've lost two stone, and then there's—' She stops abruptly, like she's said too much, and sips her tea.

'Then there's what?' When she doesn't answer I shove

her shoulder lightly, but she continues to drink her tea, so I shove it harder. 'Jemma – tell me. Is it a man?'

'No, not a man exactly.' She averts her eyes downwards, coyly, but the corners of her mouth twitch. 'Danny.'

'Oh my God, I forgot you snogged him. So is that a thing now?'

I pull myself up into a kneeling position, facing her. This is the best distraction I've had in ages, and I realize how much I'll miss Jemma and her love life updates when I'm away.

'Well, it depends what you mean by "thing". We haven't had that conversation yet – so I don't know if we're a couple or anything. But we ended up kissing after the quiz again last week after everyone else had left, and then last night he asked if I fancied going for a drink after work and as soon as he got back to the table after he bought the first round, he kissed me. We hadn't even touched our drinks yet. I can't remember the last time I've kissed anyone sober. That has to mean something, right?'

'Yeah, I'd say so,' I affirm.

'You know it's weird, Holly,' she says slowly, 'but he's the first guy in ages I've just been myself around on a date. I mean, what's the point of me pretending to be cool to Danny? He knows me. And it's the most relaxed I've ever felt with a guy.'

'Jemma, you're VERY cool when you're being yourself. That's why Danny likes you – he knows the real you.'

'Whatever. I'm going to miss you, Holly,' she says, suddenly looking serious. I pull her in for a hug and after a few moments I hear her sniff into my shoulder, like she's about to cry.

303

'No, don't.' I sniff too. 'You'll set me off again.'

'Right, I'm definitely getting out of here before that happens.' She jumps up and drains the last of her tea, before handing me back the mug. 'That tasted like pish by the way.'

'You're welcome.'

'Send me postcards,' she shouts from the gate as I wave her off.

I look at my card properly for the first time, smiling at my former colleagues' farewell messages. There's something from everyone except Richard and Melissa. Richard I get, but what's Melissa's problem? I put the card up onto the mantelpiece, next to three other farewell cards from Leah, Susie and my folks.

Nothing from Alex. As much as I'm so glad Jemma came over, and going away will be a million times easier knowing we're still mates, I allow myself to acknowledge that, for just a split second when I saw her at the door, I was disappointed it wasn't Alex.

Romantic feelings aside, I have never felt more myself since he's been back in my life. It's not like I realized I wasn't being myself – I wasn't trying to pretend to be someone else, like Jemma admitted to doing on her dates. But it's like I forgot who I used to be. I've had such a downer on my days in Mothston because of the way they ended that I never remembered that, for a long time, my teenage years were my happiest years.

Maybe that's the universe's reason for hurtling Alex back into my life – not to stay there, but to remind me of who I was and who I still want to be. It doesn't matter if he doesn't call. It doesn't matter if we lose touch again. It's sad but, let's face it, I'm used to being

304

let down by men in my life. Maybe it's time to start expecting less.

I take out my mobile and glance at it one last time and feel the desperation for it to ring evaporate from my body.

Then it only goes and rings, scaring the bejesus out of me, so that I toss my phone in the air and catch it again.

'Hello?' I gasp at the unknown caller.

'Holly, it's me.'

The voice is male, but it only takes milliseconds to register that it's not the one I'd been hoping for.

'Oh. Hello, Richard.'

The anonymity should have given it away – I've been ignoring his calls since I stormed out of his office. The last one was three days ago and I figured he'd given up.

'How are you?' I ask awkwardly, after a few seconds' silence. It would be easier if I was angry at him. Then I could just tell him to go eff himself and hang up. But I don't feel angry. I just feel really, really stupid. I've replayed our relationship in my head countless times over the last week and I can't believe I let him string me along for that long. He was never going to commit to me.

'Not great. I miss you, Holly.'

'Rich,' I sigh.

'No, hear me out. I have to admit, I was furious with you at first for storming out of my office like that. But I've thought about it and, well, you might have had a point. I'll admit, maybe I have been a bit unfair.'

'That's big of you.' Is it bad if I just hang up and turn my phone off?

'I guess I was embarrassed for people to find out—'

'Why, thanks.'

305

'You know what I mean. Because I'm your boss.'

'WAS my boss.'

'Exactly. Now that everyone knows anyway, and I'm not your boss any more, I really think we can make this work. I love you, Holly.'

Those last words make me take a sharp in-breath. Despite myself, my heart flutters at the words I've been waiting so long for him to say to me.

'It's too late,' I stammer, sliding down the wall and onto the floor. I can feel my temples throbbing so I shut my eyes and rest my forehead on my knees. 'My flight is booked, and I've given up my flat.'

'Bloody hell, Holly. That was quick.'

'I'm organized like that. I'd make a marvellous PA.'

'I'll give you the money for your ticket – and you can come and live with me.'

Why is he saying all this now? When I've been waiting for what seems like for ever to hear some sort of promise of commitment from him, why does he wait until I'm sitting here – wanting something completely different – to tell me he loves me, and he wants to have the sort of relationship I've been trying to have with him all this time.

ARE YOU KIDDING ME, GOD?

Maybe I could go back to being the person I was a few weeks ago, who loved Richard and wanted the life he's promising now. Can I really have changed so much in the last few weeks? Realizing too late what it is that I want seems to be my forte, so what if I get to Bangkok and decide that I've made the biggest mistake of my life?

'Um . . . Holly? You still there?'

'Yeah, I'm here,' I whisper. 'Sorry, Rich – this is a bit

of a headfuck. I need to think about this. Can I call you back?'

'Why don't I come over?' he says quickly. 'We can talk it through and—'

'No,' I interrupt, my voice breaking. 'I need to think about this by myself. I'm just too confused.'

I hang up the phone and burst into tears. I've never cried so much in one day. When did life get so fucking difficult? What happened to the days when I used to just have fun and take things as they come, and when making a wrong decision didn't seem like the worst thing in the world? I give in to the tears, wrapping my arms around my legs and sobbing into my elbow. And I cry and cry, thinking about Richard, and about Alex, and about Max, and even about Dean. I cry until I feel all cried out, and I feel weirdly soothed when I'm done.

I stand up and look around the room, at boxes filled with my stuff, at my passport lying on top of my rucksack with a plane ticket poking out from its pages, at Harold crawling across the mantelpiece and systematically knocking each farewell card onto the floor.

Then I look at my To Do list – with its big headers and multicoloured sub-sections and neat score-throughs and six-month schedule – and rip it up, tossing the scraps back onto the floor.

Chapter Thirty-five

ALEX

It takes several elongated seconds for the doors to wheeze open, but as soon as my feet hit the platform it strikes me. A feeling that causes a smile to dawn across my face. A feeling that I'm home.

'You look rough,' is how Kev greets me, along with a sideways handshake that becomes a hug.

He invites me with a vertical swoosh of his arms to check out his suit. It's dark grey and fits him well. The knot of a racing-green tie is bulbous but straight.

'Selling catalogue goods door to door,' he says self-deprecatingly. 'Hardly the dream, is it?'

I feel a surge of guilt. Have I ever even asked Kev what he dreams of doing?

'It's not for ever, though, eh?' I say, drawing my hands into my sleeves and shivering against the cold weather that arrived this week.

'Who knows? I just want to save enough money for a deposit on a house for me and Diane.'

We navigate through town, past the discount store that used to be Woolworths, and past The White Horse, which is under new management.

'I put my vinyl on eBay. Even Pink Floyd, till she made me take it off.'

'She sounds like a keeper.'

He beams. 'I'm looking forward to you meeting her.'

We take a left up George Street. If we were to follow the road to its end we'd reach the canal where my dad sometimes lives, but in a moment we'll turn right up a street I know better than any other.

'I'm pleased things are coming together for you, mate,' I say, spying a Vauxhall estate parked in the driveway. An anonymous silhouette appears behind new coral curtains in my parents' room. It feels like I've seen an ex-girlfriend holding hands with a new man.

Kev watches me watching my old house. 'You couldn't wait to get away from this place and now look at you, all maudlin at seeing someone else in there.'

I force myself to stop staring and we continue down the street towards Kev's.

'My parents are thinking of finally selling up themselves,' he says. 'They need a few bob now the property boom's over in Spain, so I could be out on my ear. Guess this thing with Diane has happened at the right time.'

It's only when I catch sight of Kev's downstairs curtains, shaded and drawn, that I remember why I'm here. He rotates his key in the front door and I have to try really hard not to give the game away with a grin. He steps inside and, upon turning into the living room and switching on the light, is confronted by dozens of friends and family, most of them wearing masks of Kev's face.

'SURPRISE!'

His expression unchanged by the hullaballoo, he turns to me.

'I see they only invited good-looking people,' he says, and then finally breaks into a toothy smile as everyone laughs and cheers.

I hold out my hand, and this time it's me who turns the shake into a hug. 'Happy birthday, mate.'

'So how's London?' says Rothers.

Both he and Megs have a glaze of awe on their faces. It's obviously affected for my benefit – they're far too happy to feel envy.

'Really good,' I say, hoping that will be enough to satisfy them. I don't want to think about London tonight.

'New job going well?'

'Yep, loving it.'

Megs chips in: 'Got your head round the Underground yet?'

'Not yet,' I say, forcing a laugh. 'But I'm getting there.'

Rothers wants to know if everything is as expensive as they make out. I tell them it is.

'How much is a pint, then?' he persists.

'Depends. You struggle to get a drink for less than four quid.'

They glance at one another, open-mouthed, and I use the pause to excuse myself, telling them I need to get changed and that we'll catch up properly later.

The party has barely started but the bathroom already stinks. I scour shelves and the windowsill for air freshener but find none. Inspecting my face in the mirror, I see that Kev was right – I look rough. My lips are dry and colourless, and a dark wing has formed under each eye. I force a smile, and it produces whiskers

310

of wrinkles on the flanks of my face. They don't fade immediately. I wonder whether my own perception is warped or if this is how people really see me. For the first time in my life I feel old.

I change my shirt and shave and by the time I unlock the door, there is a woman leaning against the landing wall, waiting.

'You must be Alex?' she says, extending her hand, and because she can see that I'm still unsure, she introduces herself. I should have guessed, because if there ever was a girl who matched Kev's type, then Diane is it: petite, blonde and a chest that threatens to rip the torso of her top.

'I've heard a lot about you,' I tell her. She really doesn't look like the kind of girl who collects snow globes.

'Well, don't believe anything that twat says,' she says, releasing the kind of guffaw you might hear in a *Carry On* film.

She slides past me into the bathroom and, just as I'm preparing to navigate a daisy chain of girls sitting on the stairs, yells something about the pong, which she obviously thinks I'm responsible for. I go to explain but am waylaid by Kev.

'Can you believe she did this for me?' he says, choking a little. 'My little Fledermaus.'

'Fledermaus?'

He nods, as if no explanation is required. It's only when he looks up to see my confusion that he adds: 'It's what Germans call bats. It's our pet name.'

I let it go. It wouldn't feel right taking the mickey out of him tonight, not when he's so happy. And Diane really has done him proud, getting all his friends here and decorating the house with photos of Kev as a kid for his embarrassment and our amusement. Right now he is staring at a shot of me and him aged nine or ten, before Holly moved to Mothston. We're holding fishing nets and jam jars.

Kev seems confused. 'What were we doing here?'

'Well, you were wearing a bright green shell suit, for starters.'

'Let's not get started on fashion, Noel. What were the nets and jars for?'

'We were trying to catch ghosts.'

The memory takes a moment to reform in his mind. 'Did we catch any?'

'None at all.'

I take the photo in my hand and wonder how we went from kids catching ghosts to what we are now. I barely recognize myself.

'Diane seems lovely,' I say, trying to forget the photo.

'She is.'

The Kev I once knew would have blushed at such talk but the only emotion displayed on his face is pride.

'Do you know when I realized that I loved her?' he says. It's a rhetorical question. 'I've got this test, and no one has ever passed except Diane.'

'A test?'

'I image their hair falling out. I imagine them bald, and I think to myself, if that happened, would I still want to be with them. And you know what, Al, I would. I'd still want to be with Diane. And if anyone gawped at her shiny head, I'd punch them in the teeth.'

I've never heard Kev talk like this, and I smile affectionately at him as we absorb the party. It doesn't feel so different from the parties people used to throw whenever their parents were out of town. Rothers and Megs are still glued to the sofa, still lost in their own private world after all this time. Even the smells are the same. The whiff of perfume as everyone arrives submitting to the whiff of pastry and meat when the nibbles are served. I expect the smell of spilt lager will soon rule, and by the end of the night we could be holding our noses amid the stench of vomit on carpet.

The thought causes a flashback. The night I gave Holly and Ellie a lift home at 2 a.m. Ellie had been sick and Holly was smitten with Dean Jones. I try to sweep the memory from my mind. I've spent the last week doing everything I can to not think about Holly and I don't want to ruin Kev's night by turning all sombre.

'My dad reckons he'll be here about nine thirty,' I say to sidetrack myself. 'Once his meeting has finished.'

Kev shakes his head, grinning. 'I can't believe he's set up a rebel barge club.'

'He's got three converts already. They're meeting in The Lion.'

We laugh to ourselves, strolling from room to room, taking it all in, and I realize that not everything is the same as when we were teenagers. Someone producing a tray of shots back then would have been received as a hero, but here they're swathed in a groan. And when a Spice Girls song comes on, everyone cheers. I know only one person who would have cheered back then. The skirts are longer too, the handbags bigger and more practical, and no one is trying to get off with anyone, as far as I can surmise.

Everyone asks about London, and each time it becomes

313

harder to lie about everything being rosy. Maybe Kev detects that something is bothering me and that's why he insists on leading me outside. He says he wants to show me the fish pond he has finally built after years of saying he was going to.

We duck under his washing line towards the brick structure that stands two feet high.

'So we've talked about my love life,' he says, pointing out the polyethylene lining, which is apparently less prone to leakage than a combination of brick and sealant. 'What about yours?'

I shiver in the cold. 'How many fish have you got in there?'

'Four. Two koi, two goldfish. How's Melissa?'

'Don't koi eat goldfish?'

'Only if you've got baby goldfish, but Torvill and Dean can look after themselves.'

'Torvill and Dean?'

'They dance, Alex. You want to see it, when they skate together through the water. It's something else.'

I eye him fondly. Perhaps I've been too harsh on him over the years. I guess he's like a pair of shoes that chafed because I wore them every day. I needed to take them off for a bit to realize that, actually, they're pretty comfy. Or maybe it's just Diane's effect. Either way, his life has moved forward since I left Mothston, while mine has regressed.

'Get that look off your face and answer my question, will you?'

'I haven't spoken to Melissa for well over a week.' I feel a spit of rain on my forehead. 'We should go inside.'

Kev doesn't move. 'Why aren't you speaking?'

314

I pause. Kev waits. 'She thinks I've got feelings for Holly.'

'And have you?'

'Why can't I see any fish?'

'They're hiding. They don't like the Spice Girls. Now answer my question.'

We sit on the side of the pond and, unable to fob him off any longer, it all comes spilling out. Kev says nothing for ages, his chin resting on a fist.

'Didn't you, you know, ask her not to go?'

When I fail to offer an answer, Kev opens his arms as if what he's about to say is obvious. 'You're a stupid twathead, you know that?'

'You don't know anything about it, Kev.'

'I know Holly likes you.'

I stand up, scratching the back of my neck in frustration. 'You know that she likes me?'

'She told me.'

I reject his words with a laugh. 'And when did she tell you that, exactly?'

'In the pub when I came down to London. She told me she was jealous of you and Melissa.'

I turn away from him, grabbing the washing line and leaning into it with my weight until it is taut.

'You're talking shit, mate.'

'I saw it with my own eyes, Alex. I saw it in her face. I'm telling you, Holly's got feelings for you.'

'Then why did she come around to say she wanted to go travelling?'

'Have you thought about the possibility that she wanted you to give her a reason not to go?'

I release the line and return to the pond.

'Why are there so many plants in there?'

'They shade the water, stop algae getting out of control. And they soak up toxins so Torvill and Dean and Reggie and Ronnie don't choke to death.'

Kev doesn't blink or avert his eyes from mine.

'As if I'd turn her down.'

Kev lets a shrug do his talking. *OK, if you say so*, it says.

'She knows what's what,' I argue. 'She knows I love her. It's frigging obvious.'

Again Kev says nothing, redirecting his attention towards the kitchen window, through which Diane can be seen holding a can of lager that is foaming through the pull tab. It must have gone everywhere because everyone in the kitchen is cheering.

'It's exactly the same as sixth form. Holly coming around to tell me that we won't see each other for ages, buggering off, forgetting all about yours truly.'

Kev's face turns sharply towards mine. 'Things aren't always what they seem, mate.'

'What's that supposed to mean?'

He looks into the pond, pointing at something with his index finger, his arm moving with the flow of whatever it is I'm supposed to be looking at. All I can see is a ripple on the surface of the water.

'It's like "New York, New York". Sometimes it comes on and I smile, but before Sinatra pipes up I realize it's not "New York, New York" at all, it's the theme from *Steptoe*.'

I cover my eyes with my hands, wearily drawing my fingers down my face, stretching the skin so that I must resemble a sad clown.

'What I'm saying is, she came around to see you be-

316

fore university and you spoke about whatever you spoke about, but I'm not sure your recollection of that day would chime with Holly's.'

I'm getting angry now and struggling to hide it. What the fuck does he know about what happened back then? There was only me and Holly in that room.

'I think you should just shut up, Kev. You're talking about stuff you know nothing about.'

'No, mate, you should listen for once in your life, because I know more than you think, and I've never said anything because I promised Holly I wouldn't, but, clearly, as neither of you is ever going to be honest with each other, I think it's time . . .'

Chapter Thirty-six

HOLLY

September 1999

I sit shaking in the passenger seat while Kev drums his fingers on his steering wheel. Eventually I pull down the visor to look in the mirror. Tears have made track lines in the powder on my cheeks and ugly black mascara smudges around my eyes. Wild strands of hair are clamped to my forehead with sweat and I notice that the right-hand side of my collar is higher than the left. I tug on the bottom of my shirt. The left side is longer. I've done my buttons back up wrong.

Pulling out a hairband from my handbag, I pile my hair messily on top of my head, securing it tightly.

Kev glances at me, then reaches across me and opens the glove box, grabbing a box of tissues and dropping them gently onto my lap.

'So,' he says, after I've wiped my face, 'are you going to tell me what's going on?'

I was much drunker, and much happier, a couple of hours earlier.

'I love this song,' squealed Ellie as the sound of 'A Little Bit of Luck' made its way from the house into the garden. She grabbed my hands and pulled me to my feet, singing and spilling my plastic cup of Turbo Shandy over the grass.

Several others joined us dancing and three minutes of watching the boys pull their best garage moves made me collapse in laughter on the ground again.

'Oh, don't go to university,' Ellie whined at me for the hundredth time, sitting down next to me. 'I'll miss you.'

'I'll miss you too,' I laughed, pointing at her drunkenly. Her mum and stepdad are visiting friends in Sheffield, so Ellie offered to throw an end-of-summer party before everyone either gets jobs or goes to uni. 'But you can come and stay with me in London. And I'll be back to Mothston loads to see you and Dean, and everyone else.'

'So are you and Dean going to do the long-distance thing or what?' she asked.

'Dunno.' It was true – I didn't. Who knew how either of us would feel once we were separated? No point worrying about it, I thought. What will be will be. 'We'll see what happens.'

'Still thinking of shagging him before you go, though?'

'Yeah,' I giggled shyly.

'About time – you've been a virgin, like, *for ever.*'

Ellie's been with four different boys since she lost her virginity a year ago. None of them boyfriends.

'Talk of the devil . . . *Dean*! Over here!'

Dean had wandered out into the garden and strolled over at Ellie's holler.

'Well, I'll leave you lovebirds to it,' she said, springing

319

to her feet. 'Oh, and feel free to go hang out in the spare room if you want some privacy.'

She winked mega-unsubtly, making me blush and Dean laugh, and sauntered off into the house.

'Holly?' Kev's face is a mixture of concern and impatience, and I realize I've been sitting here just staring out of the window for ages. So I lean my head against the glass and start to talk.

We were kissing for ages in the bedroom. His breath tasted of cigarettes and beer, and it was making me queasy. I kept waiting for a feeling – some kind of urge that made me want to do more than just kiss. But it never came. I felt nervous and tired. And it hit me. I didn't want to do this.

'Dean?'

'God, you're beautiful,' he mumbled against my neck.

'Do you think we could just cuddle or something?'

'Sure,' he breathed, pulling me closer and holding me there. Then his hands started roaming over my body.

'Dean, wait.'

'Holly, trust me,' he whispered into my ear. 'When you want to stop, just say stop.'

He covered my mouth with his. I felt suffocated.

'Dean, I—'

'Just relax,' he said, starting to unbutton my black silk shirt clumsily. I covered his hand with mine to stop him but he pinned my arm above my head and carried on with one hand, tugging at the last button, making it ping off and land on the floor.

'Oops,' he laughed, breathlessly. Then he began squeezing my boobs, alternating between the two. I tried to get into it – I'd quite liked the times his hands had slipped under my bra when we'd been kissing before – but this was different. It felt weird. It made my stomach clench and a wave of nausea run through me that felt nothing to do with how much I'd drunk.

'Dean,' I whispered again. I could hear voices on the landing outside the room. One of the boys was reciting the instructions of a drinking game. I didn't want anyone to hear what was going on. 'I really don't think I can—'

'Shhhh,' he breathed gently, burying his head in my chest. 'You're so sexy, Holly.' His hand was up my denim skirt and on my knickers now and he pulled them halfway down my thighs. 'You'll enjoy it if you relax.'

His hand crept back up, his fingers searching. I tried to relax. I felt guilty. I'd made Dean think I was ready. I'd come into the bedroom with him and let him kiss me and touch me. But his touch was clumsy and it wasn't making me feel good at all.

'Dean, maybe we should stop – it doesn't feel right,' I hissed, as a girl on the landing wailed 'I *still* don't get it,' while four or five others laughed, and the boy started to repeat the rules.

'Shhh,' he repeated. 'Stop acting like such a kid, Holly.'

Was he right? Was I acting like a kid? Maybe it was meant to feel like this the first time.

But when I heard him undo his zip my body numbed with fear.

'Dean, I don't want to do this.' I pressed my palms on his chest and gently pushed. 'Please, can we stop?'

What came next is a blur. The brief relief that his hand had moved away, a chorus of voices chanting 'Down it, down it, down it' outside the door, my anger being replaced by fear, a sharp pain. I let my body go limp, and I stopped trying to push him away.

I don't tell Kev everything. Just a summary. And when I'm done I turn to look at him for the first time. His eyes are the size of tea plates and he opens his mouth like he wants to say something, but no words come out. I don't know why I told him. Kev and I have never been that close and I never would have confided in him about anything before. But I needed to tell someone, and from the moment I climbed into his car I felt that if Alex trusted Kev, then so could I.

Kev turns away from me, instead staring ahead through his windscreen. He clutches his steering wheel like he's driving, even though the engine is turned off.

'Shit, Holly. You mean he—'

'No, no. I mean – I don't know.' I sigh, rubbing my temples.

'Do you want me to call the police?'

'God, no. I wouldn't even know what to say, how to explain it properly.'

'Do you want me to go in there and beat the shit out of him?'

I smile slightly for the first time. 'No, that's OK.'

'You *sure* you don't want me to kick his arse?'

I nod. Then I put my face in my hands and cry. Kev lets me, stretching his arm out to pat my shoulder awkwardly from his seat, but not coming any closer.

'Oh, Kev, I'm such a fucking idiot. Why was I even there? Dean doesn't give a shit about me. None of them does.'

'If you're waiting for me to disagree that your mates are all a bunch of cocksuckers,' Kev says after a pause, 'then forget it.'

'I'm not.' I sigh. 'And they're not my mates. Not any more.'

'Hey, whoever is being sick in there, it better be in the loo,' Ellie had yelled, banging hard on the door.

I wiped my mouth and got up to open the door, locking it again once Ellie was inside.

'Oh, it's you. Bloody hell, Hols – you look terrible.'

I was about to answer when a fresh wave of nausea hit me and I bent over the loo again, heaving heavily, until there was nothing left in me, and it was just stomach bile I was spitting into the bowl.

'It's not like you to spew,' Ellie laughed, holding my hair back. 'That's my party trick.'

Confident there was nothing left to bring up, I pulled down the toilet seat and sat on it, holding my head in my hands.

Ellie zipped open a make-up bag on the bathroom shelf and began applying bronzer at the mirror above the sink.

'Soooo,' she smirked. 'Did you and Dean do it or what?'

I looked up at her and tried to work out what to say. Ordinarily, I'd be pointing out that she was putting far too much bronzer on and was changing ethnicity in front of my eyes, but it seemed a bit irrelevant at that point.

'Kind of,' I whispered.

'Kind of?' she cackled, dropping the bronzer back in the bag and pulling out a lipstick. 'Either you did or you didn't. Urgh, you didn't puke on him, did you?'

323

I shook my head.

'Did he get it all the way in?'

'Yes, he did. That's not what I meant by kind of.' I took a deep breath. 'I didn't *want* to.'

'Yes you did, I saw you go into the room together.'

'I know, but I told him I wasn't ready. Ellie I . . . I said no. I told him to stop.'

I watched her in the mirror to see her reaction. Her hand froze at her mouth for a split second, but then she carried on gliding the pale pink lipstick over her lips.

'Did you hear me? He—'

'I don't really see what your problem is,' she said, spinning around to look at me and clicking the lid back on the lipstick.

'What do you mean?'

'So you had it off with your boyfriend. Big deal. It hurts a bit the first time. But it gets better after that. I should know, I've done it four times.'

'But I didn't want to do it.'

'So what – are you saying he raped you?'

'I'm not sure.'

'Holly, Dean Jones is *fit*. He could have any girl here. He doesn't need to rape anyone. If you're regretting doing it with him, then get over it. You had to lose it at some point.'

'Ellie!'

'What? I don't know what you expected me to say.' She sounded irritated. 'You're just wasted.'

She turned on her heel to leave.

'Oh, and make sure you don't get sick on the carpet, yeah?' she said on her way out of the door. 'My mum'll *kill* me.'

'Alex is my only real friend, you know,' I tell Kev.

'Yeah, well. That kid would do anything for you.'

'I know. And that's why I need to see him. I need to tell him how I feel.'

'What do you mean?'

I left the bathroom and stumbled downstairs, ignoring everyone, and walked out of the house, without saying goodbye to anyone.

I needed to get home. My default setting meant I was soon punching Alex's number into the mobile that Dad had bought Mum a week earlier and that Mum had passed on to me, huffily declaring that she never went anywhere anyway. The thought of seeing Alex was like an unexpected beacon of light in a big void of shitness.

I wanted him there so much that I ached.

He looks after me. Makes me laugh. Makes me feel safe, and happy. That's what I love about him.

I love Alex.

I love him so much it makes my insides hurt.

Why don't I just tell him instead of playing this stupid game with these losers? They act to the rest of the school like we're a big bunch of best friends, but behind each other's backs they're all slagging each other off and getting off with each other's boyfriends.

Alex is the only person I trust, and the only person who matters to me, and I need to see him now.

It rang. No answer. Come on, Al, pick up, I prayed silently. I let it ring out, then I tried again.

Still no answer.

My eyes welled up with frustration. He'd never not answered before. He once told me that, if he knew I was out, he moved the phone right next to his ear so that he'd definitely hear it ring if he was asleep.

Kev! I figured he must be with him, and Kev had just got a mobile too, thank God. I scrolled through my numbers and hit call.

'Hello,' came the groggy reply.

'Hey, it's Holly.'

'Holly?' He didn't conceal his surprise at me calling him. 'What's up?'

'Is Alex with you?'

'Ah ha,' he said, almost happily. 'Nope, 'fraid not.'

'Oh, shit.' My voice broke. 'I really need him, Kev.'

'What's wrong? Are you pissed?'

'No, it's not that,' I sobbed into the phone. 'Something's happened and I . . . I just really need Alex.'

'Jesus, Holly. Where are you?'

'I've just left Ellie's – I'm on the corner of her road. But I can't go back in and . . . I just need Alex.'

'Right, stay where you are, I'm coming to get you. I know where Ellie lives – I can be there in less than ten minutes.'

'I need to tell him how I feel,' I repeat.

'You're pissed,' Kev shakes his head. 'And your head is messed up after what happened tonight.'

'I'm not – I've puked up every last drop I drank, and my head's never been clearer. There's no one I'd rather spend time with, or who I look forward to seeing as much, or who I'd rather tell stuff to. I've felt this way for ages.'

326

'Then why are you going out with Dean?'

I flinch at the sound of his name.

The truth is, he made me feel special. Like Ellie says, he could have anyone, and he chose me. I felt lucky.

'I thought he was cool,' I whisper croakily, shrugging, feeling ashamed.

Kev shakes his head and looks out of his window.

'Please don't say anything about this to Alex,' I beg. 'I need to tell it to him in my own way. Kev? Please promise me you'll never tell Alex we had this conversation?'

'Why don't you let me tell him?' he says, turning back round to look at me. 'It'll be less embarrassing for everyone. Then if he wants to call you and reciprocate he can, but if he doesn't—'

Kev doesn't finish but his unsaid words hang in the air. Does he know Alex isn't interested? Is that why he doesn't want me to make a fool of myself?

'Thanks, Kev,' I say, more decisively than I feel. 'But I really think I need to tell him myself.'

'Fine,' he says grumpily, starting the engine. 'But don't try calling him again tonight because if he does feel the same you'll only go and break the little fucker's heart if you wake up tomorrow and realize you just want to be friends.'

'Fine,' I say, leaning back into the seat and letting my eyelids flutter sleepily shut. 'I promise. But I won't change my mind.'

'We'll see.' He purses his lips doubtfully. 'Right, let me take you home.'

*

When I wake up the next morning, I feel different.

Admittedly not the kind of different I was planning for. Not the happy/spring-in-my-step/seeing-the-world-through-new-eyes type different.

But I know what I need to do.

Chapter Thirty-seven

ALEX

September 2010

I wait on platform one at Mothston Station. The cafe hasn't opened yet and the shutters are still down at the ticket kiosk. For about ten minutes I am totally alone, with only the words that Kev uttered last night for company.

At first I was angry. How could he have kept something like that from me all these years? But later, as I tried and failed to find sleep on his sofa, I realized he was just doing what was right by Holly. The real nobhead was me for not being there for her when she needed me the most. Me and Dean fucking Jones. Fury swells inside me at the thought of what he did. No wonder she never came back to Mothston; no wonder the adult Holly I met when I first moved to London wasn't the same carefree one I knew back at school.

After about ten minutes of waiting alone, an overweight pigeon executes a clumsy landing onto the concrete, and a memory that had faded becomes vivid once more: waiting for my first and only date with Fiona the vegetarian right here at the station a few months ago.

Remembering what I saw back then, I walk along the platform towards the entrance area. I don't know why I care but I do. Once inside, I look up to the glass ceiling and the faecal universe that I noticed for the first time nine months ago, but it is not there. The ceiling has been cleaned. I stand there, staring through the glass at the clear morning sky, thinking about the day Holly came to see me before university, about how I blew the chance for us to be together.

At York I board a train to King's Cross and find a seat with no one else around. Tiredness creeps up on me as the train begins to roll down the country, and after a stop at Doncaster I find a toilet where I splash water on my face before examining my dripping skin in the mirror. How different would my life have been if I'd known back then how Holly felt? If I had not taken Kev's advice to 'get absent' and not ignored the phone when it rang that night? Would Holly and I be like Rothers and Megs, still sickeningly happy? Would there be a collection of little Alex and Hollys?

It doesn't matter now. That's all in the past and today is about my future. Our future.

She'll be confused at first, of course. But the look on my face will tell her why I'm there. And if it doesn't I'll tell her straight: *I love you, Holly Gordon*. We'll hold one another, right there on her doorstep, and then we'll go inside and talk, and I'll apologize for everything, for trying to make her jealous of Jane when she came to tell me how she felt, for not listening when she needed me to listen, and for making exactly the same mistakes again a week ago. I construct a monologue in my mind, tweaking and deleting and starting over as the blurred greens and browns of the countryside pass by my window.

I'm not sure how much time has elapsed when I'm startled by a hand on my shoulder. I open my eyes and realize that I'd fallen asleep. The train is stationary and the only person left in my carriage is a pencil-shaped man wearing a blue uniform. I examine his name badge and see that he is Michael, the train manager.

'Our destination,' says Michael, tilting his head and looking out of the window onto the platform.

I apologize and collect my bag, and then rub the sleep from my eyes as I make my way through King's Cross. Although it's still relatively early, there are so many people around, here in London, on a Saturday morning, and none of them knows who I am or what I'm about to do. As I take a seat on the Northern Line, part of me is desperate for someone to make eye contact, to initiate a conversation, so that I can confide everything. But of course no one does. This isn't Mothston. Things are different down here.

An overground train takes me the final leg to Black-heath, where I swipe my Oyster card against the yellow circle and begin to make my way down the high street. It's a nice area – a little village within London with a huge heath at its heart that means it doesn't feel as clogged as most of the city. I can see why Holly likes living here.

Spotting a bucket of sunflowers for sale on the pave-ment, I act on instinct and hand over a tenner to the

331

man in the shop before resuming my walk, feeling my heart thump. I take a deep breath as I wait to cross the road, reminding myself of what Kev told me last night. Holly loves me. She always has. It doesn't make me any less nervous.

The days that change everything usually pass you by. You don't realize they changed everything until afterwards. Like that day in The Lion when Dad revealed he was buying a boat, or when Holly came around to see me before leaving for uni. But right now, as I'm living this day, I know it is going to change my life for ever.

I wait for a black cab to pass and cross the road before making my way onto Montpellier Row. Holly's road. To my right is a hotel with letters missing from its sign. The Clarend n Ho el. That's kind of what this is. I've come to find my missing letters.

My hands are trembling as I leave the pavement and step onto the pathway that leads to Holly's flat. I stop for a second, take another deep breath and place my finger on the doorbell. No going back now.

The heat of the morning sun on my back is a reminder that winter is still a month or two away. Though it is warmer than yesterday, my teeth chatter, and my mind has emptied of any coherent thoughts. Suddenly I'm not able to summon all the sentences I'd constructed during the journey, and though my heart is thumping and my hands are shaking and my teeth are chattering and a sweat has started to consume my body, it doesn't matter. I know everything is going to be OK.

I hear footsteps and a hand on the door. I lift the sunflowers from my side ready to hand over in case I cannot find any words. I don't think I've ever felt this nervous in my life, even though it's Holly. The lovely, kind, beautiful, free spirit that is . . .

The door opens. It is not Holly.

Standing before me is a man wearing a sleeveless jumper and shirt. Like me, he seems confused. We stare at one another for a few seconds.

'Alex . . .'

'Mr Gordon . . .'

I realize that Mr Gordon has been holding out his hand for me to shake since he opened the door. I offer a limp shake, looking behind him for a sight of Holly.

'It's good to see you, Alex, but if it's Holly you've come to see then I'm afraid you've just this second missed her.' Mrs Gordon comes to the door, smears of mascara around her eyes. Mr Gordon puts a comforting arm around her shoulder. 'She left in a black cab a few minutes ago,' he says. 'We're about to leave ourselves, once we've got Harold in her cat box.'

My mind struggles to compute what is going, and all I can think to say is: 'Where are you taking Harold?'

Mrs Gordon releases a heavy sob, burying her face into her husband's shoulder.

'Did Holly not tell you she was going travelling?' says Mr Gordon.

The excitement and the anxiety that I have felt since I found out Holly loved me last night is suddenly replaced by total panic. It never even crossed my mind that she would be setting off so soon.

'Which airport?' I say, retreating back from the doorstep.

I am not sure whether I thank Mr Gordon for his help or not. I'm back on Montpellier Row, looking around for a black cab to take me to Heathrow, and when one pulls up a few minutes later and I take my seat in the back, I say a silent thank-you to the sky.

'Which terminal, pal?'

The driver adjusts the volume on his radio to a low thrum, sets the meter and begins to accelerate in first gear. After a few seconds he looks in his rear-view mirror, requiring an answer. A smile hatches from my lips at the ridiculousness of the situation, at my life becoming a romantic comedy.

'I'll find out on the way.'

I realize what this means: I'm going to have to call Holly to ask what terminal she is flying from, and although this falls more into comedy than romantic, it's OK. I can tell her I'm coming to the airport and that I'll explain everything when I get there.

I clutch my mobile, hand still trembling, and force myself to do it. I press my thumb against her name and the line is quiet for what seems like a month as the satellites and masts do their bit. The driver changes gear and the engine relaxes. My heart is pounding. Finally the call engages.

It has not been possible to connect your call, please try again later.

I end the call and resolve to try again once we're nearer the airport. There's plenty of time.

The driver's eyes alternate between the road and his mirror once again.

'Going anywhere nice?' he says, and I'm grateful for the distraction from the excitement and anxiety that have returned.

'Just meeting someone, actually,' I answer, placing the phone back in my pocket.

'The missus, is it?'

I smile at the thought. 'Not yet, but I'm optimistic.'

We join a bridge flanked by the slate-grey flow of the Thames. To our right is the Palace of Westminster. At the end of the bridge we take a left towards South Kensington.

'So,' the driver resumes, 'this girl worth all the trouble, is she?'

I think again of the last five months, of our hands touching in the pub, of her singing in the park, of her foot sliding across the sofa. But I don't get a chance to answer.

'My ex-wife wasn't,' he says, then uses his tongue to amputate a bit of food from between his front teeth. 'I smelt men's aftershave on her one time and you know what she said? She said it was because she'd popped into Boots.'

I try to maintain an appearance of mild interest while remembering how it felt to finally kiss her. I call Holly again.

'Can you believe that? She tried to tell me that she was looking to buy me some new aftershave. It would have been the first time in twenty years.'

It has not been possible to connect your call, please try again later.

'Like I say, you're often best off without them.' The driver accelerates along a slip road and onto the motorway, but no sooner have we picked up speed than we have to slow to a near halt because of traffic. 'You know the biggest difference between men and women?' The taxi is now at a standstill, allowing the driver to stare into his mirror in anticipation of a reply.

'Why aren't we moving?'

'Folded towels.' The driver's reflected eyes home in on mine, expecting curiosity. 'Women want all the towels in the house to be folded, and men don't give a toss.'

I imagine living with Holly. It would probably be me complaining about the unfolded towels.

Pulling the phone from my pocket once again, I compose a text to Holly.

'Is traffic usually like this?'

'I'm surprised she didn't mention it on the divorce papers – distress caused from unfolded towels.'

I force myself to sit back. 'Do you think there has been some kind of accident? Why else would we not be moving at this time on a Saturday morning?'

Another chortle. 'You're not from around here, are you?'

I glance at the sky, where a dark cumulonimbus is prowling like a playground bully. Fifteen minutes go by and still there is no reply from Holly.

'How far is the nearest train station?' I say, worried that Holly will soon be checking in.

'Southall, probably.' The driver sniffs, pointing at a line of oak trees that border the carriageway. 'About a mile and a half, as the crow flies. But you're a human, not a crow, so you're going to have to walk to the next junction and then go back on yourself. Take you about forty-five minutes, I'd say.'

Forty-five minutes to get to the station, less if I run; plus another fifteen on the train – and that's if it comes straight away. But I don't even know what terminal I need. Why isn't she replying? Even if this isn't what she wants, surely she'd respond, telling me not to come? I decide to wait it out in the cab, praying that Holly is stuck in traffic too.

I close my eyes and rest my face in my hands, resolving not to look up until I feel the car in motion again. I'm not sure how long has passed when I become aware of a traffic report on the radio.

'Turn it up, please,' I say, opening my eyes.

The driver adjusts the volume. Something about a lorry shedding its load. Reports of frozen vegetables strewn across both carriageways. Police hoping to reopen the motorway in approximately an hour. I suppress a scream of frustration and get out of the cab to see for myself the line of static traffic stretching as far as my eyes can see. I examine the colours and the shapes of the cars in each of the three lanes but nowhere can I see another black cab that might be taking Holly to the airport.

In the sky to my right I notice a passenger plane in ascent. It vanishes behind a tower block, reappearing a second later trailed by a worm of white smog, its progress appearing laboured from this distance. I tell myself that Heathrow is one of the busiest airports in the world, that hundreds of flights take off from its runways every day, that the chances of Holly being on board this plane are negligible, but it still feels as though the pilot and his crew are taking a part of me with them into the clouds: hope.

I get the urge to smash something, to let out all my frustration at having fucked everything up again, and the only thing to hand is the sunflowers. When I'm done

I sink to my knees on the hard shoulder and realize that everyone in the traffic jam will go home tonight and tell their husbands and wives about the crazy man who obliterated a bunch of flowers against the tarmac. Then I well up because while they're doing that I'll be alone when I should be with Holly. I try one more desperate time to call her but the cold, officious voice confirms what I already know: that life is not like a romantic comedy; that I am too late and it's all my own fault; and that this, after all, is not going to be the day that changes everything.

Text from Alex to Holly

I'm on my way to the airport. I love you and I'm sorry. Will explain everything when I get there xx

Text from Alex to Holly

PS what terminal are you at? xx

Text from Alex to Holly

Stuck in a jam on M4. What time is your flight? xx

Chapter Thirty-eight

HOLLY

I like children. A lot. That said, if the toddler sitting behind me continues to kick my chair for the entire duration of the flight, she's getting sold to child traffickers during the stop-off in Abu Dhabi.

I should embrace the distraction, really. Because as long as I'm focusing on that, then I'm not focusing on the fact I'm about to embark on a voyage, on my own, with no concrete plan, for an undetermined amount of time.

'Ladies and gentlemen, this is your captain speaking. On behalf of the crew I ask that you please direct your attention as we review the emergency procedures. There are six emergency exits on this aircraft . . .'

My eyes flick hungrily to the emergency exits. Why? I (mentally) slap myself around the face and (physically) relax my body into my seat. I want to do this thing.

Even though I was all 'WHAT THE BLOODY HELL AM I DOING?' the whole time I was tearing up my travel plan, I kept on shredding it until the pieces were too small to contemplate sticking back together again.

After I had hung up on Richard without telling him

categorically that it was over between us, and without insisting I was definitely, 100 per cent going travelling, I could have died of self-loathing.

Why was I even on the verge of contemplating trading in my imminent travelling adventure for domestic co-habitation, just because the potential cohabiter had snapped his fingers?

The realization I'd drifted so far from who I used to be scared me. Life was fun when I was spontaneous and happy-go-lucky but somewhere along the line I developed an irrational need to be in control. And the real killer is, when I look back over the last few years, I've never been less in control of my life.

Even though deep down I've always known my desperation to escape Mothston and the people in it was tied up with that awful night with Dean Jones, it wasn't him I blamed for it. It was me – for letting myself get in that situation in the first place. Dean shouldn't have done it, and Ellie shouldn't have made me think it was all my fault, but it was never them I hated.

Admittedly, I did derive a SMALL amount of satisfaction from hearing through Mum that Dean resents his job cold-calling to sell conservatories nearly as much as he resents his unemployed, live-in girlfriend. And likewise, when Mum mentioned a couple of years ago that she'd run into Ellie's aunt, who revealed that Ellie had been diagnosed with irreversible bowel incontinence, I found a TINY bit of pleasure knowing that she sometimes shits herself in public.

That's not HATE, though.

I was the one I really blamed.

That's why I'm not sorry Alex came back into my life,

340

even though I got hurt. He brought out the person I used to be. And on reflection, she was a better version of me.

And so I know what I'm doing now is a good thing. It's how I always said I'd do it one day. I never wanted a step-by-step itinerary, or adventures with deadlines that I can tick off once they're done. I'll go where my mood takes me, and stay as long as I'm enjoying it and leave when I'm ready for something new. And I'll come home when I'm ready – whether that's one month, six months or five years.

So I won't be rushing for the emergency exit before take-off, because my fear is etched with something else. Something I don't think I've experienced properly for a long, long time. Excitement. The scary kind that comes from not knowing what's in store. The excitement I felt as a kid when my folks were taking me to Spain and I had no idea what would be there, and where I'd be sleeping, and who I'd meet. Or when I sent off my UCAS form with my university choices, and I knew I was committing to living somewhere new with people I didn't know and doing things I'd never done before, but I didn't know where, who or what.

I've got my first three nights booked at a hostel in Bangkok, and a vague plan to spend Christmas Day in Aus with Jess, my uni mate, but other than that . . . WHO THE HELL KNOWS?

I lean back and close my eyes, smiling slightly to myself, until a forceful thud on the back of my headrest sends my head catapulting forward, making me sigh.

I turn and peer over the top of my seat at her mum, with a mildly irritated look on my face, then turn back round.

That'll teach her.

'Ladies and gentlemen, as you may have noticed, we've just turned on the Fasten Seat Belt sign. If you haven't already done so, please stow your carry-on luggage underneath the seat in front of you or in an overhead locker. Could you please take your seat and fasten your seat belt?'

Right, Holly. This shit just got real.

I slide my seat belt into its clasp and close my eyes again, thinking about what my taxi driver said earlier.

'The problem with the world,' he'd asserted emphatically, meeting my eyes in the rear-view mirror, 'is that everyone's in such a rush to get somewhere that they forget to enjoy the journey.'

Granted, he was talking about the traffic – he'd passed a massive accident on the other side of the motorway on his way to collect me and the road was a bumper-to-bumper assembly of honking horns and angry shouts, apparently.

But really, it's a metaphor for life, isn't it? What's that wanky bollocks everyone always says? 'Life is what happens while you're busy making other plans' – that's it. That's the thing with wanky bollocks – there's usually some truth in it.

Anyway, it's lucky the taxi driver knew about that accident on the motorway – I could have still been sitting on his back seat right now if he hadn't known to take a detour. Instead, I'm just minutes away from a completely fresh start.

'Ladies and gentlemen, we'll shortly be making our ascent. Please can we ask you to make sure your window blinds are open and your table trays are in the upright position for take-off? Please turn off all personal electronic devices, including laptops and mobile phones.'

Well ahead of you, Captain. My phone has been off since I left my flat. I spent all last night on the phone promising to look after myself (Leah), promising to get stoned in an Australian hippy town called Nimbin (Susie) and promising to stay in touch with news of any men I meet/fancy/see naked (Jemma). No word from Alex. I wondered whether I should call him, to say goodbye. And I almost did – I had my finger on the call button. But then my folks turned up early and I had to sit with them promising to buy a bum bag for my valuables (Dad) and to get out of the bloody dark ages and join Facebook so I can update my status and post some photos (Mum – she's got nineteen friends, apparently).

I couldn't face calling him today – I have to look forward, not back – and I couldn't bear the disappointment of constantly checking my screen to see if he'd called, and seeing he hadn't. So I turned it off as soon as I got into the taxi.

It felt meaningful at the time but a bit stupid now. Should I check it quickly now as it's my last chance?

I glance at the cabin-crew lady doing her final checks. She's trying to squeeze a duffel coat into a packed overhead locker a few rows in front, so I pull my BlackBerry out of my bag and turn it on, waiting for the screen to load up. A few seconds later it starts vibrating, and notifications of six missed calls and three text message appear. Crikey.

The first call is from Richard. Oh God, I forgot to call

him back. I'm a terrible person. Actually, no I'm not – see how he likes playing the waiting game. For months now I've sat by waiting for whatever affection he decides to throw my way, whenever and wherever it suits him – honoured that it's me he chose to give it to. I can't believe I nearly got sucked back into that yesterday. I felt so disgustingly grateful that he was telling me he loves me and offering me a place to live that I almost forgot I don't want his ridiculous, conditional, narcissistic love in his shiny, characterless bachelor pad anyway.

Nor do I, Harold concurred when I said that out loud to her. I didn't have the heart to tell her I wasn't entirely sure whether she was even invited.

The remaining five calls are from . . . Alex.

I suck my breath in and click into my messages.

Alex.

Alex.

Alex.

'Hi, folks. We're now ready to depart. Could all members of the cabin crew please start making their way towards their own seats, ready for take-off?'

What does Alex want? After a week of radio silence, he decides in my last hour in the country that he really needs to contact me? After a week of me hoping he'd call. A week of me trying to work out what I'd say if he did.

I click on the first text message, and take a sharp breath – my annoyance at his timing turning into something else. Something I can't quite describe.

I click on the second message. My heart is palpitating like I've just taken three Pro-Plus and washed them down with a can of Red Bull.

344

'Can you put your bag under the seat in front of you, please?' The cabin-crew lady, suddenly beside me, makes me jump. 'And *that* needs to be turned off now.'

Clicking into the third message, I stare at the words.

'Is there a problem?' she says impatiently. Her tone snaps me back to reality and I shake my head.

'No,' I whisper, turning off my phone and slipping it into the back of the seat in front of me with trembling hands.

She pauses, peering at my face, which I'm pretty sure is devoid of colour.

'Are you feeling OK?' she asks, her tone warmer, her face registering concern.

'Yeah,' I mumble, as my mind processes those three words from Alex. The three words I've been waiting to hear from Alex since that rainy September, eleven years ago. 'I feel fine.' I force a smile. 'Thanks.'

She nods, then continues quickly down the aisle to complete her final checks, before walking briskly back to her own seat and strapping herself in.

And I do feel fine, I realize, as the plane makes its bumpy journey across the runway.

I feel different somehow, I acknowledge, as it lifts smoothly up off the ground, and heads towards the clouds. But I feel fine.

Chapter Thirty-nine

ALEX

October 2011

I pull the book from my satchel and hold it aloft for the class to see.

'Who can tell me what *Romeo and Juliet* is about?'

Bhumi Khan folds her blazer tightly across her front and then raises her arm. Three or four others follow suit.

'Not seen it,' answers Gareth Stones, who isn't one of the three or four. Slumped into his chair, his body is almost linear.

I ignore him. 'Bhumi?'

'It's a love story, isn't it?' she answers. 'DiCaprio and Danes get it on.'

Stacey Bamber looks at Bhumi as if she's just farted. 'Danes and DiCaprio both die, fool. It's about not always getting what you want.'

Stacey nods, satisfied with her answer.

'You're both right,' I adjudicate. 'It's a love story and a tragedy, but at its heart it's a story of two feuding gangs. The Montagues and the Capulets.'

Gareth's eyes awaken for a second, but he immediately remembers his disinterest. Which is fine. Holly was right: I was concentrating on the wrong half. Gareth is never going to read Shakespeare in his time or mine. My strategy now is to hold the attention of as many of the others as possible by making the syllabus relevant to their lives. If the work interests them, it follows that Gareth won't have a captive audience for his juvenility. This is how I'll articulate it in my interview next week.

I circulate copies of the play. Gareth has a query.

'Yes, Gareth?'

'Is it true that Mr Rodgers is nailing Ms Pritchard?'

Bhumi gasps, then covers her open mouth with her palm. There are sniggers, but most of the class is rapt, eager for my response.

'Gareth, I'll be happy to have a discussion on nailing when I'm confident you know anything about it.'

Gareth's face turns crimson amid the guffaws of his classmates. He cannot seem to muster a comeback, and I worry that I've gone too far. What if he submits a complaint to Mr Cotton? He'll never appoint me Head of English then.

I review the clock above the door. Five minutes until we can all go home. My thoughts once again start to linger on what lies ahead tonight when Gareth straightens himself.

'I guess we can discuss it now, then,' he says, scratching his armpit. 'Seeing as I've been nailing your mum.'

The room falls into a silence punctuated only by the whistle of the autumn wind through the tall conifers adjacent to the gym. I haven't yet formulated a response of my own when Kenny rises to his feet, slowly but purposefully, and strides towards Gareth. I know instantly that I

347

need to intervene, but it's as though I'm in a dream where something terrible is happening and I cannot move.

Gareth's frame retracts so that his chair scrapes against the floor. The rest of the class looks at Kenny and Gareth, then me, then Kenny and Gareth, as if they're spectators to a game of tennis.

I shuffle from behind my desk. 'Sit down, Kenny.'

Undeterred, Kenny grabs the front of Gareth's shirt before I'm close enough to come between them. Gareth is stiff with fright, even though Kenny is a good six inches shorter than him. He might have turned out to be an innocent bystander at the stabbing, but a month in a young offenders' institute seems to have earned Kenny a reputation as someone not to be messed with.

He draws Gareth nearer.

'I'm not even joking, you best shut the fuck up about people's mums,' he threatens, just as I take him by the shoulders.

But I'm redundant. Having said all he apparently wanted to say, Kenny returns to his seat while the rest of the class gawp at Gareth. He shrugs his shoulders to show that he is not defeated but his face, completely drained of colour, betrays him.

'OK, I think we'll call it a day.' I take a few seconds to steady my voice and think about what to do next. 'Kenny, stay behind, please.'

The class stands in slow motion, the usual Friday-afternoon stampede replaced by a disbelieving shuffle, girls whispering to one another, boys lifting the tops of their jumpers over their mouths to hide cackles and smirks. Bhumi is the last out, leaving Kenny and me alone.

'Why isn't Gareth here? Why is it just me in trouble?'

Sitting at my desk, I bury my face in my hands for a brief moment. Any other day and I'd be able to think about this lucidly. I examine the clock again, and I know the next few hours are going to feel like an era.

I exhale wearily. 'You're not in trouble, Kenny.'

'Why am I here then?'

'Because I want to make sure it stays that way. Something tells me you and Gareth wouldn't have gone into the corridor and shaken hands. I just want you to stay here until he's out of the way. I've got things to do anyway, we don't even have to talk.'

I pretend to mark some mock exam papers and after ten minutes of silence I release Kenny and follow him into the now sleepy corridor. He nods goodbye as we part, and there is nothing hidden in the gesture, no malice or disgruntlement or resentment. It feels like progress.

I get there an hour early, but I'm too fidgety and nervous to sit, so I take up a position midway along the metre-high barrier where I'll be able to see her arrive. I check myself and regret my outfit. These brogues resemble canoes with chinos, and they look too new. She'll take one look at me and either laugh at my attempt to be hip or be freaked that I'm dressed like I'm going on a date. I attempt to scuff the shoes on the barrier, without success.

Needing a distraction, I draw my phone from my pocket.

'I thought you were meeting Holly?' is how Kev answers.

'I'm an hour early.'

349

Kev snorts. 'I wouldn't expect anything less from you, cockermouth.'

'The thing is . . .' I hesitate. 'Holly doesn't know I'm here to meet her.'

HOLLY

I stretch my arms and legs as far as the ceiling and seat in front of me will allow, blinking. I must have dozed off. It's nearly four o'clock in the morning according to my watch, which is still on Melbourne time.

'Whaa ime issin unden?' I yawn loudly.

'Eh?' asks Ryan, yanking his headphones out of his ears.

'What time is it in London?' I repeat.

'About six in the evening, I think.'

'Crazy.'

I'm bored, and too uncomfortable to get a proper sleep, so I pull out the carrier bag I shoved under the seat in front of me, and empty my airport purchases onto my tray.

With the tiny koala bear Babygro over my hand, I use my fingers to walk the matching bootees over onto Ryan's tray.

'G'day, mate!' I say in a babyish voice.

Ryan laughs and grabs the Babygro, regarding it thoughtfully while biting his lip.

'Can't believe I'm going to be a dad in six months,' he sighs eventually. 'And that I'm moving to London. And that I have to drink my beer warm from now on.'

'Get used to it, dude,' I tell him, grabbing the Babygro and repacking the bag. 'And that warm beer thing is just a myth, perpetuated by you Aussies.'

We sit in silence for a few minutes, me leaning against my window and staring out at the clouds. It's weird to think I'll be back on British soil in less than an hour. The past twelve and a bit months have flown by. Before I went away, a year would drag on endlessly, but this has gone in the blink of an eye. When I think back to my flight out of London, it seems like a lifetime ago. So much has happened. And there are people who have come into my life who feel like they've always been there.

'You sad to be back?' asks Ryan, reading my thoughts.

Am I? I think about all the adventures I've had. The sights I've seen. The drinks I've drunk and the sunshine that's soaked into my skin. And then I think of home. And my folks. And my friends. And Harold, who hurtfully replied to the postcard I sent her with a message from York, saying she's happier now than she's ever been, and that she's now known as Harry. I think of summer picnics on Blackheath Common and pubs with log fires on winter nights.

'No,' I grin, truthfully. 'I loved every minute and wouldn't change a single bit for the world, but I'm proper excited to be back.'

ALEX

'She's not expecting you to be there?'

I hadn't planned on telling anyone this little detail, lest they make me doubt even more the wisdom of what I'm doing. I suppose there was a part of me that hoped Kev would reassure me.

I look around. Half of London seems to be waiting for someone. To my left is a tall, goateed man wearing a

351

black suit, patent shoes and chauffeur's cap. To my right a man of sub-Continental appearance is dressed in beige trousers and a short-sleeved white shirt. Handwritten signs inform me they are waiting for Kerrigan and Lovejoy respectively, and these formalities cause me to consider abandoning this whole idea. Kerrigan and Lovejoy will be escorted to their cars and driven home in comfort to their loved ones, who will probably have a coq au vin on the hob. What am I going to do? Carry Holly's bag and look on idly as she works out which tube we need. I don't even have any money for a taxi. We'll have to take a detour to a cash machine. Just what you want after a twenty-three-hour flight from Melbourne via Dubai.

Holly's email said she would kip on Leah's sofa tonight and come to see me tomorrow. I should have been patient.

'I'm sure it'll be fine,' reassures Kev unreassuringly.

A horrifying thought occurs in my mind: what if I've got this all wrong? More than a year has passed since she rang me from a hostel in Bangkok and explained why she didn't reply to my calls and messages. We'd waited eleven years, she said, and I finished her sentence in my mind. Had I read too much into her tone, imagined promises that she did not make?

Since then, we've said nothing about us. A couple of times she called, a snatched conversation here and there, always cut short by a dying battery or an adventure waiting to be had. Occasional emails filled me in on her travels: swimming off Bondi Beach; a flat tyre in the outback that meant she had to sleep in a hire car; cookery lessons in somebody's house in Chiang Mai; the horrors of a ping-pong show recommended to her and some girls from her hostel by a cab driver in Bangkok. Isn't it entirely conceivable that she shared all these adventures not just with girls from her hostel, but with someone new, that my year of celibacy has been misguided, and that this is why she planned to see me tomorrow, to break the news gently?

'What are you up to?' I say to distract myself.

'Stripping wallpaper off the spare room – that's my Friday night.'

'Where's Diane?'

'Downstairs. Watching telly. She's been throwing up like a bulimic.'

'Nice.'

'At first I was checking my watch, waiting for the afternoon to come, thinking she'd be all right then, but it turns out the name's a con. They should call it morning, afternoon and all-through-the-night sickness. Doctor says it lasts up to sixteen weeks.'

I know we're at the age where everyone is having kids, but I still can't get used to the idea of Kev as a dad. Not that I think he'll be anything other than great. Torvill and Dean and Reggie and Ronnie want for nothing. I just always presumed I'd be first. Deep down, if I'm really, really honest, something inside me saw myself as being superior to him – as if he was Lennie to my George in *Of Mice and Men*. Which I know is absurd. He's beaten me to every significant milestone in a man's life: kissing with tongues, losing it, getting a job, buying a house.

'Anyway, I best get back to the stripping, mate.'

'I'll come up and see you both soon.'

'That'd be good.'

I slip the phone back in my pocket and begin to scan every face that passes through Arrivals, finding myself increasingly anxious as travellers come and go with their wheeled suitcases and their backpacks and their plastic bags full of duty free. The scrum around me becomes less intense. Kerrigan and Lovejoy are led away. I use my phone to check her email for the umpteenth time. She definitely said Friday. My abdomen aches with nerves and a touch of despair. I start to prepare myself for disappointment.

HOLLY

'If my bag doesn't come out soon I'm going to fall asleep on my feet,' I groan, allowing my eyelids to droop with the hypnotizing motion of the conveyer belt.

'If my bag doesn't come out soon I'm going to scream,' Ryan counters, and the same orange case that's done four circuits reappears.

'If my bag doesn't come out soon I'm going to kill myself.'

'If my bag—'

'THERE'S MINE,' I interrupt, as my rucksack glides past. 'Quick!'

Ryan runs after it and brings it to me. 'There you go, kiddo.'

'Thanks. So this is it,' I exclaim, hauling the bag up onto my back. 'Give my love to Jess, won't you, Ry? Tell her I miss her and we need to meet up loads now we're all back. Especially after the baby's born.'

Jess had reluctantly broken up with Ryan, who she met

working in a bar in Melbourne, when her expired visa forced her to come home. Then when she phoned him a month later to tell him she was pregnant, he booked straight on to my flight to come and be with her. My old uni friend and I have got much closer since I spent Christmas with her in Melbourne, and I've become great mates with Ryan too.

'Thanks. Hope your godson likes his koala gear. When will you get to meet him?'

'Tomorrow, I think,' I say excitedly, straightening the twisted straps on my rucksack. 'I'm actually kipping at Leah and Rob's tonight, but Leah said he'll be in bed by the time I arrive.'

We grin at each other for a second or two then stick our fists out for our trademark fist bump, with a 'BOOM' and a rocket noise. Then I start the walk towards Arrivals.

'Can I still pull that off now I'm thirty?' I turn back to enquire.

'You never could pull it off, H. Now get out of here. I hate goodbyes.'

ALEX

And then, in the slipstream of a gaggle of students, she is there, and though I've been waiting for her for an hour – for a year – it somehow takes me by surprise, and I get an urge to shout her name like Rocky to Adrian. Until I spot a man walking beside her.

Blond, stocky, wearing a vest. Almost certainly Australian. Suddenly my body is consumed by a fierce dread. But after a second or two he starts to walk in a different direction and relief filters through my every fibre.

I take her in. Her hair, tied in a knot that fireworks into several directions. Her face, freckly and younger somehow than when I last saw her twelve months ago. Her clothes: jeans that are ripped above the knee, Converse trainers and a mustard beach T-shirt that cuts off just before her belt to expose a line of tanned belly. She looks . . .

. . . more beautiful than anyone I've ever seen.

The man is gone now, and it appears as though Holly glances my way, but it is like she doesn't see me, because she looks away and continues walking. One step, two steps, three steps, and then she double takes, confusion etched on her face, but her expression quickly fades into something else, something happy. She changes course, quickening her pace, stopping a couple of feet from where I am standing. For a few seconds we stand there grinning broadly at one another, neither of us speaking.

'Your taxi finally made it through the traffic jam, then?'

She chuckles sweetly at her joke; I open my arms for her to step into, my heart racing.

'Yep, I've been waiting all this time.'

Her backpack makes it impossible to hug her properly, but I don't want to let go. Eventually she draws herself away from me.

Settled by her warmth towards me, I point to her backpack. 'Let me take that.'

Holly scrunches her face dismissively. We look one another up and down, and for just a second we're both unsure how to proceed until she holds out her left hand

and says: 'Come on, we've done enough waiting around. Let's get the tube.'

I take her hand in mine and this time, unlike all the other times that have gone before, she doesn't let go.

THE END

Acknowledgements

Laura and Jimmy . . .
Continued thanks to our agent Lizzy Kremer, for her general brilliance and brutally honest feedback that helped shape the book into what it is. We're also extremely grateful to the entire Transworld team, in particular our editor Harriet (mushroom-in-lasagne argument aside), both September and her predecessor Mads for their ace publicity ideas, and Lisa for our lovely cover. We also owe a debt of gratitude to our mutual friends who've had to put up with our constant book chat.

Laura . . .
It would take pages to list the friends who have inspired, helped or supported me in some way while this book was being written, so I'll just mention Gemma Fensome, Emma Baird and James Gill, who either had to live with me or work with me during the process, and have been brilliant cheerleaders and constant sources of humour. And limitless gratitude to Mummy, Daddy, Susanna and David for the fact I grew up surrounded by love, encouragement and laughter.

Jimmy . . .
I need to thank James Osborne for his advice on teaching, and Keren David, Lee MacDougall, Grace King and Molly Kat for their suggestions and encouragement. Huge thanks also to Mum and Mike for their constant support down the years.

A big thank you to all bloggers and online
book reviewers who have been
so enthusiastic and supportive of
The Best Thing That Never Happened To Me.
A special thank you goes to . . .

Kevin Loh (I Heart . . . Chick Lit)

Emma Louise (Emma Lou Book Blog)

Shaz Goodwin (Jera's Jamboree)

Jade Craddock and Stephanie Pegler (Chicklit Club)

Jennifer Joyce (Jennifer Joyce Writes)

Samantha Bates (The Book Corner)

Evelyn Chong (Eve's Chick Lit Reviews)

Karen Cocking (My Reading Corner)

Melissa Puli (Chicklit Club Connect)

Stacey Woods (It Takes A Woman)

Laura Delve (Laura's Little Book Blog)

Laura Lovelock (She Loves To Read)

Leah Graham (Chick Lit Reviews & News)

Chloe Spooner (Chloe's Chick Lit Reviews)

Lucy Walton (Female First)

Rachel Smitten (Rachale's Reads)

Jenny Davies (Wondrous Reads)

Meet Laura and Jimmy . . .

There are many brilliant comedy duos: Laurel and Hardy, The Two Ronnies, French and Saunders, Mitchell and Webb . . . Now Jimmy and Laura join the ranks! We picked their brains, which turned out to be hilarious and alarming in almost equal measure . . .

How did the two of you meet?

Laura Tait: We were on the same journalism course at uni and, shortly after we started, a bunch of us rebelliously skipped a media law class to go to the pub.

Jimmy Rice: Someone suggested a game of pool and Laura was my doubles partner. That was the first time we spoke properly.

What were your first impressions of each other?

LT: That he was ace at pool AND very competitive, and I had a funny feeling that if I messed the game up for us, he wasn't going to be gracious about it. Thankfully, we won.

JR: She was doing shots of After Shock during the game, which made me question her commitment to victory. That aside, I noticed that she laughed a lot.

Who's the sensible one?

LT: Me.

JR: Me.

LT: No way. What about the time you bought an arthritic rescue cat just to impress a girl?

JR: Well what about the time you left your passport on the plane in Croatia?

LT: What about the time you tore the last page out of the book a friend had been reading throughout a group holiday?

JR: What about when you couldn't get to your toiletries for the whole week in Portugal because you forgot the combination lock on your vanity case?

N.B Laura and Jimmy are still arguing about this.

How do you plan out the story?

LT: Good planning is even more important when you're writing with someone else because we each need to know exactly what is happening in each other's chapters for continuity. So we have lots of discussions before we go off and write independently. We start with the general idea – the theme and the plot of the book. Then we go into more detail: who the characters are, and how everything comes about. It's only once we have a clear, detailed chapter plan and in-depth bios for the main characters that we start to actually write it.

JR: Things do change throughout the process – one of us will call the other and say 'I know this is meant to happen, but if this happens instead will it mess up your latest chapter?' and the other will say 'Yes, but you're right – that's better . . . I'll change it.'

When you're writing, what does a typical day look like for you?

JR: I'm quite disciplined about it. My alarm is set for 8 a.m. and once I've got a brew I'll write until late afternoon, either at my desk or in a cafe. I try to set aside some time in the evening to sit with a notepad and think of ideas.

LT: My alarm is set for 8 a.m. I snooze it. Eventually I get up and set up camp with my laptop. Then I make breakfast. Then I realise I can't work in a non-spotless house, so I tidy it. Then it's lunchtime. During the course of the afternoon I usually have emails to respond to and remember there's something I urgently need to order online, like a picture frame for a poster someone bought me three Christmasses ago. Then, after dinner, I really get down to it and once I'm in the zone I just write and write, and I'll still be sitting there writing when the sun comes up.

How do you fit writing in around your other jobs?

LT: I write and edit for my full-time job, so the last thing I want to do when I get home at night is open my laptop and write some more, so it's usually weekends or days off work that I get most of my material written. But I use evenings to do things like think about my next chapter and jot down ideas, or read Jimmy's latest chapter.

JR: When I worked full-time I made the most of the fact no one in the office had a view of my screen. Now I'm freelance I leave myself four or five writing days a week.

Have you always been 'only friends'? And did you find writing the romantic bits difficult?

LT: We really have. We've got a close-knit group of friends from uni who all still hang out and go on holiday together, so before we started writing the book we didn't really spend much time together just the two of us. So we have got much closer, but only as friends. I've never felt awkward writing the romantic bits, but they're probably the scenes we've had to work on the most so maybe on a subconscious level it's difficult.

JR: Our agent suggested in an email that our romantic scenes would improve if we pretended that we'd slept together. Although we both replied to the email we've never actually brought this up when we've been together.

LT: It's a good thing no one can see how hard you're laughing through email.

How well do you think you know each other?

LT: Really well. We've been friends for eleven years but have got to know each other much better since we started writing together. I think co-writing only works if you develop a good sense of how the other person thinks, and what they find funny, and how they'd react in a certain situation.

JR: And how they take their tea.

Who's funniest?

LT: Jimmy does really make me laugh – he's incredibly perceptive but at the same time lacks the filter most people have about what is polite or appropriate to voice, so he comes out with things that everyone else is thinking but wouldn't necessarily say out loud.

JR: Laura's chapters are funnier than mine. She's funny in real life too, often unintentionally. Stuff happens to Laura that would *only* happen to her. Like the time she dropped the entire contents of her handbag in the middle of a busy three-lane road.

Like Chalk and Cheese (but in a good way)

Drink of choice?

LT: Mojito. Crushed ice, loads of mint.

JR: Tea. Strong, half a sugar.

Dream job?

LT: To play the lead in a Broadway musical. I can't sing, though. Apparently that matters.

JR: To play up front for Liverpool. I actually played at Anfield once for a work thing and scored. It was being filmed. I definitely didn't make the cameraman edit my goal and put it on YouTube.

Book you're reading right now?

LT: *Funhouse* by Diane Hoh. I recently bought the entire collection of Point Horror books on eBay. Whenever someone catches me with one I pretend it's 'for research'.

JR: *Hard Times*, Charles Dickens.

Favourite food?

LT: I'll eat anything but usually opt for fish or seafood – and I love sushi.

JR: I'll also eat anything apart from fish – the smell makes me nauseous.

Perfect night in?

LT: Mates, red wine, board games, records, cheese board.

JR: Sitting alone at my desk with a laptop, the words flowing onto the page.

Weirdest celebrity crush?

LT: David Bowie as the Goblin King in *Labyrinth*.

JR: I knew she'd say that. I had to think hard about this one, and even consulted my housemate, before settling on Karen Brady.

We hope you've had as much fun reading

The Best Thing That Never Happened To Me

as we did.

If you did enjoy it, please consider leaving
a review, or get in touch with us on Twitter
using @TransworldBooks and #thebestthingbook.

We'd love to hear what you think.